THE HEART WANTS

What Reviewers Say About Krystina Rivers's Work

Something Between Us

"This is a very good debut novel. Krystina Rivers uses her personal experience of being in the military during Don't Ask, Don't Tell to bring us a captivating, second chance romance. I was invested almost immediately. …Second chance romances are one of my favorite tropes when done well. And *Something Between Us* was done very well. I look forward to reading more from Krystina Rivers. She is a new author with a bright future."—*Sapphic Book Review*

"The fact that said relationship started while they were both in the military, had to hide because of Don't Ask, Don't Tell, and reconnect after the policy has been repealed and they're both civilians gives this second-chance romance a special flavour, all the more so as the characters' motivations to join the military in the first place are very different. All in all, it was an enjoyable read and I'll check out the author's next book. And bonus point for the characters drinking my favourite wine, Brunello di Montalcino."—*Jude in the Stars*

Visit us at www.boldstrokesbooks.com

By the Author

Something Between Us

Last New Beginning

An Atlas to Forever

The Heart Wants

THE HEART WANTS

by

Krystina Rivers

2024

THE HEART WANTS

ISBN 13: 978-1-63679-595-9

THIS TRADE PAPERBACK ORIGINAL IS PUBLISHED BY
BOLD STROKES BOOKS, INC.
P.O. BOX 249
VALLEY FALLS, NY 12185

FIRST EDITION: AUGUST 2024

CREDITS
EDITOR: BARBARA ANN WRIGHT
PRODUCTION DESIGN: SUSAN RAMUNDO
COVER DESIGN BY INKSPIRAL DESIGN

Acknowledgments

The idea for this book started percolating in my mind while my wife was deployed to Africa a couple of years ago. I was working on *An Atlas to Forever* (behind on my deadlines as I frequently find myself) but the idea of an idealistic soldier for whom service had been engrained from birth wouldn't let me go. I finished Atlas and knew this story had to be the next one I would write. Being a wife at home while your soldier is deployed is hard and gave me plenty of emotional fodder to draw from. I had so much fun fleshing out Reagan's and Sydney's personalities as well as what brings them together and pulls them apart. I also just love the idea of two people who are meant to be together despite the world—and their own self-sabotage—doing everything it can to keep them apart.

This book is a little different in that it takes place chronologically (for the most part) over fifteen years and we get to see young and naïve Reagan and Sydney experience first love and first loss and slowly come into themselves as they grow into adults, something I've never written before, but it was a lot of fun.

Thank you, Sandy, for not turning away when I brought this crazy idea to you. I so appreciate your advice, guidance, and support. Thank you, Barbara Ann, for being the best editor around. You make the editing process fun, and I learn so much from each and every set of comments you send me. Thank you for working with me through my many flaws, including my nearly fatal loquaciousness. Rad, thank you for believing in me and creating such an amazing platform that uplifts and supports queer authors. Thank you to Ruth, Cindy, and everyone behind the scenes at BSB doing the things I don't even know exist. Also a big thank you to Inkspiral Design for your fantastic cover. You brought exactly what I was hoping for to life. I'm so grateful to publish with the amazing BSB team.

To the writing community as a whole, I thank you. Without you, I'd never have written my first book, no less be publishing my fourth. I love how everyone is a cheerleader for each other. I imagine that this is what it would feel like to play a team sport. Readers, reviewers, other authors, no matter what category you fit in—and it may be all three—I'm honored to be a part of this team.

To all my family and friends, I wouldn't be here without you. Thank you for all of your love and support. Kris, the queen of book titles, thank you from keeping me from titling this book with my first idea…I shudder at the thought. Ana and Morgan, I can't imagine this journey without you. Mom, Mom Angel, Cheryl, Catey, Mindy, Dad…I am beyond grateful for all of you.

To all the LGBTQ+ military servicemembers who have served past, present, or future, thank you for your service. While your government may not have always supported you, and your fellow servicemembers might not have always seen you, know that your service matters. As a veteran, I know that our wars are not always right, and our laws are not always just, but I honor your dedication and your sacrifices to answer the call in service of our nation.

Last but not least, to my wife, Kerri. Not only could I have not written this book without both your Army officer intel and attorney insights, I would have also never had the confidence to have finished one book—no less four. You have been with me on every step of this journey, and I love you even more for it. It is hard to believe that by the time this book comes out, we will have been together for almost twenty-three years and out of those, we have spent about four of them apart due to the military's whims. You are my first love, my forever love, my best friend, and forever the object of my heart's deepest want. I love you so much and am grateful for every moment that we have had together and every memory still to come. There is no one else I want to walk beside through this crazy life.

Dedication

To all the LGBTQ+ military servicemembers who have served—in silence or openly—past, present, or future

PROLOGUE

Present Day

Reagan rocked back on her heels and breathed in the scent of roasting coffee. She was slightly embarrassed to admit that she preferred tea, but that didn't stop her from savoring the rich, nutty scent. There was something about the aroma that said, "Good morning, world. I'm coming for you."

As an Army major—soon to be lieutenant colonel—it was how she liked to greet every day. Even on days like this when she didn't have to work. The cacophony of café sounds were normally a soothing buzz. But this morning, a patron was talking on the phone so loudly that people on the street could probably hear.

The self-importance was something to behold. Reagan wanted to tap the blonde on the shoulder and remind her she wasn't the only person in Coffee and a Kick, and she should try to not treat it as her own private office.

"Listen, Bill, the installation was obviously not completed with appropriate workmanship. The contract that your client signed clearly stipulates the finished product shall be free of defects for a period of not less than one year. My client had to close their entire deck because the metal is so rusted. It's been four months." The voice was familiar, but Reagan couldn't quite place it. She had a lovely voice despite the volume being annoying as hell and the topic being about as interesting as paint drying. She wasn't hard on the eyes, either, in that gray, pinstriped skirt suit, heels that looked painfully high, and legs that were shapelier than seemed fair. "Bill. You're not hearing me—" It was her turn in line, but apparently, she couldn't pause her conversation, so she stepped to the side and gestured for the person standing between them to go ahead.

Reagan's heart hit the floor with a nearly audible splatter. The familiar voice made sense. Sydney Adams, the only woman Reagan had ever loved, the woman she'd never thought she'd see again after their impromptu and heartbreaking reunion in Munich a few years ago, stood four feet away. Granted, she'd almost completely lost that southern accent Reagan had loved, but it was still the same voice.

Sydney gaped at her, and the guy on the phone spoke so loudly, Reagan could hear his tinny voice saying, "Sydney? Hello?"

She blinked at Reagan like she'd seen a ghost; she had, really. Finally, she weakly said, "I'm gonna have to call you back, Bill." And hung up as poor Bill was yelling something about needing to finish the conversation now.

"Sydney Adams...your hair is longer." *Great job, Captain Obvious.*

She tilted her head, arched an eyebrow in the way Reagan had always been jealous of. "Uh, yes. It's been this way for a while."

Uncomfortable silence. Reagan's thoughts were on hiatus, though she couldn't tear her eyes away. "Are you...here on vacation?" The words popped out without thought and were silly, but last Reagan had heard, Sydney was never moving out of Boston.

Sydney chuckled nervously and rubbed at the hollow at the base of her neck. It had always been a tell of hers. "No, I live in the District now."

"What? No. *I* live here." Knowing that something—or someone—was able to get Sydney to move when she hadn't been enough stung. A lot.

The frozen thoughts thawed when Sydney laughed. "I can't believe it's really you. You look amazing." She beamed, and those pesky butterflies started up in Reagan's stomach, just like they had the first time they'd met, and the dimple in Sydney's right cheek popped.

A throat clearing behind Reagan reminded her that they were both in line at a coffee shop, and Sydney was up.

"Um, can I buy you a cup of coffee? For old times' sake?" Sydney said.

Reagan should have felt anger or hurt, but she felt happy, maybe, or at least curious and decided to embrace it. "Why not?" It wasn't like they'd left things on bad terms in Munich. Reagan had simply realized Sydney was never going to want her as much as she wanted Sydney. And would never be willing to sacrifice anything to make it work. Reagan had resolved to move on and stop hanging on to the hope that they'd be reunited and live happily ever after.

Sydney gestured for Reagan to step to the counter. "A Big Jake and a large Saguaro, please."

"What the hell are you ordering, and what kind of place is this?" Sydney squinted at the menu.

"Cowboy themed. Do you still like the same thing?" There'd been a time when Reagan had gotten them coffee every weekend morning from the shop near her Monterey, California apartment.

"Yes."

"She'll take a large Sheriff Woody with one extra sugar."

Sydney handed a credit card to the barista. "You're apparently my coffee hero once again, but what did you just order?"

As they stepped to the end of the counter, Reagan said, "You're in a Wild West coffee bar, and they name their drinks accordingly. How'd you miss the theme when you came in?" She didn't think it possible to miss the garish decorations, complete with fake cacti and an inoperable—she hoped—mechanical bull.

"A heated conversation with an arrogant archnemesis attorney gave me tunnel vision." That cheeky smile had always been Reagan's kryptonite. "I couldn't focus on the menu while keeping my responses as sharp as a samurai sword." She mimed parrying an attack.

"I'm no expert, but I don't think that's how you fight with a samurai sword. Regardless, the ambiance is bizarre, but I guarantee, it's the best cup of coffee you've had since Italy."

"I'll be the judge of that. But what am I drinking?"

"A Sheriff Woody is a standard coffee, medium roast, with an extra shot of espresso, two creams and two sugars, but you have three." Did Reagan see that drink her first time here and think of Sydney? Yes. But that was only natural, wasn't it?

Sydney's brows furrowed. "Hmm. From *Toy Story*, right?"

"Of course. Sheriff Woody is a good guy. Reliable. Not exactly boring but nothing flashy, thus the standard coffee. He's sweet yet doesn't lie down and take things, thus the sugars and the espresso shot." Had Reagan asked a barista one morning when she was feeling particularly nostalgic about the drink? Yes. But she was happy she had so she could answer the question now. There was nothing weird about that.

She was certain of it.

Sydney laughed, and Reagan gravitated toward her. Without her permission, for the record. "Ah. I was prepared to be offended, but Sheriff Woody is cute. What about yours?"

"The Big Jake is named after John Wayne's toughest cowboy character, so it's a double shot of espresso, and the Saguaro is a white tea with a hint of vanilla and prickly pear. Because it's hydrating. Or something." Embarrassed about her encyclopedic knowledge of the menu, she looked at her hands.

"Still not a fan of coffee but a seeker of the caffeine in the morning, huh?"

Reagan was saved a response when the barista called their order. Sydney handed Reagan her espresso and tea first before snagging her own drink. Reagan blew on her espresso twice before taking a sip and wincing at both the burn and bitterness, but it was her routine. She lived and died by routine.

Sydney bit her lip, laughing at the wince. "Would you want to sit for a bit? Catch up? Do you have time? I'm supposed to be heading into the office, but I'll text my assistant and let her know I'll be late."

Reagan was still shell-shocked but couldn't help her curiosity about what Sydney had been up to. It had been four years since they'd last run into each other. Though their story had started eons before that. They'd practically been babies. It was ancient history, really.

PART I: ANCIENT HISTORY

Naples, Italy, Fifteen Years Ago

CHAPTER ONE

R eagan still hadn't gotten used to the differences between American coffee shops and Italian ones, though in fairness, she'd only been in Italy for a few weeks. Italy, although bustling, appreciated a slower pace to life, including coffee. In the States, everything was rushed: order, drink, get out. Ideally, drink after leaving. The Italians seemed offended if someone tried to take their coffee to go.

It was a lazy Saturday, and Reagan had nothing to do but luxuriate in her espresso and croissant before she went to tour the Castel dell'Ovo. She'd rather have a nice pot of tea, but when in Rome—or Naples in this case—espresso it was.

"Café, please. With cream and sugar," a woman who sounded like she was from somewhere in the American south said to the confused barista.

"Un caffè?" The barista nodded but didn't look confident. The tourist wasn't going to get what she wanted the way things were going. Reagan felt bad for her. If she hadn't spent four years in high school studying Italian, she'd be lost too.

"Maybe." Shit, that accent was cute.

She tapped her shoulder. "Excuse me, ma'am. Can I help you? I don't think she understands what you're trying to order."

A beautiful, doe-eyed woman with white skin, about her own age, turned to her. "Oh, I would be so appreciative if you could. I just got here yesterday, and I haven't started my crash Italian class yet. And I forgot my translation book." She was adorable with those huge blue eyes, a smattering of freckles on her shoulders, and that southern drawl.

"Of course. What do you normally like?" Reagan wanted to ask where she was from. But first, coffee.

"I was trying to get a coffee with cream and sugar to be easy, but I'd prefer something a little sweeter. Like a mocha or something? Do they do those here? Maybe a pastry?" She smiled, and a dimple appeared in her right cheek, awakening an unfamiliar muscle deep inside Reagan, followed by the fluttering of a thousand wings. She gulped air and tried to channel her military bearing to keep her composure. She simply *couldn't feel* what she was feeling and shook it off. Or tried to.

"Not exactly, but I have an idea. You like chocolate?"

"I do." Her smile got bigger, and Reagan's insides clenched a little harder. It was unacceptably pleasant.

Reagan ordered a marocchino for her new friend, an espresso for herself, and two chocolate croissants. She took a chance and said, "Italians don't like to-go. Since we're probably the only Americans in here, any chance you'd want to eat together?" Reagan feared the flutters this woman inspired but couldn't ignore the impulse to spend more time with her. Get to know her. It was inappropriate, but she was compelled.

"Sure. All my friends are still sleeping—jet-lagged—but I've never been out of the country, so I want to enjoy every second. I'm just too excited to sleep." Her eyes looked a little wild. "Thank you so much for your help. I know I studied how to order, but I couldn't make my brain find all the words. My jet lag, I guess—I swear, I'm pretty smart, generally. But you're my coffee hero."

Reagan's ears felt hot, and she couldn't believe her boldness when she said, "Some call me coffee hero, but you can call me Reagan. Reagan Jennings." She stuck out her hand.

The stranger took it and said, "Sydney Adams. Nice to meet you."

Reagan liked the sound of her name as it rolled off those lips. The arrival of their coffee reminded her to let go. Her hand was so incredibly soft. Softer than what seemed possible. Reagan was used to her own hands, calloused from six years of field exercises and physical training.

"Well, thank you again. Cheers, Reagan, my new friend slash coffee hero." Sydney lifted her cup.

Reagan brought their cups together before blowing twice and taking a sip. She winced. It was hot and bitter, but that was espresso.

She wished the Italians embraced green tea, but she was committed to acquiring a taste for espresso. Like anything, if she put her mind to it and worked hard enough, she could make it happen. "So where are you from, Sydney Adams?"

"I'm a student at Vanderbilt, but I grew up in Virginia—and West Virginia, I guess—but Virginia feels more like home. I'm doing a semester abroad here." Her voice was like honey, laying a sweet layer over every word that graced her full lips. Reagan would happily just sit and listen to Sydney give a monologue. "What about you? Are you here for school too?"

"No, I graduated from West Point last year and am in the Army. I'm in Naples for a few months, but I'm permanently stationed in Germany. At least for another year and a half." Reagan held her breath, awaiting Sydney's reaction, hoping she was ambivalent or supportive of the military. *Most* people were, but that wasn't always the case.

"Oh wow. That's impressive. My dad was a SEAL and had tried to get in but was rejected, so he did ROTC instead. He respected academy grads but also said they were punks, so who knows." She laughed nervously. "I'm sorry, that was rude."

Reagan didn't think a *punk* could make it through the four years of hellish intensity of West Point, but Sydney's laugh was so melodic that she couldn't hold even a modicum of irritation. Plus, it was her dad's opinion, not hers. "It was the toughest years of my life. But it was also amazing, so…" She shrugged as she trailed off.

"Sorry, I didn't mean to offend. I really don't know enough about it to make a judgment." She laid her soft hand on Reagan's forearm, and Reagan was ready to overlook any transgression.

"No offense taken." When Sydney just stared, she added, "I promise. If your dad was here, I might give him a hard time but not you." Sydney's face blanched, and Reagan worried she'd misstepped. To change the subject, she said, "How long are you here for?"

The tension melted from Sydney's posture. "Until early December. And I'm so excited. I've heard we'll have three-day weekends pretty much every week and can explore the country as much as we want. Even the rest of Europe if we can afford it. Not sure how much of that I'll be able to do, but—" Her face went red, and she covered her mouth. "I can't believe I just said that."

Reagan suppressed her smile. "I get it. And honestly, you might be able to afford more than you think. There's this goofy airline that somehow charges, like, one euro for flights all over. It's a little bizarre, but nearly free is nearly free, even if each seat has a vendor sponsor."

"Really?" She stared, wide-eyed, as though she didn't believe it. "I can't even imagine."

Reagan laughed. "It's true. You board, and they're like, 'Welcome aboard, today's flight is sponsored by blah blah mobile phones.' Then everyone claps when you land. I try not to think about why, but I haven't heard of any safety issues, so it's probably fine."

Sydney's eyes went wider when she choked on her coffee, and even that face wasn't unattractive. Reagan was a little embarrassed at herself. It wasn't like she had any reason to believe Sydney was gay—she certainly didn't look like the stereotype, but Reagan didn't think she did, either, even with her short hair—and regardless, it wasn't like Reagan was in a position to do anything about it.

"Sorry about my bad timing. I didn't mean to make you choke," Reagan said and rubbed the back of her neck, looking anywhere but at Sydney's face. Unfortunately, her eyes found their way to the swell of her breasts, the tops visible above her shirt. Shit. She could do better than this. She had plenty of practice suppressing any *unnatural*—as far as the military was concerned—urges.

Sydney took a sip of water and coughed a little more. "No, no. Not your fault at all. My mama always tells me to take more care when eating and drinking, but I clearly never listen." She flashed that smile again, and Reagan squeezed her thighs together as tightly as she could. For her own well-being, she should make an excuse and leave, but she felt an inexplicable pull to be near this girl. Become her friend.

"Well, regardless, I'm still sorry."

Sydney rolled her eyes. "Anyway, where in Germany are you stationed?"

"Wiesbaden." When Sydney's brows furrowed, Reagan said, "A little west of Frankfurt."

Sydney's shoulders relaxed as she said, "Ah. I haven't been there, but I know where that is. Wiesbaden sounds like something out of a World War II documentary."

"It's not a terribly exciting place, but it has some lovely hot springs, and it's the center of German champagne. Which…isn't French but isn't terrible."

"I don't know enough about champagne to know the difference. I've mostly had horrible frat party stuff, you know? Or maybe you don't. Do they have frats at West Point?"

Reagan chuckled. "Not so much. Not drinking in general, either. We occasionally did it once we were old enough, but there's so much at stake: career, education, networking opportunities, status. It was worth it to some, but in my family, career is everything, so…" She shrugged, wondering if Sydney would be able to understand.

"I get it. I know it isn't exactly the same, but I'm a scholarship kid, so I can't screw around, either. I have a good time, but I'm not a party kid. Can't afford it. I have plans." She waved her arm in a half circle as she dragged out the word plans for several seconds.

"Grand plans, huh? What's next from here?"

Sydney took a sip and licked a small spot of foam off her top lip, causing Reagan to swallow hard and squeeze her thighs even more. "Graduate Vandy at the top of my class, full ride to a top five law school, move to an appropriately liberal city, partner within five years, and marry an appropriately upwardly mobile woman within ten years, even if we have to do it in Canada. But I'm sure we won't by then. And that's it. Ten-year plan."

That answered the gay question. *Shit.* Not a fact that would make Reagan's life easier. "Wow. That's…specific. And you don't care which law school you go to as long as it's a top five?"

"I'd prefer Stanford. I mean, as a lesbian, I'd love to live in the gay mecca of the Bay Area, but I'm pretty sure anywhere is better than Podunk West Virginia for the ladies."

Reagan's jaw dropped a bit at Sydney's openness, both in shock and a little bit—okay, a lot—of envy. But Sydney must have interpreted her reaction as disdain because she said, "I'm sorry. Gay is a taboo thing in the military, isn't it?" She looked at the table. "I, uh, understand if you can't be my friend."

"No!" Reagan was as surprised as Sydney looked when she yelled and tried to sound less…something…as she continued. "I mean, I don't think less of you at all. It's illegal for people in the military to be gay, but it's fine for me. No, I mean to me." Could she sound any more of a dolt? She couldn't *be* the gay woman she was. Or at least, she couldn't act on any of *those* feelings. Despite how much she might want to.

"Ah," Sydney said, her cheeks a little pink. The embarrassment mirrored Reagan's own, but she was praying hers was less apparent. Sydney cleared her throat. "You said your career was really important. What are your plans? I mean, you know my ten-year plan, so it only seems fair."

A ten-year plan? She'd had a twenty-five-to-thirty-year career plan since she'd been able to walk. "Uh, my ten-year plan is to be a major and preparing to make lieutenant colonel. Beyond that is to make general. That's, like, the twenty-five-year plan, but general is my mission. Even if it's just brigadier general, though I'd prefer a few more stars."

"That sounds pretty lofty, but there's something about you that screams you're the take-charge sort. Do you come from a long line of generals?" Sydney ran her hand through her long blond hair that looked like it would be as soft as silk, and Reagan desperately wanted to touch it and find out.

She cleared her throat in an attempt to clear that impulse. It wasn't particularly effective. "No, I come from a long line of colonels who wanted to get that star and didn't. I'm going to be the first. I have three younger brothers, and if one of those twerps gets it before me, I might just die. I'm pretty sure at least two will get it too, but I *need* to be the first."

"A little sibling rivalry, huh?" Sydney chuckled. "I wish I knew what that felt like."

"You don't," Reagan said flatly. Sibling rivalry was the worst. If they didn't have it, she was pretty sure she and her brothers would be a lot closer. "Siblings are great, but they're also kind of horrible when your parents teach you that you need to be the best. I think my brothers hate me a little because I finished top of my class at West Point, and now, they have to as well."

"That doesn't sound fun."

Reagan was captivated by Sydney's long fingers as she tore a small piece off her chocolate croissant and popped it in her mouth. When she licked a flake off her index finger, it was like the Mojave

Desert was transported into Reagan's mouth, and a few grains of sand lodged in her throat. She coughed and tried to clear them. She dabbed at her watering eyes as she tried to steer them back into safe territory. "No siblings for you?"

"I have a brother, but he's only twelve, so there's no rivalry. He's more like a nephew, but he's my only sibling, so no actual nephews to compare our relationship to." She shrugged and took a sip again, seemingly fascinated by a divot in the counter between them.

"Is there a story with that age gap? A second marriage or something?"

Sydney's face blanched, but she calmly said, "No, just a surprise. But tell me more about Italy. How long are you here?"

Reagan noticed the change of subject and accepted it. "I've been here a few weeks, and like you, I'm determined to take advantage of my every nonwork hour through year-end, when I go back to Germany, and while I'm there too. I'm going to savor my time in Europe."

"Oh yeah? What were you planning to do today to take advantage of this beautiful place?" Another small bite of the croissant and her tongue peeked out again as she sucked the fingertip into her mouth to capture another fricking flake. Reagan squeezed her eyes closed.

"I was heading over to Castel dell'Ovo and then along the water for a while. Maybe grab pizza for lunch. What about you?"

"I was also thinking Castel dell'Ovo and then see where the wind took me. Maybe to bed." Her little laugh was enchanting, and Reagan told herself again that she needed to shut this down. She should change her plans. She should not be thinking of Sydney in bed. "Would you want to join me? At least until I can't stay awake any longer?"

Reagan knew exactly what the right answer was. She also knew what her answer was going to be. They were not the same. But it wasn't like hanging out with Sydney was a crime. Maybe spending a little more time with her would help Reagan get it through her head that Sydney was and would have to remain firmly in the friend column. She could do this.

CHAPTER TWO

By the time Sydney sleepily made her way back to her dorm, she could barely keep her eyes open, but she'd had the absolute best day.

"You look awfully smiley for not being able to hold your head up," Aliyah, Sydney's best friend and roommate, said.

"Well, you look awfully tired for having slept all day rather than enjoying the sights," Sydney countered.

"And sass. What *have* you been up to today?" Aliyah stared at Sydney intently with brows raised as she continued smoothing cocoa butter on her dark brown skin.

"I just toured around. Walked along the water and visited some castle thing. What I told you as you were falling asleep." At Aliyah's pursed lips—she'd never been able to keep secrets from her—Sydney said, "With a girl. A really fucking hot girl." She fanned her face with a magazine just thinking about Reagan.

"Girl." She leveled her gaze at Sydney. "You've been in this country for twelve hours and you've already found a girlfriend? You've got more game than my boy Dwayne Wade."

"I don't have a girlfriend. Just a huge crush. One I'm seeing again tomorrow." Sydney was embarrassed at how she squealed "tomorrow" but was thrilled when she and Reagan had decided to tour the other castle in Naples the next day.

She'd had the best time walking along the water with Reagan and hadn't wanted it to end, afraid if she went back to her hotel to sleep, she'd never see Reagan again. She'd been trying to get up the nerve to ask Reagan to sightsee together again but hadn't managed it before they were about to say good-bye.

Reagan had looked so nervous biting her lip and looking down when she'd said, "I was thinking of touring Castel Nuovo tomorrow if you'd like to join."

"Earth to Sydney," Aliyah said as she waved her hand in front of Sydney's face.

"Sorry, jet lag catching up with me I guess." She laughed nervously at the fib. "What'd you say?" She couldn't stop her yawn.

"Sure. Jet lag." The disbelief was palpable in her voice. "You were imagining making out with your new girl. We both know it. Anyway, spill. How'd you meet her? What does she look like?"

"She helped me with my order at a coffee shop, and we ended up touring together." Little flutters of excitement danced in her belly as she thought about how her body had reacted when Reagan had touched her arm. "She's gorgeous. Like a model. Tall, thin, amazing arms, brown hair in a pixie cut. I normally prefer longer hair, but her face was pretty—so fucking pretty—that it was like her hair somehow made her face even prettier because it didn't distract from it, you know? She's white, and her skin was pale, as though she hadn't spent much time in the sun, delicate almost, but her hand when I shook it was calloused, her grip firm and anything but delicate. Sometimes, her posture was weirdly ramrod straight, but then she'd relax a little bit and look more comfortable until she caught herself again. It was adorable." She sighed.

Aliyah mimed gagging, then laughed. "You're a lovesick puppy."

"Whatever. But I don't even know if she's gay. I came out, but she didn't respond. Then, I got worried that she'd have an issue with it because she's in the military, but she seemed okay and asked to meet up again tomorrow. It's weird. I don't know what to think. She probably just wants to be friends." Sydney wished with her whole heart that they would be more but knew that was unlikely. But she was determined to enjoy their time together, no matter what it led to.

"Sydney and Reagan sitting in a tree. K-I-S-S-I-N-G." Aliyah laughed, and Sydney threw her pillow at her. Aliyah caught it. "You're going to have to try harder than that to actually hit me. I can't believe you call yourself a lesbian."

"We don't all have to be athletic you know. Some of us are happier with academics. That doesn't make me less of a lesbian." Sydney was exhausted with people thinking that just because she was gay, she was sporty.

"I'm sorry, you know I don't really think that." Aliyah sat on Sydney's bed next to her and bumped their shoulders together.

"It's just so frustrating. I feel like everyone looks at you and knows you're gay, but I continuously have to deal with frat bros hitting on me and proactively telling everyone I'm gay before they assume that I'm straight. So I'm a little rabid about it and make situations awkward."

"I know my little uncouth bestie. But think about it this way. You get to pass as straight in the world when you need to. And you're always white. I don't have either of those luxuries." She wrapped her arm around Sydney and squeezed.

"We're both fucked, aren't we? You more so than me. Think we'll ever get to a point in society where the color of our skin and who we love really don't matter?" She sighed and lay her head on Aliyah's shoulder.

"No." She scoffed.

"But we'll keep trying," Sydney said. "Together."

"Ab-so-fucking-lutely. And in the meantime, you'll hang out with your Army hottie tomorrow."

"I most definitely will." Sydney couldn't stop the smile that spread across her face. "Did you want to come? I know I've only talked about her looks, but we had such a good time together. She's such a kind person. We were walking along the Lungomare, and there was an elderly woman who was having a hard time with a little cart. She ran over and picked the cart up and put it onto the sidewalk for her. It was the cutest thing. And I think you'll really like her."

Aliyah pursed her lips. "Mmm. I think I'll let you do your thing tomorrow. I don't want to cramp your style. But if you keep hanging out, I'll want to meet her. I need to make sure she's good enough for you."

Sydney really hoped they'd keep spending time together. They'd only spent a few hours together so far, but, between her attraction and how much fun they'd had, Sydney had a feeling that this could be the beginning of something kind of amazing. Before she found out, though, she *had* to get some sleep.

❖

When Sydney walked into the café the next morning, Reagan's mouth went dry. The day before she'd been wearing jeans, so Reagan hadn't seen her legs, but today she was in flip-flops, with short jean shorts and a plaid button-up shirt with the sleeves rolled up to almost her elbows. But the legs beneath those jean shorts were something else.

"Hey, you," she said in that perfect southern accent. "You already ordered for me."

Reagan realized that she was unconsciously standing at parade rest, which she found herself doing a lot when she was nervous. It was one of those weird things no one had told her about life after West Point. When nervous or uncomfortable, all sorts of bizarre habits might start to reappear, but she was consciously trying to break herself of it. "I did. I knew you'd want something sweet, so I took a chance. I hope that's okay." Reagan was suddenly nervous that she'd overstepped.

"Of course. Thank you. I appreciate it." She pursed her glossy pink lips and blew on the small cup. Reagan gasped when she felt the light breeze as it ricocheted off the coffee and toward her face. Sydney took a sip, and Reagan watched the corners of her mouth curl up. She smiled back, pleased with herself that she'd made a good choice. "That's amazing. What is it?"

"It's just a caffè latte but with sugar. I thought about getting you the marocchino again but wanted you to be able to try something new. And a chocolate croissant, of course. Because a day in Italy without a chocolate croissant is a day only half lived."

"I just knew I was going to love this country. And I'm so happy I met you. You're showing me all the ropes." She smiled and laid her hand on Reagan's arm. Reagan resisted the urge to lay her other hand on top. "And I'm eternally grateful. I can't wait to see more with you today."

Reagan's chest warmed. She cleared her throat to buy a few seconds to come up with the right words. "I think guide might be a little generous, but my high school Italian classes do come in handy. I wish I could've studied it more at West Point, but it isn't a strategic language, so I studied Russian instead."

Sydney squeezed before pulling her hand away, and a chill ran through Reagan at the loss of warmth, despite the heat in the bar. "Wow. Russian *and* Italian. Impressive. And even if guide doesn't ring true to you, it feels right to me, or maybe even lifesaver. I'd still probably be coffee-less if not for you. And that would be a terrible shame." Sydney shook her head and sighed dramatically.

Reagan laughed. "Okay, lifesaver is way over the top."

Sydney shook her head. "Absolutely not. I'd have never gotten a palatable coffee yesterday if not for you. I'd have been a sad, hollow shell of myself trying to stumble around Naples, jet-lagged and bleary-eyed."

Her smile made unfamiliar muscles inside Reagan contract in a way that would have been pleasurable if Sydney wasn't one hundred percent off-limits. She took the last sip of her espresso, eager to be out in the sunlight with other things to focus on. "Shall we head out and be each other's tour guides?"

Sydney took her last sip too. "Yes, I'm so excited." She also took her last bite of croissant and sucked the tips of her index finger and thumb. Again with the fingers? Reagan's heart rate doubled, and she jumped out of her chair on instinct. She wanted to get them moving as quickly as possible. "Are you okay?" Sydney asked.

"Of course," Reagan said much too quickly to be natural. "Just eager to see the castle." She silently chanted to herself to *act natural* as they headed toward the Piazza del Municipio even as her heart felt like it was fluttering in her throat. She distracted herself by pointing out the sights. "That's Neptune there on that fountain."

Sydney gasped. "It's beautiful."

"Hard to believe it's been moved six or seven times since it was sculpted in the fifteen hundreds, isn't it?"

"How?"

"Craftiness. They can disassemble parts of it, and some of the statues were added later." *See, you can be normal. Act the tour guide.*

Sydney looked at her, wide-eyed. "How do you know all that?"

"Just a good memory, I guess. It's nothing special, really." She stared at the ground, uncomfortable.

Sydney stepped in front of her while they waited for traffic to clear so they could cross the street and grabbed her elbows. "That's impressive. Why are you being shy about it? I *wish* I had that kind of memory."

Reagan looked up and felt tongue-tied.

"I don't know you that well yet, but you impress the hell out of me." Sydney's fingers pressed lightly into the sensitive skin of her inner arms, and she used every bit of self-control to not sway toward her.

She always felt like she was walking a tightrope with an abyss of inadequacy below her. Even though she was the oldest of her siblings, nothing she ever did was good enough; she wasn't smart enough, fast enough, tough enough. Graduating top of her class should've meant she was the best of the best of the best, yet those fears of always falling short were consistently there. Her pesky gay urges also didn't help, and she lived in fear that someone would find out and point and yell, "She doesn't belong here! She's *gay*."

Yet something about Sydney chased part of that away. Even though she had to be more obviously gay when around Sydney—her gaze lingering too long—it was like she knew she could be her true self for the first time in her entire life. "Thank you," she finally whispered.

The light hadn't turned, but traffic cleared, so pedestrians pushed past them, but Sydney just held on, lips pursed. "Uh, looks like it's clear to cross." Reagan pointed her chin toward the intersection.

"Oops." Sydney ran her thumbs lightly along Reagan's skin one more time before letting go. It was barely even a touch—nothing more than a hint of a graze—yet Reagan felt like she was on fire where those thumbs had apparently *claimed* her. *Hell.*

Sydney was in the street before Reagan caught up. "Why're you running?"

"There's so much to see." She moved her hand in a wide arc. "Look at how beautiful this all is."

"If you look past the graffiti."

Sydney laughed. "Well, sure, but that's just part of the city. One of my professors told me that you have to look twenty feet ahead and not directly in front of you." She stopped and turned in a circle. "Seems accurate."

Reagan looked at the litter in the street and then out at the sun shimmering off the water. "Huh. I hadn't thought about it that way, but you're right." However, if she looked into the distance, she couldn't look at the beautiful woman standing next to her, which was a shame.

Sydney grabbed her hand, pulling her toward the towers of the castle. "Come on." She didn't hold her hand for long, but it was long enough that Reagan prayed no one from her unit was around, even as she relished those smooth fingers against hers. She took a step and tripped over her own feet. *Great.* Apparently, being around Sydney turned her into a klutz.

Sydney squeezed her hand. "Are you okay?"

"Yeah, sorry, the sidewalk was a little less even than I thought." She laughed and ran her free hand through her short hair, idly wondering how long it was going to take her to grow it back out. "Let's try this again." She took a step, and when she didn't stumble, she released Sydney's hand with regret.

They spent two hours wandering the stone halls and ramparts of the "new" castle. They stood on the roof as they neared the end of their self-guided tour, shoulders nearly touching—so close that if they both breathed in at the same time, Reagan was pretty sure that they did touch—forearms on the wall.

"That's Vesuvius there," Reagan said, pointing at the volcano looming a mere thirty miles away.

"It's so beautiful," Sydney said, and the corner of her lips curled up.

"But they say it's one of the most dangerous because it's still active, and this area is so densely populated."

Sydney looked at her, that small smile having bloomed into a full one that continued to set off sparklers in her belly. "You're kind of like an encyclopedia. I like it." A gust of wind blew off the water and ruffled her hair, and she grabbed it with one hand as best she could, huffing at the minor annoyance as she continued to look at Reagan.

And Reagan felt so self-conscious. "It's nothing." She laughed nervously and pointed at the bay. "Just a good memory and curiosity."

"That's so cool. I'm super jealous. School must've been a total breeze." She looked back at the water. A gigantic yacht floated by, and Reagan wondered what it would be like to be so wealthy you could relax all day in luxury like that.

"Not exactly," she said but didn't want to get into military academy politics or the pressure of having to always be the best. "When do you start classes?"

"Tuesday."

"Are you excited?"

"I am." Sydney's eyes lit up. Apparently, she was a little nerdy. Reagan could relate.

"What are you studying?"

"International business, international law, Italian literature, and the archaeology of Pompeii."

"Impressive. And a lot. Wow."

"I can't afford to fall behind on my credits, and I only get my tuition covered if I'm full-time, so..." She shrugged. "My best friend who came too is only taking two classes and has plenty of time to sightsee—which is why she's still in our room sleeping right now—but I'm going to make it work somehow." She sighed. "I'm not going to miss out on anything. Except for maybe some sleep." She laughed and shrugged.

Reagan fought the urge to tuck a loose strand of hair behind her ear and stuck her hands forcefully into her pockets. She couldn't let this little infatuation take root, but my God. She was so attracted to Sydney, it should have been criminal. Oh wait. It was. Fuck.

When Reagan's stomach growled loudly, she covered her mouth. "Oh my God. How embarrassing." Though it was a little bit of a relief to take her mind off her attraction.

"I like it." Sydney said and bit the side of her lip. "It makes you seem more..."

"Uncouth?" Reagan clearly hadn't had enough to eat after her ten kilometer run that morning. Sydney studied her until Reagan worried she saw some flaw. Maybe she had something on her nose. She rubbed it self-consciously and prompted Sydney again. "More what?"

"Human."

She didn't seem human? What was that supposed to mean? Reagan was pretty sure it couldn't be good. It was probably because of her freakish memory. "Uh, since my stomach has so loudly spoken, why don't we go grab some lunch?"

"Sure. What'd you have in mind?"

"Pizza. If you haven't had a buffalo mozzarella Neapolitan pizza, you haven't lived."

"Those are some pretty big words there." She stared at Reagan incredulously.

"It delivers." Of that, anyway, she was confident.

CHAPTER THREE

Sydney couldn't suppress a groan when the first bite of pizza hit her tongue. It was like heaven on a fork. The spiciness of the sauce, the extra creaminess and tang of the mozzarella. "Holy shit," she said around the bite. "I don't think I've ever had something this good in my mouth in my entire life."

Reagan's eyes went wide, and Sydney realized what she'd just said. She scrambled to come up with something to correct her overly sexual gaff, but the only things that popped to mind made it worse, not better. It wasn't like she'd even had sex yet. She almost had a couple of times, but it just hadn't felt...right, so she'd pulled back. Her girlfriend at the time had been pissed, but Sydney wasn't willing to fake being ready.

She chewed to buy herself time, but thankfully, Reagan changed the subject before she could make even more an ass of herself. "We should have the caprese salad next time so you can see how good the buffalo mozzarella is on its own." She pressed her lips to her fingertips in a chef's kiss.

Sydney was certain her cheeks had to be as red as the rose in the vase on the table but was happy to hear Reagan still wanted there to be a *next time*. "I appreciate you taking me under your wing. This has been great. Especially while my friends are being lame and sleeping."

Reagan's tone stayed light, but a sadness crossed her face as she said, "I'm happy to keep you company while your friends get used to the time zone. It's been fun."

"Oh no! I didn't mean I only wanted to use you this weekend. I hope you still want to be friends and hang out. I've had so much fun the last two days. I feel like I've known you forever, not just since yesterday." It was weird how close they felt. Sydney hated the thought of losing that or the thought that she'd hurt Reagan's feelings.

That muted smile bloomed again, and an invisible weight lifted. "Same. I don't think I've ever vibed with someone as quickly as you."

"Cool," Sydney said. Taking a chance, she continued, "Well, we should make plans to get caprese soon. I'm assuming you'll have to work tomorrow, and I'll be starting school in another day, but you've been an amazing part of my Italian experience so far, so let's keep it rolling."

"How about Thursday evening? We can go to my favorite trattoria. You can bring your friends if they're ready to interact with civilization by then." She laughed, and Sydney was excited but felt a little pang of regret that the little bubble they'd lived in that weekend was going to burst. Infiltrated by outsiders. Not that she didn't love her friends, but things felt delicate with Reagan. She didn't want her friends to be weird about it. Especially Aliyah.

She focused on the excitement and ignored the twinge of disappointment. "Sounds great. I'll ask."

As Sydney walked home after dinner, ready to fall into a deep sleep in her oddly small and not terribly comfortable bed, she *might have* obsessed slightly over every second with Reagan. Every glance, every touch, every word. When she'd grabbed Reagan's hands in the street, they'd had a moment. She couldn't quite get a read on Reagan's feelings, though. She assumed the Army thing made it harder for her, but it felt like she was interested one minute and just wanted to be friends the next.

It wasn't that Sydney would turn away a friendship, but she wanted more. Longed for it.

❖

Reagan was finishing her last set of squats at the gym when Air Force Lieutenant Mari Greene, an acquaintance of Reagan's who worked in the section next to hers, grabbed two twenty-pound weights from the rack and said, "Do you want to grab dinner tonight?"

"I can't. I have plans."

"Ooh. A date?" Mari said and waggled her eyebrows. "Where'd you meet him?"

She hated this. "Just some friends. We're going to Trattoria Petrucci."

Mari started alternating reticulated curls as she said, "Nice. I love that place. But you really should try dating some of these Italian men. They are something else." She fanned her face and whistled. "They seem spoiled and self-important, but who cares when you're looking for a fling. I'm telling you. And they *love* American women."

If only she was interested in men. That would have made life so much easier. Alas, she wasn't, and honestly couldn't envision herself having casual flings anyway. She wanted to lie and say she had a boyfriend back home, but that was against the honor code too, so she stuck as close to the truth as she could. "I'm not here for very long, and flings aren't my thing. I'm focusing on enjoying my time. No complications."

"To each her own, but you're missing out." She set the weights down and took a sip of water.

"Catch you later. I've got to hit the showers." Reagan felt a little queasy. She hated having to avoid a love life, but she was going to have to until Don't Ask Don't Tell was repealed. There were rumblings that it might be coming. But until it did, she'd keep figuring out ways to tap dance around why she didn't date without outright lying.

❖

Sydney's friends were more fun than Reagan had been expecting, though she still found herself gravitating to Sydney at the quaint cocktail bar they ended up at after dinner. "What did you think of the food?" Reagan asked when she plopped on the couch next to her.

"It was amazing. That crudo was simple yet melt in your mouth and so fresh. I haven't had many meals that fancy. Not that it *was* fancy. But it was nice." Sydney stumbled as she backtracked and turned a little pink, rubbing at the hollow at the base of her throat.

Reagan wondered if she was nervous or self-conscious or something else. "I've been there before but had more fun tonight than alone. I'm glad we were able to enjoy it together." She lifted her glass. "Cheers to fun and new friends."

"Cheers." Sydney clinked their glasses and took a sip of her cosmopolitan or whatever it was. It was bright pink and in a martini glass and looked classy yet fun. Reagan was a simple girl and stuck to beer or wine, though she had broadened her wine tastes significantly since she'd been in Europe. The martini glass looked at home in Sydney's hand, though, and Reagan wished that she was more sophisticated and could pull off a drink like that. But she was pretty sure she'd look silly.

"Sitting down there on the water was peaceful. And gorgeous. And that cat…so cute."

"I don't think the waiter thought he was all that cute as he weaved around our table. But I'll admit, I gave him a couple of bites of shrimp." She shrugged and looked a little sheepish, but Reagan was happy to see her blush had receded.

"Me too," she whispered. "I was afraid I was going to get caught, but I didn't care *that* much. I don't think they'd ban me for life if they caught me."

"Couple of rebels we are. Rebels *with* a cause." Sydney lifted her glass, and Reagan clinked them again.

"What are we cheersing over here, kids?" Aliyah dropped into a chair adjacent to the couch and held out her glass to join in. It was weird when someone younger than Reagan called her a kid, but whatever.

Sydney was adorable as she said, "Just our inner rebelliousness."

Aliyah stared at them with her brows raised. "You two? You're, like, the least rebellious people I've ever seen." She pointed at Reagan. "Little Miss West Point, I bet I could toss a quarter at your bed, and it would bounce four feet into the air."

It was embarrassingly true, but Reagan stayed silent and took a sip.

"And you." She pointed at Sydney this time. "Little Miss I Can't Go Out Because I Have a Paper Due in Six Weeks." She scoffed and took a sip of her drink.

Sydney sat up straight. "Hey. That paper was, like, seventy-five percent of the grade. And I'm currently at the top of our class. I intend to stay there," Sydney said, her voice holding a haughty tone that Reagan hadn't heard before but liked. Really, really liked.

"Yeah, but six weeks before it was due?"

"Stop exaggerating. It was four weeks, and it needed to be an outstanding paper." Sydney exhaled like a bull getting ready to charge and shook her head. "As you know, if you procrastinate, you'll never get there. Or it'll be a mad dash at the end, and the quality will be inferior."

Aliyah snorted, but Reagan was too busy watching Sydney to pay much attention. She looked so beautiful all fiery-eyed in irritation. "Are you trying to say *I* submit things of inferior quality?" Aliyah said, mock horror in her voice.

Sydney laughed and shrugged.

"Are you buying this?" Aliyah said. "Six weeks or four weeks or whatever is way earlier than you need to write a paper. Am I right?"

It wasn't until the conversation had gone silent that Reagan realized they were both staring at her. She rewound the last few words, a trick she'd learned at West Point when not paying close attention in class or when a firstie was yelling at her for some violation. "Don't look at me. My ideas of a wild Friday night at West Point were writing papers or polishing my boots or using an old toothbrush to ensure no speck of dirt marred the baseboards. I'm a sad example of collegiate life." When Aliyah and Sydney just stared, Reagan worried she'd made herself seem like the biggest loser to ever take a breath. "I mean, we still had fun, but we were so busy, it was low-key. Academy life is... different. But I'm pretty fun now, aren't I?"

"Of course," Sydney said.

Aliyah waited a beat before she said, "Pshh." But she smiled, so Reagan figured she couldn't be too bad.

Sydney threw a cardboard coaster at Aliyah's chest like a Frisbee. "Don't be rude."

Aliyah made a show of rubbing her breastbone as though the coaster had been a boulder rather than a tiny piece of cardboard, and Reagan truly laughed that time. "Fine, fine," Aliyah said. "You're both all right, I guess."

"Not sure what to do with all the flattery," Reagan said and made a show of rolling her eyes, but they all laughed, and Reagan felt surprisingly comfortable.

"It occurs to me that we could call ourselves the Dead Presidents Society," Aliyah said and laughed.

"What?" Sydney said.

Reagan looked back and forth between them, waiting to understand.

"Because we all have dead presidents' names. Your name is Reagan, as in Ronald." She pointed at Sydney, "Your name is Adams, as in John and his son John Quincy. And me." She tapped herself on the chest several times with her thumb, "My last name is Monroe, as in James. Thus, the Dead Presidents Society. Know anyone with the last name of Madison or Washington? We could invite them to join." She leaned back in her chair with a self-satisfied smile.

Reagan choked on the wine, and as she wheezed, trying to catch her breath, Sydney patted her back softly.

"Are you okay? Just take slow breaths." The pats switched to slow circles, and even as tears stung Reagan's eyes because she was coughing so hard, the skin beneath Sydney's hand burned. "I mean, she wasn't even that funny."

That set off another round of coughing, harder this time.

"Don't be a bitch, Syd. It was funny. Though maybe not *that* funny." Aliyah and Sydney both laughed, but Reagan was pretty sure they were laughing at her, not with her. "Imagine when I hit her with quality work."

For the life of her, Reagan couldn't figure out why she was laughing so hard. Though the gasping for air was more from Sydney rubbing her back than the Dead Presidents Society.

Sydney dialed what felt like seven hundred numbers for her prepaid calling card before the weird European phone ring started. It was the first time she'd tried calling the States since she'd been in Italy and wasn't used to the process.

"Hello?"

"Hey, Mama." She hadn't realized exactly how much she missed her mother until they were on the phone. "It's so good to hear your voice." She scooched up higher in her bed and pulled the rather limp and scratchy gray comforter around her chest, trying to find a more comfortable position.

"Hello, dear. Miss you too. How's Italy?"

She tried not to gush, but it was hard. "It's so amazing here. Everywhere I go, I think, nothing can get more beautiful than this, and yet, somehow, I find something even more beautiful around the next corner. And the food...I can't even start. It's like I've died and gone to heaven."

"I'm so happy for you. I can't wait to see photos. I'll live vicariously through you."

"You could come visit."

"I would love to, but I can't swing that money right now. Your father and I used to talk about going, but..."

Sydney's jaw clenched at the mention of her father. *Dick.* He was supposed to have been a hero. But he had completely fucked over her mom, brother, and her. He'd insisted his wife shouldn't have a job because he could take care of them all. Except that he hadn't made a single responsible financial decision in his entire life. Or in his death. *Dick.*

"I'm sorry, Mama, I'll send all the pictures to you. It'll almost be like you're here. And in a few years, I'll be making all that lawyer money, and I'll bring you and Noah back so we can see it together." She needed to keep her eye on the prize. Nothing was more important than financial security because she'd never had it growing up.

"I can't wait. Have you made any new friends?"

"I've been hanging out with Aliyah a lot. She's my roommate again, and..." Sydney wasn't really sure what, if anything, she should say about Reagan. Her mom wasn't a huge fan of the military. Understandably, all things considered.

"And?"

She was going to have to learn to hold her cards closer to her chest to be a good attorney, but her mother had always been able to see through her. "I've made a new friend. A good friend. She's an American, but she's living here now."

"Oh, a girl who is a friend or a girlfriend? Or a crush that you're hoping to convert into a girlfriend?" Sydney could picture her mom at the kitchen table, a mug warming her hands, trying to pry all the details out of her. Since it was bedtime in Italy, it was about four in the afternoon in West Virginia. Her mom was probably having decaf tea after an hour of tending to her tiny portable vegetable garden.

"A friend who is a girl…but also a crush maybe?"

"How'd you meet? Is she studying abroad too?"

Sydney absolutely wouldn't lie to her mother—never had, never would—but if she could omit the tiny military detail, it would make life easier. "She saved my life in a coffee shop."

"What on Earth happened in a coffee shop that necessitated lifesaving? Were you choking on a scone?" Her voice sounded like she wanted to laugh, but a hint of fear was also woven into the tone.

The thought of needing the Heimlich in the café was a little amusing. The thought of Reagan's arms wrapped around her, even preparing for the Heimlich, sent tingles along her arms. "Not exactly. She helped me order, saving me from a decaffeinated day of sightseeing. I was so jet-lagged, I would've never made it."

Her mom's laugh, rich and full, made her feel wrapped in a warm hug. "Whew. Glad to hear it was only metaphorical."

"Without Reagan's caffeine help, I could've fallen asleep while on the castle I was touring and tumbled over the side to my death. So it really preempted a life-and-death situation. And anyway, we ended up sightseeing together. She's been my unofficial tour guide, and it's been lovely."

"Interesting theory, dear. Anyway, *is* she a student too?"

Dammit. "No, she graduated last year."

"Backpacking around Europe before she gets a real job?"

"No, she's an Army lieutenant stationed here."

The complete silence on the other end was deafening.

"Did I lose you, Mom?"

"No, sweetheart. I'm still here. Just a little startled. Are you sure you can trust her?"

"All we've been doing is sightseeing, Mom. She's been nothing but kind and helpful, and we've been having a lot of fun. That's all it is. It's a break from real life, and I'm going to enjoy it. You have nothing to worry about." Sydney wasn't sure why her mother didn't trust *any* service member. Her father had been killed in action, and after his death, they'd found out the true level of his betrayal, but it seemed like any disdain should have been targeted at him versus the entire military.

But even though Sydney had a gigantic crush on Reagan and dreamed about them being a couple, it wasn't likely to happen. Reagan had that whole Don't Ask, Don't Whatever thing, and it wasn't like it was practical. Sydney lived in Nashville. Reagan lived in Germany, and who knew where she'd end up next. They had their lives all planned out, and it didn't involve trying to follow the other around the world.

But she could continue to dream about what it would be like.

CHAPTER FOUR

Reagan sat in her government supplied rental car at the Metro station, waiting for Sydney with more pent-up anxiety than was healthy. It was really scary having her two worlds overlap. But she was getting promoted, and it would be nice to have a friendly face do the pinning. It was true that she'd only known Sydney for a couple of months, but they'd been spending a lot of time together, and they felt... close.

She'd been so nervous a few weeks before when she'd asked Sydney to come to her promotion ceremony. She wasn't sure Sydney would have any interest; they didn't talk about her job very much. In fact, Sydney seemed to avoid talking about anything military. If the topic came up, she quickly changed the subject.

But even though this promotion wasn't a big deal—it was almost automatic based on time in grade—it was still an important step on her goal of becoming a general, and she wanted her best friend to be there for it. So while they had been wandering the grounds at the Caserta Royal Palace, Reagan had wiped her sweaty palms on her jeans and plucked up the courage.

"You really want me to be part of your ceremony?" Sydney had said, eyes wide.

"Yeah, I'd love for you to be there." Reagan was embarrassed at her stammering. It should have been no big deal. Yet it had felt like one.

Sydney's smile had grown bigger, and God help her, there was that dimple. "I'd love to," she'd said.

And now, here she was. Nervous about seeing a girl she had a secret crush on in front of a bunch of soldiers who could report her if they suspected something. But brimming with excitement too. She wondered if Sydney would find her attractive in her uniform. That was a thing for some people, though she was wearing her ACUs—her combat uniform—rather than her ASUs—her service dress uniform—so it wasn't as dashing.

The time for agonizing was over because Sydney emerged from the station looking radiant in a white sundress with a few large flowers scattered across it. The blue flowers made her eyes pop more than they already did, the red ones accented her glossy red lips, and Reagan did what she could to steady her breathing. She couldn't take Sydney on base while gaping at her.

"Hey, you," Sydney said and slid onto the passenger seat.

"Hi." She cleared her throat, still searching for her military bearing. "I love this dress."

"Thanks." Sydney smiled and looked away.

Reagan closed her eyes and took a deep breath. She needed to center herself to get through this. "You have your passport, right?"

"Right here." She pulled it out of her purse. Reagan opened it and looked, needing to see what Sydney's photo looked like. Dammit. She was cute even in her passport photo. It was so unfair.

"Looks okay?"

"Of course," Reagan said and made a quick U-turn to head back to base.

She handed her ID and Sydney's passport to the uptight gate guard at the booth. "Good morning," the Italian soldier said in heavily accented English. "What is your guest's purpose today?"

"She is coming to my promotion ceremony."

"Very well. Proceed." He sounded almost like he was in pain as he said it, but he still snapped to attention and saluted her. "Have a good day, ma'am."

She returned his salute as much as she could from the car and drove in. Once they were clear of earshot from the gate, Sydney whispered, "Do they do that every time?"

"Do what?" The corner of Sydney's lip was caught between her teeth, her eyes a little wider than normal, and my God, she looked amazing. Regan had to tear her gaze away for safety.

"Call you ma'am and salute?" she said, miming a very limp salute.

"Uh, yes. It's standard procedure, though I think the foreign MPs don't really like saluting baby officers like me. He wasn't very happy about it."

"Huh."

Reagan very much wanted to ask what Sydney was thinking, but before she could ask anything, Sydney said, "So what happens next?"

"Ceremony, you pin me, I change into civvies, we go have dinner and a drink to celebrate. If you want, that is." God, she sounded so inept. Why couldn't she just be normal with Sydney? Have a natural conversation. It wasn't that hard with the rest of the world.

"Of course I want to celebrate with you. This is a big deal."

She sighed in relief. "Cool. We could invite some of your friends if you want. Or not. Either way." The rambling was getting out of hand. Reagan was an adult. A West Point grad. She *could not* let a woman fluster her this way.

"Let's play it by ear if that's okay. Unless you want more people here to celebrate. Which is totally fair."

At least Sydney was a little ramble-y too. Though maybe that wasn't a good thing. But God help her, it set those horrible flutters loose in her belly again. She was so screwed.

❖

Sydney didn't know what she'd been expecting when she walked into the room where the ceremony was to take place, but it wasn't some tired, eighties-vintage, windowless conference room that felt like it sapped all the life from her. Except that being in the same room with Reagan always gave her life and turned everything into Technicolor, like when Dorothy landed in Oz.

This dismal conference room challenged that effect, but still, every time she looked at Reagan, everything felt a little lighter. And what was it about a woman in uniform? The clothes, the combat boots. She wouldn't have thought boots sexy, but something about the confidence Reagan exuded in them was hot as fuck. Or maybe it was everyone saluting and calling her ma'am.

It took everything in Sydney not to shove her up against every wall and kiss her into next Tuesday. Clearly, that wasn't an option, but she should have received a medal of commendation for her ability to resist.

"Attention to orders," someone in the room yelled, and everyone in uniform jumped to stand. Sydney almost leaped out of her seat in the front row. It felt like a flash mob was about to overtake her, but she quickly realized no one was surging forward. "The president of the United States, acting upon the recommendation of the secretary of the Army has placed special trust and confidence…"

Sydney ignored the rest of the words and simply enjoyed staring at Reagan. She was almost directly in front of her, staring at some unseen point in the back of the room, but she looked so professional, regal.

Sydney was brought out of her single-minded focus when the guy said, "Ms. Adams, will you please step forward to pin the new rank on First Lieutenant Jennings?"

She jumped up, feeling gawky. Like the nerdy teenager she'd always been, even though she was twenty-one now. She stepped in front of Reagan like she'd been told to do and pulled the new rank out of her purse, ready to put it on Reagan's chest before she realized she needed to pull the old rank off first. As she fumbled to hold on to her purse and the new rank and grasp the old, Reagan's eyes flicked to hers, and a small smirk appeared at the corners of her lips, but it was enough that Sydney's heart rate doubled.

Before she could even smile back, Reagan's gaze was again trained on the back of the room, her face as serious as it had been before. Sydney grabbed the edge of the rank with the gold bar on it and pulled, but that just pulled Reagan's blouse away from her chest, so she used two fingers of the hand holding the purse and the new rank to press on the shirt. It wasn't lost on her that she was touching between Reagan's breasts. "Sorry," she whispered.

The corners of Reagan's lips curved again, but her gaze stayed on the back of the room. Sydney finally got the old patch free; it really shouldn't have been such a challenge since it was only affixed with Velcro, but it was apparently the strongest Velcro in the history of the world.

She took the new patch with the embroidered black bar and pressed it into Reagan's chest. Reagan let out a puff of air. Sydney did too. She ran her fingertips up and down the small patch a few times. She had to make sure it was firmly attached, didn't she?

Reagan's eyes flicked to hers as well for a half of a second, and Sydney took a step back.

"Congratulations, First Lieutenant Jennings," the DJ or whatever said.

"Congratulations," Sydney whispered. "Thank you for letting me be a part of this."

Reagan finally broke the stiff posture and smiled. "Thank you," she said and pulled Sydney into a quick hug.

Sydney's arms answered instinctively, wrapping around her. The stiffness of the uniform was rougher than she expected, but Reagan's breath against her ear felt anything but stiff. She wanted to savor the moment, but she couldn't because Reagan was pulling away as quickly as she'd pulled her in and was moving to shake the hand of someone else.

Everything moved so quickly while Sydney was still in a haze from being so close that she could feel Reagan's exhales on her cheek. She smiled and shook people's hands and wondered if she looked like a cartoon of a woman with stars instead of eyes. She hoped not. She knew that would be an issue for Reagan, and she'd never do anything to damage her career. So she tried to play the best friend role as best she could. And after all, it wasn't like there was anything going on.

After what felt like a breath and an eternity all at once, they were walking back to Reagan's car.

"Thank you again. It was really nice having you here. This wasn't a particularly exciting promotion or anything, but it was awesome having a friendly face do the pinning."

Sydney thought about what to say. She didn't want to gush, but she did want Reagan to know how much it meant to her that she'd been included. "I've never done something like this, and it was super cool. So thank you."

"Would you mind if we swung by my place so I can change before dinner? I promise, it'll be a quick stop."

Seeing Reagan's home? Yes, please. "Of course. Fridays are off days for classes, so I'm free until Monday." Sydney realized she could've been implying something she hadn't meant to with giving her availability through Monday but was relieved when Reagan didn't seem to take it that way.

"Perfect. I'm only a few minutes from here."

When they pulled up to the *estate* Reagan was staying in, Sydney gasped. "*This* is your *flat?*"

Reagan was adorable with her nervous chuckle. "Sometimes, our accommodations when we're TDY are a little better than normal." She shrugged.

"You could say that. Well, I haven't seen your place in Germany, but this is gorgeous."

The house looked like a mansion. It was four stories and was a gorgeous beige color with a red roof. It wasn't just the house; the grounds were also amazing. It was like a photo out of an Italian calendar.

"I don't have the full building if that makes you feel better. Just the top floor. Though it's lovely." She led Sydney up three rather steep flights of stairs before opening a beautiful wood door with intricate floral carvings into a voluminous space.

"This is amazing," she said without thought. It looked exactly as she would picture a historic flat in Italy should have looked. Reagan gave her a glass of water and went to change, leaving Sydney to explore. It was a little barren, and it was strange that Reagan didn't have a single photo, but maybe she had to pack lightly regardless of the length of assignment?

Sydney wandered onto a quaint balcony off the living room. It looked out over the city, and she was again struck by how close this building was to such a vibrant city and yet, seemed to be a world away too.

"This is my favorite spot," Reagan said as she joined her.

"It's beautiful."

"I can't tell you how many evenings I've spent sitting out here with a glass of wine, watching the city bustling below."

"I can certainly understand why." Sydney wished, hard, that Reagan would step just a little closer, but instead, she leaned against the railing a few inches away. Sydney craved even a casual brush of their arms. Although she had loved Reagan in uniform, she looked just as amazing in her khaki capris and light pink, short-sleeved, button-up with brown flip-flops.

"Shall we head out? I missed lunch because I knew I was going to cut out early and am starving." Reagan inclined her head toward the door. Sydney felt reluctant but knew it would be weird to come up with an excuse to stay, so she agreed, and they were on their way again in Reagan's tiny smart car.

"I couldn't help but notice that you don't travel with a lot of knickknacks or mementos," Sydney said when they were pulling out.

"My dad moved us around a lot when I was little, so I got used to traveling light. I have a small photo album that I always take with me but otherwise, just the bare essentials."

"No wall of photos at your place in Germany?"

"Nope."

"No porcelain buffalo from a family trip to Yellowstone on your mantle?" Sydney felt silly when she giggled at her own comment.

"Never went to Yellowstone with the family, and even if we had, nope."

"Huh."

"Huh, what?"

"That just seems strange. My mom is pretty sentimental and keeps little souvenirs from everyplace we've been, mostly little places we could drive to on the east coast and camp. She'd spend the entire trip looking for the single perfect souvenir. In Myrtle Beach, it was a little shell turtle with adorable googly eyes. In Boston, it was a Boston Tea Party tea set, of course. I also have a perfect souvenir from every trip sitting at home in my bedroom. We moved around a lot too, but those little trinkets were the most important things we moved with us. Those and books."

Reagan chuckled. "If you used professional movers, I'm sure they hated you."

"Ha. Movers? Not so much. But I love those little things. As corny as they are, I go home and look at them and smile at all the fun times we've had. They're worth the world to me." She shrugged, knowing she probably sounded childish but wanted Reagan to really know her. "Every time I pick up my crab Beanie Baby from the time Mom and I went to Maryland, I smile and laugh at how my mom gushed over the crab cakes at one random hole-in-the-wall. If she could have married a food, she would've run off to Vegas with it."

Reagan cackled. "That's sweet. I'm jealous."

"No way." Sydney swatted her shoulder.

Although Reagan didn't pull her eyes from the road as she expertly maneuvered through traffic at a terrifying pace, a hint of a smile crossed her lips. "No, I'm serious. My family is so by the book about everything. We've done some traveling but nothing whimsical or silly. It's always strictly regimented to ensure we don't miss anything." She dropped her tone to mimic a man. "Zero seven thirty, breakfast; zero eight hundred, lock and load; zero nine hundred, arrive at battlefield; zero nine thirty, commence battlefield guided tour." She shook her head and returned to her normal voice. "Souvenirs? I think not. No clutter is permitted."

"That's so sad." Sydney couldn't imagine life being so regimented from start to finish.

"A little sad, but it's all I've known." She shrugged. "I mean, I've had opportunities to live in and visit a lot of amazing places. Some blah ones too, but those stories are not worth telling. But I'm not great at spontaneity as a result. We never changed plans midstream. I'm not *that* bad, as I know plans are only good until the mission starts, but I'm not spontaneous."

"What do you call this?" Sydney pointed at them and the car.

"Dinner. Everyone has to eat, right?"

"But you didn't plan it all out, did you? We're doing this spur-of-the-moment, aren't we? Do you even know where you're taking us?" Sydney didn't think Reagan was as uptight as she claimed. "Also, you pivoted that day that we met and toured with me."

"We still did my exact itinerary that first day. No changes other than I had company. And I had this idea of an early dinner and celebratory drink this morning, so still following my plan. Flexibility but not spontaneity." Finally, at a stoplight, she looked at Sydney with an expression that said, "Challenge me on this, but I'm right." That cocky look did *something* to Sydney's belly.

"Okay, okay. I concede. But give me time." Something about the idea of making Reagan step out of her comfort zone sent a little thrill through her.

"I'll believe it when I see it," Reagan said as she pulled into the parking lot of a restaurant along the water.

Even if Reagan didn't believe it possible, Sydney was committed to breaking her out of her rigid box—at least a little bit—before she had to head back to the States, and that thought sent a wave of warmth across her skin.

As they walked to the entrance to the restaurant, Reagan said, "Oh, did you want to invite any of your friends for dinner? Or drinks?"

Sydney looked at her watch. It was only four thirty, which gave her the perfect excuse to not invite them. "Nah, Aliyah and a few of our other classmates took the train to Rome and aren't due back until later. They might even end up staying so they can experience the night scene or something."

Reagan stopped and stared. "Oh, I'm sorry. Did I keep you from that with my dumb ceremony? You could've said no. It wasn't a big deal."

Sydney rolled her eyes. "First off, it was a big deal to me. When am I going to have another chance to do that? Second, they were planning to spend the full day at the Vatican. Total overkill. We did that the last time we went up, and I don't need another whole day there." Sydney didn't mention that *everyone* wasn't planning to do the Vatican again, and she could've toured the Colosseum, but once Reagan had invited her to the ceremony, she wasn't going to miss it.

Reagan's touches sometimes lingered slightly longer than felt normal. Sydney knew it was forbidden, but she hoped there was something a little deeper there and couldn't help but jump on every opportunity to spend time with Reagan and try to find out.

CHAPTER FIVE

Bringing Sydney back to her place after their amazing dinner didn't seem like the smartest move when she was trying to keep some emotional distance, but when Sydney suggested they head somewhere else for another drink, Reagan realized how much she wasn't ready for the night to be over. But she didn't want to drink and then drive, so she suggested heading back to her place and letting Sydney crash in the guest room.

It was one of the least thought-out plans Reagan had ever had, but despite it making things more difficult for her self-control, she wanted to spend as much time with Sydney as she could. She was well and truly damned if she did and if she didn't.

"Thanks again for having me over." Sydney smiled sweetly. "I just thought we didn't quite celebrate enough at dinner."

"Fair enough. How about a glass of Brunello? That feels pretty celebratory, right?" It was her nicest bottle of wine, and she'd been sitting on it for weeks.

"I don't know enough about wine to weigh in, so whatever you think is fine with me."

"Yet."

"What?"

"You don't know enough about wine yet. I'm pretty sure we're going to get to enough wineries that you're going to learn a lot more."

"I like the sound of that." Sydney smiled and nodded. "When should we start?"

Reagan laughed. "Tomorrow? It's Saturday, after all." *What was she doing?* "There's a winery up in southern Tuscany that's on my list. We could hit it up if you don't have other plans." She shrugged and pulled out her corkscrew, nervously going to work opening the bottle as she waited to hear Sydney's reaction.

Sydney leaned back against the counter, and when Reagan looked up, she said, "Sounds fun." She looked so gorgeous in that dress, and the way she had her hands resting on the counter behind her highlighted surprisingly defined shoulders.

Reagan swallowed hard, trying to relieve the sudden dryness. "Cool." *What a nerd.* "Should we sit out on the balcony?"

Rather than answering, Sydney took the glass Reagan was offering with a sultry smile and headed to the door. Had her fingers lingered for a second longer than normal? The base of Reagan's throat fluttered, and her heartbeat thundered in her chest as she watched Sydney's hips sway as she walked.

By the time she got her wits together and caught up, Sydney was already settled in a chair on the balcony with her right leg crossed over her left, and Reagan struggled to not stare at the flex and release of her perfect calf. She dropped into her seat and forced herself to look at the city. "What's your favorite color?" It was a ridiculous question, but she had to say something to get her focus off Sydney's body.

"Where did that come from?"

Reagan took a sip of wine, soothing her still-dry throat, as she stared pointedly into the distance. "Just a question."

"Red."

"That doesn't surprise me at all."

"No, blue."

"Wait, which is it?" Reagan was surprised she was indecisive about anything. Especially something as innocuous as her favorite color.

"It's a more difficult question than you think. Because it depends on the moment and on my mood. Sometimes, it might also be orange."

"How does your favorite color morph depending on your mood?"

"I like blue when I'm mellow, thinking about the ocean. I think I told you I spent a few years in Virginia Beach, and one summer, my mom saved up enough that we took a road trip to the Florida Keys. And that water was so blue and turquoise and aquamarine. It was beautiful, kind of like here. So when I'm feeling mellow, or want to feel mellow, blue it is."

"Okay. So why red or orange?"

"Orange if I'm out having a blast, or I feel like I'm living the lyrics of that 'Walking on Sunshine' song. Orange is my *everything is going my way* song. And red, well, red is my strong emotion color. If I'm super angry or fired up or passionate."

Was she feeling passionate now, and that was why she'd said red first? "Huh. And you don't feel like you lean toward one more than the others?" It seemed so bizarre to not have an actual favorite.

"Nope."

Reagan couldn't stop herself from asking, "What's your favorite color in this moment?"

"Red."

"Why are you particularly fired up today? It seems like it's been chill."

"You." Sydney sucked in a sharp breath. "I mean, it's been a really exciting day for you."

"Shouldn't that be an orange day? Because everything is going the right way?"

Sydney bit the side of her lip, which was entirely unfair and hampered Reagan's ability to think rationally, an ability she normally prided herself on. "Well, it's orange for you. But not necessarily me. Anyway, what's *your* favorite color since we are getting so deep here?"

"Blue. Deep blue to gray blue," Reagan said without a thought. Thankfully, she didn't tack on the, *the same color as your eyes*, that almost followed it. She shook her head at herself.

"Huh. Now, I would have seen you as a gray person."

"Gray? That's so…bland. Am I bland?" She had a lot of rules and things to live by, but bland wasn't how she saw herself. Sydney thinking her bland was horrifying.

"No! A bland person wouldn't savor chocolate croissants like you do. They'd probably have a slice of toast. Or not even toast. Just bread. A slice of bread without butter. But gray feels like a military quest, down to business, no-frills sort of color."

Reagan slumped in her seat. "Exactly. Bland." Was that who she'd become? Who she'd always been? It was a sobering—and depressing—thought.

Sydney dragged her chair next to Reagan's, making one of the worst metal-on-concrete sounds Reagan had ever heard, and placed a hand on her knee. "Absolutely not. Just because you aren't a free spirit doesn't make you bland. I mean, I'm not a free spirit. But you are amazing. And special. And fun. I've had more fun with you in the last few weeks than I've had with anyone. You make the world a better place. And I'll fight anyone who tries to say something different."

"You really think I'm not boring? Because I do. I read books for fun. And run. It's weird, isn't it?" Reagan hunched in her chair, feeling exposed, head spinning. She'd had a glass and a half of wine at dinner, and although this was her first glass at home, she felt more buzzed than she'd thought. Clearly, her judgment was impaired.

But God, Sydney looked pretty framed by the setting sun in front of them.

"Some people might see that as boring, but I think it's fantastic. *You* are fantastic. I've never known anyone quite like you before, *First Lieutenant* Jennings."

Hearing her rank, while sexy, was also like hearing the needle scraped across the top of a vintage Beatles record. What was she doing? Reagan jumped up, yanking her knee from beneath Sydney's hand. "I need another drink. How about you?" Her voice sounded like Screech from *Saved by the Bell*, but Reagan didn't care. She needed space. She. Could. Not. Do. This. She couldn't feel this. So she fled. Like an adult.

"Uh…" Sydney started as she stared at Reagan's half-full glass.

Shit. Reagan couldn't believe she was going to do this because it certainly wasn't going to help the sober and rational part of her mind, but she tipped the wineglass back and downed the contents in two gulps.

"Uh." Sydney's gaze flicked between her own glass and Reagan's. "Sure. I'm ready." She tipped her glass back too and took one impressive swallow.

Drinking Brunello like that was a crime.

"I'll be right back," Reagan said while still completely distracted by the beautiful column of Sydney's neck. The muscles in Sydney's throat flexing as she swallowed shouldn't have been sexy, but they were.

Jesus.

Reagan grabbed Sydney's glass by the stem, very careful not to touch her hand, and practically ran inside. She squeezed the glasses harder than was safe. This was not good. To buy herself more time, she set the glasses on the counter and went into her bathroom to splash cold water on her face. Her hands shook, and she tightened them into fists as she squeezed her eyes closed, desperately trying to banish the image of Sydney with her cherry red lips and wavy blond hair, but it was burned on the backs of her eyelids.

"Lieutenant Jennings," she whispered as she made eye contact with herself in the mirror. "You are going to march back out there and act civilly. Make small talk and drink one small glass of wine without touching her or letting her touch you. You'll talk about the weather, football, anything so there are no lulls in the conversation. You graduated from West Point at the top of your class through sheer will and determination. You can resist these little urges. You've got this."

She splashed water on her face, resolved to stop feeling anything inappropriate. That resolve was quickly tested, however, as Sydney waited for her in the kitchen, leaning against the counter like she owned it. *Fuck.*

"I was starting to wonder if you'd gotten lost. Especially when I saw the glasses still empty." She lifted her now full glass. "Hope you don't mind that I divvied up the rest."

"No, of course not." That was not the small pour Reagan had been planning. "Sorry I kept you waiting." She didn't make a move to grab her glass. She didn't trust herself to get that close.

Sydney pressed her lips together and winced. "Do you mind if we stay inside? I was getting a little chilly." She ran her free hand up and down her arm, and Reagan realized she had goose bumps. "This dress isn't very warm, you know?"

"Sorry. Do you want a sweatshirt or something?" Reagan felt guilty that she hadn't realized Sydney had been uncomfortable.

"Sure, thank you."

Reagan grabbed the first sweatshirt hanging in her closet, a West Point zipper hoodie. When Sydney took it, Reagan grabbed her wine and quickly moved to the other side of the kitchen in an effort to keep distance between them. "It's surprisingly cool tonight. I wasn't expecting it." *Great job, talking about the weather. Just stick to the plan until you can escape to bed.*

"I would've brought a sweater or something if I'd known. I'm just not used to everything being in Celsius yet." She giggled. That was cute too. "Thanks for this hoodie. It's warm."

"Of course. Are you a football fan?" God, she sounded like a dork jumping from topic to topic without even a breath. Apparently, Sydney thought so too as she laughed loudly and choked on a sip of wine.

"You're all over the place this evening. My dad was a Washington fan, so I guess I cheered for them, but I'm not a huge fan."

"Well, Washington kind of sucks, so it's probably good you aren't a super fan." Reagan shrugged, trying to be casual before changing the subject again. Because that was totally normal. "What do you think of the wine?"

"Aren't you going to tell me who your team is?" Sydney squinted at her. "Why are you being so weird?"

"I'm not weird. You're weird." She knew she wasn't being clever. She was one thousand percent weird. "But my team is Kansas City. My dad retired as the garrison commander at Fort Leonard Wood in Missouri, but he was also stationed there two other times when I was younger, and that was when I was learning about football."

"That's wild. Where all have you lived?"

Reagan thought for a moment. She'd really lived all over but tried to start at the beginning. "Where haven't I lived seems more like it, but I was born in Washington at Fort Lewis, but we also lived in Texas, Oklahoma, Missouri three times, England, Kentucky, Germany, Georgia. All over, really."

"Wow. That's a lot. I know that's tough growing up."

"For sure. It was like every time I made a good friend, either my dad was getting sent somewhere or theirs was. I tried to stay in touch, but after a while, the letters or emails trailed off, and that was that." She shrugged. She was used to being a loner, which was why her friendship with Sydney was so odd. "You dealt with some of that too, didn't you?" she said, remembering Sydney's father had been a SEAL.

"A little. But by the time I was in middle school, we stayed put. Sort of." Sadness flashed across her face, and Reagan wanted to ask why, but Sydney shook herself, and a smile that looked a little too bright flashed across her face. "What's your favorite?"

Reagan took a sip to buy time because the first thought that popped into her mind was: here. That moment. But there was no way she could say that.

Sydney's overly bright smile softened into a genuine one. "Don't overthink it, just tell me."

That real smile did her in. "Here," Reagan croaked, unable to stop herself.

Sydney's eyes darkened. "Really?" She said it so quiet, Reagan could barely hear her.

Reagan nodded.

"Like Italy? Naples?" Sydney bit her lip as she looked at Reagan with eyes too blue for their own good.

"Like now. This moment." Reagan was playing with fire, but she couldn't stop. Something about Sydney tonight…she couldn't look away. Sydney stared at her with that perfect mouth, lips slightly parted. "I…" She stopped and took a sip of wine.

Sydney took a step toward her.

Reagan took a sip, then another without tasting the wine and felt paralyzed. Unsure.

Sydney grabbed a piece of lint from Reagan's shirt. "You just had this fuzz." She held her index finger out with a tiny spec of gray on it before pursing her lips and blowing it off.

But she didn't move away.

"Thank you," Reagan mumbled. She looked at the floor, too nervous to look up. But she watched as Sydney ran a finger down her forearm until she loosely interlaced their fingers. Lightly squeezed.

Reagan's mouth was painfully dry. She cleared her throat, but it was like she'd swallowed a handful of sand.

"Are you okay?"

Reagan took a sip of wine, then pointed at her throat. "Just a tickle. I should probably have water instead." She shrugged. Her head was light. Was it the wine or Sydney?

Sydney was staring at her mouth, and she licked her lips reflexively. She didn't know if she wanted Sydney to lean in or move away—that had to be the wine—but as Sydney drifted closer, Reagan caught sight of the West Point emblem emblazoned across the chest of her sweatshirt, and every reason this was impossible flooded back.

Honor. Integrity. Selfless service.

Fuck.

She stepped back and pulled her hand away more sharply than she'd meant to. The hurt that flashed across Sydney's face was like a sucker punch, but Reagan couldn't give into this need, no matter how badly she wanted to.

❖

Sydney's entire being deflated when Reagan pulled away.

She'd been trying to feel her out all evening and thought Reagan had been giving her green lights. Well, except for her sudden need to refill drinks that weren't empty. Okay, looking back, that had been at least a pink light. She'd thought Reagan was just nervous.

But now that the strong "no" had been issued by actions if not words, Sydney didn't know how to fix it. She didn't know if words *could* fix it based on Reagan's tight expression.

Reagan's chest rose and fell, and Sydney felt the need to backpedal. Pretend what she'd been thinking wasn't what she'd been thinking. "I'm sorry, I didn't mean to…I mean, I wasn't trying to…I…I'm so sorry if I—that I—misread."

Reagan sighed so hard, a napkin sitting on the counter fluttered. "I want to. God, do I want to, but I can't. I can't believe I'm admitting this out loud, but you have no idea how sorry I am that I can't." She closed her eyes and ran her thumb and middle finger in opposite directions across her forehead, as though she was trying to stretch the stress off her face.

"I don't understand. We're alone." The harm of two adults doing something in the privacy of Reagan's home was something Sydney couldn't grasp.

Reagan winced. "I know. Fuck the Army, and fuck Don't Ask, Don't Tell. Can we sit?" She chuckled, and Sydney's heart dropped. "On opposite sides of the room?"

Sydney's instinct was to run home and lick her wounds. But she couldn't. Not when Reagan was still willing to talk. Maybe she could still sway her. And there was something about Reagan that she couldn't run from, so she nodded and followed her into the living room after grabbing her glass from the counter.

"I've always known I wasn't really interested in boys. In high school, my friends were boy crazy, but I threw myself into track and cross-country and student government and my job. I loved all those things and needed them for my academy application. Yet, they were all excuses to not date. Not that it kept me from developing a crush on Tatiana, the head cheerleader and salutatorian, who I was competing against for valedictorian." She rolled her eyes and paused to take a drink.

Sydney wanted to say something, but the appropriate response eluded her. She understood being in denial to yourself, but did this mean Reagan *was* gay?

"But then came West Point and Molly Baker." Reagan sighed. "She was a year ahead of me, and she'd been in my student chain of command when I was a lowly plebe. She took me under her wing, and at first, it was just a little hero worship. Natural. But over the next three years, we grew closer and closer, and I realized that I definitely had a crush. And it wasn't unrequited. But we were both too dedicated to allow anything to go any further than a hug that lasted a breath too long. We were bound to the honor code. 'A cadet will not lie, cheat, steal, or tolerate those who do,' and a relationship would require lying, since homosexual acts were a crime. Then one night, we were on pass in New York City. We'd been out drinking and dancing at a club, and we kissed. It was brief, a mistake. We both pretended it never happened, and we lost touch after she graduated. And..." She dusted her hands together and shrugged.

"So the honor code is what you still live by, even though you're not at the academy? Why is what you do at home an issue?"

Reagan chewed her lip, eyes filled with sadness. "I'm sure to someone who is so out and unashamed, it doesn't make sense, but the military has laws that only apply to military personnel, the UCMJ, and under that, any homosexual conduct is illegal. Kissing, holding hands." She swallowed hard. "Sex. It's all grounds for prosecution and a dishonorable discharge."

"But no one is here. Who's going to know?"

"Me. I can't willingly break the law. We have these other values, similar to the honor code. They're called the core values, and by taking my commission in the Army, I have agreed to abide by them. Loyalty, duty, respect, selfless service, honor, integrity, personal courage. If I sit here and convince myself to do the wrong thing—no, the illegal thing under the law—just because no one is watching? It means I have no integrity, and without integrity, I can't really embody any of the other values. I don't think I'd be able to look at myself in the mirror if I didn't have integrity." She looked so downcast. So lost.

"But it's an unjust law. It's not illegal to be gay in the real world." Sydney couldn't fathom being forced to pretend to be something she wasn't. It wasn't fair.

"I know. But I have chosen this life, and I have to abide by the rules I agreed to when I swore in. And maybe they'll change. I pray they change because I don't want to be old and alone. And I'm not going to marry some dude just to have a family. But until the law changes, this is who I am. Closeted lesbian Reagan Jennings, who sticks to herself and doesn't—can't—get involved with anyone. But this is my life, my career, and I'm not going to change it." The earnestness in her eyes was painful. "No matter how attracted to someone I am."

It felt like the air had been completely let out of Sydney's balloon, and she was left with a sad, floppy shell. "What does that mean for us now?" She hated asking. Was terrified of the answer, but she couldn't stand waiting. She needed to know if Reagan was going to cut her out of her life or if they could go back to being friends. Best friends. The idea of spending time together as only friends without the *possibility* of more was awful, but the idea of never seeing Reagan again was unbearable.

"I...I should stay away from you."

Sydney wanted to throw up.

"I don't want to. I'm not sure that I can even if I did, knowing you're still here for another two months. For that matter, I hate the thought of you leaving. You've become my closest friend."

"You have no idea how relieved I am to hear that." Sydney tried to dampen her smile so as to not seem like an eager puppy but knew she was failing.

"You are the first person I've acknowledged my sexuality to. Obviously, Molly knew, but we never talked about it. Ever." She shrugged, but the vulnerability on her face made Sydney's heart stutter.

"Wow. Really?" Sydney couldn't believe she could walk around holding that big of a secret without ever sharing it.

Reagan nodded. "I feel like we were friends in another life or something. I don't know. But you make me feel safe, and I'm drawn to you in a way I've never felt before."

Sydney wanted to squeeze her hand but tightened her fingers around her glass instead. "It's the same for me. Every time I see something fun or new, I think 'Reagan would love this,' and I try to remember to tell you about it. Everything just feels *better* when we're together. And if you need me to just be your friend, I can do that. I promise. You've become my closest friend too. Well, you and Aliyah, but in different ways." Sydney didn't know how she'd be able to force her feelings away. She didn't mention that every time she saw Reagan, she was sure her heart would hurt a little. But she'd take whatever she could get. "And I hate the thought of leaving and never seeing you again too." She added the last part as the thought was a little devastating. She'd do whatever she needed to, and maybe, someday in the future, things would change, and everything would become possible.

When Sydney lay in Reagan's guest bed later that night, she hoped that she could live up to the promises she'd made. At least to the point where Reagan couldn't tell when she was hiding her true feelings. She'd thought about going home that evening, but both she and Reagan were too buzzed to drive, and calling a taxi seemed like too many euros that she didn't have.

Yet, no matter how much she hated the fact that Reagan had rejected her that evening, a tiny part of her was jubilant that she knew for certain that Reagan *had* feelings for her. *Was* attracted to her. It was only the military that kept them apart. She also appreciated that Reagan had been open about why they couldn't be together, even though she wanted it.

And although Sydney needed to be realistic, she couldn't help but dream about a day when Don't Ask, Don't Tell was repealed. Obama had apparently recently made a statement reiterating that he intended to end it, but there was no timetable. But to Sydney, the most important thing was that it *would be* rescinded.

And although Reagan wasn't exactly who she'd envisioned for her long-term, the magnetism between them was hard to deny. Sydney had a need to be around her that she'd never experienced. And Reagan was funny, incredibly attractive, upwardly mobile—though not in the way Sydney expected—and perfect in every other way. If two people really wanted to make something work, they had to be able to find a way. Nothing was impossible.

But she couldn't let her heart run away with itself. She still had law school and a job and making partner to conquer before she settled down. Yet she couldn't help but wonder if Reagan could be the person she was supposed to settle down with.

CHAPTER SIX

The drumming of Reagan's fingers on her desk was more soothing than it had a right to be. She was likely annoying the hell out of everyone in her office, but she was cranky and tired and moody, and she'd take whatever type of comfort she could find.

She tried to work, but every time she did, her mind kept floating back to the last few weeks and Sydney. She couldn't believe how everything had played out. Sydney almost kissing her. How furiously she'd wanted it. Yet, she'd somehow managed to find the self-control to stop. To push her away. Sort of, anyway. And smooth it over. The vineyard should have been romantic, but somehow, they'd managed to keep it light and friendly. Distinctly *unromantic*. It was like talking about their attraction and how it was an impossibility had taken away some of its power, and they were able to just hang out without all the heavy stuff sitting between them like the humidity on a sticky August afternoon in Fort Leonard Wood, Missouri.

At least, that was how Reagan felt, and she hoped Sydney felt the same. She'd been worried that, even after the vineyard, Sydney might be too attached, and Reagan had tried avoiding her, but they'd both found a way to be mature about everything.

Which was a relief because the thought of not spending Sydney's remaining time here together—as much as they could, given Sydney's school and Reagan's work schedule—was heartbreaking, so she was thankful that they were back to hanging out as friends.

But God, Reagan wished there was someone—anyone—she could talk to about all of this. All these impossible feelings still wormed their way into her consciousness at the most inopportune times, like while she was lying in bed at night trying to sleep, and now, while she needed to work. But there wasn't anyone.

She wasn't out to her parents or siblings or friends. In fact, it was in becoming such close friends with Sydney that she'd realized exactly why she didn't consider anyone a close friend. She'd never been completely herself with anyone before. But with Sydney, she'd slowly opened up until she could reveal the real her. Granted, she hadn't come out to Sydney until a few nights ago, but she hadn't been actively hiding it, either. They could just talk about anything and everything, and it was…real. She'd never said the words "I'm gay," out loud, yet everything had poured out of her on Friday night. She wished she could talk to Sydney about how she was really feeling, but that was impossible. She needed Sydney to be strong and knew if Sydney realized just how conflicted Reagan still was, it would be a lot harder.

And God help her, she'd invited Sydney to stay with her for a couple of weeks after her course ended. If she needed Sydney to be strong before, she *really needed* her to be now.

What bullshit Don't Ask, Don't Tell was, an archaic law that had no place in today's military. She knew of people who were gay but discreet, but she simply couldn't do that. Integrity was the most important trait a person could possess. Once someone lost their integrity, it was impossible to get it back, and she wasn't willing to sacrifice hers for anything.

Not even for the first girl who'd ever made her question whether it was all worth it.

"Are you trying to send a Morse code message to Russia?" Lieutenant Greene said as she passed.

"Huh?" Reagan looked at her for a clue.

Greene raised her brows and looked pointedly at Reagan's hands.

"Oops." She smiled, chagrined, and covered her tapping hand with the other one to stop the pitter-patter. "Sorry," she said and shrugged, determined to focus on her work and stop lamenting.

"Why are you so…agitated?"

"I'm not." Which wasn't the truth, but it wasn't like Reagan could get into why. That was all part of this hellish conundrum. Greene wouldn't be who she would confide in anyway, but it would be nice to have the option to talk to *someone*. Especially now that Sydney was going to be staying with her for two weeks. She needed someone as a sounding board because she might've just made the biggest mistake of her life.

❖

"Can I help you carry some of this down?" Reagan asked on Sunday morning when Sydney opened the door.

"Nope, this is it," Sydney said, laden with a pack on her back, a suitcase in one hand, and a massive duffel bag in the other.

"I don't think you can even fit in the stairwell carrying all of that." As if to prove Reagan's point, Sydney was halfway through the doorway when her duffel and suitcase collided with each other and the door frame behind her. Sydney's momentum caused her to tumble into Reagan's arms as she lost her grip on both bags.

Reagan grabbed her, something she'd been getting used to. She congratulated herself when, once Sydney seemed to have her balance back, she squeezed Sydney's arms and released her. She didn't savor that moment with Sydney pressed against her. Not even a little bit. She was purely performing a public service. "Are you okay there?"

Sydney's face was perfectly pink in embarrassment, though Reagan didn't understand why. She tripped at least once every time they hung out. She was probably going to have to catch her daily. It was no big deal. And not something she was going to enjoy. Not at all.

Sydney giggled, and Reagan's abs tightened. "Sorry, I'm so clumsy. I try to be more coordinated, but I'm just not sure how." There was that giggle again. Damn.

"Maybe you should try a yoga class with me. It's good for coordination. There's one on base. You'll tone a lot of muscles you don't even realize you have. Not that you need to tone your muscles. You look fine—more than fine—I mean, not..." *Jesus.* Reagan felt her own face going hot as she stumbled around words she had no business saying. Or thinking. "I just—"

"Don't worry about it," Sydney said and smiled. "I didn't take offense. Maybe helping to strengthen the tiny muscles I don't know exist *will* help with my coordination. I'll take you up on a class when we aren't catching the last few Italian bucket list sites."

Reagan exhaled and felt a lot better. She hadn't offended Sydney; that was the last thing she'd ever want. "Okay, cool. There's a class Tuesday evening. You could take the train down to the base and meet me after work? The station is only a block away." She didn't want to sound too hopeful, but the idea of sharing something else with Sydney filled her heart with a little bubble of joy.

Sydney shrugged one shoulder. "Sure. Why not?"

❖

Reagan sat in her car Tuesday evening, waiting. Sydney had enjoyed yoga so much the week before that she'd asked to come back again, and this was their last chance before Sydney headed home the following Monday.

Reagan couldn't believe how fast the last week had gone and felt dread deep in the pit of her stomach at the thought of Sydney leaving. Sydney had quickly become the best friend she'd ever had, but she was afraid they'd lose touch once Sydney was back in her real life. She'd been toying around with inviting her up to Florence for a couple of days as a going-away gift. Reagan had a pass so they could have a long weekend, but she was afraid Sydney would shoot it down because she was worried about money and was adamant about Reagan not paying for her.

Every thought was wiped from her mind, however, when Sydney emerged from the train station doors. Last week, she'd been in leggings, and this week, she was wearing short shorts that should have been illegal. Had her legs somehow gotten longer? Sydney walking toward her was sexier than Ursula Andress coming out of the water in the white bathing suit in *Dr. No*.

"Hey, you," Sydney said, sliding onto the passenger seat of Reagan's rented Smart car.

Reagan coughed. "Hey," she managed.

"Fancy meeting you here. How was your day?" Sydney smiled, and there was that dimple again.

Lord help me.

Sydney somehow was radiating sunshine and all the beauty in the world. Reagan needed to touch her. Swipe that wayward tendril off her forehead. Squeeze her hand. Anything to be closer.

Instead, she clenched her jaw and squeezed the wheel tighter. She pushed in the clutch and slid the car into first, focusing all her attention on it so she wouldn't have the ability to think. She had no idea how she was going to keep a casual conversation going for the few minutes between the station and base.

When she'd invited Sydney to stay with her, she'd felt like she had a handle on this little crush. They'd given it a name, talked about it, demystified it. The crush didn't control her anymore.

Until Sydney moved in. And they saw each other at the softest and most intimate moments of the day. As they sat on her rooftop patio drinking a cup of espresso in the morning. As they had both fallen asleep on the couch watching *Julie & Julia* last night.

Sydney had had a very strange look on her face as Reagan had cleaned up their empty wineglasses and the cheese and bread board. No. It wasn't *strange*. It was hungry. And not for more cheese. For Reagan. She'd almost dropped the glasses when she'd recognized it. Because although Sydney's eyes were heavy and her breathing was slow from just being awoken, there was a need there that Reagan had immediately recognized.

For the first time in her life, Reagan had understood the meaning of "bedroom eyes" that she'd read about in romance novels. She'd ached to wrap Sydney up in her arms and kiss her. Hold her. Simply share the same air with her.

It was impossible, but seeing those heavily lidded, needy eyes had called to Reagan in a way she'd never expected. A way she'd never felt before. She needed it to stop, but God, she didn't want it to.

Part of the problem was that, at the end of the night, when she was relaxed and tired, seeing Sydney in her soft cotton pajamas with that relaxed and sexy face felt like a kill switch on her self-control, as if there had been a power outage, and her self-control board had been fried. And she didn't know who had the skill set to repair it. She certainly didn't.

And now…she had no idea what to do. She only had a week left with this temptress, and then, she might never see her again. She wanted to weep at the thought in both relief and sadness. She had feelings, complicated feelings that she couldn't put a name to.

She wasn't sure what Sydney had been saying their whole drive; she'd just been smiling and nodding the whole way back to post and through the checkpoint and across the base, but now they were parked, and she no longer had the excuse of keeping her eyes on the road.

"What do you think?"

Reagan finally looked at Sydney with no idea what she was asking. "Sorry, I was focused on parking. What do I think about what?"

There were those damned dimples again. "Gelato after yoga?"

"Of course. Who doesn't want gelato twenty-four seven?"

While heading to gelato later, Sydney said, "You don't think I'm indecent in these shorts? I wasn't comfortable wearing them, but my leggings were dirty." Giggle. "I guess I could've worn sweatpants, but it felt too warm out for that. Even though it's December."

She looked a tiny bit indecent. Or decadent. Or delectable. Or any number of words Reagan couldn't think of. And now she couldn't tear her eyes away from Sydney's legs as they walked. "No, I think you look fine." *Great.* "But if you'd be more comfortable, we can grab it to-go and take it back home. Or we could walk around while we eat. It's beautiful tonight."

Sydney gave her a soft smile. It was sweet and adorable and reminded Reagan to stop objectifying her. "Okay."

Reagan had spent the whole class trying to flow in the spirit of anti-objectification. And still—in warrior two while she was facing Sydney's back—she couldn't help but appreciate the delicate line of her neck. The way her arm muscles flexed when the instructor reminded them to tighten their muscles to the bone. So she'd slammed her eyes closed with the force of Fort Knox closing the vaults and focused on breathing.

And now she got her reward for all that amazing self-control. She made eye contact with the server and handed him her receipt. She ordered a stracciatella, and Sydney ordered a peach.

"Want to walk?" Reagan asked once they received their cups of gelato. "A cold front is moving in tomorrow, so it's probably our last night to be able to walk outside. Especially with gelato."

"*Benissimo,*" Sydney said with gusto and swooped her fist through the air.

"Your accent was nearly perfect there."

"I love how it rolls off the tongue." She said it three more times, each more emphatic as she spun in circles on the sidewalk.

"Easy there." Reagan chuckled, but Sydney spun a little too hard into her as she hit an uneven portion of the sidewalk.

"Oops," she said sheepishly. "What am I going to do without you to catch me every time I stumble?"

"Be more careful, I guess. Or perhaps not spin around like a ballerina on old narrow sidewalks?"

"You make it sound so simple, but sometimes, the night just calls for twirling." She looked so innocent and happy. Like nothing existed in the world other than them. "And this was one of those moments. Luckily, you were here to catch me."

"I guess you'll have to find a new catcher when you get home." Reagan laughed as she said the words, even though the thought of Sydney leaving and finding someone else was like a dagger.

Sydney must have felt the same because she placed a hand on Reagan's arm. "No one can replace you." Reagan tried to scoff, but Sydney said, "I mean that. I love our friendship. I don't know how to describe it, but I swear, no one will ever replace you. Even if they're also a master of catching me."

Reagan swallowed hard. "I don't think I've ever been so close to someone in my life."

They stared at each other for too long. Luckily, tourist season was mostly over, so no one was bumping into them on the sidewalk. Although Reagan hadn't committed to the idea yet, she couldn't stop herself from saying, "What would you think about going up to Tuscany for the weekend? I have a pass, so we could go up on Thursday afternoon and back Monday. Plenty of time before your red-eye home that night."

Sydney chewed her lip, rubbed the hollow at the base of her neck. Reagan could see the excitement behind the uncertainty, though. "That sounds really expensive, and I'm, well, I'm a little over budget—"

"Don't worry about that. It's a going-away gift. An early Christmas present. I'm not a student, and I don't have any bills. I want us to share this experience." Reagan stumbled over her words. She couldn't believe she'd said that. Not because it wasn't true, but because it was.

"But we've been to Florence. We don't need to waste money going up there and getting a hotel." Sydney tried to walk again, but Reagan held her in place with a light touch.

"We just did a day trip to Florence and didn't have time to see hardly anything, but I've heard all of Tuscany is wonderful. Let's go up for the long weekend, stay in the countryside, ride bicycles along the city walls in Lucca, have dinner on a rolling hill, hike, whatever. Or maybe Cinque Terre instead. It's your last hurrah, so we should make it a good one. Who knows when you'll come back here? When we'll see each other again." Reagan knew she was playing with fire, but she so wanted this. She could keep her feelings in check for a few more days while she and Sydney had a once-in-a-lifetime experience. "Please? It'll be so much fun. You're going to regret it if we spend your last weekend wandering around Naples again. Seeing. The. Same. Old. Stuff." She huffed as though that was a hardship. It wasn't. She loved Naples but wanted their last weekend together to be special.

Sydney looked like she might be starting to soften, so Reagan grabbed her free hand and squeezed, swinging it back and forth as she said, *"Please."* It was probably the silliest she'd ever been in her adult life.

Sydney rolled her eyes but smiled. Big and perfect. "Fine. If it means so much to you. But you're not paying for everything."

Reagan nodded but would pay for as much as she could. Sydney had been living on her savings since she hadn't been working in Italy, and those had to be dwindling. Reagan was lucky. She had no student loans, no car payment, no credit card debt, nothing. And it wasn't like she made bad money. She was saving and investing a ton, and she really wanted to splurge—as much as she could without Sydney knowing—so she could treat her to a good time.

CHAPTER SEVEN

Sydney had been reluctant to go to Tuscany. Her funds were running low. She'd actually started using her for-emergencies-only credit card the previous week so she wouldn't completely run out of cash. And she was sure her bank was going to charge her a fee if her balance fell much lower, which would eat away at it even faster.

But as the idea started to sink in and Reagan nearly begged her to say yes, the butterflies always present when she was with Reagan started to do huge swoops in her belly. She wondered if they were spelling out Reagan's name like someone doodling in a high school notebook. And she was so happy she'd listened. She couldn't imagine a better way to spend her last few days in Italy. And even though Reagan had been the one to put a "Do Not Enter" sign on the relationship door, she certainly had a lot of romantic ideas.

They'd ended up staying three nights in Riomaggiore, at the southern end of the Cinque Terre, five beautiful villages perched on a cliffside overlooking the Mediterranean Sea that had the most beautiful sunsets she'd ever experienced. That morning, they'd headed south toward Florence and had spent the last full day renting bikes and riding them around the medieval city walls of Lucca before checking into their bed and breakfast and wandering the streets of Florence.

The B&B Reagan had found was quaint, right along the Arno River, and seemingly within walking distance of everything. There'd been a small amount of confusion surrounding the bed situation that Sydney was not sad about. Something about the B&B owners not being

Italian and listing the room as a double versus two singles or something like that, so Reagan had booked them only one bed. A double bed that looked very small.

Sydney knew nothing could happen, but it was fun watching Reagan squirm when she spoke to the owners.

And now she appreciated the feel of Reagan's arm next to hers as they sat at the top of the steps at Piazzale Michelangelo, watching as the sun made its fiery descent into her last night in Italy while the bronze replica of Michelangelo's *David* stood guard behind them. The setting sun turned the sky bold pinks and oranges, but it gave the buildings of Florence a soft pink glow that would stay in her memory forever. It was odd how comfortable the silence was between them while they were immersed in the soundtrack of one of the busiest tourist attractions in the city. People were bustling all around, speaking all different languages, some louder than others, and the smell of toasting bread permeated the air as paninis were grilled at a food cart behind them, causing her stomach to grumble. Even though it was only four-thirty.

Reagan sighed. She sounded content but with a little sadness underneath. Sydney felt it too. She couldn't believe she was going home in just over twenty-four hours. "What was your favorite part of this weekend?"

"That's a tough one." Sydney pursed her lips as she thought back to everything they'd done. "That dinner on the hillside at the Tuscan winery was amazing, but I think my favorite was when we walked from our hotel on the path along the cliffs up to Monterosso and then took the boat back. It felt like every step we took was prettier than the last. And the smell of the ocean air. I've never experienced anything like that in my life." She giggled. "Hell, I never even dreamed something like that existed. God, that makes me sound like a bumpkin, doesn't it?"

Reagan laughed and bumped her shoulder. "Not even a little. I've traveled around Europe, spent time all over, and it left me speechless too. I don't know if I liked the hike or the boat ride more. Both were gorgeous."

Sydney would add a third option for her favorite part: doing it all with Reagan, but she wasn't going to voice that. "Same. I would've thought I would have enjoyed the boat more—and it was amazing—but I think I preferred the hiking. It was just so breathtaking."

"Given your aversion to exercise, I would've also expected you to like the boat ride better." She flashed a cheeky smile.

"Hey, I like *some* exercise. Just not running. Perhaps you're rubbing off on me."

"Maybe you'll continue your new love of yoga when you get home and think of me when you do it." It felt like Reagan was staring pointedly at the horizon so she didn't have to look at Sydney.

A lump lodged itself squarely in Sydney's throat. She tried to swallow it and force a smile, but the realization that this was their last evening together felt like it was suffocating her. Sure, she'd *known* it was their last, but the idea that after tomorrow, she had no idea when—or if—she'd see Reagan again made her want to cry. She couldn't believe how quickly their time together had gone. "Not sure if I'm going to make it to those sunrise classes at my school's gym, but there's something about moving my body that way that speaks to me. Everything feels better after yoga." If only it was a cure-all for missing someone.

Was Reagan wiping her face? She looked away, and Sydney didn't want to turn far enough to see her because that would be weird. Could Reagan be as sad about her leaving as she was? A shiver raced through her as she felt cold and empty at the thought of Reagan wanting her but being unwilling to go after what their hearts both wanted.

Reagan cleared her throat. "Are you cold?"

"Just a little. It isn't bad, but this sweater isn't quite enough. I wish I had an actual jacket now that the sun is down." That was partially true. She shivered again, and Reagan leaned into her.

"We still have a little while before dinner. Now that the sunset is over, why don't we head over to the Christmas Market? It's still outside, but at least we'll be moving around." Reagan jumped up as though her bout of melancholy was magically behind her.

The smile on her face helped cheer Sydney up. She didn't want to ruin the night by pouting, and Reagan extending a hand to help her up helped too. Even more when she ran her thumb across the back of Sydney's hand once, twice, and held on for an extra moment. She tugged, and when Sydney followed her down the stairs, she let go. Sydney desperately searched for a reason for her to hold it again but came up empty.

They walked in silence for a few minutes, their shoulders occasionally brushing. As they crossed the Arno, Sydney was again struck with how beautiful Florence was. This was the first time she'd seen it at night, and it was stunning. "We haven't walked across the Ponte Vecchio yet," Sydney said, pointing at the beautiful three-arched bridge to their left. "It's the oldest bridge in Florence, right?"

The covered stone bridge lined with shops reflected on the slow-moving river, but the twinkling lights under the arches gave it a magical look.

"It is. We can't miss that. Do you want to go for a walk after dinner to let our food settle and check it out? I'm not sure what time all the shops close, but I'm sure it will be beautiful even if they're closed. Maybe more with fewer tourists."

"You know we're tourists too, right?"

"We're different. We live here. Sort of."

"You live here," Sydney corrected.

"Until tomorrow, you live here too. And I'm only here for another month before I head back to Germany. But for now, we are *Italiano*." She said the last word with a heavy Italian accent, and Sydney giggled.

"Okay, you win," Sydney said. "I'll be *Italiano* for one more evening." She didn't try to imitate the accent, but Reagan still smiled as they both leaned against the side of the bridge and held eye contact. Significant eye contact that made Sydney forget about the cold breeze cutting through her. It made her forget that she had to leave tomorrow. It made her forget every damn thing other than this woman and this moment. Reagan's tongue darted out for half a second, and she bit her lip in that exact spot. Sydney squeezed her hand into a fist to refrain from reaching out and rubbing that spot with her thumb. She so desperately wanted to kiss her, but after her clumsy attempt that was gently rebuffed, she wouldn't dare.

A bike passed by behind them and rang its bell, ending their moment as firmly as if a rogue wave of the icy Arno below had splashed them. Reagan jumped back. "We'd better hurry, or they might run out of mulled wine."

Sydney didn't know what mulled wine was and doubted they would run out, but she understood Reagan needed space, so they walked together in a silence that had Sydney wondering what-if an awful lot.

After a few more blocks, Sydney could see some wooden booths all with cheery red-and-white striped awnings and lots of twinkly white lights. She pointed. "Is that it?"

"It is. Looks like Christmas, doesn't it?"

Sydney nodded. And as though a Christmas angel was waiting for their arrival, an orchestra suddenly started playing "Sussex Carol."

"Look at that, they're welcoming us in," Reagan said.

Sydney looked around in wonder as they stepped into the piazza. It was the first moment she felt ready for the holiday season. The little wooden booths were full of holiday gifts, trinkets, food, ornaments. She'd never seen anything like it.

She didn't realize she'd stopped until Reagan tugged her hand again. "Why don't we get some mulled wine, and then we can wander around and look at all the shops to see if there's anything you want to get for your mom?"

"Perfect. Though, aren't you getting anything for your parents or brothers?"

Reagan hadn't dropped her hand, and her fingers were so strong, yet so soft. Sydney didn't want to call attention to it, but her heartbeat started galloping. "No, uh, I'm on a TDY, a temporary duty, right now, and I can't take leave, so I'm not going back. And we aren't huge gift givers anyway. My parents are more experience-type people. I'll probably Skype the family on Christmas Day, but that'll be it."

"That sounds so...lonely." Sydney hated the thought of Reagan alone on Christmas.

"It's no big deal. It won't be the last time. Duty calls, you know?" She cleared her throat and pulled Sydney into the longest line in the food area of the market. "Have you ever been to a Christmas Market before?"

A clear change of subject, but Sydney understood there were things a person sometimes didn't want to talk about. She had plenty. And Reagan's hand was still in her own. "I haven't, but it looks great so far."

"Wait until you try this wine. I'd get a snack, but we have dinner reservations, so...we'll have to save that for the next time we're in a Christmas Market."

"I like the thought of us going to another one of these together."

"For sure. We can't just lose touch, can we? I know you have to go home, and I have to go back to Germany, but we're going to stay in touch. We'll do this again." She spoke so fast that Sydney had to strain to understand all the words, given the volume of chatter in the market, but she liked that she made Reagan nervous.

"We will." Sydney felt shy and ran her fingers through her hair, shaking it out. "You're my…best friend."

There was that eye contact again. Sydney's entire body vibrated with it, and she felt a jolt in her center. "You're mine too."

Their moment, however, was interrupted by it being their turn to order. Dammit.

Reagan ordered them gluhwein that appeared in two steaming boot mugs. Sydney sniffed the top of the mug, and her mouth watered. She could smell the alcohol, but it was a little spicier and fruitier than normal. She winced as she burned her tongue when she impatiently took a sip but delighted in the flavors. "That's delicious. It's a little like warm sangria but with, I don't know…cloves and cinnamon and a lot of flavors I can't quite pinpoint. Is this an Italian drink?"

"Not exactly. It's more German, as the entire Christmas Market, or Christkindlmarkt, is a German thing. But it's perfect for a chilly night."

Sydney leaned in closer, pretending to be colder than she was as an excuse to stay close to Reagan. "It'll help us stay warm while we find the perfect souvenir for Mom."

"So you guys get little tchotchkes for each other even when you're traveling separately?"

A little embarrassed, Sydney said, "This is the first time I've traveled without her, but it feels like the right thing to do. Oh my gosh, look at how cute this wooden thingy is." She pulled them to a booth with hundreds of wooden circular contraptions that looked a little like a merry-go-round, each with several tiers like a wedding cake and little propellers at the top that were spinning.

"Those are amazing, aren't they? They're Christmas pyramids or something in German that starts with a W and has twenty or so letters. The heat from the candles rises and makes the propeller spin, which turns all the levels. I don't know why they don't have any candles lit here, but they're really neat." She spun the top propeller with her index finger, and the three layers below also spun. "Do you think your mom might want one of these? They're kind of magical."

Magical was right. Especially if they were propelled by a candle. "That feels more like a real Christmas gift than a kitschy souvenir, but I do want to get her one. Christmas is only a couple weeks away." She bent over to look at them all closely and marveled at how intricate they were. One had little nutcrackers and ballerinas all over it. Which was cute but not quite right. Another had a Nativity scene, but her eyes fell on one with trees and forest animals. She gasped.

"What is it?" Reagan asked.

"This one." She lifted it up gently. It seemed so fragile. "It's perfect. My mom will love all these little animals."

After Sydney paid, they wandered the stalls, ate samples of flamed cheese—which Sydney was heartbroken she couldn't buy because of her imminent departure and didn't eat more of because she didn't want to spoil dinner—and had another mug of wine. Reagan didn't grab her hand again, and Sydney was beyond disappointed about it.

"Oh, look at that." She pointed at a cuckoo clock, but it was an Italian version with a little Pulcinella, the mascot of Naples, that came out and had a glass of wine at the top of the hour. "It's like the combination of German from this amazing market but with the exact perfect amount of Italian kitsch."

Reagan laughed Sydney's favorite belly laugh. "That's adorable. Do you want to get it?"

Sydney had wanted to find her own memento, but after seeing how much the Christmas pyramid was, she really couldn't justify spending any more. She was already going to have to pick up as many hours as she possibly could as soon as she got back so she'd be able to pay off this credit card before March. It was a disheartening thought, but she wouldn't change a second of the extra time she'd spent with Reagan. "Oh no. I'm fine. My souvenir is this mug and my memories with you. This whole time has been magical. I don't need another little knickknack to remind myself of this trip. Every time I close my eyes, I'll remember all these moments and smile."

She cleared her throat at the sudden emotions burning there. Reagan stared at her, and Sydney's heart lurched at the intensity. She reached out and squeezed Reagan's hand. She couldn't even remember what she was supposed to be doing. Or saying. But a thousand chains wouldn't have been able to prevent her from touching Reagan in that moment.

And holy shit, Reagan was interlacing their fingers again. Sydney drifted closer to her. How was she supposed to not kiss her? Luckily—no unluckily—the shopkeeper interrupted them, and Reagan dropped her hand like she'd been burned.

She mumbled something that sounded like "sorry" as she took a step back. Sydney felt her heart break a little at the clear pullback. She wished more than anything that she could get Reagan to break her own rules just for one night. But she couldn't. And certainly not while standing in a crowded market.

At dinner, Reagan seemed a little detached, which made Sydney feel hollow, but she was very pleased when Reagan said, "Still up for taking that walk to the Ponte Vecchio?"

"That sounds great." It felt like the air had gotten colder, and she surreptitiously moved closer to Reagan as they walked, hoping she could steal some of her body heat and using any excuse to get closer.

"When does school start back up?" Reagan said after they'd been walking for a few minutes with seemingly no direction in mind.

"Not until February, so I'll have plenty of time to work to—" Sydney barely caught herself before she admitted to having to work to pay off her credit card. She really didn't want Reagan knowing how she'd gone into debt for this interlude.

"Work to what?"

"Oh, just replenishing my savings. Since I wasn't able to work over here like normal, I need to build up some savings again."

Reagan turned them left, and the bridge was in front of them. The Ponte Vecchio was probably the most famous bridge in the west, other than maybe the Golden Gate and the London Bridge, and it did not disappoint. "Wow," she whispered.

"Gorgeous, isn't it?" Reagan said.

"Gorgeous doesn't feel like a strong enough word. Resplendent? I wish I had the words to describe it, but it's too perfect. It's like everything Italian personified and then covered in Christmas."

Reagan laughed and took her hand, encouraging her to follow. Most of the little shops were closing up for the night, but the twinkly white holiday lights crisscrossing over their heads still illuminated the way.

"I thought it would be cooler seeing the bridge from the outside, but it has a whole different charm and appeal crossing it, doesn't it?" Sydney said.

She wondered if Reagan realized that she'd forgotten to drop her hand as they walked. Was that a sign that maybe she did want more? God, Sydney did so badly. Those butterflies started doing the massive swoops in her belly again. "Is this your first time on it?" Sydney wasn't sure why she thought Reagan had been there before.

"It is. And worth the wait." Reagan smiled, and Sydney's knees felt a little weak.

As they were nearing the midpoint of the bridge, Sydney noticed a gap in the shops. She pulled Reagan to the closest of the three archways where they could look out at the river and leaned against the wall that hit just above her hips.

They both laughed as they rebounded against the wall, and Reagan said, "Let's take a picture to remember this moment. I think this iPhone is supposed to take pretty good shots."

"Sure." They turned and put their backs to the water while Reagan held up her phone. She snapped a few pictures and flipped the phone around to look at them.

"Ugh. Pointed too high. This would be much easier if they had a camera on the side with the screen."

"Maybe Jobs will figure it out in the next model." Sydney shrugged and used it as an excuse to get closer to Reagan and angled her head toward her. Reagan's scent was intoxicating, and Sydney wondered if she'd look as dreamy as she felt in the photo.

"We look great in this one. Do you want me to email it to you?" Reagan flipped the phone so Sydney could see, and they did look great. So happy and relaxed after what had been a perfect night.

Sydney had a burning in the back of her throat that made it hard to speak. "Please," she said with as much excitement as she could muster and faced the water. "I love Italy," she said, mostly to herself as she gazed out at the inky river beneath them, willing her heart to slow to a normal cadence.

"Are you excited to get home?" Reagan asked.

"That's a loaded question." Sydney chuckled and tried to decide how candid she wanted to be. "I'm excited to see my mom. I really miss her. I'm excited to spend Christmas with her and my grandma." She sighed and brought her gaze up to meet Reagan's. "I'm less excited to leave this magical place." She swallowed hard and plucked up her courage. "To leave…you."

"I know. I hate it too," Reagan said, her voice barely a whisper. When she tucked a lock of hair behind Sydney's ear, Sydney closed her eyes and leaned into the contact. That unmistakable smell of what she now knew to be Reagan's lotion flooded her nose. It was clean and crisp and a little like fall.

Sydney opened her eyes, and Reagan had gotten closer. Much closer. Sydney wanted to lean in the rest of the way but feared getting rejected again. Knowing Reagan felt so strongly about doing anything that could endanger her military integrity, Sydney stood as motionless as the bust of the ancient Florentine gazing at them from across the bridge.

She stared at the line of Reagan's full bottom lip, pink and glossy and calling to her like a siren. Yet, she stayed still, unwilling to break the moment or make Reagan pull away. A little voice inside her head screamed, *kiss me*. She brought her hand to Reagan's wrist, where it lay lightly against her collarbone as though she wasn't sure what to do with it and held it there. She wanted Reagan to be sure that she wouldn't stop the next step.

And finally—after what felt like months of waiting—as though Reagan could hear her internal voice, she kissed her. Sydney thought she heard a whispered, "I can't," just as Reagan's lips grazed hers.

It was the lightest brush at first. Sydney felt the quiver of air against her face when Reagan let out a shaky breath. She seemed so hesitant, but when Sydney curled her fingers into Reagan's light jacket and pulled her closer, she groaned and deepened the kiss.

The hand at Sydney's neck slid into her hair, and Reagan lightly scratched her blunt fingernails along Sydney's head. Sydney pulled her closer until their bodies were flush, unwilling to allow even a millimeter of space in between them any longer. Their tongues lightly glided together, and Sydney thought angels were singing. She'd kissed a few women in her life and one unfortunate guy, but she'd never felt this way before. Like she wanted to rip off Reagan's clothes but also just hold her and protect her from the outside world.

However, well before Sydney was ready to stop, Reagan broke their kiss. She rested her forehead against Sydney's, eyes closed, but moved away a fraction. Just enough so that their bodies were no longer touching. "What the fuck am I doing? I'm so sorry. I can't. God help me, I want to, but I can't. I don't mean to play with your emotions, but I just couldn't help myself. You look so perfect. You *are* so perfect. I'm sorry."

Sydney's heart broke. "Please don't say you regret this. You just did what we so desperately wanted. What *we've* been wanting for months. You didn't do anything wrong."

"But I did."

Sydney couldn't help but notice that she *didn't* say she regretted it, though. She tilted her head until Reagan made eye contact. "You didn't. It's an innocent kiss. Okay, not entirely innocent, but not the end of the world. We're in Florence. Everyone knows what happens in Florence, stays in Florence."

Reagan laughed. "*Does* everyone know that?"

"It's common knowledge. And one little kiss—maybe even three or four—isn't going to send you to Army jail."

"Technically, it could." Reagan winced.

"Luckily, there's no one on this bridge. It's just the two of us, a few jewelers closing up shop, and that creepy statue over there. I don't think anyone is going to report you. I'm not. No one will ever know except us."

Reagan closed her eyes and took a deep breath. She tilted her head from side to side a few times before saying, "We're just two friends saying good-bye. Tonight is all we have. Tomorrow, you go home, and I go back to my real life. In the closet with a padlocked door. But tonight, maybe we can pretend to be two students without any baggage." A hint of a smile flashed on her face.

"Exactly that. And if we are two students with no baggage, I think we can kiss again. I mean, that's something that you can't do just once, right?"

Reagan bit her lip and pursed them as she seemed to mull the idea over. "I know I shouldn't. I'm afraid I'm going to regret this. I'm afraid it's going to ruin my career. But you're right. I can't believe I am going to say this, but I'm going to break the rules just this once. Pretend I'm someone else. Pretend we can be something else."

Although the need to pretend to be someone else hurt a little bit, Reagan's lips on hers again softened the blow. This second time, she wasn't tentative at all. Reagan pressed her lips to Sydney's with the confidence she exuded while in uniform, and it was sexy as hell. Sydney lost herself in the moment and no longer cared who they had to be, but she desperately didn't want this night to end. Ever.

They stayed tucked away in the corner of the shops on the bridge for what felt like hours, kissing until their lips were swollen, and Sydney's body ached with need. Until her heart screamed to tell Reagan how she felt. This had to be love, didn't it? She'd never felt this way about anyone. But she knew she couldn't say those words. Not tonight.

When Reagan finally broke their kiss, she said, "You make me feel like I've just run a world record pace marathon. I want to stay here and kiss you forever, but I think, maybe we should take a break. Before someone finds us."

Sydney hated it, but she knew Reagan was right. Italians had a funny thing about PDA, and being gay was still taboo. She was also having a hard time keeping her wandering hands *over* Reagan's clothes.

So, true to her word about pretending to be someone else, Reagan took her hand, and they walked. Along the banks of the Arno, along the deserted streets of Florence, past the long-since-closed booths at the Christmas Market. They talked about what felt like everything and nothing all at the same time until the sky began to lighten.

"I have an idea. Do you want to watch the sunrise at Piazzale Michelangelo before we head to bed for a few hours? It feels like the perfect way to end this perfect night," Reagan suggested.

Sydney couldn't believe they'd been walking all night, but she was game for another hour before getting some rest. When they finally fell into bed together, she was grateful for the one bed, removing any question of their sleeping arrangements.

After they kissed and kissed and kissed until they couldn't stay awake any longer, she rested her head on Reagan's shoulder, and Reagan pulled her close. She'd yearned to do more than kiss but knew it was impossible. She knew when they woke up, they'd have to go back to being good friends again. She'd give Reagan a hug at the Naples airport, but that was it. No kissing, no lingering touches. Because tomorrow—no, later today—Reagan had to go back to being Lieutenant Jennings, and she had to go back to being Vanderbilt Junior Prelaw and Finance Major Sydney Adams.

And she couldn't stand the thought of her first time also being her last time with Reagan. So wrapped in a cloud of Reagan and longing for what could never be, she held on to her fiercely as she drifted to sleep as though she could hold on to that moment forever.

Part II: The Past

Monterey, California, Eleven Years Ago

CHAPTER EIGHT

Reagan had been at the Naval Postgraduate School in Monterey for a few weeks and was still adjusting to the cool temperatures after a whirlwind few months. Three months ago, she'd been in Iraq, where she'd been for the previous eleven months as the intelligence officer for an engineering battalion assisting local communities to rebuild bridges. Two months ago, she'd returned to the sweltering heat of Fort Bragg, North Carolina and found out she'd been selected for a master's degree program in defense analysis at the Naval Postgraduate School with a follow-on assignment to Morocco. Three weeks ago, she'd moved to California to get settled before the school year started. And it couldn't have worked out more perfectly.

The next three years were like a gift to keep her on track for her planned career transition to a foreign area officer as soon as she put on major and was eligible. It was still a few years away, but the Morocco assignment was a perfect broadening assignment, a perfect stepping stone, until she was eligible for major.

She was sure she would've appreciated the climate in central California after she'd graduated from West Point or even after she'd left Germany, but now, after nearly three years in the Middle East on back-to-back deployments, she thought she was freezing to death. It was fifty degrees, and she was pretty sure it was colder than the North Pole.

As she put on her long-sleeve thermal shirt and leggings, a stocking cap, and gloves, it looked like that was where she belonged. But she didn't care. She didn't want to be cold and had a long twelve mile run on the calendar that day.

She turned left out of the gate, heading along the bay toward downtown Monterey. The view was amazing. As someone who'd spent a lot of time growing up in the middle of the US or Europe, she never took this ocean view for granted. She had earbuds, but she always left one out. Partially for safety but also because she wanted to hear the ocean crashing against the shore.

The first mile was always the worst, and Reagan gave herself a minute to pause and stretch at the knee-high wall at the top of Fisherman's Wharf. She'd felt a few alerts on her phone and pulled it out of her arm strap to see who was pinging her at six in the morning. On the display was an alert from Facebook: "You have a nearby friend."

She barely used Facebook and wasn't sure why on earth she'd be getting an alert but wondered if perhaps someone from her West Point class was nearby, as they were practically the only friends she had on the damn app other than family. Out of curiosity, she opened it and almost dropped her phone. Sydney Adams was showing as less than a mile away. In fact, it kind of looked like she might run right past her on her way out to Sunset Beach. Jesus Christ.

It felt like she'd taken a punch to the gut. She hadn't seen Sydney in almost four years. Not since their formal good-bye at the airport where they'd shared an awkward hug as they'd swallowed back tears because they'd been in public.

She still couldn't breathe but didn't want her run to take all morning, so she forced herself to start running again but didn't pay one iota of attention to the ocean. All she could think about was that dimple, that soft southern accent, that beautiful smile. Everything she'd been obsessed with four years ago. And for some time after if she was being honest. Sydney had been her heart's first real want. Her first crush. The first kiss she'd had that had meant something.

As they'd been saying their teary good-bye—their real, uncensored good-bye—Sydney had asked if she could friend her on Facebook. Reagan had barely used it back then, but she'd pulled out her laptop before taking Sydney to the airport and sent her a friend request. She'd also sent the photo of them on the Ponte Vecchio.

At first, they'd messaged every day. But that had quickly slipped to somewhere about every week. And then once a month. Then, they'd just interacted with each other's public posts on their walls.

And then came the girlfriend. Reagan couldn't stand seeing them taking selfies all over Nashville, but one of them kissing had done Reagan in. She didn't block Sydney—though she'd wanted to—but she did snooze her posts and just stopped going on Facebook altogether. It was easier.

And now, with no warning, she was less than a mile away. What was Reagan supposed to do with that? Should she pretend like she hadn't seen it? Should she message her and see if she wanted to catch up? What if Sydney still had that girlfriend? Harmony? Reagan had always hated that name. Maybe she and Harmony were in Monterey for a romantic getaway. Her stomach curdled at the thought, even though she hadn't had anything other than a small orange to eat so far.

Looking back, she was sure she had been wearing rose-colored love glasses because of the romanticism surrounding Italy. Also, the taboo aspect of her longing being illegal under the UCMJ had probably made it seem so much more intense than it had actually been. And she'd also been so much younger. Four years didn't sound like a lot, but she'd changed since then. She'd never even had a girlfriend at that point, and now she'd had a couple, though she was currently single. It was hard maintaining a relationship with someone when she was deployed.

Regardless, she'd really enjoyed Sydney's friendship. They'd had such a good time playing tourist together, and they'd just clicked.

She spent the next three miles thinking about it. Agonizing over it. Overthinking it. She briefly wondered if she'd simply see Sydney somewhere along this trail. No, Sydney had never been an early riser, but maybe something had changed by now.

But she didn't see her on her run. She didn't run into her at the little coffee shop she stopped at for her shot of espresso and hot tea. She'd learned that little trick when deployed because she'd never acquired a taste for coffee, and coffee in the DFACs was particularly disgusting. But she still liked the hit of caffeine, so she'd taken to having a shot of espresso with a tea chaser.

She took a luxurious shower—with water that could have been hotter, but at least she'd been feeling mostly warm by the time she got back from her run—and ate the croissant from the coffee shop. It was lovely.

She savored every perfect bite of that croissant in an attempt to not look at her phone. Delay making a decision. But she needed to stop procrastinating. Tomorrow was Sunday, and if Sydney was in town for the weekend, she might be heading home tomorrow. And not taking action was a decision in itself.

Reagan obsessed over the what-ifs. She didn't want to seem pathetic if Sydney had a girlfriend. Or that she was trying to steal Sydney away from someone.

Reagan realized she was being silly. She was still Facebook friends with Sydney and could check her relationship status to see if she was seeing anyone. Publicly anyway. She held her breath as she opened Sydney's profile and scrolled down…

Relationship Status: Single

Her heart did a little skip.

She told it to stop.

This was ridiculous. She wouldn't obsess about contacting an old friend from school, so why was she complicating things with Sydney? She opened the nearby friend section and tapped Sydney's name. She could message her from right here. She typed in a somewhat awkward and generic: *Hey, stranger. Long time. I don't even use this app, but I got an alert you were "nearby" in here. Are we both really in Monterey?*

She hit the send arrow before she could spend another second obsessing about it. Because holy shit, she'd just done that. And holy shit, it was Sydney fucking Adams.

She flipped to that long-ago selfie from the Ponte Vecchio and smiled. She shook her head at her silliness and put her phone down. She busied herself pulling out the syllabi for the classes she'd registered for, checking to make sure she had all the required books. She always felt it was crucial to be prepared on the first day to set the tone. But before she'd even had a chance to pull all her textbooks out, her phone dinged.

Sydney had responded: *OMG! Haven't seen your name in forever. In Monterey with a few girlfriends but heading home tomorrow. You?*

Reagan: *Here for about 18 mos. Grad school. Where do you live these days?*

Sydney: *Really? I'm at Stanford. Like 90 minutes away.*

Reagan's heart did a little somersault at that revelation, but before she could respond, Sydney texted again: *Want to grab a drink later?*

Before she could over think it, Reagan quickly typed: *When and where?*

❖

Reagan stood outside of the Elephant and Crown bar along the water. Oh my God, she was really doing this. She was going to see Sydney Adams for the first time in four years, and her heart felt like it might beat right out of her chest. Simply reaching out to Sydney had been a huge leap for someone who really liked everything in life to fit in its neat little box. She didn't change her routine. She didn't veer off the course. And yet, she had today and was feeling a little nauseated about it. Well, nauseated but happy. Gleeful. She wasn't sure the last time she'd felt this excited for something. Or this nervous.

She spotted Sydney first. She looked stunning. More than stunning. She was in a white, scoop-neck shirt and a chic leather jacket paired with jeans and tall boots. She jumped up when she saw Reagan and ran to her, wrapping her in the biggest hug.

Sydney pushed her back to arm's length, looked her up and down, and pulled her back into another hug. "I can't believe you're really here. You look fantastic!"

Reagan wasn't nearly as dressy as Sydney was in her fashionably holey jeans and a flannel with the sleeves rolled up, but she hoped she looked passable. "It is so great to see you. And you're the one who looks fantastic."

Sydney pulled them back to her table. "Tell me everything. How are you?"

"Everything is a pretty lofty goal." Reagan chuckled. "But I'm good. Really good. A few months ago, I was in Iraq feeling like I might literally sweat to death, and now I'm sitting here in a bar in what feels like a cold version of paradise looking at my favorite friend whom I haven't seen in ages." Reagan felt herself smile big. Seeing Sydney felt even better than she thought it would.

"Oh God, Iraq." Her face went a little white. "How long were you there for?"

"Eleven months but my battalion was doing important work, so it was rewarding. But I don't want to talk about that. Tell me about you. Are you at Stanford Law?"

She beamed, seemingly recovering from the Iraq revelation. "I am."

"That was your top choice, right?"

"Good memory. Yes. I applied all over and got in pretty much everywhere."

Of course she had, Reagan thought.

"But I'm happy to be in California for now. I interned in Boston this summer and have only been back for about a week. I start my final year of law school next week."

"Grabbing your dreams with both hands. I'm not surprised." She wanted to grab both of Sydney's hands and squeeze them to have an excuse to touch her but managed to resist. Probably no incidental contact was the better course of action since her time here was going to be fleeting. Although, her mind told her all the feelings she'd been feeling back in Italy were stronger in her memory than they'd been in real life, her heart wasn't getting the memo now that they were face-to-face.

Sydney shrugged, seemingly feigning nonchalance. "So what made you check your nearby friends on Facebook today? After I heard from you, I checked your wall, and it looks like you haven't posted in a long time."

"Yeah, your guess is as good as mine. I've never heard of nearby friends, so I was surprised when I got the alert. I swear, I've never set that up. Can you see my location?"

Sydney's eyes went adorably large. "I have no idea. Shit, now I need to look. That feels like a violation of privacy." She pulled out her phone.

"Well, you're the attorney—"

Sydney stuck up one finger to interrupt and said, "Not an attorney yet."

But Reagan didn't let that stop her. "I think you could figure out if you have a case. But it's just one of the many reasons I haven't been on. Too much risk of too much information available when deployed, you know? OpSec is one of the most important things when deployed."

Sydney's cheeks lost a little of their glow. "OpSec?"

"Operations security. Remember the old-timey posters from World War II in your history textbooks that said, 'Loose lips sink ships'?" When Sydney nodded, she continued, "Kind of like that. You have to be careful about saying where you are, what your schedule is. Pretty much anything could be targeted or hacked by unsavory people and used to exploit weaknesses that we may not even know exist. It's safer to not post than to think about censoring every word. Plus, I've never been that into it." She shrugged, trying to play off the seriousness, but the remaining color in Sydney's face drained away.

"Jesus, I hadn't really thought of that. It's terrifying. Were you ever in real danger? Did you have any close calls?"

Reagan took a sip of her gin rickey to buy herself a minute. She didn't want to lie, but she certainly didn't want to get into the details— she never spoke about what had happened—and decided to make a joke instead. "There was a time or two where things got a little hairy, but I've got nine lives, so it's all good. I must've gotten them from the cat my grandma had when I was growing up. Buster. He was a super sweet boy, and I'd get to stay up half the night with him during the summer when my parents would send me and my brothers to see her." And changing the subject was always a good tactic.

"Aw, Buster. I love that name for a cat."

"So you're a cat person?" Reagan said.

"Not really. We couldn't have pets when I was growing up." Sydney looked away.

"Were you...allergic?" Reagan asked, unsure why she was being so weird.

"No, it just didn't work in our small apartment. And we moved a few times, which makes having a pet hard too."

"Ah." Reagan didn't really understand, but that was fine. There had always been some things Sydney didn't want to talk about. Her father and her finances, specifically. She was fine leaving it for now. "What about now? Do you think about getting a cat or a dog?"

Sydney laughed. "No. The idea is appealing, but I graduate next year, and it wouldn't be fair. I'm going into big law. I've got an offer from the firm I interned at this summer in Boston, and the hours for a first-year associate—hell, the first five-plus years—are brutal. It wouldn't be fair to get a cat and leave him home alone for fifteen or more hours a day, you know?"

Reagan shuddered. "Why would you do that to yourself?"

"I don't want to say money, but the answer is...money." She shrugged as she ran her middle finger around the shallow hollow at the base of her throat, Reagan's favorite tell. "I've never had any financial security, so I picked a job where I'm certain to find it. The hours are brutal, but the money is fantastic. Especially as you move up."

While Reagan had never been rich, they'd always been comfortable, and she'd never worried about their stability. She wanted to ask Sydney more, but this wasn't the time. "I could see that."

"What about you? Any kittens or puppies or fish in your future?"

"Nah. I'm not here long, then heading to Morocco for two years, and I don't think I can take a pet. And after that, I'll hopefully be able to put on major and can switch tracks to become a foreign area officer."

"Does that mean you'd get out of the military?" Sydney said, her eyebrows rising slightly.

Was that a hopeful look? Reagan winced at the thought. "No, it's a slightly different trajectory from my current path. FAOs mostly work as diplomatic personnel in embassies or other installations in a strategic partnership with the host government. Stuff like that."

"Sounds glamorous. I can see you fitting right in."

Sydney's smile was as potent as it had always been, and Reagan found herself squeezing her thighs tightly, just as she'd done the first couple of times they'd hung out in Italy. It was a strange feeling, and, God, did she want to stare and never look away. She couldn't believe she was sitting in front of Sydney Adams after all these years.

CHAPTER NINE

Sydney couldn't believe it when Reagan had slid into her DMs this morning. Although she'd never forgotten about Reagan, as their messages had slowly tapered off, Sydney had stopped seeking her out. She probably hadn't seen her name in more than three years. But seeing it was a jolt that had sent shivers of anticipation down her spine.

She knew she shouldn't feel that way. But the memory of their last night together in Florence—their kisses, falling asleep in each other's arms—made her feel warm all over. She still dreamed about that night, even if she'd never admit it to anyone. Surely not her ex-girlfriend, Harmony, whom she'd dated for more than two years. Not even Aliyah, who was still her best friend and had attended Stanford with her. Aliyah had graduated with her MBA in the spring and was just taking pity on Sydney by continuing to live together, even though she'd accepted a position as an investment banker and was making dough. Aliyah could move to a condo in a trendy neighborhood in San Francisco but continued to live with Sydney and their third roommate, Jessica, in Menlo Park. Certainly, she deserved the truth.

But there was no way she *wasn't* going to see Reagan. She and her roommates had plans to go whale watching, but she'd begged off. How could she not? Jessica hadn't known anything about Reagan, but Sydney had given her the highlights when she'd told them she might be busy for the rest of the evening. Not that she thought they'd fall into bed. She didn't sleep around, and while she'd stopped following the news around that anti-gay policy years ago, she assumed Reagan's situation hadn't changed.

They'd been understanding if a little sad that she was blowing them off, but sitting across from Reagan, she had no regrets. Even if it was terrifying thinking of Reagan deployed to the country that had taken Sydney's asshole of a father from her.

"What do you think about dinner?" Sydney said when there was a brief lull in the conversation. Her stomach had just rumbled, but she didn't want to put an end to their night.

"I am in favor of the meal, generally. It's always hard for me to sleep if I'm hungry." Reagan smiled, and Sydney couldn't help but laugh.

"No, goober. How do you feel about dinner tonight. With me?"

"If that's on offer, I'm definitely in favor. What do you have in mind?"

"It's my first time here, so I don't have any recommendations. Do you have any places you like? If you like it here, we can stay too. Or I'm fine going somewhere else." Why did Reagan always reduce her to a rambling dork? It was embarrassing. She'd spent the summer eviscerating opposing counsel, admittedly using the written word, but still. Nearly an attorney, she was supposed to be fast on her feet and agile. Reagan robbed her of those talents.

Reagan tapped the table with her index finger. "Hmm. I've only been here for a few weeks, but…" She pursed her lips and seemed to be mumbling to herself. "It's Saturday night, we don't have a reservation, but not bar food. Ooo." She perked up and looked at Sydney as she said, "How do you feel about a picnic? There are some nice beaches around here, and we can climb around on the rocks to find someplace private to just relax and watch the sunset."

There went Reagan again, planning the most romantic dates imaginable, even though they weren't dating. Just like she'd done over and over in Italy. But it wasn't like Sydney could say no. She loved the idea of spending time with Reagan, whether or not romance was on the table. "I am in favor of picnics," she said, hoping Reagan would pick up on her subtle teasing.

"Let's close out, and we can grab food and pick up my car to drive to the beach," Reagan said.

"Isn't there beach right here?" Sydney asked, perplexed.

"Yes, but with the shape of the bay, we're looking more northeast here. And there's so many people. It's hard to relax. There'll be people over at Asilomar, but there's more beach to spread out on and little nooks and crannies you can find to hide in. I mean, not that I'm trying to hide you. A little privacy would be nice. But it's also not like I'm trying to get you to a secluded place for something…Jesus." She dropped her head in her hands. It was nice watching her get flustered too. It made Sydney feel better about her earlier ramblings.

"No worries. I get it. And if we're not even looking west, the sunset probably won't be very exciting," Sydney said and laughed to break up Reagan's awkwardness.

Reagan took them to a Middle Eastern carryout window weirdly tucked into the back of a souvenir shop, where they both grabbed falafel wraps and fries and walked a few blocks to Reagan's car, which was… surprising.

"Is this seriously your car?" Sydney said as they approached a bright yellow, oddly shaped, half truck, half station wagon thing. It was so much brighter than anything she would have picked for Reagan. She knew the one she'd had in Italy was a rental, but the dark gray Smart car was still what she'd been picturing.

"It is. Hop in. It grows on you. It's…sexy-ugly. And it's a Subaru. Or a Lesbaru, as I like to think of it."

Sydney had so, so many questions. She didn't even know where to start as she climbed into the surprisingly comfortable seat. "I've always pictured you in your old Smart car. I don't really know why. Clearly, it was a rental, but this is…the opposite."

Reagan let loose a huge belly laugh. "I hated that damn car. I mean, it got the job done, but no one felt safe doing one hundred and seventy kilometers an hour on the Autostrada in that tiny ass thing. The only time I've picked that small of a car since was when I was back in Italy for a few days."

"Ah," Sydney said, feeling a twinge of irrational jealousy that Reagan had gone there without her.

"How about you? Have you been back?"

"I wish," Sydney said, feeling the weight of sadness that she hadn't been able to take any true vacations since Italy. She'd gotten a full ride to Stanford, but that didn't really account for the ridiculous cost of living in the Bay Area. She supposedly had room and board included, but that didn't go very far. "I dream of taking my mom and Noah, my brother, who I can't believe is going to be sixteen, on a trip to Europe. Or anywhere. Maybe in a few years, once I'm a senior associate. Until then, I doubt I'll have the time or money. And I still have a year left of school." She sighed, hating how poor they were and wishing she could fast-forward to a time when she would be secure and could take care of her mom and maybe even help her brother with college. She could visualize it and did so regularly when she meditated to help manifest it.

"That makes sense," Reagan said.

They rode in silence for a couple of minutes, and Sydney tried not to obsess over what she should be saying. They hadn't seen each other in years and had so much to catch up on, but her heart was racing with nerves. She didn't want Reagan to feel sorry for her because she was still poor.

"We need something to drink," Reagan said as she turned into a liquor store parking lot. "Give me one sec, and I'll be right back. Unless you want to come?"

"No, surprise me." Sydney decided she'd rather have a minute to recenter herself.

As Reagan walked away, Sydney shut her eyes and regulated her breathing. In for four, hold for seven, and slowly out for eight. She didn't think she had a real anxiety issue, but things felt a little overwhelming sometimes, and she'd learned about this breathing trick when researching meditation and visualization and used it whenever she needed it.

With her mind quiet, she could easily understand why spending time with Reagan had both her heart and mind racing, but she had the clarity to remind herself that she'd always had an emotional connection to Reagan. Even just as friends, she was closer to Reagan than anyone, so it was not surprising that her body was having an extreme reaction.

And by acknowledging that fact and accepting it, her body was able to settle down. Her heart returned to normal, and the tightness in her chest dissipated. Perfect timing as Reagan slid back into the car and placed a paper bag on the floor behind Sydney.

"Ready?" she said.

It was a quick but beautiful drive along the beach until Reagan decided they were at the perfect spot and pulled the car onto the sandy shoulder. "We're here?" Sydney said.

"Looks like a good spot to me. Will you grab the food?" Reagan grabbed the paper bag with their drinks and a blanket from her back seat and led Sydney down a maintained sand path that opened to a small beach. There were a few couples sitting on it and one family with two small children and a dog running and jumping in the shallow, frothy water left behind as the waves broke farther out, reached their termination point on the beach, and retreated.

Sydney thought they might sit there, but Reagan kept heading down the beach. "Where are you taking us?"

"I ran over here a week or so ago. I think there's a perfect spot a little farther ahead. Are you good to walk for a bit?"

Sydney didn't want to curtail whatever Reagan had planned, but she also didn't want wet sand to mess up her most expensive boots. "Sure, but let me take off my shoes. I should've brought flip-flops."

"This isn't where I saw this evening going, either, but I think it's perfect," Reagan said as she slipped off her own canvas Sperry's. "I always thought the ocean would be warm in California, but this beach cured me of that."

"I want to laugh at you, but I thought the same thing. I wasn't able to tour Stanford before I moved out here, and I have to say, I was woefully unprepared for central California weather. But I love the wildness of the ocean here. It's more stunning than the Atlantic."

"Totally." Reagan guided them a little closer to the ocean as they neared what appeared to be the end of the beach, but when the waves receded, she walked around an outcropping of rocks and into a deserted stretch of sand.

"You really found all this on a run?"

"Yeah, though we aren't there yet."

They walked for a few more minutes, around another outcropping, and then climbed over a small hill of rocks that Sydney wished she'd been wearing hiking shoes for before they finally came upon another deserted section of beach. It didn't really seem all that different than the ones they'd already passed, but Reagan seemed excited.

"And here we are," she said, spinning in a circle with her arm outstretched. "No cars, no people, but a rocky shore for the waves to crash against and provide a little more drama. The road and trail have curved away from us here a bit too."

"This is nice." Although Sydney would have been happy stopping earlier, this was better than the spots they'd passed.

Reagan spread out the blanket, and once Sydney sat, she pulled out a bottle of red wine, a small pack of clear plastic cups, and a liter of water. "I thought this would make the setting better. It's a screw top, but it was the best screw top they had." She gave Sydney a crooked smile.

"I have nothing against screw tops, myself. I heard somewhere that they actually keep the wine fresher." Sydney certainly didn't have the pedigree, even after their crash course in wine in the Italian countryside, to judge.

"Yep. There's nothing like the sound of a corkscrew turning and the pop that it makes, but corks let in more air over time. Regardless, for an impromptu sunset beach picnic, this is a lot easier." She poured them both glasses and handed one to Sydney. "To long-lost—but never forgotten—friends."

She tapped their cups together, but Sydney felt like she'd missed a little something. "To found again friends," she corrected.

"I like that. I'm happy I found you today. Not sure how it happened, but I'm glad I plucked up the courage to reach out."

"Why'd you need courage? We've always been friends." Even when they hadn't been talking, Sydney still thought of their time together fondly. Felt close to Reagan. Thinking about it now, she realized that might have been weird since they hadn't actually talked in more than three years. And in truth, it was possible a small crush still lingered. But she certainly wasn't volunteering *that* information.

"Not courage, exactly." She coughed and looked away. Took another sip of wine. Sydney wondered if she was buying time. "More like I thought we'd stay in touch—friends forever, you know—and we didn't, and I wasn't sure if you wanted to hear from me." Reagan paused, stared at the ocean. It didn't feel like she was done, so Sydney waited as Reagan took a sip and cleared her throat. "It kind of felt like you drifted more when you started dating that girl. I didn't know if that was still a thing. I was afraid to overstep."

Oh. Could Reagan be harboring a few feelings too? "Harmony? We were together for a couple years but have been over for some time. She's at Michigan now."

"Nice. Wait, not nice." She turned with wide eyes. "I don't mean I'm happy that you maybe got your heart broken, I just mean…I—"

Sydney laid a hand on her arm. "It's fine. I know what you meant." She wasn't entirely sure she did. Maybe Reagan meant she was happy Sydney was single, but that didn't really make sense if Reagan was still living under that horrible DADT policy. But she didn't want Reagan to continue spouting words she didn't mean. "We had a good time, but it wasn't right for either of us. No heart breakage." That wasn't entirely true. She'd thought her heart was breaking after Harmony's accident, when she hadn't known what was going on, but once she'd found out Harmony was okay, she realized her heart had never been in play anyway.

Reagan nodded. Sydney didn't think there was anything else to say on the topic without making things worse, so after a rather pregnant pause, she leaned back on her elbows and watched the waves crash against the rocks. They sat in silence as the sun slowly made its way closer to the horizon. Sydney missed comfortable moments like this one. Reagan was the only person other than her mom she'd ever experienced them with.

"Are you hungry? We should eat our food, though it's probably cold," Reagan said.

Sydney hadn't noticed, but once Reagan said it, her stomach grumbled in response. "My stomach says yes."

Sydney watched Reagan's shoulder-length hair sway around her face as she dug in the food bag. She'd thought Reagan had been beautiful with her pixie cut, but this hair, just longer than shoulder-length, framed her face like it had been born to.

Before she knew what she was doing, she reached out and brushed her fingertips along the silky ends. "I love your hair longer like this." Reagan looked up, her mouth in a little O, and Sydney quickly said, "Sorry," as she dropped her hand. What the hell was she doing?

"No problem. I just wasn't expecting it, so you startled me." She handed Sydney her wrap. "I still had my West Point pixie cut back in Italy, huh?"

"Pixie cut, yeah. West Point?"

"In high school, I had long hair, but when I got to Beast—the cadet version of basic training the summer before school starts the first year—they convinced me to chop off my hair in a bob. Worst decision ever. Rather than being able to pull my hair back in a bun, it was constantly in my face. So as soon as I could, I went pixie cut because then, it's never in the way. The regular maintenance to keep it short was a pain, but the ease of ten seconds to style my hair daily was worth it. But I missed my hair, so I've been growing it out for a few years. I like it better now."

"Me too," Sydney said softly but kept her hands to herself that time.

As the sun melted into the water and the sky blazed bright orange and red, they caught up on Reagan's life. They touched on her deployments again, though Sydney still felt like she was holding something back, and discussed Reagan's brothers and how they were doing. Apparently, the Naval Academy one, Jasper, had also graduated at the top of his class, but her other two brothers had both graduated number two, and Reagan and Jasper hadn't let them hear the end of it.

As the sun disappeared below the horizon and the sky was a vibrant pink and dotted with fluffy pink and blue clouds, they talked about Sydney's life. Law school, how she enjoyed living in San Francisco and around a large population of gay people for the first time in her life—amazing—how often she got back to see her mom and brother—not nearly as often as she liked as it was an expensive trip, though she didn't share that.

As full dark came upon them, they still lounged on the beach and slowly sipped the last of their wine. "Have you read the final *Wheel of Time* book yet?" Reagan asked.

"No! It's out?" When Reagan nodded, Sydney said, "I don't read much other than law textbooks, case studies, and court decisions these days. Law school is a drag." She sighed, wishing she could put off the start of the semester for a few more weeks.

"You don't like it?"

"Yes and no. It's so much damn work when classes are in session. I feel like I do nothing but read, write, and study for twenty hours a day. It's exhausting. But also fun. I like picking apart arguments and structuring a counterpoint. At the same time, it's also my last year, so although I'm ready to graduate and make my way in the world, it's also the true end of my youth. After this, I'm a real adult. Which feels a little scary."

"I get that." Reagan had to be fibbing.

"Shit, why am I here complaining to you, someone who has been defending our country for, like, six years, serving in war-torn areas, about being afraid to grow up?" Sydney felt silly and childish.

"No, really. I do get it. It's weird. Sometimes, I don't feel ready for the level of responsibility laid upon me. But I have to step up, as I'm sure you will too when the time comes. You're amazing, Sydney Adams."

Sydney could feel her face flushing and said a silent word of thanks that it was now full dark and would camouflage her embarrassment. "Thanks," she finally stammered. "You're pretty great yourself."

A comfortable silence again came upon them until the sea lions, whom Sydney hadn't seen on the walk in, started barking. Sydney jumped and was thankful she'd already finished her wine.

"You okay?"

"Yeah, they just startled me. I guess it's surprising they haven't been serenading us all evening, isn't it?"

"It's probably a sign that we should head back. It's getting pretty late." Reagan pulled out her phone, and the light of the screen blinded Sydney for a moment. "Oh shit. Yeah, it's already after ten."

Sydney couldn't believe it, and yet, she could. It felt like that always happened when they were together. "What I really can't believe is that my roommates haven't been texting me like crazy, worried some deranged soldier has murdered me at the beach." Sydney laughed, but Aliyah was a worrier. She shot off a quick text just to let her know all was well.

"You guys are leaving tomorrow to head back up to school, right?"

"Yeah." Sydney hated the thought now that she'd had an afternoon reconnecting with Reagan. It wasn't nearly enough.

"Do you want to borrow that book? We could swing by my place to pick it up before I take you back to your hotel."

Unsure if she'd have time to read it before the semester started but unwilling to bring the evening to a close and unwilling to say good-bye to Reagan for who knew how long this time, Sydney said, "That would be great. Thank you." Borrowing a book meant they'd need to see each other again soon, didn't it?

She also hadn't asked about that anti-gay policy. She wanted to ask but was afraid as well. Spending time together this evening had convinced her that she hadn't gotten over Reagan, even a little bit. She struggled to not casually touch her at every opportunity. That wouldn't be fair because at the end of the day, Sydney wasn't really in a position to date anyone, especially not this woman.

She was only in California for nine more months before she'd likely be heading to Boston for the foreseeable future. And Reagan was going to Morocco for who knew how long and then where? Their lives were incompatible, yet that need to be around her—to talk and laugh and spend time together—was so strong that Sydney didn't know how she could go back to no contact at all after tonight.

CHAPTER TEN

The day hadn't been anything like Reagan had planned. She was supposed to go for her run, do an hour of yoga, eat her salad for lunch, look at a few apartments, and start preparing for classes the coming week.

Instead, she'd spent the entire day thinking of Sydney before they'd met up, immersed in Sydney while they were having drinks and dinner, and somehow ended up back in her billeting room with Sydney under the guise of letting her borrow a book. Yet, they'd been there for more than an hour, and it was coming up on midnight. Thankfully, it was only Saturday, and classes didn't start until Wednesday.

She'd just poured them both another glass of wine and found the bottom of the second bottle they'd opened together that day. It had been hours since she'd opened the first on the beach, but she had a buzz simmering that had her coming to terms with the fact that she'd been wrong that morning. Her perception of the intensity of her feelings toward Sydney hadn't been skewed by time, and they'd come roaring back, perhaps stronger than ever.

If Sydney's giggle was any indication, she was also feeling a little buzzed. "Okay, Amy Adams in *Trouble with the Curve* or *Julie & Julia*?"

"That's easy. For sure *Trouble with the Curve*. She's a total badass in that movie. Attorney and baseball savant?" She fanned her face. "Though redheads are not my type in general." Reagan wasn't sure how they'd gotten on to this strange little game. But it was fun. "My turn. I've got a good one. Rachel McAdams in *The Vow* or *The Notebook*?"

"That *is* a good one." Sydney pursed her lips and bounced her shoulders as she thought about it. "She was delightful in both, but I'm going with *The Notebook*. I normally prefer darker brunettes, but the epic love story that was *The Notebook*? Chef's kiss. Sure, they both die in the end, but could there be a more romantic way to go? That movie just proves some people are meant to be, no matter the odds. The heart wants what the heart wants." Sydney's face went soft and dreamy as she smiled.

Reagan realized she desperately wanted to kiss her. She'd felt the pull all evening, but she almost succumbed. Thankfully, Sydney didn't seem to notice. Reagan tried to keep things light. "But how about a movie where those two get together? Rachel and Amy? My God, that would be amazing." She fanned her face again.

Sydney tapped her lips with her index finger. "Hmm, but would you be able to own that movie safely?"

"Safely?" Reagan said, not sure what she meant.

"You know, cuz gays are illegal and all?" Her voice had the slightest slur. Yep, definitely a little tipsy.

"Not anymore." Reagan felt her big smile, the one that only came out when she was a little tipsy too.

Sydney gasped and jumped up, and the wine in her glass sloshed a little close to the rim. "Does that mean that your closet, the one that was locked up tighter than Fort Knox, has been…demolished?"

"I never thought of my closet like that, but, yeah. Gone. As soon as the ban was lifted a few years ago, I flew home and came out to my parents. They didn't really understand how I could have kept this from them. My dad still doesn't fully understand how I'm still serving, even though the ban is over, but he's coming around. They both love me and are fine. They haven't met either of my girlfriends, but they weren't serious, so it didn't make sense."

Sydney clutched at pearls she wasn't wearing. "Wait a second. You went from being in the closet to having two girlfriends at once?" She stared, eyes wide and mouth slightly open.

Reagan choked on her wine as she laughed. "If that's what you heard, you're definitely drunk. Enough for you." Reagan tried to take her glass, but Sydney stepped out of reach, laughing.

"It's what you said, so I think you're drunk too." She laughed even harder, and Reagan joined in. It wasn't even all that funny, but somehow, she couldn't stop until tears were rolling down her face.

When Reagan finally got herself under control, she pointed at herself and said, "Single now. In the past two years, I have had two nonserious, nonconcurrent girlfriends. That's it. Also, I can't be that drunk because I came up with the word nonconcurrent. Boom."

That led to another round of laughter before Sydney plopped on the couch next to her again. "We're a little bit of a mess," she said. "But we're not going to go back to not being friends, right? I mean, we live less than two hours away from each other. I've missed you. I've missed…us." She swirled a slightly unsteady finger between them.

Relieved, Reagan said, "I've missed you too. Let's not go back to that. Maybe we can have weekend study sessions." She almost said, "weekend study dates," but managed to change it. Although she was now free to pursue Sydney as far as the military was concerned, even her wine-addled brain knew it wasn't the right choice. Sydney had the power to completely break her, and when it came down to it, they were both only temporary residents with very different plans for the following year.

"Yes. And we also need to talk about Rand and the rest of the Two Rivers crew and how they save the world."

"Ooo, book club. I love it." Reagan chuckled at the sleepy but sweet expression on Sydney's face as her head rested against the back of the small love seat. And she was going to need to rent a house sooner rather than later if Sydney was coming back. No "two people in one bed" trope again. Though that one night they'd slept in the same bed— with Sydney's head on her shoulder—in Florence was a memory she treasured.

But it couldn't be repeated. "And on that note, we should probably get you back to your friends. It's nearly three in the morning."

"Probably a good idea." Sydney ran a finger along Reagan's flannel collar. "But how? I don't think either of us is fit to drive."

"True, so how about if I walk you home, and I'll call an Uber from your hotel?"

"Wouldn't it make more sense for me to just take an Uber from here?" Her brows furrowed.

Reagan didn't want to tell her that she didn't feel comfortable putting a very tipsy Sydney into a car with a stranger. Reagan herself was in a better position to defend herself than Sydney was. She'd had a lot of combatives training in the Army and seemed to be handling the quantity of alcohol a little better. But she didn't want Sydney to think she was babying her. "It's a nice night for a walk, isn't it? Plus, by the time we walk back to your hotel, I'll be sober."

"That seems reasonable. If you promise not to walk back alone. That's not safe," Sydney said.

"Agreed. I'll take a car back here."

"And I will sit with you and wait for it to come."

"You drive a hard bargain," Reagan said, chuckling.

"I'm nearly an attorney, you know. It's in the training." Sydney bit her lip as she stared at Reagan, and an unwelcome fluttery feeling started between her legs.

Reagan jumped up and downed the last of her wine and took their empty glasses to the kitchenette in her room before extending a hand to help Sydney up.

The walk back to the hotel should have taken less than a half hour, but Sydney insisted on stopping at the end of Fisherman's Wharf to ballroom dance as the topic of Amy Adams in *Enchanted* came back up. "I just want to date someone who will twirl me when the need strikes, you know?" she'd said.

"We aren't dating, but I'm your friend. Is the need striking now? I'm happy to twirl you as a stand-in," Reagan answered immediately.

And so she twirled her. Right there at three thirty in the morning at the top of the wharf. By the time Sydney had stopped twirling, she fell into Reagan, too dizzy and out of breath with laughter to stand on her own, so Reagan guided them to a bench.

Funnily enough, it was the bench Reagan had been stretching beside that morning—yesterday morning—when she'd gotten the Facebook alert about Sydney that had started this wild ride of a day. They talked about nothing and everything until the sky started to lighten.

"How did we put the sun to bed last night and then sit here as it wakes up this morning without sleeping?" Sydney asked on a yawn.

"I've no idea, but it's the second time we've done it together. Do you want to grab breakfast? I'm starving."

"I'm in favor of breakfast, especially with you," Sydney said, reusing Reagan's phrase from the night before.

They grabbed breakfast burritos at a small shack on the municipal wharf before Reagan lived up to her promise and walked Sydney back to her hotel and took a cab home.

As she lay in bed, reliving every moment of that completely perfect day, Reagan couldn't decide what to hope for with Sydney, but she knew she needed to buckle up because it appeared things were going to get a lot more interesting, and Reagan feared they would pull her right out of both her routine and her comfort zone.

❖

The first week of classes was always a whirlwind. Sydney had exchanged a couple of texts with Reagan since she'd been back in Menlo Park, but they hadn't made any definitive plans to see each other again. She desperately wanted to. Especially with tomorrow being Friday, and the weekend looming in front of her. Although she had work to do for school over the weekend, it wasn't an insane amount, and she was pretty sure that if Reagan wanted to meet up, she could use one of the two cars she, Aliyah, and Jessica shared. They also had two bicycles, and normally, Sydney rode one all around Menlo Park and Stanford, preferring the bike to the stress of finding somewhere to park.

But this weekend, she was hoping to make a longer trek. Back down to Monterey. But she needed an invite first. "Hey, Mom," she said as she swiped to answer and put her phone on speaker.

"How's my soon to be lawyer smartie pants?"

Sydney really hoped her mom stopped calling her a smartie pants when she actually became a lawyer, but she wasn't sure that she would. "I'm good. First week of classes was good. Securities law seems like it's going to be dense and boring as hell but important. I think agency and partnerships should be more fun. I had that professor last year, and she's funny. All in all, a good first week. What's going on with you and Noah?"

"At almost sixteen, Noah knows everything now." Her mom sighed, and Sydney envisioned her rolling her eyes. "But he's taking calculus, and soccer practice has started already. He's probably going to make varsity, which is making him more popular with the girls, God help me. But he's a good boy. Helping Grandma with odds and ends around her house and doing all the yard work here too."

"I'll have to see if I can make it home for at least one of his games. And staying busy with you and grandma will help keep him away from the girls." Sydney laughed and shook her head. Noah hadn't looked or acted like a lady's man when she'd seen him at the start of the summer, but kids at that age changed so fast. And he was handsome.

"I hope so, and we would love it if you could make it for one of his games, but we understand that you're busy. And plane tickets are so expensive."

"I have money saved up from my internship this summer, Mom. Send me the schedule, and I'll see if I can get a cheap flight out there if I book something early."

"I'll email it."

"Thanks, Mom. I'll let you know what I find," Sydney said.

As she spoke, her phone dinged, signaling an incoming text from Reagan. She picked it up and felt the smile as she read it:

Kinda late notice, but u want to come down this weekend? Just rented a house and moved in today. It's sweet. Right on the water. Maybe we could study together?

She wanted to text back immediately but also didn't want it to seem like she'd been waiting all week for an invite. Which she had been, but Reagan didn't have to know that.

"Sydney, honey, are you still there?"

And she needed to pay attention to her mom. Whom she was on the phone with. "Yeah, sorry, Mom. What did you say?"

"I just asked what you're doing this weekend. Something with Aliyah?"

"I'm actually heading down to Monterey."

"Weren't you just there last weekend?"

Shit. She hadn't thought this through. "Yes, but I ran into the craziest blast from the past. Do you remember Reagan from Italy?"

Her mom's long pause told Sydney everything she needed to know. Her mom still wasn't going to approve of her spending time with someone in the military. But Reagan was nothing—absolutely nothing—like her father. "I see."

"Mom, Reagan is a good person. She's probably the most honorable person I've ever met. I know Dad was horrible. A liar and a cheater, but that doesn't make every single person bad, does it?"

"Not every single person, but the way we were treated after he died…it's disgraceful." Sydney heard a rattle, like her mom was trying to set her teacup back into its saucer, and then a deep breath. "I'm not saying they're all bad. I'm just saying the military isn't always a good influence on people, especially when it comes to doing the right thing. I just worry about you. I'm sorry. I'm sure your friend is lovely. Just, please, be careful, okay?"

"I will, Mom. I promise."

As soon as Sydney hung up, she texted Reagan back:

Sounds fun. Can't wait to see your new place. Your room was fine but a little cramped lol. I don't have class tomorrow. Should I drive down tonight? Or do you have classes tomorrow?

Reagan: *You could do tonight? That works. I have one class in the morning, but that's it.*

Sydney: *Let me check with my roommates, but tonight should work.* Sydney knew she shouldn't get so excited, but after seeing Reagan last weekend, the need to see her again was irresistible.

❖

Reagan was not prepared for Sydney to come down that night. Luckily, the place was furnished, and she didn't have much, so it wasn't like she'd moved in fifty boxes—everything fit into one duffel, a rucksack, and a deployment bag—but still. Good God.

She scrambled around all afternoon, getting supplies, cleaning, buying food, all so her place would be presentable. And yet, she hadn't even thought of asking Sydney to wait until tomorrow to drive down. She wanted to see her.

She checked her watch again as she pulled her sheets out of the dryer. The house was furnished, but she didn't trust the sheets or towels, so she'd bought two sheet sets and several towels and had washed them twice to get them soft before making both beds in the house.

Thirty more minutes until Sydney got there. She didn't have time to cook—and didn't really have the talent anyway—so she'd wait another ten minutes before she called in an order for dinner. Pizza and red wine was a classy dinner, wasn't it? Classy enough, anyway.

She was surprised when the pizza showed up seconds before Sydney did, but it worked out well. "This place is great," Sydney said as she walked into Reagan's living room.

"Yeah, when I'm on a temporary assignment stateside, I always try to rent a house if I can. Even short-term, it's normally cheaper than billeting. Or a hotel, as you'd probably call it. It's hard to believe that this place, where I can sit on the front porch and hear the ocean, is cheaper than that dinky room, isn't it?"

Sydney spun in a circle as she took the place in. "For sure."

"Being a government servant has perks, I guess. Let me show you your room, and we can sit on the porch if you'd like and have dinner. Sorry it's just pizza, but it was a busy day."

"You didn't have to do anything special for me." For some reason, Sydney's southern drawl was more prominent. More like when they were in Italy. Reagan hadn't realized it until then that Sydney had lost a lot of that charming accent.

"It wasn't like I did anything major. Just new sheets. I don't trust the linens in rentals. That's probably a weird quirk since I don't have an issue in hotels, but…I'm not sorry about it. The sheets I got at the NEX seem great."

Sydney squinted at her. "The…NEX?"

"Sorry, I forget you don't know all the acronyms. The military loves them. The NEX is the Naval Exchange. It's like the Navy's version of Target. There is one at the Naval Postgraduate School where I've been living and go to school. Anyway, you have brand-new sheets on the guest bed."

"Fancy. I was going to invite you up to my place next weekend, but I have two roommates and no guest beds, so hanging out at your place might be better when we have our study dates. Study sessions, I mean. Not dates." Sydney chuckled nervously, and Reagan decided to take that moment to get them both wine. The thought of dates was…scary.

When she returned with wine in hand, Reagan said, "All settled?"

Sydney nodded. "I never realized how much I love the ocean and its sounds until this past week," she said as they sat at the cute little table on Reagan's porch.

"Kind of the same. I've spent a lot of my life landlocked, and although I've been near the ocean before, it didn't have the same allure as here. In Italy it was so much…I don't know, tamer, maybe?"

"Yeah, it was gentle. Here it's like, 'bitch, don't mess with me.'"

Reagan chuckled at that imagery. "Exactly that."

"Tell me about your first week in school. What are you studying?" Sydney said.

"It was good. I'm in a defense analysis program revolving around information strategy and political warfare."

When Sydney just stared, Reagan said, "It's basically a program to get us thinking about our intelligence efforts, diplomacy efforts, etc. and how they can be used to help us influence strategic conflicts for the better and potentially win conflicts that the US is directly or indirectly involved in."

"That's a lot of words, but I'm not sure how they all work together," Sydney said and laughed.

"Sorry, we love to use twenty words when two or three would be sufficient. How about this, the program is to help prepare us to effectively influence and improve the national security strategy? I was selected to attend this program, so it's an honor."

"That makes a lot more sense," Sydney said around a bite of pizza. "Not that I can judge our government complicating things that should be simple as pie. Lawyers do it a lot too." She shrugged and took another bite.

"I haven't dealt with a lot of lawyers, but TV certainly supports that."

"It's probably a little overplayed but partially true. And as an aside, how the hell do you sniff out all of the most amazing food places. This is fantastic."

Reagan still hated being the center of attention or having compliments showered upon her, and she scratched her neck nervously. "I, uh, read a lot of reviews. And I don't like to cook, and thus eat out a lot and try new restaurants regularly. I still have that overachieving memory, so I remember everything I've read as well as everything I've eaten, so I revisit the wheat and blacklist the chaff."

"I love that I get to reap the benefits."

"I *love* that you doubled down on my farming metaphor." Reagan laughed.

"My mom grew a lot of tomatoes, basil, and spinach when I was growing up, which basically makes me a part-time farmer. Or a tangential farmer."

"Tangential? That's what you're going with?"

"I could say I'm farmer adjacent if you'd prefer."

Spending time with Sydney reminded Reagan that what she would really prefer was spending as much time as absolutely possible with Sydney, even if it wasn't a great move. In fact, knowing that a relationship was possible but ill-advised made spending a lot of time together foolish, but Reagan was a glutton for punishment. She didn't think she could even half-heartedly try to stay away and wasn't going to try. Who knew when their paths would cross again? She wasn't going to waste a second of what they could have. Even if that could only be friendship.

CHAPTER ELEVEN

When Reagan woke the next morning and went for a run, she could feel the lingering impact of the wine she'd shared with Sydney the night before making her legs sluggish, but she wouldn't change any of it.

Sitting on her porch, listening to the crashing waves, and sharing a meal and wine with Sydney had been so low-key perfect. The only way it could have been better was if they'd spent time snuggling on her porch swing. No. Jesus. That would massively complicate things since being more than friends wasn't an option. Her feelings for Sydney were already too strong to casually date, but casual is all they could have since their time in California was limited.

Reagan spent the rest of the day studying at home with Sydney, but she'd made a dinner reservation for them at a seafood place on Cannery Row. Its food and water views were both supposed to be amazing, and she looked forward to sharing it—platonically—with Sydney.

The setting didn't really affect the food itself. Some of Reagan's favorite places were little hole-in-the-wall establishments that didn't have a menu beyond a tiny chalkboard, but when sharing with other people, someone special to her, the setting was the Luxardo cherry on the cocktail.

Reagan had been vague on dinner plans because she wanted it to be special and a little mysterious. The look on Sydney's face when they settled into their booth along the window overlooking the water made it all worth it.

"This is…gorgeous. Where'd you hear about this place?" Sydney said.

"I think I read about it in *Condé Naste*. The review said the ambiance amplifies the already fantastic food, so I have *very* high expectations."

Sydney sighed and looked around. "Don't take this the wrong way, but why on earth did your girlfriends break up with you? You plan the most romantic hangouts, and we're just friends. I don't understand how someone could leave you."

"Wow. That's a loaded question." She cleared her throat. "Maybe I'm an asshole as a girlfriend."

"I don't believe that for a second. You couldn't be so sweet and kind to me and an asshole to someone you're dating. Not possible." She squeezed Reagan's hand too briefly, and Reagan had an urge to grab her and press that hand back against her skin.

She grabbed her wineglass and took a sip instead to keep her hand occupied. "No, you're right. I'm not an asshole. But I'm not a great girlfriend."

"That just doesn't seem possible."

Reagan's heart fluttered at the thought of Sydney thinking of her as a girlfriend, or even just as girlfriend material, yet she knew she was fundamentally to blame for her previous relationships not going anywhere. "It's more like who I am that makes me difficult to date. I have a demanding job that requires me to leave. Sometimes for long stretches. And sometimes without much notice. It's not exactly a characteristic women look for in a girlfriend, you know?"

Sydney nodded, and Reagan felt like she could see the realization dawning on her face. She was relieved that Sydney had gotten the message that, even though she was out and single, she still wasn't in a position to date—not that she knew if Sydney was interested anyway—yet her heart broke a little as every traitorous fiber of her being wanted to pull Sydney into her arms and kiss her the way they had that last magical night in Florence.

"Ah," Sydney finally said, her face a little pale.

Reagan should have left it at that. She knew it. Yet, she continued, "I've deployed twice in the last four years—three times, if you count Italy—and that can be hard. But I was more serious about my career than I was about either of them, and at the end of the day, I want to make general. And the only way to do that is to answer when the Army calls. Sometimes before."

Sydney's face lost its last bit of color. Reagan needed to change the subject before she ruined this meal. She finally settled on, "How's Aliyah doing? Did you say she's still your roommate?"

"She is. She's taking pity on Jessica, our other roommate, and me by living with us even though she graduated with her MBA from Stanford and is making bank." She chuckled, and it soothed Reagan's raw soul after the difficult discussion about her exes. "She swears she loves living with us and says it keeps her grounded in a world where she's surrounded by a bunch of cis, white, straight men who've never experienced a second of adversity."

Reagan smiled, remembering how ballsy she'd been at twenty when they'd met. "She's definitely a powerhouse. I'm so glad she's doing well for herself. I guess all members of the Dead Presidents Society are doing well, huh?"

Sydney barked a laugh. "Oh, I forgot all about our secret society. Yes, I think so. I'm the laggard here still in school, but I'm optimistic for the future. I've had great internships each summer, so I think I'm going to catch up to you both. And soon." She winked.

Reagan's skin tingled. She had absolutely no doubt of that. Sydney's future seemed the brightest of anyone she'd ever met, and she was happy that, since they'd reconnected, she might now get to see it.

❖

"So you're going down to Monterey this weekend? Again?" Aliyah asked as she opened a bottle of wine for them.

"Yeah," Sydney said. It was Wednesday night, and she planned to drive down the following afternoon while Aliyah was still at work. She and Reagan had fallen into a surprising routine. She hadn't expected to spend nearly every weekend together. She hadn't expected to turn down the cute girl in her securities class who'd wanted to study together at her place to prepare for their midterm. The twinkle in her eye had said she had something else in mind too. She was cute, and Sydney wanted to be interested.

But still, she'd turned her down. And why? Because she was too busy half mooning over her best friend. Well, her best friend next to

Aliyah. She'd started leaving things at Reagan's house. She'd started thinking of the room she slept in as hers rather than Reagan's spare.

It wasn't like she and Reagan were dating. It felt like they'd fallen into the exact same routine as Italy. They'd become best friends again, best friends who touched too much, spent too much time together, and did too romantic of things together to be purely platonic, but they weren't dating either.

"Are you sure you guys aren't dating? You're in Monterey all the time." Aliyah huffed as she sat and handed a glass of wine to Sydney.

Sydney took a sip and said, "This is good. And, yes, I'm sure we're not dating. We're just friends." That was true, though Sydney didn't know if she was happy or sad about it. Okay, she knew. She was both.

"What about your other friends? We miss you. We were supposed to be having a grand year together before you move to Boston next year, and now I'm always hanging out with Jessica. And it's not that I don't love her. She's great, but I miss you. I thought *I* was your best friend, but it certainly doesn't feel like it anymore."

Sydney felt like a sumo wrestler sat on her chest. She hadn't realized how badly she'd been neglecting Aliyah. "I'm so sorry. You *are* my best friend." She moved to the couch to take her hand. How could she explain her feelings about Reagan when she didn't really understand them herself? "Things with Reagan are complicated. She's my friend, but I have this *need* to spend time with her. I don't really know how to explain it...it's like there's something inside me pushing me to be with her. It was like this in Italy too, but we're freer now. We haven't done anything. We touch more. Casually, I mean. We stand closer together, and it feels like we both look for ways to touch. That's not exactly right, but I don't know how else to explain it."

Aliyah's brow furrowed. "So why don't you just go for it and actually date? She's in the military, and it seems like loads of people in the military end up in DC. That's close to Boston. Sort of. And you'd probably be really happy if you ended up in DC."

"I think we both know it would be a mistake, and her military service is a nonstarter for me anyway. She told me she's deployed twice since Italy to Iraq and Afghanistan and doesn't try to hide how her job is the most important thing for her. I couldn't handle her deploying. Not after my dad. And she's moving to Morocco next year. You know how much I hate being a six-hour flight from my family, so there's no way I'm going to Morocco. Our lives are simply incompatible."

"You really wouldn't be willing to try something long distance for a while? Since you have this weird connection that defies explanation?" Aliyah said.

"No. Our lives won't work together. I want to settle down and work for one firm. Make partner. Have enough money to help my mom and brother. I need to be able to stand on my own. Support myself. My mom drilled that into me. I can't do that if I have to move every two years. And after Harmony, I'm not ever doing long distance again."

"Yeah, that whole Harmony thing was fucked-up. Though I think you might be a little shortsighted here. Harmony and Reagan are very different. As are your feelings I think." Aliyah took a sip of wine and readjusted on the couch. "Regardless, I miss you. I don't care how obsessed you are with her. Bring her here sometimes. And maybe you and I could hang out during the week."

"You're never home before eight. How are we going to hang out during the week?" Sydney asked, her irritation rising. But she squelched that. She needed to stifle her silly crush on Reagan and do a better job spending time with Aliyah, just not this weekend.

She'd already promised Reagan, after all.

And by the time Saturday morning rolled around, she was completely infatuated. Again. It was her own fault.

"What do you think about going to the coffee shop to study today? I forgot to buy more creamer, and it might be fun for a change of scenery, don't you think?" Reagan asked that morning.

"Sure. And a change of scenery might give me a little life for the memo I'm working on. It's deadly boring," Sydney said and rolled her eyes.

"Cool. What do you think about a little hike in Big Sur in the late afternoon? It's so beautiful down there."

Sydney felt stressed at the idea of stopping studying early to go hiking—she had a big midterm coming up next week—but Reagan looked so earnest and happy. How could she refuse? Maybe she could study more when they got back after the hike. She was pretty sure that people who hadn't gone to law school, even those who went to the hardest undergrad programs in the country, couldn't understand law school hell. Regardless, there really wasn't much of anything that she wouldn't do for Reagan. God help her.

"Sure. Sounds fantastic."

Except that it wasn't just a "little hike." Reagan, in her typical "let me plan the most romantic non-dates in the history of the universe with a woman I'm only friends with" way, had a picnic basket backpack, and it was less than an hour from sunset as they continued to climb.

Sydney could only assume that there was another breathtaking sunset picnic in their future. Although she was enjoying the hike and the easy conversation, how was she supposed to sit next to Reagan and have a picnic with a beautiful backdrop and continue to see her as just a friend? She hadn't wanted to admit it, but after talking to Aliyah earlier in the week, she'd been questioning everything about her relationship with Reagan, and this was torture.

"Our picnic spot is just ahead."

They rounded a bend, and Sydney's jaw dropped. The trees opened to a clearing, and it felt a little like they were standing on top of the world. The hillside dropped off about fifty feet in front of them, and beyond it, the rocky coastline of California curved, and the fickle beast that was the Pacific continued to mercilessly pound the shore. "This is so beautiful," she said as Reagan moved into the clearing and pulled a blanket out of her backpack, spreading it out on the ground.

"Right? A classmate mentioned he'd come upon it with some buddies when they were hiking this week, and I thought it would be a perfect place to have a casual dinner. The sunset should be perfect this evening." As she spoke, she pulled out containers with veggies and hummus and different cheeses, a bottle of wine, and two plastic cups. The cups were fancier than the ones they'd shared the first evening in Monterey; these had stems.

Once Reagan popped the cork and poured them both a glass, Sydney said, "Here's to memories. We've had a lot of spectacular ones, almost exclusively due to your planning, so thank you."

They plinked their glasses together and held eye contact as they sipped. Sydney resisted the urge to close her eyes as she swallowed and instead watched every muscle in Reagan's face and neck. She moistened her dry lips with a quick flick of her tongue. It took the hoot of an owl to break the tension, and Sydney had never felt more grateful for an owl in her entire life.

"This is good," she said gesturing to the wine.

"Yeah," Reagan said. "Thanks for coming with me. It's nice up here, isn't it?"

"It really is." Sydney was happy she had a sweatshirt on, but that was typical no matter the time of day or year in that part of California. The surprising part was that there was no fog on the horizon or rolling up the hillside.

They both reached for a piece of cheese at the same time, and their fingers brushed. They pulled away, then both reached forward, touching fingertips again. Tingles ran up Sydney's forearm, and she hoped Reagan hadn't seen her shudder.

Reagan turned her hand to give Sydney the go-ahead gesture. "Please, you go first."

Sydney placed a small slice of cheese on a cracker, but instead of eating it, she held it toward Reagan just below eye level, daring Reagan to take it with her mouth.

Reagan's eyes flicked to her outstretched hand before she leaned in and took the snack with her teeth.

Sydney felt a burst of air leave her as Reagan's lips grazed her fingertips, her eyes remaining on Sydney's the entire time. Sydney was confident she'd never experienced so sexy a moment in her entire life. Not in the entire two years she and Harmony had been together. What was she doing?

"If you're going to feed me," Reagan said, "I should return the favor." She grabbed a chunk of blue cheese, but rather than putting it on a cracker, she held it between her thumb and index finger.

Sydney's pulse pounded in her ears, and a throb started between her legs. She hesitated as she questioned the wisdom of what she was about to do before she gave up and leaned in. She gently took Reagan's fingers in her mouth up to the first knuckle and slid her tongue behind the cheese to guide it from her fingertips. Her eyes fluttered closed, and Reagan moaned. She ran her tongue around both of Reagan's fingers for good measure and gently sucked before she leaned back.

Sydney held her eyes closed as she chewed, savoring every exquisite second. When she finally blinked, Reagan was staring at her with such wanton lust that it took everything Sydney had to keep herself from leaning in again and taking those beautiful lips. But even as Sydney told herself to stay strong—reminded herself of how much she needed to keep it together—she realized she was already leaning.

"How do you hold this much power over me, Reagan? Why do you plan dates like this when anything more than platonic is a mistake?"

Reagan bit her lip as she stared. "I don't know what on earth you're talking about." But the expression on her face said differently.

"I don't know how to live in this moment—all alone and with the sun about to sink into the water—and not kiss you. The memory of us kissing on that Florentine bridge is so strong in my memory, even today. Anytime I'm feeling low, I think about it, and it gives me strength. Do you think of it too?" Sydney whispered.

Reagan's throat bobbed as she swallowed, but she nodded. She took the fingers that had just been in Sydney's mouth into her own as though savoring the taste of Sydney that might still remain, all without breaking eye contact.

Sydney's breath froze in her throat. She couldn't remember why kissing was a bad idea. In fact, it was the only thing in the universe that could possibly make sense, so she leaned, paused right before their lips touched, and connected with Reagan's gaze. She had to be sure she wasn't alone. Had to be sure that Reagan wanted this as much as she did.

Reagan's nostrils flared as she ran her fingers into Sydney's hair and pulled her the rest of the way. Their lips together were like heaven. Sydney quivered, moaned. Her lips softened, and Reagan's opened, her tongue tracing Sydney's bottom lip. Her heart thundered and felt like an out-of-control freight train in her chest when she greeted Reagan's tongue with her own.

Kissing Reagan was an ethereal experience. Sydney felt dizzy, and she grabbed Reagan's shoulder to ground herself. Her fingers dug into the soft material of the sweatshirt, and she used it to pull herself closer, scooting across the blanket until a clanking startled them both, and they pulled away.

The knife on the little cutting board had knocked the bottle of wine over. Luckily, Reagan had stuck the cork back into the top, so it didn't spill, but she scrambled to right it. "Oops," she said with a sheepish smile when she looked at Sydney again. "Not sure where that came from."

"Really? That's what you're going with?" Sydney could tell her exactly where it came from. Exactly when the yearning started. And it was four years ago, on the other side of the world. And she was pretty sure it had never gone away. Not even when she was with someone else.

"Well, no. I mean, I know where it *came from*. I'm just not sure where my self-control disappeared to." Reagan's chest rose and fell rapidly, probably as quickly as Sydney's.

"Yeah, that was...something. A lapse?" Sydney weighed the words in her head, but they felt all wrong. "No, not a lapse. I think it was a conscious moment. When you fed me that cheese and cracker."

"When you swirled your tongue around my fingertips. That's when I knew we were going to kiss, but I...I think it was a mistake."

Sydney knew she was right, but it was like a dagger. "I know. I know. You're going to Morocco in a year."

"And you're going to finish law school and go work at some big muckety-muck firm. Probably Boston, right?" Reagan's shoulders fell when she said the word.

"Yeah, unless I get a better offer."

"So, *if* we pursued something, we'd only have a handful of months. And then..." Reagan trailed off as she mimed an explosion and fluttered her fingers as though remnants of their hearts would scatter in the wind.

She looked so beautiful in the soft pink and orange light of the sky, and Sydney burned with the need to kiss her again, even with the hopelessness of their situation. A stroke of desperate inspiration struck. "I don't see how this could work in the long-term any more than you." Reagan nodded sadly. "But I haven't seen you in four years, and within hours of seeing you again, the need I felt for you was back. Stronger than ever. I'm not sure if it ever went away. So how is fighting this thing any easier?"

Reagan sucked on half of her lower lip before she said, her tone flat, "Nothing about this feels easy."

"Exactly my point. What if we keep it casual, undefined. But if we want to kiss, we kiss. If we want to hold hands, we hold hands. We see what happens over the coming months with no promises of forever.

Perhaps by giving into it, the need between us will fizzle out. And if not…well, we'll cross that bridge when we get to it." She shrugged one shoulder.

"Casual," Reagan said slowly, as if testing out the word. "No labels but follow our instincts. If, next summer, there's something to pursue, maybe we can figure out a way or maybe not."

That wasn't exactly what Sydney meant, but she didn't correct her. She wanted to kiss her so badly. Talking time needed to be over. She smiled and crawled around the blanket so the food and wine weren't between them and sat with her hip pressed against Reagan's, facing her. Her back was to the ocean and the sliver of sunlight remaining above the horizon. The view in front of her, however, was much more enticing.

Reagan pushed off her elbows until she was sitting up and ran her thumb along Sydney's jaw. "My instincts are screaming, more kissing," she whispered.

Same, Sydney thought, but rather than speaking, she pulled Reagan's lips to hers. Their last kiss had started slowly, but this one was full of the passion they'd both been repressing for so unbearably long. Their tongues moved together with a sense of urgency Sydney had never felt before. Reagan massaged Sydney's hip, urging her closer. Sydney squeezed Reagan's breast but hated how many layers of clothing were between her hand and Reagan's flesh.

Frustrated with the angle and the crick she was getting in her neck, Sydney climbed onto Reagan's lap, straddling her. In the moment since she'd broken their kiss, Reagan's lips found Sydney's neck. Her breath tickled Sydney's skin as she peppered kisses along her collarbone and throat.

Sydney needed to feel Reagan's skin and slid her hand under her sweatshirt and up her back. Reagan yelped and pulled away. "Holy shit, your hand is cold."

"Sorry," Sydney said but left her hand exactly where it was. "You'll get used to it, right?"

"Maybe. But I think this will help," Reagan said as she surprised Sydney by lying back and pulling Sydney on top of her, effectively pinning her cold hand beneath Reagan's body.

"Spoilsport," she said, only halfheartedly because lying on top of Reagan wasn't a hardship.

Reagan ran her thumb along Sydney's jaw. "You are so fucking beautiful. I can't believe I am lying here, holding you, kissing you. I used to dream about this."

"Me too," Sydney answered before lowering her face back to Reagan's and getting lost in her.

They lay like that, making out, hands exploring over clothes until long after twilight gave way to darkness. When they finally decided to head back, they hiked to the car holding hands, carefully stepping in the pool of red light from Reagan's headlamp. She grabbed Sydney's hand while she drove them back to her house and placed it on her thigh, her thumb lightly rubbing back and forth the entire way back up Highway 1.

Sydney desperately wanted to invite Reagan back to her bedroom but knew the timing wasn't right. She wasn't ready. She wasn't sure where things were going between them, but her heart was already involved where Reagan was concerned, it always had been, and she didn't want to hop into bed and regret it. Sex meant something to her. So did Reagan. Reagan also didn't seem ready, either. They kissed again one last time before bed, and as Sydney lay down to sleep, she pressed her fingertips to her swollen, well-kissed lips and took a moment to thank whatever higher power had brought Reagan back into her life.

Reagan woke the following morning, and at first, thought she'd had the best—and cruelest—dream of her entire life. Kissing, no, making out with Sydney for hours on that hiking trail, and it all felt so real. She'd been dreaming of kissing Sydney for years, but she didn't realize she hadn't dreamed it before she padded into the bathroom and looked at her face. Her lips were still swollen, and she had a small hickey where her neck met her shoulder. She hadn't dreamed any of it.

Sydney was sleeping in her guest room, wearing one of Reagan's marks. She hadn't meant to leave it, but as they'd been brushing their teeth after getting changed for bed, Reagan had seen a small purple mark on the inside of Sydney's collarbone. She remembered specifically enjoying that spot, the closest she could get to Sydney's breasts without taking off her shirt. Apparently, she'd enjoyed it a little too much.

She'd so wanted to ask Sydney to come to bed with her, but something inside her had told her it was too soon. Sure, they'd known each other for more than four years, but for something as significant as sleeping with Sydney, who was so important to her, she felt like it wasn't time yet. They'd only just decided to take things as they came. Take whatever felt natural. And it felt right to wait.

As she neared the end of her run, she passed their coffee shop from the day before and decided to cut her run a little short and grab coffee since she hadn't gotten creamer. As she pulled the door open, the smell of cinnamon rolls was so strong, she could almost taste them and knew she'd be walking out with at least one.

A cheery, fresh-faced teenage girl with acne-dotted white skin and braces said, "Good morning, what can I get for you?"

She ordered her expresso, tea, and two cinnamon rolls, but stumbled when she got to Sydney's order. "I think I need a large medium roast with an extra shot of espresso, two creams, and maybe two sugars." Reagan squinted, trying to visualize what Sydney had ordered yesterday.

"Of course." The barista bit her lip. "Are you getting coffee for the girl you were in here with yesterday?"

"You remember us?"

The girl's cheeks flushed, and she quickly said, "Her order was so specific, and she was nice. She had three sugars in her coffee. Not two."

"Great. Three sugars. Thanks." She gave the girl a big smile and made sure to leave her a hefty tip.

A sleepy-eyed Sydney was just emerging from the bathroom when Reagan walked in the door. "Already back from your run?" she said, looking Reagan up and down.

"Yeah. I also got coffee because I realized in all the excitement yesterday, I didn't get creamer." She lifted the drink tray. "And I got two cinnamon rolls because they smelled so good." And because of the salacious way Sydney was staring, she said, "See something you like?"

"I'm not sure if it's the coffee, the cinnamon rolls, or you that has me most excited."

"Oh?"

Sydney ran a fingertip down her bare arm. "Just kidding. It's you all yummy and sweaty. I want to touch your abs, but I'm trying to be good." She bit her lip, and Reagan felt desperate for her.

"I want to kiss you, but I'm gross."

"Hmm." Sydney took everything out of her hands and set it on the table. "Yet, I just don't care," Sydney said as she pressed her body into Reagan's and kissed her as though they hadn't seen each other in months.

Sydney's fingers danced along the exposed skin of Reagan's back, and her hips pressed forward in reflex. When Sydney's lips parted, Reagan opened hers and lightly stroked their tongues together. Her skin was aflame, and she spun, pressing Sydney against the wall and sliding her thigh between Sydney's.

"Oh my God." Sydney sank her teeth into Reagan's bottom lip before she tipped her head back, leaving the entire column of her throat for Reagan's mouth, and it was a lot more than she'd had access to the night before. She first kissed the little love bite she'd left, then around the edge of the tank top she was wearing. She desperately wanted to pull that tank top down and uncover the tight nipples she could see through the thin material, but she resisted the call and kissed her way back up.

Rather than claiming Sydney's mouth again, she rested her forehead against Sydney's. "How do you do this to me? You test every shred of my self-control."

"Me? You come in here all sweaty in a sports bra. How am I supposed to keep my hands off you?"

They stood like that for long moments, breathing. Reagan wanted to kiss her again but stepped away. She needed to shower and get more clothes on.

They ended up spending the day cuddling on the couch and studying for their respective programs with frequent kissing breaks, which were much safer once they'd both showered and dressed in real clothes. When Sydney left to drive home that evening, Reagan was sad but also on cloud nine.

Her heart sang with the elation of finally getting to hold Sydney's hand. Kiss her. Hold her. All with no fear of punishment or a complete derailment of her career. She knew they weren't making any promises. They couldn't. But she was going to drink in every second. And try not to count the moments until next Thursday when Sydney was back.

CHAPTER TWELVE

It had been three weeks since that fateful hike and kiss, and each Thursday through Sunday had been picture-perfect.

But this weekend, Aliyah had requested that they all hang out and go to a drag show in San Francisco. The show sounded fun, but Reagan had classes on Friday, so she couldn't head up until the afternoon, and traffic had seemingly been sent from the depths of hell to try her patience, and for a second, she wished she was in a snowplow and could simply plow all these cars out of her way. All she wanted to do was gather Sydney in her arms and hold her and kiss her into next week. But they were going to have to be social, and Reagan felt the preemptive loss.

When she finally arrived—after three hours, double what it should have taken—it was six. But Sydney must have been watching out the window as she came running out the second Reagan parked.

"You're *here*," she screeched as she threw herself into Reagan's arms.

Reagan was pushed back a step until she hit her car, but she savored the feel of Sydney like she would after a long deployment, even though it had only been a few days. Reagan pressed her nose into Sydney's hair and relished the uniquely Sydney smell that was like freshly blooming cherry blossoms in springtime DC. *God, how could she feel so perfect?*

"You're a sight for sore eyes." She was acutely aware of the soft give of Sydney's breasts against her own and grateful that her internal filter stopped her from describing that.

Sydney leaned away just enough to brush a light kiss across Reagan's lips. "Do you want to come inside?"

"Yeah, let's go see your place." She grabbed her assault pack from the back seat and followed Sydney upstairs. She was a little self-conscious carrying around a camouflage bag, feeling like she was screaming for attention, but it was all she had.

"I'm sorry traffic was so ugly. I guess that's an advantage to me coming down there on Thursdays," Sydney said as they walked up the stairs to her third-floor apartment.

"I just hate that we lost a whole day together." She felt pouty, yet she didn't want to make Aliyah hate her by always stealing Sydney away.

"Me too...but no one is here now if you want to start the grand tour in my room?" She pulled Reagan toward a hallway.

Reagan quickly took in the living room and kitchen and the first open door in the hallway as a bathroom before Sydney led her into the second door on the left. She had barely dropped her bag on the floor when Sydney slammed the door closed and pushed her against it.

Reagan grabbed Sydney's hips as their lips collided, and she pulled her as close as their clothes would allow. Sydney slid a thigh firmly against Reagan's center. All the oxygen in her lungs left her in one puff at the heavenly sensations that raced through her. She tilted her pelvis, grinding harder against her.

"Fuck, how do you feel so perfect?" Sydney said and pushed into her.

Reagan slid her hands under Sydney's shirt, stopping to cup her breasts through her bra. She ran her thumbs back and forth across the silky material until she felt Sydney's nipples harden.

A door slammed somewhere. Reagan dismissed it, but Sydney leaned back, sucking Reagan's lower lip before giving it one last light kiss. "Damn Aliyah's timing."

They were both still breathing hard as Reagan said, "Well, we're here to hang out with her, so, and I say this with regret..." Reagan looked at Sydney as she trailed a finger across her lower lip, along her jaw, and down her throat, until she came to the top of her shirt. "We should probably get out there."

"Fine," Sydney said and sighed but interlaced their fingers as she pulled Reagan into the living room.

"Ronald Reagan." Aliyah stood in their living room in her power suit, hands on her hips like Wonder Woman. "Why've you been holding my girl captive down in Monterey for all these weeks?"

"I don't know what she told you, but there's been no bondage involved."

Aliyah folded forward laughing, and Sydney rolled her eyes. When she righted herself, Aliyah pulled Reagan into a tight hug. It was an intimate hug, familiar. Almost as though because she and Sydney were close, she and Reagan had to be too, best friends by extension. "It's good to see you, Reagan. Glad you're finally out of that damn Harry Potter closet you've been chained in."

"Me too. Life is a lot easier when you aren't suppressing half of it." Reagan was still surprised at the genuine connections she could make with people once she didn't have to evade—because she'd never really lied, just dodged—every personal question lobbed her way. "I hear you've done well for yourself too, Ms. Big Shot Private Equity Manager."

"I wouldn't go that far, more like private equity bitch. But I can't complain about the money, even though the commute sucks. And the hours are tough."

"You're telling me," Sydney said. "She's rarely home when I go to bed."

Aliyah grimaced. "It's why I invited the *lovebirds* to hang out up here for a weekend. Now, let me fire up the grill. Who wants a drink?" Aliyah shrugged out of her suit jacket and tossed it on the back of the couch as she opened a sliding door and revealed a microscopic balcony that had one chair and a grill.

"She loves that behemoth," Sydney said conspiratorially. "We could actually fit three chairs out there, but it's her favorite thing, so Jess and I can't deny her. Plus, she's a grill master. Wait till you have one of these steaks. Fantastic."

"I heard that," Aliyah yelled.

"I hope so since I complimented you," Sydney called back.

Reagan's chest felt warm seeing their closeness. "You're awfully cute, you know that?" She squeezed Sydney's hand and pulled her closer for a chaste kiss.

"Ugh, get a room, you two." Aliyah mock gagged as she crossed to the kitchen.

"We're here at your request, your royal highness. You can't complain about us," Sydney said.

"If only Jess was here to back me up. Sheesh. Well, now that you've both come back up for air—"

"We weren't making out, drama queen."

Sydney tried to interrupt, but Aliyah didn't stop talking. "Do you want beer or cabernet? Vodka?"

"Whatever is fine. What would you prefer?" Reagan asked.

"Wine," Sydney answered, even though Reagan had addressed the question to Aliyah.

"Glad you're making decisions for all of us, Sydney," Aliyah said and laughed. "Luckily for you, that's what I was thinking too. Up top." She held her hand up for a high five, and Sydney stared at her like she had three heads.

"That's new." She tilted her chin at Aliyah.

"Sorry, too much frat bro energy at work, but still, don't leave me hanging." She raised her eyebrows while her hand was hanging out in the air.

"I got you," Reagan said and gave her a high five.

"Thank you, Reagan. At least *someone* knows what's up."

Sydney shrugged and grabbed a bottle of wine from their small countertop wine rack as Aliyah grabbed the steaks she'd had marinating in the fridge. "Will you bring out a glass for me? I'm going to get these babies cooking."

As soon as they all sat around the table and Reagan took her first bite, she knew Sydney hadn't been lying about Aliyah's prowess with the grill. The steak was flavorful and cooked to perfection, as were the broccoli and potatoes that also came off the grill. Sydney's fingers tracing little patterns on her thigh the whole time made the meal even better. And more frustrating. It was going to be a *long* night on the couch.

Sydney stood and cleared their dishes. "That was amazing, but I feel like I'm going to be off red meat for weeks." She patted her stomach and walked into the bathroom.

Aliyah, who'd been jovial all evening, spun in her seat as soon as the door closed behind Sydney and angry whispered, "What exactly is going on between you two?"

Caught completely off guard, Reagan fumbled her words. Who could have predicted the affable Aliyah would transform into Ms. Hyde the moment they were alone? "Uh, what do you mean?"

"You know." She waved an arm down the hall where Sydney had disappeared. "What are your intentions with her? She was fucked-up over a bad breakup last year, and she already had daddy and abandonment issues. And now you, little Miss Long-Lost Military Love, shows up out of the blue? What. Are. Your. Intentions." It was clearly a question but stated flatly. A demand.

But Reagan didn't dare not answer. "To spend as much time with her as I can while our orbits are overlapping. I can't ask her for more than that, even if I wanted."

Aliyah's lips pressed into a thin line. "You're setting her up to break her heart."

"No," she said immediately. "That's not my intent at all. We both know a future after California is uncertain, but we just couldn't fight... *us*...anymore. We've both wanted it for too long. But I'd never hurt her if I could help it." Reagan wanted to loudly emphasize her point, but they were keeping their voices low.

Aliyah shook her head slowly and pursed her lips. "You two are going to rip each other's hearts out, and you're *both* in denial about it. *Jesus* help me."

It was a possibility, but it was one Reagan couldn't let herself dwell on. The other flicker of hope rattling around in her head was, what if she *could* get Sydney to come with her? It was absurd, but, God help her, she wasn't going to want to say good-bye in a few months.

"Well, one of you needs to pull your head out of the sand about this. And you better not hurt her, Reagan. I swear, I'll hunt you down in whatever country you end up in and cut you."

Reagan struggled to not show any reaction. West Point had taught her to mask her emotions, but Aliyah's hard stare rivaled the meanest Firstie. Reagan sighed in relief when the bathroom door popped open, and Aliyah's posture relaxed, and she smiled pleasantly, as if she hadn't just been threatening Reagan a breath before.

"Shouldn't Jess be home by now?" Sydney checked her watch as she walked into the room.

"She was having a drink with a few classmates but should be home any minute." Did Aliyah's face soften a little when she talked about Jess? Reagan was pretty sure it had, and she wondered what that was all about.

As if summoned, the front door opened, and in walked an attractive woman with brown skin and a round face. Jessica, Reagan assumed.

"Jess," Aliyah said, confirming her hunch. "If you're hungry, there's a plate on the counter covered in foil." And, yeah, her face definitely softened.

Once introductions were made, Jess grabbed her plate, and they all moved to the couch to chat and laugh for hours. She and Sydney sat with their hips pressed tightly together, and they held hands or traced fingertips along thighs, but she wanted Sydney to herself. She sighed in relief when Sydney yawned and proclaimed it time to go to bed because they'd have plenty of time to hang out the next day.

They brushed their teeth together as they did at Reagan's, but when Reagan asked for sheets for the couch, Sydney said, "Please stay in here with me."

Her eyes were wide and vulnerable, and Reagan would have given her anything. She ran her fingertips along Sydney's jaw. "I want to, and I want *you*, but I really don't want our first time to be when we can hardly keep our eyes open, have huge steaks digesting, and we're sharing walls with two other people."

"I know. I just meant sleep next to me. Not *in* me. I want you too, but tonight isn't the night. After sharing you all evening, I want to hoard you. Fall asleep in your arms. It's not like it's the first time we've shared a bed."

Sydney's sly smile took her back to that long ago night in Florence. The one Reagan had relived over and over again after Sydney had gone home. Holding Sydney in her arms, the beauty of waking up with her nose filled with the cherry blossom scent of Sydney's hair. That night, her heart had been filled with pain and pleasure knowing that it could never be more.

Thankfully, she'd been wrong, even if it was only short-term. For now. And she couldn't think of a better way to spend the now than sharing a bed with Sydney.

CHAPTER THIRTEEN

Sydney woke the following Friday morning alone in Reagan's guest room. She'd thought maybe she and Reagan would share a bed again when she'd arrived the evening before. Unfortunately, Reagan had other ideas, so here she was: alone and unhappy about it. She checked the time on her phone.

Reagan had probably already left for class. Unfortunate because Sydney always enjoyed seeing her in that sexy uniform. It wasn't fair that she was so attractive in that drab, digitized, shapeless camouflage. Was it her aura of power? Maybe? Or maybe drab colors just looked good on her.

It was a little fortunate that Reagan was gone, though, because Sydney had plans for that night and needed time to execute. A romantic dinner, candles, wine, a walk along the ocean, and hopefully—Sydney took a deep breath to settle her nerves—she would take Reagan to bed.

She never moved fast in that arena. She'd made Harmony wait nearly nine months, but Sydney was particular about sex. Making love wasn't something she took lightly. But she'd been ready to sleep with Reagan after their first kiss and had been driving herself crazy for weeks, stopping them even when her internal voice kept screaming for her to keep going.

Something inside told her tonight was the night. And she was going to start the night off by making her signature dish: homemade pappardelle pasta with butter tomato sauce and roasted vegetables. She'd love to be able to take Reagan out to a fancy dinner, but funds were tight. So she'd make the simple but tasty recipe that she'd learned from her grandmother so long ago. She'd stopped at a farmer's market on her way down and bought fresh cherry tomatoes, along with broccoli, asparagus, basil, and a nice local bottle of cabernet. She'd swung into a specialty grocer to find the rimacinata semolina flour and a high-quality butter, both of which were crucial. And to let the pasta dough have enough time to set before she rolled it out, she needed to stop lazing in bed and get to work.

Serendipitously enough, her mom called, putting a needed end to her daydreaming about having sex with Reagan. Though an hour later, when she was kneading the dough for the noodles, she was still a little irritated and stressed about her mom's request. Why had she told her that she was making Grandma's homemade pappardelle pasta? She hadn't mentioned that things had been getting more serious with Reagan and that they were kind of seeing each other, but Mom had certainly jumped on that.

She'd been down on the military again, and Sydney had begged her to keep an open mind because Reagan was amazing. And that had ended with Sydney promising that she'd ask Reagan to come home with her for Thanksgiving. That felt too serious. Scary. Stressful. But as Sydney considered it, she realized she wanted to see her family and didn't want to be away from Reagan, given their limited time together, so she'd agreed.

Sydney spent the rest of the afternoon cooking and studying. Her arms were tired from the kneading, rolling, and cutting. Her legs were tired from standing for so long. And she was stressed about not having spent enough time studying.

But it was all worth it when Reagan got home, and Sydney greeted her with a glass of wine and watched that slow smile creep across her lips. Sydney hadn't dressed up, but she was wearing jeans that made her ass look fantastic and a low-cut blouse that she hoped would drive Reagan a little wild.

"Something in here smells amazing. Is it for me?" Reagan asked as Sydney handed her a glass.

"No, I made it for my girlfriend, so you'll have to get out of here before she gets home. Sorry." She shrugged a shoulder and smiled.

"I guess I'd better hurry. Can I have at least a little kiss before I go?" She stepped toward Sydney with her eyebrows raised.

Sydney made a show of being put out. "I suppose so. But you'd better be gone before she gets here."

"Yes, ma'am." Reagan dipped her head—towering over Sydney more than usual in her combat boots—and kissed her. Her lips were firm but softened as Sydney slid her hand around Reagan's back and under her blouse.

Sydney untucked Reagan's T-shirt until she could slide her hand against bare skin. She loved the feel of the soft skin of Reagan's lower back.

"Are you *sure* I can't persuade you to spend the evening with me instead of your girlfriend?" Reagan said before opening her lips and deepening their kiss.

Sydney's mind spun as Reagan squeezed her ass, and her tongue slowly stroked Sydney's before it retreated and stroked again. Sydney couldn't help the groan from deep in her soul. She wanted to kiss this amazing, sexy woman for the rest of her life. She pressed her hips into Reagan and pulled her closer. "I guess I could be persuaded. You are a pretty good kisser."

"Pretty good?" Reagan said, a look of mock horror on her face.

"Hmm. Better than passable?"

Reagan's jaw dropped, and her brows drew together. "That sounds worse than pretty good."

"I mean, I don't want you to get too big of a head." Sydney laughed.

"Too big of a head, huh?" Reagan said and surprised Sydney by tickling her.

She yelped and tried to step away, but Reagan moved too fast and had her pinned against the wall before Sydney could react. "I guess I'll just have to give you another demonstration of my prowess."

Without giving Sydney a moment to take a breath or prepare, Reagan's mouth took hers again. But this time, she was demanding. She kissed with an abandon that felt foreign but also luscious. Her mouth broke free of Sydney's, and she kissed along her jaw, nipped at her earlobe.

Her mouth was setting Sydney's skin on fire. The flutters in her stomach moved south and turned into a throbbing between her legs. She squeezed them tighter and realized Reagan's thigh had slid between her own. She wanted to tear all their clothes off but reminded herself that she had garlic bread in the oven that would burn if she didn't get it soon. And she wanted that night to be special. Something they'd both remember. Not something that started with clothes flying off in front of the door.

"Okay, okay. You're a good kisser." At Reagan's raised brows she said, "A fantastic kisser. You have the most wonderful lips that mine have ever had the privilege of tasting."

"That's better. I'm glad you're willing to give my lips the credit they're due." She brushed those wonderful lips lightly across Sydney's and then stepped back.

Thank God for the wall behind her, or Sydney wasn't sure if she'd be able to hold herself up.

"I'm going to go change. You look amazing, and I'm all here in this potato sack." She used two fingers to shake her blouse. "I'll be right back."

Sydney stayed exactly where she was until Reagan's door closed, and she sighed in relief. She wasn't expecting Reagan to test her resolve to eat dinner, but God, had she. When she finally steadied her uneven breathing as much as she could, she went to the kitchen to check the bread and put the finishing touches on the meal.

When the door clicked behind her, Reagan sagged against it. She didn't know how she'd kept her bravado up while pressing Sydney against the wall like that. Sydney's teasing had goaded her, but that kiss had tapped into a deep need, and she'd lost herself in the moment. She desperately wanted to slide that beautiful, wine-colored blouse right over Sydney's head and bury her face between her breasts.

She was hoping that night would be their first time, but whatever Sydney had made smelled so good, Reagan had been ready to drop to her knees and worship her. And she wanted their first time to be slow and romantic. Not hot and fast and against the wall, though she hoped there would be plenty of time for that later.

Her shaky hands opened the Velcro on her blouse and unzipped it. She undid her web belt and tried to take her pants off before taking her boots off, which made her almost fall over. She rolled her eyes and sat on the bed. After agonizing over her clothes for longer than she wanted to, she settled on the best she could, given the lack of notice. She put on her favorite cream-colored skinny pants and a light and flowy navy blouse that she half tucked into the pants. If she'd had more time to think, she could've picked out something better, but she was impatient to get back.

Sydney had been busy. She'd lit three tapered candles in holders Reagan didn't know the house had come with. The table was set with placemats she also hadn't known were there and had large flat bowls filled with delicious-looking pasta.

Sydney had refilled their wineglasses and was standing there with a hip cocked and a smile that made love swirl in Reagan's chest. When she could finally manage words, she said, "What are we having tonight? It looks as good as it smelled when I first walked in."

Sydney gestured for her to sit and then followed her into the adjacent seat. "Homemade pappardelle pasta with butter tomato sauce and roasted vegetables."

Reagan was impressed. "I didn't know you were a chef too."

"Hidden talents and all, but maybe you should try the food before committing fully." Her tone was teasing, but there was an underlying self-consciousness too, so Reagan quickly swirled a few noodles on her fork, speared a piece of broccoli, and placed it in her mouth.

She would have fawned over the meal even if it hadn't been amazing, but she didn't have to fake her reaction. "Oh wow, Sydney, this is perfect." She closed her eyes as she continued chewing, savoring each burst of flavor. "The pasta is so light but chewy. The sauce is mild, but the longer it's in my mouth, the more flavors come out."

When she opened her eyes again, Sydney was staring at her with a huge smile. "I'm glad you like it. It's my specialty. I want to say everything I cook is this good, but it isn't. I mean, I'm not a bad cook, but this dish is special. My grandma taught it to me when I was a kid. We used to make it for special occasions."

"What is the special occasion today?"

Sydney rolled her lips in for a beat, seeming to think about her answer before she finally said, "You. And me. Us. That's it."

"Well, I'm honored to be the recipient of your special occasion meal. Now, stop staring at me and eat. This is too perfect."

"Okay, okay." She twirled pasta on her own fork, and Reagan was mesmerized for a moment watching Sydney's lips wrap around the fork and slide its heavenly contents into her mouth. Reagan thought about Sydney's lips wrapping around her nipples, her clit, and rather than fighting off the surge of lust that burned through her, she embraced it. She let the pleasure of it invade every cell of her body as she took another bite.

They didn't speak for a couple minutes. The only sound was their forks clanking against the plates and the crunch as they both took bites of garlic bread in between bites of the pasta. Reagan finally broke the silence. "I think this is the best meal I've ever had. Truly."

That sweet smile grew on Sydney's lips, and everything in Reagan felt like a gooey mess. And suddenly, it came into focus. She loved Sydney. She thought she had before, thought she was falling, but watching Sydney smile at her like that sealed the deal. She wanted to blurt out the words but decided to wait until the moment felt right. She didn't think they'd make it through the night unsaid, however.

"You're welcome. I really am glad you like it." Her face got a little tighter before she said, "On a completely unrelated note, I talked to my mom today."

"Oh?"

Sydney rubbed the hollow at the base of her throat. "Yeah, she's weird about the military and was a little less than thrilled to hear we're growing closer. Seeing each other."

"Oh." Reagan said again, this time with a heavy heart. She rarely met people who had a bias against the military, and the fact that Sydney's mom felt that way hurt. Pretty badly.

"I told her to please reserve judgment because you're amazing, and she said, 'Bring her home for Thanksgiving.'" Sydney winced and took a sip of wine. "I don't want you to feel like you have to win her over, but I also want her to like you, and if she gets to know you, she'll love you. I—" She looked like she wanted to say something else but stopped herself.

"I wish I could go home with you for Thanksgiving, but my whole family is getting together this year, so I've got to go to Missouri. All my brothers are coming." Reagan felt sad but also a little relieved. The thought of being put on display for Sydney's mother and needing to win her over was terrifying, given her current disposition.

"Oh," Sydney said, her shoulders falling. "I didn't want to be away from you for a whole week. I know that sounds stupid, but a week sounds so long."

Her eyes looked so sad that before she even thought about it, Reagan said, "Do you want to come home with me? I know you haven't seen your mom or brother in a while, but maybe you could split the week since you don't have classes? Go home for the first half and meet me in St. Louis on Wednesday?" She hadn't thought about what it would mean for Sydney to go home with her, but she was sure it would be fine. Her parents were doing okay with her being gay, and her brothers hadn't even blinked.

"Uh, maybe? Will you come home with me for Christmas? If you're going to steal me from my mom for Thanksgiving, I'll need to give her something, and us being there for Christmas might do it."

Terrifying. "Sure. My parents are going somewhere for Christmas, so I'm free."

Her smile bloomed again, and when she squeezed Reagan's hand, the terror that had seized her receded. Some.

"Why don't I clean all this up, and then, would you like to go for a walk along the water while we let our dinner settle?" Sydney said.

"A walk sounds great, but let me clean up." Reagan jumped up before Sydney had a chance to protest and grabbed their plates. "You probably spent all day making this. You shouldn't have to clean too."

As they walked along the bay, Sydney smiled when Reagan took her hand. It felt like they were meant to do that. Their hands fit perfectly, and everything just felt...*right*.

They talked about their classes and the weather and a funny story Sydney's mom had told about Noah and a girl he was trying to flirt with. He'd ended up tripping over a parking stop and bruising his shin. In perfect comedic timing, Sydney tripped as she finished the story. Reagan caught her as she always seemed to.

Reagan laughed sweetly. "Apparently clumsiness runs in the family. But I'm sure he's not nearly as cute as you are when he trips."

"Luckily, I have you to catch me." Sydney's breath caught at the intensity in Reagan's eyes. It didn't fit with the lighthearted mood. "Are you okay?"

Reagan lightly grazed her lips across Sydney's. "There's something I need to talk to you about, but can we go home? It's too… open…out here."

"Of course." Sydney felt nauseated and tense, worried that whatever Reagan was going to tell her was going to be bad. Fundamentally shift them somehow.

Reagan shook their joined hands. "Relax. It isn't anything bad, but it's something I feel like I need to tell you before we go any further."

When they got back and settled on the couch, Reagan looked uncomfortable, so Sydney lightly kissed her. Despite Reagan's reassurances, Sydney still felt dread at what Reagan was going to share, but she wanted to get whatever it was out in the open. "What did you want to talk to me about?"

Reagan nodded. Blinked. "Will you sit next to me, not look at me like you're looking into my soul?"

"Sure." She scooted, pressing their hips together.

Reagan brought their hands to her mouth and turned them until she could kiss the back of Sydney's hand. She sighed. "You know I deployed twice. The first time was Afghanistan. I was a company commander. That went smoothly. Little scuffles here and there, but I came back with everyone I went out with."

Sydney felt a little relieved that this wasn't about them, but knowing something bad had to be coming sat in her stomach like a lead weight. She squeezed Reagan's hand.

"But the second time, I went to Iraq. I was the battalion S2. Uh, the battalion intelligence officer embedded within an engineering brigade. We were trying to rebuild some of the infrastructure that had been damaged by friendly fire and insurgents. Part of my job was providing intelligence for that effort. This included working with the Iraqi Army intelligence to gain intel, but my secondary mission was to help transition certain intelligence tasks over to the Iraqis. Our bases were close, but most communication and training happened remotely.

I'd never met my Iraqi counterparts. I'd just spoken to them over the phone or on shitty video calls, and I felt like they were having a hard time understanding some concepts."

She let out a shaky breath, and Sydney wanted to gather her in her arms but settled for rubbing her leg instead, hoping it would help settle her nerves, made sure she knew that Sydney was here for her. No matter what.

"So I advocated, hard, for us to meet in person. The Army refused to let me and my team travel to them, but four months in, I convinced the Army that we needed to let them come to us, despite their reservations about an inside threat. I was ecstatic. So was the officer I was closest to. He was a go-getter and wanted to stop relying so heavily on us. The first time we trained together, everything went off without a hitch, but the second time…" She cleared her throat. "They'd been betrayed by someone. We were really careful about keeping the details of their travel arrangements under wraps, but somehow, insurgents found out. They managed to plant a bomb on the truck, but the timing was off. The assholes probably timed the truck to blow up a few minutes after arriving at our base in the hope that they could take out our intelligence building." She sniffed. "Do you mind if I get some water?"

Sydney tried to jump up. "I'll get it for you."

"No. Thank you. I'll grab it."

Reagan pointedly didn't look at her, and Sydney felt cold without her as she dreaded what was coming next.

She heard Reagan sniff in the kitchen and couldn't leave her alone in her grief. Reagan was leaning over the sink with her head hanging. Sydney wrapped her arms around her from behind and pressed her face against Reagan's back.

Reagan tensed, but Sydney didn't let go, and Reagan relaxed into her. She pressed Sydney's hands into her chest.

"You don't have to keep talking about this if you don't want to," she whispered.

"No, I haven't talked to anyone about it. And I feel safe with you. I need you to know before we go any further." Sydney moved with her as she took a deep breath, let it out. "The truck was held up at the gate. Something about a delivery in front not having the right paperwork. My friend Jane was an MP and the OIC on duty at the gate that day.

We'd been…flirting off and on. Nothing serious, just fun. But when the enlisted MPs were dealing with the delivery truck and traffic started to back up, she left the guard shack to talk to the Iraqi intelligence guys. She'd known they were coming and didn't want to leave them out there like sitting ducks, but when she approached the truck, it exploded."

Reagan's breathing accelerated, and Sydney tried to soothe her by rubbing her collarbones.

"I tried to run out there, but someone held me back. My friends— Rai'd Sahel, head of the Iraqi intelligence group, and Jane—were both killed. Along with the other Iraqi soldiers and two US soldiers who happened to be in the vehicle behind them."

"I'm so sorry, Reagan." She squeezed tighter, wishing she could protect Reagan from the hurt.

"It's war, right? We all know the risks, but Sahel was a good man. He was doing his best to make his country a better place for his three children. And Jane, she was two years behind me at West Point, though I didn't know her there. She joked that I'd tortured her during Beast, but I don't remember at all. We'd kissed a couple times, and I liked her. As a person. She had three brothers, just like me, but she was the youngest rather than the oldest. And it was my fault. It was war, but I was responsible."

"No—" Sydney tried to say.

"Look, I know I didn't strap the bomb to that damn truck, but I'm the one who pushed for in-person meetings despite my superiors' concerns. It hurts that I made a bad call. They teach us at West Point that bad decisions will happen, and you can't agonize over them. You have to accept it and move on. It's what I did. I was given a couple days' of quarters that involved talking to behavioral health, and then I had to get back at it. Working with Sahel's colleagues. Men I hadn't met. And it was fine. It was hell, but it was fine. But I sometimes wonder what all of their lives would be like today. Not just Sahel's and Jane's but all ten of the people killed. Would they be doing important work? Or would their numbers have been called anyway, just in a different way? Could I have done anything to stop it?"

Reagan stood tall without dropping Sydney's hands, and her head fell back. Sydney squeezed even tighter, as though she could stop the hurt as Reagan took long slow breaths. She turned in Sydney's arms and finally made eye contact for the first time since she'd started talking. Tears slid slowly down her cheeks. Sydney wiped them with her thumbs.

"I know it was the right choice having them come. I know they learned and took things back to their unit. But I *hate* that it happened. That the world lost them." She pulled Sydney into her arms and buried her face in Sydney's neck.

Sydney held her, rubbed her back. She hoped that she was helping by being there. By still loving her even as Reagan experienced her darkest moment again. She wasn't sure how long they stood there, but she hoped Reagan found sharing cathartic.

When Reagan finally pulled away, she gave Sydney a watery smile. "Thank you for listening, holding me, not running. I'm sorry I got all crybaby-y."

"Don't be ridiculous." They both laughed, and Sydney prepared herself to be vulnerable too. Reagan certainly deserved it. "I'm sorry you went through all of that, but thank you for sharing. For trusting me. I want to know you. All of you. Be here for you. Because I love you. I have since Italy. I think that's why Harmony broke up with me. She always said it felt like I was holding part of myself back, and I thought she was being ridiculous, but the more time I spend with you, the more I realize she was right. I couldn't love her with my whole heart because a piece of it has only ever belonged to you. Even though you were never mine, you still owned me. And since we've been together, that little piece that loves you has gotten bigger, and I don't know why I was waiting to make love to you. We don't know what the future holds, but we have now. And I want to enjoy every moment of love that I can."

Reagan licked her lips. "Of all the ways I imagined you telling me you love me, I never thought it would be standing in my kitchen, tears still drying on my face, but I love you too."

Sydney surged up to capture Reagan's lips. They tasted a little salty, but they opened to grant access to Sydney's seeking tongue. Reagan's hands were in her hair and on her back. Then, they were under her shirt and were sliding it up and over her head.

Reagan leaned back and stared. Even though she'd seen Sydney in a bra before, she was looking at her as though it was the first time. She was wearing new underwear, a red lacy set she'd splurged on at

Victoria's Secret for just this occasion. Reagan cupped her breasts and ran her thumbs over her nipples through the material.

Sydney groaned and pressed forward, seeking more pressure.

"I love this bra. Is it new?" Reagan's voice was raspy. Sexy.

Sydney couldn't find her voice, so she simply nodded.

"Does it have a matching piece that I'm going to find soon?"

Sydney wished she had a bottle of water, her mouth was so dry from the intensity of Reagan's gaze.

"Will you come to bed with me?" Reagan said.

"Yes," Sydney whispered. It had been her plan all day—for days, really, and was the reason she'd bought those new underwear—and she wasn't turning back now. She needed to feel Reagan naked. Under her. Over her. Everywhere.

CHAPTER FOURTEEN

Reagan felt so raw, so open, as she hooked her finger into Sydney's and drew her toward the bedroom. By opening up about her deployments, Reagan had unlocked a door within herself that she hadn't known was there and let Sydney in. All the way in. Into places Reagan hadn't realized she'd been guarding. Places untouched since long before Iraq.

In her bedroom, Reagan leaned down for another kiss, but after the lightest of grazes, she pulled back. "You're sure? I don't want to pressure you if you're not ready." She thought she might die if Sydney said she wasn't but never wanted to push her.

"I don't think anyone has ever tried to take care of me like you do." Sydney cupped Reagan's cheek and rose up onto her toes as she kissed her. She ran the tip of her tongue along Reagan's lower lip, and Reagan opened for her. Sydney's tongue slowly entered, stroked until Reagan's knees felt weak. It wasn't like they hadn't done this before, but every pass of her tongue felt different tonight because she knew they weren't going to stop.

Reagan's hands shook as she reached for Sydney's jeans. She wanted, needed, to see her. While she worked the stubborn button, Sydney opened Reagan's top and slid it down her arms until it could go no farther, and Reagan released her grip. She fumbled. "Damn you, button. Why do you hate me?"

Sydney giggled and pushed Reagan's hands away, her own fingers taking care of the task much more quickly. She shimmied her pants down her legs. "Damn skinny jeans for being so difficult. They should make a wind pant version so when the need strikes, you can just whip them off."

Reagan laughed and was preparing to say something, but Sydney stepped out of her jeans. Seeing her in nothing but a red lacy bra and panty set sent every thought in Reagan's mind on vacation. Her mouth went dry, and her clit throbbed. She didn't realize her shirt had slipped from her arms until Sydney kicked it to the side. "Thank you," she finally managed.

Sydney's brows furrowed. "For what?"

Reagan's tongue felt a little swollen, but she swirled a finger at Sydney and finally was able to string a few words together. "For this, sexy, fantastic, present you're giving me. I know they're your clothes, but it feels like a gift to me." She could see Sydney's dark nipples through the lace, still hard and calling for Reagan's tongue. Her pussy looked completely bare behind the lacy underwear and was begging for Reagan's kiss.

"Seen enough yet?" Sydney said, her tone teasing.

Reagan dragged her eyes back up. "Looking is half the fun, but, yeah. Will you wear this for me again, though?" She swallowed, trying to quench the dryness in her throat. "Soon?"

"Absolutely." Her southern accent was a little stronger, and Reagan wondered if it was because she was more open too. Relaxed. Her most genuine self. "Now, let's get these pants off you."

Her fingers were nimbler than Reagan's, and she flicked the button and had the pants around her ankles within seconds. "I'm sorry I don't have fancy underwear for you."

Sydney ran her finger around the waistband of Reagan's cotton bikinis, and all of her stomach muscles clenched as a surge of wetness found its way to her center. "Don't underestimate the power of simple black. These are tantalizing."

Reagan hoped Sydney was going to slide her fingers inside, but instead, Sydney pressed a kiss between her breasts and in a line along the top of the bra cups. Reagan wished she'd been wearing a low-cut bra, but she still shivered as Sydney's warm, wet tongue licked along the top. She arched her back, hoping Sydney's tongue might slip below that cup, but either Sydney didn't realize what she was aiming for or was torturing her on purpose.

Sydney straightened and walked Reagan backward to the bed. "Lie down," she whispered, her voice husky.

Reagan did as she was told without thinking. The look in Sydney's hooded eyes took her breath away.

"Will you show me how you touch yourself when you're alone?" *Oh God.* How could she do that? The idea of Sydney watching her while she touched herself had desire blazing through her veins, but she was barely comfortable with sex in general, and the thought of being on display like that terrified her. "I'm…I'm not sure if I can. I'm…a little self-conscious." She fought the sudden urge to turn off the bedside lamp and crawl under the covers. She wasn't embarrassed by her body—she knew it was toned—but she wasn't that experienced, and she'd been so busy repressing every sexual urge for so long, she felt like her sexual awakening had been a little stunted. She was petrified of disappointing Sydney.

"Hmm." Sydney bit her bottom lip and crawled onto the bed and knelt next to her. "Can I still touch you?"

Reagan nodded, and Sydney ran her middle finger from Reagan's lips down her chin, between her breasts, along her abs, and ending between her legs as she traced up and down Reagan's slit through her underwear. Reagan's breath came out in a burst, and she pushed her hips into the mattress so she wouldn't surge up into Sydney's hand and embarrass herself.

"Relax," Sydney said. "You can trust me."

Those simple words broke through the self-doubt. Reagan sat up and kissed Sydney as the tightness in her chest loosened, and she allowed herself to cup Sydney's breast as she'd been thinking of doing since she'd taken her shirt off. She gently squeezed, and Sydney groaned; she ran her thumb back and forth across the nipple again, and Sydney gasped. Reagan slid the lace of her bra down, exposing Sydney's breast fully for the first time and took it in her mouth.

"Yes." Sydney's breathy encouragement empowered her, and she pushed Sydney onto her back, straddling her hips. "God, you're beautiful."

"I've never felt as beautiful as I do when you look at me like that." Reagan shimmied her hips, aching for pressure, and Sydney reached between them again. Something about Sydney was making her feel bolder, and she slid her hips back and forth along her fingers.

"These are in the way," Sydney said as she ran her hand under the elastic at Reagan's hip.

"They are, aren't they? Yours too. Though they've been lovely to look at." Reagan ran her palms over both of Sydney's nipples—one exposed to her and the other still behind the lace.

"Let's remedy that," Sydney growled. She sat up and reached behind Reagan, flicking her bra off with minimal effort. Before Reagan could do the same, Sydney took her breast in her mouth, and the alternation of licking and the light grazing of her teeth had Reagan's fingers trembling too much.

When she slipped for the third time, Reagan said, "Wait."

Sydney looked up. "What's wrong?" Her eyes were wide, chest heaving.

"I just needed you to stop so I could do this," Reagan said as she finally released Sydney's breasts from their lacy captor.

A slow, sexy smile spread across Sydney's face. "Well, don't be so scary about it next time. You can take clothes off me anytime—absolutely anytime—you want."

"In that case, let's get your underwear off too." That maneuver wasn't sexy, but the feel when Sydney stretched out on top of her without a stitch of clothing between them sure as fuck was.

Reagan thought Sydney was going to straddle her, so she was surprised when Sydney slid both her legs in between Reagan's and pushed her knees apart before rising up and looking unabashedly at her.

She felt self-conscious that she hadn't gotten waxed like Sydney. She meticulously trimmed her hair, but she wasn't expecting Sydney to be completely shaved. She'd always been too embarrassed to get a Brazilian but wondered if Sydney would be turned off by her hair, despite the fact that it was neat and shaped.

She was about to apologize, but Sydney spoke first. "You are so fucking hot, Reagan. Seriously. Those abs are chiseled by sapphic goddesses. You're so wet for me. I can't wait to bury my face in your pussy."

Reagan thought she might be lying except for the flush on her face, the slight flare of her nostrils, the rapid rise and fall of her chest. Yet, Reagan couldn't stop herself from saying, "You really think that? You aren't sad I'm not waxed?"

Sydney raised her gaze to Reagan's face. "Are you kidding me right now? You're the most unbelievably sexy woman I've ever seen. In my life. I get waxed because I prefer it for myself, but waxed, trimmed, natural, I'd want to bury my face in your pussy no matter what." She ran a finger around Reagan's clit, down to her hole, and back up to her clit again.

Reagan pressed her hips up into the contact this time.

"Oh God," Sydney whimpered.

Reagan's own whimpers stayed in her throat as Sydney maintained eye contact while she slid down Reagan's body and lifted first one thigh and then the other over her shoulders. Reagan barely heard the, "I love you so fucking much," right before Sydney spread her open and brought her mouth to Reagan's clit.

A quiet yelp escaped Reagan's lips at the first contact, but she quickly found a rhythm with Sydney's tongue. Sydney's dexterous fingers tugging her nipple brought out another cry as she found just the right pressure on the most sensitive parts of her body. She thought she might sing. Until Sydney's other fingers found their way to her entrance.

Sydney's mouth left her, and Reagan reared up to see why she'd stopped. "Wha—"

"Is this okay?" she asked, eyes earnest, and Reagan didn't think she even realized how close Reagan had been and how removing her mouth had been torture.

Feeling desperate, she groaned, "*Please.*" She flopped back. Apparently, she was willing to beg.

Sydney chuckled as she lowered, and the vibrations were wonderful, yet Reagan couldn't focus on them because Sydney was sliding a finger into her, and all the breath left her lungs. When Sydney started moving that finger and her tongue at the same time, Reagan gasped for air. All the muscles in her body seemed to be reacting on their own timetables. Her fingers grasped at air, reaching, trying to find something to hold on to as an orgasm screamed through her entire body, harder than she would have thought possible. She found the seam along the top of the mattress, and she held on as if her life depended on it, pulling on it every time another contraction erupted through her.

When Sydney's slow tongue strokes switched from pleasure to overstimulation, she gasped, and Sydney seemed to know. She stopped moving, pressed a kiss to Reagan's outer lips, and crawled back up her body. Sydney somehow also knew that Reagan still needed pressure against her clit and lightly pressed her thigh where Reagan wanted it. She peppered kisses along Reagan's neck that she only vaguely registered before laying her full weight on her. "Is this okay?" Sydney asked.

Her words felt slurry, but Reagan said, "Perfect." She tried to ask for just a minute to recover from the most intense sensations she'd ever felt, but those words came out unintelligible. She didn't even try to say them again but pulled Sydney to her as tightly as she could.

Sydney might have fallen asleep for a few minutes or maybe hours, but she awoke on her back with the most magnificent sensations all over her body. Was she being kissed by fairies? Everything felt alight in pleasure. Her hips rolled up in response to a sensation she didn't realize was there until she was already reacting to it.

"Hey, you," Reagan said, and the rest of the evening came back into focus. "I was wondering how long I could touch you before you came back to me." She lightly nipped at Sydney's collarbone before traveling farther down to take Sydney's nipple between her lips.

"Holy shit," Sydney said as Reagan's teeth ever so lightly grazed her nipple. It was ninety-nine percent pleasure with the tiniest hint of pain and felt so amazing.

Reagan looked up. "Bad holy shit or good holy shit?"

"Good." She wasn't proud of herself, but she pulled Reagan's head back to her breast as Reagan's fingers never stopped their motion. She needed her mouth. She needed her fingers. She *needed* Reagan like she'd needed nothing before. She'd also never been much of a sex talker in her life, but Reagan made her *need* to speak. She couldn't come up with anything particularly eloquent, but as Reagan's perfect pressure pushed her higher and higher, she heard herself saying, "Yes, yes, right there, yes, yes, *yes!*" as she shattered into too many exquisite pieces to count.

"How did you...you're amazing...I don't think I've..." Sydney ran through half phrases as Reagan kissed her chest, her collarbones. She kissed both Sydney's nipples, making her jump. "Hey. Give me a minute here." But even that little jolt didn't dim the smile she could feel across her face.

"Your wish is my command," Reagan said and lay next to her before rolling Sydney until her head rested on Reagan's shoulder. She loved how it felt.

"It's like the first time we shared a bed together. Except fewer clothes."

Reagan laughed. "That was nice, but I like this a little better."

Sydney didn't want to give in to sleep. She didn't want the night to end, but her eyelids felt too heavy. Yet she smiled as she drifted off knowing there'd be more nights like this.

When Sydney woke the next morning, the bed next to her was empty and cold. Where was Reagan? She rolled out of bed, hoping Reagan wasn't having second thoughts and padded, naked, into the kitchen.

There she found Reagan making breakfast. She had sausage cooking in one pan as she fried eggs in another.

"Why'd you sneak out on me?" Sydney said.

Watching Reagan's eyes slowly go wide as she took in Sydney— and presumably, her nakedness—was the funniest thing Sydney had seen in a while. Reagan kept staring, and Sydney felt it was important to remind her of her cooking tasks.

"Don't forget the eggs."

"What?"

"The eggs." Sydney pointed.

A full three seconds later, Reagan said, "Oh right," and spun back around to swirl the pan. Looking at something other than Sydney apparently helped her find her voice too. "You can't just come out here in all your naked perfection and expect me to not get distracted. I thought I was going to bring you breakfast in bed, and suddenly, here you are. Naked. And amazing. But naked. It's kind of the first time I've seen you standing naked, and it was a little surprising, and—"

Her babbling was so adorable, Sydney had to wrap her arms around her from behind. There was no choice. She was the most beautiful, adorable, amazing, sexy person Sydney had ever known. And she didn't care if the eggs burned. She was pretty sure Reagan had more. She *needed* to touch her, so she did.

The eggs did burn as Reagan took her in the kitchen. She'd turned off the burner, but the slight smell still permeated as Sydney came while sitting on the kitchen counter with three of Reagan's fingers buried in her. She'd never think of that smell the same again.

By the time she drove home on Monday morning—she'd stayed as late as possible for more time with Reagan—Sydney's muscles felt individually tight, but overall, her body was loose and relaxed in a way that was wholly unfamiliar. She'd almost skipped class for the first time ever because she hadn't wanted to leave, but Reagan had convinced her to go. She was right, but Sydney would be counting the milliseconds until she could be in Monterey again.

CHAPTER FIFTEEN

Reagan whistled "Jingle Bells" along with the background music in the airport as she stood next to Sydney, waiting for their suitcases to come around on the belt before they'd meet Sydney's mom at the curb. She still couldn't believe Sydney had convinced her to come to West Virginia to spend Christmas with her family. They weren't supposed to be all that serious, and yet, she was going home to meet Sydney's mom and brother and grandmother?

In her heart, she knew she was kidding herself about this being light. They felt serious, they'd both admitted to loving each other, but there was that ticking time bomb looming. The truth of Aliyah's accusations—of them sticking their heads in the sand—made her nauseated, but she was terrified to ask Sydney about the future.

"You don't have anything to be nervous about," Sydney said as she squeezed Reagan's hand.

If only she really knew. "That's easy for you to say. My family wasn't predisposed to hate you when you came home with me."

"Well, my brother doesn't. Oh, there's mine." She pointed at her dark purple bag as it came out on the conveyor belt.

Reagan stepped in and grabbed it. "I don't think that really helps. I can bond with a teenager. Moms with a predisposition to think soldiers are bad news…" She shrugged. She knew it wasn't the right time to ask but couldn't stop herself. "What happened with your dad? You've never talked about it except that he wasn't a great guy, and he was killed in action. But I don't understand how that caused her to hate the entire military."

Sydney went a little pale. She opened her mouth but didn't say anything. Then, she opened her mouth again but said, "There's your bag. Your *deployment* bag, right?"

Okay. Clearly, they weren't going to talk about this now. She grabbed her bag, and they headed toward the curb. A white SUV that was older than her and had definitely seen better days pulled up. A surly looking teen sat in the passenger seat looking at his phone, but as soon as the car stopped, a woman with blond hair, pale skin, and a strong resemblance to Sydney jumped out of the car and yelled, "Sydney, my baby!"

She came running around and swept Sydney into a huge hug. They rocked back and forth, and a pang of guilt struck Reagan for depriving them of seeing each other at Thanksgiving. She felt weird standing there watching them while holding their bags, but what else was she supposed to do?

She dragged the bags to the back of the car, but when she got there, she couldn't figure out how to open the liftgate. She tried feeling for a button, but no luck.

"Can I help you with that?" a deep voice said from behind her, catching her off guard.

"Oh, hi, you must be Noah," Reagan said.

There was no way he was anyone else. He had the same blond hair and blue eyes as Sydney, but his accent was still strong—stronger than Sydney's had been, even in Italy—and he was about six feet tall, which meant he would tower over Sydney and still had several inches on Reagan. But where Sydney was soft, with subtle, beautiful curves, he was all beanpole. Tall and gangly. She was sure he was going to be a handsome man, but for now, it looked like his limbs were too long for his body.

"I'm Reagan." She stuck out her hand.

He shook her hand with a firm, if a little sweaty, grip. "You guessed right. Here." He stepped around her and reached in a spot where Reagan swore she'd tried, and the back opened.

She tried to put the suitcases in, but Noah beat her to it. She wasn't used to that. She and her brothers had been taught that they were all equal and didn't need to help each other. She'd always made sure it didn't look like she needed help when they were around. But it was sweet.

"Thanks. I swear, I looked for the handle there."

He looked less surly now than he did when they'd pulled up. "Yeah, it's weird." He looked at his mom and sister, who were still hugging like they hadn't seen each other in years rather than a few weeks. "Mom, Syd, come on. I have practice." A hint of whine entered his voice, and Reagan could tell he was only sixteen, even though he was already a giant.

Sydney and her mom finally broke apart, and Reagan felt a pang of relief. "Don't be jealous, Noah Doah." She pulled him into a hug rather than introducing Reagan, leaving her to stand there awkwardly once again.

Reagan turned to their mom. "Hello, I'm Reagan Jennings." She extended her hand.

Sydney's mom's expression was markedly cool, but she took her hand as she said, "I'm Alice. These two rude and ungrateful kids are mine."

"Ha, ha, Mom," they both said at the same time.

"Mom, this is Reagan. My girlfriend," Sydney said.

"I know," Alice said. "We introduced ourselves."

"Why don't you sit in the front, Noah, and I'll sit in the back with Reagan?"

"Wha? You're going to let *moi* sit in the front seat. Just because you have a girlfriend now? This is a first. I'm a foot and a half taller than you, and you still call shotgun based on seniority."

"Whatever. Just get in there." She shoved him toward the passenger door.

Reagan found their interactions cute. So much more relaxed than the competitions with her brothers.

She focused on being on her absolute best behavior. Once they got to the house, she tried to help Alice with everything. She offered to take out the trash, get everyone drinks, and move the car from the street into the garage. She also doted on Sydney. Not that she didn't normally, but she was extra attentive. Alice seemed a little warmer but not much. Her stare was still very suspicious, and it had been one question after another. Where'd you grow up? What was your GPA? What are your plans for the future? How many siblings do you have? Are your parents still together? What do your brothers do for a living? How do you feel about my daughter?

At that last question, Reagan had hopped up and said she'd get Alice and Sydney another glass of wine just to get away. While working on the cork, Noah popped up seemingly out of nowhere and asked for one too.

"I'm sorry, Noah," she said. "But you're gonna have to ask your mom." She felt for the guy. He looked tall enough to drink. But with five years before he'd be old enough to have a drink at a bar, she wasn't giving him anything. Especially not when his mom already hated her.

"I think you're winning her over. What did you do to her in a past life?" He chuckled, and his dimple, a twin to Sydney's, appeared. Yeah, he was going to be a lady-killer when he grew into his height.

"You know she doesn't like the military, and I'm Army through and through." She resolved to pin down Sydney that night. "I have to win her over in spite of my service, I guess."

He gave her a thumbs-up and laughed. It was a deeper version of Sydney's, which made her feel like she already knew him a little. "You're doing great. She's smiling a lot more than when we first picked you up."

"Thanks, Noah," she said as she left the kitchen holding three wineglasses between her fingers.

"Thank you, Reagan," Alice said when she handed her a glass and settled on the couch next to Sydney. "Tell me what your family normally does for Christmas."

"We don't have any traditions. We moved around a lot, and my parents were more into taking trips over the holidays than the traditional decorating and gift giving. Also, my brothers and I all played sports, so sometimes, we'd have tournaments over the Christmas week that they would take us to. Now they just do whatever. This year, they planned a big family Thanksgiving with my grandma and are doing an extended cruise now. They're...different." Reagan had never thought about not having holiday traditions, but being with Sydney's family made her a little envious of what she'd missed. "They're supportive of me and my brothers, but we don't have the closeness of you three. It's really sweet."

Alice chuckled. "Well, I was going to give you a hard time about stealing my baby girl for Thanksgiving, but you were just so kind about us now, I don't know if I can."

"I'm really sorry about that. I would have loved to have come here, but my grandma is getting up there in years, and with us not doing Christmas this year, I really couldn't miss it."

"And it wasn't like she twisted my arm, Mom. I saw you for four days before the holiday. And I'm here for *two full weeks* now. There was no *stealing me away*."

Alice huffed. "Fine, fine." She took another sip of wine. "What sports did you play, Reagan?"

It had been feeling like the inquisition since Reagan arrived, and she was hoping Alice would tone it down soon, but she continued playing along. She knew she needed to make Alice see she was more than an Army captain. "I was always a runner, so cross-country and track. I also played soccer in high school, but it was too many sports in college." She'd intentionally said college rather than West Point, which felt a little weird, but she thought it was better to downplay the military portion.

"Do you still run?"

"I do, yes. Most days." She prayed she wouldn't be the center of conversation all eight days of her visit.

"Okay, Mom, that's enough of putting her to the question, don't you think?" Sydney squeezed Reagan's thigh.

Reagan was exhausted from all the talking. She'd told Alice all about her brothers, all the places they'd lived growing up, if her mom had worked, how often she'd seen her grandmother. She needed a break.

"What do you mean?" Eyes wide, Alice's face was a picture of innocence. "We're just getting to know each other, aren't we, Reagan?"

She put on a smile she didn't quite feel and said, "Yeah."

"Mom, we're tired. Let's just go to bed, huh?"

"You have had a long day of traveling. Sorry if I've been grilling you too much, Reagan. I won't keep you up any longer. I have you set up in Noah's room, and he's going to sleep on the couch."

"That sounds great."

At the same time, Sydney sharply said, "Mom."

"Don't you take that tone with me, Sydney. This is my house and my rules."

Quietly Reagan said, "Sydney, it's okay. Really."

Sydney grunted, "Fine. I'll show you the way. Good night, Mom."

"Good night, Alice."

Sydney practically dragged Reagan down the hall, and when she closed the door to Noah's room, she said, "I cannot believe her. She's been grilling you all night like you're a felon, and now this? You have to sleep in Noah's room?" She growled. The problem was, she was still adorable, even when she growled.

Reagan ran a thumb along her jaw. "It's fine. Seriously. We've only been together for a couple months. Maybe she thinks we aren't sleeping together. And anyway, we *are* under her roof. I'm okay sleeping in your brother's room." She was mostly okay with it, though now that she and Sydney were sharing a bed regularly, she was sad at the thought of not sleeping next to her for a week.

"Oh my God, she's not that naive." Sydney rolled her eyes and huffed.

"Seriously, though. We'll be fine for a week. And it's not like we could have sex in your childhood bedroom."

"Why not?"

"Because it's your childhood bedroom. What if your mother heard us?"

Sydney pouted. "We had sex at *your* parents' house."

"That was different. First, that wasn't my childhood bedroom. I've only stayed in that house a couple of times. Second, we stayed in the room over the garage, so there was no chance of anyone hearing us." And Reagan honestly didn't care if her family knew they were having sex, but she wasn't going to risk Alice's good graces for her libido. Despite how compelling it might be.

"Fine." Sydney's shoulders slumped. "I just sleep better when we're together." She kissed Reagan chastely.

Reagan pulled her hips in until their entire bodies were flush. "Me too. But this is fine." She kissed her like she meant it. She tried to bottle an entire night's worth of emotion into that kiss but kept it short. She feared Alice getting too suspicious of how long they were taking. "I love you. Now go to bed. Sleep well."

Reagan lay awake in Noah's bed, staring at the poster of Alex Morgan on one wall and Lionel Messi on the other. It certainly could be worse. He could have *Baywatch* posters or something. But the day just kept playing through her head. Was she doing enough to win Alice over? Noah seemed to be a pushover, but Alice…she was tougher.

She couldn't sleep and thought about sneaking over to Sydney's room just to hold her but was too afraid of getting caught. And Alice's question about her intentions had her obsessing about what came next. It was going to be May before they knew it, and Sydney was going to take the bar and probably move to Boston. And what was Reagan going to do?

Go to Morocco. It was the next step on her unwavering journey to general. She couldn't turn it down, especially not after her schooling. And she wouldn't want to. It was her dream.

A creak at the bedroom door drew her attention, and the silhouette of Sydney appeared in a sliver of light from the hallway night-light. "What are you doing here?" Reagan hissed, fearful of Alice hearing.

"Shh. I'm just coming to talk. I can't sleep." Sydney tiptoed as she crept into the room and slid in next to Reagan. "I wanted to apologize."

"Your mom is just protective. I just wish she didn't hate the *idea* of me quite so much."

Sydney ran her fingers through Reagan's hair. She looked so beautiful in the low moonlight sliding around the edges of the curtains. Her hair was piled on top of her head in a messy bun, but it looked like a little halo. "She was rude, and I'm sorry."

"It wasn't like she was asking terribly intrusive questions." *Except for the intentions question.* But she wasn't going to bring that up. Reagan pulled her down until her head was resting on Reagan's shoulder. If Sydney was going to risk her mom's wrath by sneaking in, they might as well cuddle. She pulled out Sydney's hair tie and massaged her head.

"I thought she'd have relented by now and seen how great you are. Maybe she'd be weird for like an hour, but I'm disappointed she's taking so long."

A laugh bubbled out of Reagan. "You really thought she was going to be weird for an hour after a lifetime of hating the military?"

"Shh," Sydney said as she placed her hand over Reagan's mouth. "You're being too loud."

Reagan grabbed her hand and kissed each fingertip before bringing the hand to her chest. "Then, maybe you shouldn't have snuck in here against her wishes."

"I can't believe she's making you sleep in Noah's dirty teenage boy room. We aren't sixteen. She has to know we're sleeping together." There was a whine in her voice reminiscent of Noah's. Reagan chuckled and wondered if being in her childhood home brought that out more.

"Did she ever let you and Harmony sleep in the same room?" Reagan was ninety percent sure of the answer and was hoping it might settle Sydney's frustration.

"No, but I didn't sleep with her until we'd been together for, like, nine months, so the first time she came for a visit, I didn't care. After that, she came up with a lot of excuses not to come home with me." She sighed and burrowed into Reagan.

Reagan rubbed her back. "Wait. Did you say you didn't have sex with her for *nine months*?"

"Uh, no?"

"Liar. Nine months. I mean, that's fine, but we barely made it a month." Reagan knew Sydney didn't sleep around, but nine months was a really long time. Reagan hadn't spent nine months with either of her girlfriends. Collectively.

"I know." She let out a long-suffering sigh again. "Yes, I made her wait nine months. It wasn't that I was trying to tease her, but I was a little hung up on *someone*." She tapped Reagan's chest. "And she was my first, so I wanted it to be special. But my mind was preoccupied with you, which, at the end of the day, is what made her break up with me, even though I should have done the job months before she did."

Reagan's chest felt like jelly at those words, and she continued slowly rubbing Sydney's back. Her breath was warm on Reagan's throat, and she savored the intimacy of the sensation. She tightened her arms. "I want to ask you something that I know you don't like to talk about, but I want to know you. Everything about you." Reagan was afraid to ask about her dad, but she needed to know. Especially now that she was trying to change Alice's mind.

"Okay." The reply was more of a breath than a true word.

"I know your dad was killed in action when you were about eleven, but what happened?"

Sydney's sigh let Reagan know she wasn't surprised by the question. "I don't like to talk about him. He wasn't a very good man. To me, he was a great dad. When he was home, he was attentive and loving. He taught me to throw a baseball, even though I was a girl. You don't know this, but I *love* baseball, even though I'm too clumsy to play. Anyway, he took me to my father-daughter campout with the girl scouts. He was the best dad."

She took a huge breath in and sighed it out. Reagan shifted from rubbing her back to massaging her neck, and she shimmied infinitesimally closer.

"But being a good dad doesn't make you a good husband or a good man. From what my mom told me and what I could pick up from conversations I eavesdropped on between Mom and Granny, it started small. He didn't want her to worry about going to work once she'd had me, and as he PCS'd around the country, it would be hard for her to keep finding new jobs. Especially ones that he didn't deem beneath her. He said he didn't want his friends to see *his* wife working at the gas station on base. He said she should focus on me and not worry about paying the bills. He could handle it all, and she shouldn't have to bother. But there was always some good reason why he couldn't fill up her prepaid calling card so she could talk to Granny. He slowly isolated her from her friends and family. Even when he was deployed, he wouldn't let her have access to the checking account. He just gave her a generous allowance. That should have been a huge red flag, but at that point, she'd just accepted that was her life, you know?"

"Mm-hmm." That didn't seem like the woman who'd been interrogating her all evening, so she must have found her gumption later.

"When Mom was notified that he'd been killed, she was devastated. I was thirteen, but Noah was only four. Granny drove over to be with us, thankfully, but as Mom dug into their finances, she began to understand why he'd shut her out. He had a terrible illegal gambling problem. He'd taken out a second and third mortgage on the house without Mom's knowledge. He'd told her he was putting a bunch of money into the stock market and an IRA, all lies. He'd spent every dollar they had."

Reagan couldn't imagine the betrayal Alice must have felt as she'd peeled back layer after layer of treachery. She wished she could go back in time and have him court-martialed before he'd had a chance to inflict so much harm. A Naval officer being that much of a scumbag made her sick. And the fact that he'd called West Point grads punks? Somewhere that his thirteen-year-old could hear? What a piece of shit.

"Mom had to sell the house and barely broke even between the sale and his life insurance. We moved to a small apartment away from the water in Virginia Beach, but she still couldn't support us. We ended up moving to a tiny place in Richmond, where things were a little cheaper before she finally gave up and came back here to West Virginia. She lived with Granny for a few years until she'd socked away enough money to buy this place. So when you say it's my childhood home, that's true, but it isn't. We hadn't even lived here for a year before I went to college."

"I'm so, so sorry, sweetheart. That's inexcusable, and I wish you hadn't gone through it." She wished she could do more than swear at the injustice of it all and hold her.

"I think part of it is that she hates the person she allowed herself to become when she was with him, her head in the sand, unwilling to stand up to him. But she also thinks everyone he worked with knew and said nothing, even his superior officers. I mean, it was going on for a long time, so different units, different commanders. A lot of people should have known and did nothing."

"I want to say that isn't possible, but I can't. The loyalty among brothers-in-arms is sometimes misplaced. But I hate that you and your mom and Noah were all victims." She pressed a kiss to Sydney's temple.

"So now you know why my mom lumps you in with the scum of the earth. But you're *nothing* like him, and if she can't see that, it's her hate blinding her. Maybe me telling her that you followed the rules so closely, you wouldn't even kiss me when we were in Italy because it was illegal would help." She laughed, and Reagan hoped she was kidding.

"Please don't." It seemed so ridiculous now.

"I wouldn't. It was just a funny thought."

"Thank you for trusting me. I know it isn't easy to talk about, but I want to know everything about you."

Sydney leaned up on her elbow. Her hair flowed down and tickled Reagan's face, but she didn't mind. She wanted to turn her face into it and lose herself in the scent. Sydney ran her thumb along Reagan's lower lip, making her shiver. "Me too." She replaced her thumb with her lips, and Reagan sighed. Everything felt okay in the world when she was kissing Sydney.

Sydney only waited a breath, however, before deepening their kiss and bringing her hand under Reagan's shirt to cradle her breast. Reagan wasn't sure how Sydney could take her from zero to a thousand in the span of a second, but it seemed an innate talent.

She forgot all the reasons she'd been resolved not to have sex and gave in to the tidal wave that was Sydney, showing her how much she loved her with her body for the rest of the night.

❖

Sydney was lost in thought the next morning in front of the coffee pot, willing it to brew faster, when her mom said, "You're up early."

Sydney jumped. "Jesus, Mom. Why are you sneaking up on people?"

"I walked into the kitchen as I always do, shuffling my feet as I always do. If you hadn't been dreaming, you would've most certainly heard me."

Her mom, direct as ever, reached around Sydney to grab the mug she'd gotten out for herself, pulled the coffee pot off the maker, and poured herself some while the pot was still brewing. "What are you doing? It isn't done yet."

"You don't have to wait. It's got a fancy feature that keeps the coffee from percolating out unless the pot is in place."

"Huh." The coffee, in fact, wasn't trickling onto the hot plate. "Thank you," she said when her mom grabbed another mug from the cupboard and poured a second cup before replacing the pot.

"Sit with me," her mom said and pointed to the small table in the kitchen nook. "I've missed you." She placed her hand on Sydney's arm and squeezed.

Sydney wanted to have a relaxing morning, but she also needed to address how her mom had treated Reagan. "Me too, Mom. But can you please try to be a little less abrasive with Reagan today? It was like you were cross-examining a witness yesterday. I promise you, she's nothing like Dad. She's the most honest person I've ever met. She'd never lie or hurt me."

"I'm sorry, I know I was a little difficult yesterday. She seems great."

Sydney just stared.

"Really, I liked her."

"You have an odd way of showing it, Mom."

"I just want you to be careful, dear. She's in the military, so even if she doesn't mean to, she's probably going to hurt you. She won't have control over where she's sent, and you've worked so hard to stand on your own two feet. You don't know what it's like to be completely helpless."

"But I do, Mom. Growing up and seeing you struggle while being too young to do anything. It was horrible. It's why I decided to become an attorney in corporate law. I'll earn plenty of money, and I'm *never* going to be dependent upon anyone." She took too large a sip of hot coffee, but the burn helped quench her frustration.

"I see the way you look at her. I see that she loves you too. And I just worry that you're going to throw everything away to chase her into a world that won't have your back. I don't want you to make the same mistakes I did."

Sydney had no plans to throw away years of hard work. She loved Reagan with all her heart, but when it came down to her security or being with Reagan, she'd choose security. She had to.

When Reagan came back all sweaty and sexy from her run, Sydney felt herself holding back. Hopefully not enough to notice, but she needed time to think. They'd agreed they weren't looking to the future, but how could that be true when they loved each other? She tried to relax and enjoy the rest of the Christmas break, but the future was going to have to be addressed at some point, and she could only see one way.

It was going to destroy her.

CHAPTER SIXTEEN

S pring in central California was weird. The early months of the year were the nicest, and Reagan had spent many weekends at the beach with Sydney, but as spring got into full swing, the weather got cooler. The fog started to ruin afternoons at the beach, and it became harder to mark the passage of time as the weather one day was the same as the next for months.

It felt like they were stuck in a moment in time, and Reagan wished they could stay there forever. They needed to talk about the future, but the thought was terrifying. Sydney hadn't yet accepted her offer from that Boston firm, but she'd implied that she would. She'd echoed the same words she'd said months ago when they'd first started dating: "I'm going to take it *unless I get a better offer.*"

What did that mean? A better offer from Reagan? *Should I ask her to move to Morocco with me?* It seemed impossible. Sydney had had her eye on a corporate law job since they'd met years ago, and how could Reagan ask her to give that up? Conversely, how could she walk away from something that was so special, so different from anything she could have hoped for in her wildest dreams?

But their lives were too different. Was there any possibility of Sydney changing her plans? Reagan felt heartbroken at the thought of losing her after their months of perfection and also at the thought of Sydney giving up on her plans.

"What's got you in such deep contemplation up there?" Sydney asked from where she lay, her head in Reagan's lap.

Reagan jolted. They both lounged on the couch, supposedly reading. "Nothing. Just reading." She turned the page, hoping her suspicious timing would go unnoticed, and ran her fingers through Sydney's hair to distract her.

She purred when Reagan applied a little more pressure around the crown of her head. She turned her head and bit Reagan's hip through old Army PT shorts, apparently unconvinced. "You haven't turned a page in at least five minutes. If you want me to believe you, what was the gist of the last sentence you read?" She giggled as she pulled the book out of Reagan's grasp.

"Uh." Caught, dammit. She really didn't want to talk but also wasn't going to lie. "Okay, fine, I was just thinking about what happens after this summer. What's next?" Her heart felt like it was fluttering in her throat. "But it's too soon to talk about it, right?"

"Yeah, I mean, I'm graduating in a few weeks, but I still have to take the bar." She took Reagan's hand and held it against her chest, squeezing it. Reagan was pretty sure her heart was beating a little fast too. "I thought maybe I'd stay down here for a few weeks while I prep. I mean, it's full-time studying, but I could do that just as easily from here as I could anywhere. If you'll let me, anyway."

"Of course. I'd love to have you here seven days a week rather than the three and a half I currently get."

She smiled her perfect smile and said, "Great."

"Yeah." Reagan was sure her expression had to be dreamy as she brushed a few strands of hair off Sydney's face.

"I finally got graduation tickets, by the way. You're still planning to come, right?"

"Of course. You still want me to borrow an air mattress from MWR for when your mom takes your bed, and Noah sleeps on the couch, right?"

"Please. It isn't ideal, but it's only a few nights."

"I don't mind sleeping on an air mattress for three nights." Reagan leaned down and brushed her lips ever so lightly against Sydney's. "I can't wait to live with you full-time here, though."

"Me too."

Reagan knew that it couldn't last forever, but the thought of spending every single day together felt unbelievable.

❖

Sydney had thought nothing could take the shine she was feeling off, but the look on her mom's face that morning had managed it, and now that she was alone in the car, driving down to Monterey, it was all she could obsess about. Her graduation had been great, and her valedictorian speech had gone better than she could've hoped, especially given how nervous she'd been. Everyone had so much fun at the little celebratory barbecue in her apartment's minuscule courtyard. It had just been her, Reagan, her mom, Noah, Aliyah, and Jessica, her favorite people. Reagan had even gotten them all tickets to do the Alcatraz tour that weekend, which Noah had eaten up.

Then, today had rolled around.

Reagan had stayed overnight but had left around six that morning to head back to Monterey for class. Sydney had gotten up with her and given her a kiss to keep them both warm until Sydney could move her stuff down that evening. But as Sydney had sat at the tiny table enjoying her coffee and reminiscing about all the fun times she'd shared with Aliyah and Jessica in that apartment, her mom had come out of the bedroom and sat with her.

It had been fine at first, just talking about the weather. Then, Noah had gotten a little restless. Her mom had told him to go lie down in her room since it was empty. When she'd sat back down, however, she'd had a serious look on her face and let out a huge sigh, and Sydney had known that whatever was coming next was going to be bad:

"Mom" Sydney asked.

"I have to tell you a couple things. About my health and about your dad."

Sydney's heart fell, and she struggled to take a breath. Her chest felt like it was in a vise. "What's going on?"

Her mom's hand shook as she reached for her coffee cup. "I'm sorry to throw this at you after such a great weekend, but I might be sick. I haven't told your brother because I want to know for sure before I do. I had a mammogram last week, and they found a lump. I'm having it biopsied on Thursday. It might be nothing, or it might be something. I'm trying not to worry, but it's a little terrifying. Breast cancer took your Aunt Violet from us when you were a toddler, so we're higher risk."

Ice flooded Sydney's veins, and bile swelled into her throat. She reached for her mom's arm. "No, I'm sure you're going to be fine. I won't allow anything else." There was no other acceptable course. She *needed* her mom. Period. End of story. "Is Grandma going with you to the biopsy? I can take a couple of days off studying to be with you. Drive you and all that." She couldn't imagine her mom going through that without someone to hold her hand.

"There's no reason to worry yet," her mom said, but Sydney felt the muscles of her arm quiver. "The odds are that this is nothing. As my doctor told me, most lumps, even those in high-risk women, come back benign. I just wanted you to know so you could send positive thoughts into the universe. And, yes, your grandma will be there with me."

Of course Grandma would be there. They only lived a couple of miles apart. Sydney felt a pang of regret about living so far, but opportunities in West Virginia were practically nonexistent for corporate law positions. Lucrative ones, anyway. "Okay, but I can still come." She could be a little more frugal about her savings until she started her job in the fall.

"Don't even think about wasting your money. I'd love you to be there, but you need to study. Someone is going to have to take care of me when I'm ninety. Noah might, but I'm betting it's going to be you." She chuckled.

"Well, I'll be thinking of you and sending all the good thoughts to the universe, but I'm sure you won't need them. This is nothing. And even if it's something, technology is so much further ahead than it was twenty years ago. If it *is* the *Big C*—which it isn't, but if it is—you're going to kick that bitch's ass." Sydney faked a confidence she didn't feel because the thought of her mom having cancer terrified her beyond anything, but she'd never want to add to her stress.

"Thank you, Syd. I've been terrified since the mammogram, but talking about it makes me feel lighter." She took a big breath and let it out.

"Why'd you wait to say something? You know I'm here for you for whatever, right? It's the three musketeers against the world." She sat her coffee mug down and grabbed both her mom's hands.

"I know. You can always trust family. Except when you can't." Her mom grimaced, and her shoulders fell.

"What's that supposed to mean?" She, her mom, Grandma, and Noah had always been there for each other.

Fortunately—or perhaps unfortunately—her mom hadn't stopped there.

Sydney sighed as she changed lanes, and anger coursed through her veins. It turned out that the family that couldn't be trusted was her dad, and she still couldn't believe the bullshit that her mom had told her about *willful misconduct* and how it had led to the denial of death benefits, even though his behavior hadn't been any of *their* faults. Her mom had tried to fight, but the Navy had denied them again and again until she'd given up. Her dad was a scumbag, and the Navy had punished them for the sins of her father. It was disgusting.

She knew Reagan was not at all like her dad, but she couldn't deny that the story had planted a new seed of doubt. It wedged its way into a crack in their foundation that she hadn't even realized had existed. But it was there now.

She'd been toying around with the idea of trying something long distance, but after her mom's revelations, she didn't think she could trust the Army to protect her or Reagan. Her mom had done everything right, yet they'd totally fucked her. And how could Reagan be so devoted to an organization who could so cruelly fuck over a widow and two children?

And, Jesus. What would she do if her mom's lump was cancer? Cancer. Fuck. She couldn't imagine her mom going through that. What would happen to Noah?

Sydney had to pull over on the side of Highway 101 to calm her nerves. Insistent tears made it hard to see as she imagined a world without both her mom and Reagan. She felt nauseated but shook her head and squeezed the wheel tighter as she reminded herself that her entire life had been spent planning to take care of herself, and now she had to secure her mom and Noah's future too.

When she pulled up to the curb in front of Reagan's house, she was pretty sure she'd gotten her fear under control, even though she felt like she was seconds away from tears. She was relieved to see Reagan's weird yellow car. If ever she'd needed to fall into someone's arms, it was that day. She'd been expecting to be sad because of her mom and Noah's departure, but she hadn't been expecting to be completely blindsided by everything else.

"Hey, babe," Reagan called from what sounded like the kitchen. "How was the drive?"

"Hey," she called back. "Nothing eventful." A complete lie, but for some reason, she couldn't—or maybe wasn't ready to—share either of her mom's bombshells.

"Why don't we eat dinner, and I can help you bring in all of your stuff, okay?"

When Reagan looked over her shoulder as she stirred something in the wok and smiled, Sydney's words dried up. She walked up behind Reagan, wrapped her arms around her, and pressed her cheek against Reagan's back, nodding.

"Are you okay?" Reagan said.

Sydney could feel the muscles of her back working as she did something to the pan, but the feel of her, the smell of her, calmed Sydney in a way she wasn't expecting. Holding her made it feel like everything was somehow going to be okay. She didn't know how, but somehow, it had to be. "Yeah," she said, actually feeling it for the first time since she'd said good-bye to Reagan that morning.

Reagan had been spinning the words, "unless someone makes me a better offer" in her head for more than a week. What could she offer Sydney that would be better than Boston? She had to go to Morocco or give up on her lifelong dream of getting a star. She couldn't even comprehend what life as a civilian would look like. What would she do? Who would she even be?

However, the idea of life without Sydney felt too bleak to comprehend. They'd started all of this with no promises of a future, but the future was coming whether they wanted it or not. And in some ways, she was ready to get back out into the world and put some of her new skills to work. But leaving Sydney made her feel like her heart was breaking.

Lost in her own musings while pretending to study, she apparently missed Sydney trying to get her attention until she stepped in front of her. When Reagan looked up, Sydney said, "Did you hear me?"

"What? Sorry." She flashed a chagrined smile.

"That transfixed by diplomatic strategy, huh?" She smirked, and Reagan's heart did its normal flip-flop. She wasn't sure what it was about that little quirk of the lips that sent her insides spinning like a tornado.

"Yeah, it's fascinating. Really." She pushed her textbook off her lap and pulled Sydney onto her. "But you are infinitely more fascinating." She pressed her lips against Sydney's neck. "What was I too distracted to notice?"

"Mmm." Sydney tipped her head to the side and threaded her fingers into Reagan's hair, massaging, and it did the trick.

Reagan ran her hand up Sydney's waist and under her shirt, groaning when her fingers found the soft skin that lay beneath.

"You can't distract me with your feminine wiles, Miss Jennings," Sydney said, but rather than pulling away, she pressed her mouth to Reagan's, clearly wanting to be distracted. After what felt like seconds, Sydney pulled away and rested her forehead against Reagan's, still breathing heavy. "I said you couldn't distract me with your wiles."

"Obviously, you were lying."

Sydney laughed, and Reagan ran her finger along her jaw. "What I should have said was, I don't want you to distract me because I'm hungry." Her accent always got a little thicker when she was turned on. Or tired. Or hungry.

"Hungry for me?"

"Oh my God, Reagan." There was exasperation in her voice, but Reagan could hear the want threaded in it.

"That wasn't a no." Reagan took it as an invitation to start kissing the beautiful column of her throat again.

"No," Sydney said, yet she lifted her arms to let Reagan pull her shirt over her head when Reagan ran her thumbs along the top of her jeans.

"I'm happy to stop if this isn't what you want," Reagan said as she reached for Sydney's bra.

"Um. Not no."

Reagan mourned the loss when Sydney stopped massaging her head, but she quickly recovered when Sydney reached back and took her own bra off, swatting Reagan's hands out of the way. She cupped the outsides of Sydney's breasts but ignored the nipples that were straining toward her. "If you want this, I need a real, 'Yes.'"

Sydney's look smoldered as she pressed her hands against Reagan's. "Yes," she whispered.

At the simple word, Reagan stopped teasing them both and ran her thumbs back and forth across Sydney's nipples.

"God, yes. Please, yes." Sydney arched her back, forcing Reagan to apply more pressure.

Reagan wrapped her lips around Sydney's nipple and licked, sucked, worshiped it as it hardened in her mouth. She slipped her free hand between Sydney's legs and ran her fingers, teasing, along the seam of Sydney's jeans.

"Too many clothes," Sydney breathed. She stood and pushed her pants and underwear down, kicking them somewhere. Reagan lifted her hips and slid her leggings down, kicking them away.

The heat of Sydney's gaze as she watched Reagan yank her sports bra over her head sent a rush of wetness between her legs. Sydney straddled her lap as she captured Reagan's mouth and made up for the time they'd lost removing the last of their clothes.

The words, "I love you so fucking much," slipped from Reagan as she traced her fingers up and down Sydney's back before cupping her butt cheeks and pulling her firmly against Reagan's lower belly.

"I love you too," Sydney said, her hips beginning to rock.

Reagan had to feel more of her, so she ran her hands around Sydney's hips and along the tops of her thighs. When she reached her knees, she changed direction, caressing her inner thighs. The closer she drew to the apex of Sydney's legs, the more Sydney tried to push forward, encouraging Reagan to touch her rather than tease, but she wasn't quite ready. "For someone *so very hungry*, you don't seem particularly interested in food right now."

Sydney lifted her head from where she'd been kissing a fiery path along Reagan's collarbone. Her tongue peeked out, moistened her lip. When Reagan's thumbs caressed her smooth outer lips, Sydney said, "You fill me up."

It was so quiet, Reagan could barely hear, but she knew she hadn't misheard. She pressed her lips to the delicate skin between Sydney's breasts as her thumbs found the delicious wetness between Sydney's thighs and spread it up and down her already slick folds.

She grazed both sides of Sydney's clit without touching the top where Sydney needed her most, but Reagan wanted to savor every second. When she reached Sydney's opening again, she slid one thumb inside until her palm pressed against Sydney's body. She finally gave in and applied light pressure to Sydney's clit with her other thumb.

Sydney pushed hard against her, sliding, and trying to force her to give the touch she craved. "More," she groaned.

The need to please overtook the need to savor, so Reagan removed both hands and flipped them over. She laid Sydney on the couch with one foot on the floor and the other bent closer to her hip. Reagan sank onto the floor and took Sydney into her mouth. She ran her tongue from the top of Sydney's labia over the top of her clit and down until she dipped briefly inside.

Sydney's fingers weaved into Reagan's hair, but rather than massaging like she'd done earlier, she pulled Reagan closer. "Please," she said as her hips began to thrust. Reagan used one hand to steady them and the other to slide two fingers into Sydney, replacing her tongue, which she glided up and down Sydney's swollen clit.

She focused on Sydney's pleasure as her breathing grew faster and harder, her fingers rhythmically scratching in time with Reagan's tongue. Yet the words *better offer* continued to bounce around Regan's head like a pinball hitting every bumper on its way down to the flippers, only to be launched back up again.

When Sydney called her name as she came, Reagan couldn't imagine anyone else in her future. She *needed* Sydney and had to figure out how to make it work.

CHAPTER SEVENTEEN

When Sydney opened her eyes, the room was relatively dark, but light was filtering in through Reagan's sheer curtains, so it couldn't have been too late. She lifted her head from Reagan's shoulder where it had been since they'd moved to the bed, she'd given Reagan her second orgasm, and they'd fallen promptly to sleep.

But the rumbling in her stomach forced her awake, even though all she really wanted was to remain snuggled in the beautiful cocoon between Reagan's body and the fluffy comforter. She pressed a kiss to Reagan's collarbone and headed to the kitchen.

How was Reagan not hungry? Sydney had been starving when Reagan had waylaid them earlier. Not that she regretted the waylaying itself—she'd completely forgotten her need for food—but now that she was awake, it was back.

They really needed groceries, but neither of them had taken the time to go shopping, so pickings were slim. She pulled out some aged white cheddar, gouda, spinach, basil that she was surprised hadn't gone black and mushy, and frozen bread for some grown-up grilled cheese. She figured she'd make two because Reagan had to be hungry too. She was never going to be Julia Child, but she could make a solid grilled cheese.

She painstakingly assembled the nearly perfect grilled cheeses while the pan heated up and couldn't decide if she wanted Reagan to join her or if she wanted to serve her late lunch in bed. While the first option would be convenient, there was something appealing about the idea of an afternoon in bed with a grilled cheese as the cherry on top.

Sydney's phone buzzed on the coffee table, and she ran to check it. It was only a news alert, but it reminded her that her mom was supposed to hear the biopsy results today. She knew her mom would call as soon as she heard but fired off a quick text anyway.

Sydney: *Any news from the doctor yet?*

Her phone buzzed as soon as she set it on the counter again: *Nothing yet. On pins and needles but fingers crossed for good news. Grandma is here with me. I'll call as soon as I hear.*

The smell of her grilled cheese didn't feel so appealing. Her mouth felt full of sand. This waiting was the worst. She was swirling the pan when arms cocooned her from behind, and warm breath rushed over her ear when Reagan said, "I don't like it when I fall asleep with you but wake up alone." Reagan rocked her hips from side to side and brought Sydney with her.

Sydney relaxed with a comfort that shouldn't have been foreign but still felt a little odd. How could standing there with Reagan feel so right and make her so guilty at the same time? It wasn't like anything she did affected the biopsy results. But it still felt like a betrayal that she could be so content when her mom's life hung in the balance.

Still, she melted, unable to stop the primal need to seek comfort. Even if she didn't tell Reagan what was going on, she needed help to feel whole. "I was hungry because *someone* tried to starve me earlier."

Reagan nipped the bottom of her earlobe. "The only reason I was successful was because you *wanted* to be distracted." Reagan's right hand slid up Sydney's long T-shirt and cupped her breast. "Do you want to be distracted again?" she whispered.

The wetness coating Sydney's thighs strongly disagreed with her grumbling stomach.

Reagan laughed at the rumbling and said, "Apparently, your hunger is overruling me."

"I'm so weak, I need sustenance to continue." She turned off the burner, moved the pan to the back of the stove, and spun in Reagan's embrace. She was delighted to discover that Reagan hadn't bothered putting on clothes and drank in the perfection of her body. "I always want you, but not as much in this moment as I want the fancy grilled cheese I just made. You're going to need to hit pause on your sexy thoughts until my grumbling stomach is satisfied."

"Fine, fine." Reagan held up her hands as she stepped back. "Thank you. Why don't you go put clothes on while I plate these?" She tipped her chin toward the pan.

"Are you afraid I'm going to distract you too much with my luscious nipples?" Reagan rubbed her fingers enticingly across them, and Sydney gazed with need as she tried to remember what she was going to say.

"Uh, no. Okay, yes, but I'm starving," Sydney finally said with more conviction than she felt and watched as Reagan walked backward from the room, not breaking eye contact until she turned the corner.

Sydney took a deep breath as she turned back to the stove. How was she going to do this? She put it out of her mind as she used the spatula to move the sandwich perfection to plates, checked her phone one more time to make sure her mom hadn't texted back, and headed to the table. She managed to not obsess over anything for a few minutes while they ate and chatted about cheese and how it was God's gift to humanity.

However, she was blindsided when Reagan said, "I'm not sure how to talk about this, but I don't want this thing with us to end in July when you leave to take the bar."

"Um." Sydney scrambled to decide what to say. What to think. She didn't either, but they'd always known this was temporary. "I don't want it to end, either, but I don't see any way around it. I'm going to Boston, and you're going to Africa." She tried to be casual despite it feeling like her heart was in a vise. Which tightened even more as the color drained from Reagan's face.

"Why don't we try long distance? I mean, there's amazing technology these days for video calls and stuff. I get thirty days of leave a year and will happily spend it all with you, wherever you want to go. You can visit me whenever you want." Reagan grabbed her hand and squeezed it. "I can't imagine saying good-bye in a few weeks." She brought Sydney's hand to her mouth and kissed it.

Sydney's chest constricted, and tears pricked her eyes. She didn't want to say good-bye, but it was hopeless. She'd toyed with the idea of something long distance to buy more time for them, but it wouldn't work. "I don't think I can do it. I tried long distance with Harmony, and that went down in flames."

"But she wasn't right for you."

"No, she wasn't, but long distance was hard regardless. We'd had a fight, and she got in an accident and was in the hospital for a week, and no one thought to call me. I thought she was giving me the silent treatment, and I was freaking out. When I found out the truth, I was devastated. Distance is horrible. And it's not like I'm going to have time to visit. I'm going to be a first-year associate. The only things I'm going to have time for are working, sleeping, and eating. We'll never see each other."

"I love you. I can wait for you."

"For two years? That's untenable." Sydney threw her hands up.

"For however long it takes. I'll see you on all my leave, and eventually, your schedule will free up." The pleading in her eyes was shattering Sydney's heart.

"And then what? You're going to continue to move all around the world. And I'm going to stay in one place. Boston. Close to my family. Is getting stationed in Boston even a possibility at some point? Are there Army bases there?"

Reagan's shoulders fell. "No, nothing for my career path. Most Army installations are in the south, with a sprinkling elsewhere, and nothing within commuting distance to Boston." Her eyes were red-rimmed, and Sydney could see the tears collecting there, though none had fallen yet. "I hate to even ask, but what if you took a brief pause in your very detailed life plan? I'll only be in Morocco for a year or two. You could come live with me. We could start our lives together, and I'll try to get stationed someplace better stateside. I should have enough pull. What about DC? There are loads of places I could end up there, and I bet there are lots of corporate law jobs."

"So I'm just supposed to pause my life while you lead yours? And how is that going to work for me to move to Africa for two years? And isn't being gay illegal there? It's not like I'd be able to get a work permit. I'd be *totally* dependent on you." Sydney was clenching her jaw so hard that her molars were aching. How could Reagan ask her to give up everything? Her mom finally telling her the truth about her dad and what the Navy had done to them reminded her she couldn't sacrifice her career—her financial security—for love. Her mom had loved her dad too, and look how that had worked out for them.

"What if we got married? The DoD recognizes gay marriage now. It would be like any other marriage. You would PCS with me." Her tears were flowing now, and Sydney was being ripped in two. She didn't understand how Reagan could expect her to just give up everything—her life, her plan, her financial security, her ability to take care of Noah's college and her mom in the future, all of which Reagan knew was important to her—and in exchange, they were going to get married?

She laughed and choked on the tears in her throat. "Of all the ways I dreamed a marriage proposal might happen in my future, this wasn't it. This is, without a doubt, the least romantic thing I've ever heard. No, I'm not going to marry you so I can get stuck on a fucking Army base in a country that wants to murder us for being gay. I can't believe you right now." Sydney shook off Reagan's hand, stood, and started pacing. "And even if all that worked out and we came back to the States and I got a job in DC, aren't you going to have to move every two years? Isn't that how the Army works?" She tried to keep her tone even, but the hurt in her heart was making her voice shrill. She could barely breathe.

"Yeah, but I could probably cycle in and out of DC every two years, maybe."

"Maybe? That's still a lot of moving. I don't *want* to live a nomadic lifestyle. I told you one of the first times we met that I wanted to graduate top of my class. Check. Full ride to a top law school. Check. Appropriate corporate law firm. Check. Now comes making partner, finding an appropriate upwardly mobile woman, and getting married. Follow the plan. Security. Financial safety. That doesn't come if I don't establish myself. If I'm moving from city to city, country to country."

"Please, Sydney, I wasn't...I wasn't trying to control you. I...I love you. I'll do anything for you. For us." Reagan's voice was high. Squeaky.

"You won't leave the Army for me."

Reagan stared. Her mouth moved, but no words came out.

Sydney's blood was rushing in her ears and drowning out her compassion. She didn't really want Reagan to leave the job she loved, her calling. So how could Reagan ask it of her? And that outrage drove the rest of her words. "You won't even consider making a change to be with me, but you want me to give up my future, my stability, my entire life plan? Typical military response that my mom has been warning me about." Sydney hadn't even fully understood why two weeks ago, but she did now.

It didn't matter how much she loved Reagan. A piece of her, a piece she wanted to believe was right, thought that maybe her feelings were being amplified by the impending end. The knowledge that, no matter what she felt, they had an expiration date. She hoped that once she and Reagan went their separate ways, the feelings that were breaking her heart would dissipate quickly.

Because she had to protect herself. And be able to look out for her mom and brother. And with the possibility of something going on with her mom? There was no way she could pack up and move to Africa. She risked a look at Reagan again. She was paler than Sydney had ever seen. Shoulders slumped. Tears falling freely.

"I'm sorry. I didn't mean to be so harsh." She hated herself for her cruelty, but she needed it as armor. "But you have to see how unfair that is. I don't want us to end, but there's just no way. Long distance is simply a painful way to delay the acceptance of the inevitable. We both knew where this was going. We don't fit into each other's lives after this. You know it too. I can see it in your body."

"I *know* there's a way we can make this work. Maybe we can't see it now, but I believe there's a way. I love you too much for there not to be. It's why I think we could try long distance for a while until we can discover that way."

"I want that to be true, Reagan, but it isn't." Sydney wanted to sit and cry. She hated this, but she'd finally accepted that they were kidding themselves. "The longer we prolong this, the worse it's going to be."

"What? No. You can't mean that." Reagan grabbed her hand, touching her for the first time since she'd pulled away after that ridiculous marriage proposal.

Sydney didn't want to mean it, but she did. She finally understood that they were only making it worse for themselves. "I—" She was cut off by her phone buzzing on the coffee table. "I need to take that."

"What? We're in the middle of—" Reagan started to say, but Sydney couldn't hear anything else as her mom's number flashed on the screen.

Her heart dropped to the floor. "Mom, hey. Have they called?"

❖

How could Sydney ignore her to answer a phone call? It didn't make any sense. Especially when they were having the most important conversation of their lives. Reagan wanted to grab her by the shoulders and force her to pay attention. Given Sydney had just ripped her heart out, it wasn't fair of her to leave her bleeding there while she took a *phone call*.

"Mom, hey. Have they called?"

That made more sense but still. This was the only real conversation they'd ever had about their relationship. Their future. And Sydney just switched gears to answer the phone?

Sydney nearly fell back onto the couch. "No, Mom, please tell me that's not true...Well, you're going to beat it. I know you are. *We're* going to beat this. I'll be with you every step of the way."

Shit, something bad was happening.

"I know I don't have to, Mom, but I'm going to—" She popped up and started pacing again. "I'll figure out the bar and studying, but I'm going to be there for you. You aren't going through this alone. I'll head out tonight. I'm not sure when I'll get in. I'll text you, but I'll be there tomorrow."

Reagan wanted to throw up. Despite Alice's bias against her profession, Reagan still liked her. If something was wrong with her, Reagan's heart broke for all of them. Selfishly, she knew this was also going to fuck their ability to talk things through. Reagan couldn't go with her, but maybe she could sneak away in a couple of days. She hated the thought of Sydney going through something without her support.

"I love you, Mom. We're gonna get through this. I'll see you tomorrow."

Reagan had been trying to give her space, but when Sydney dropped her phone on the floor and buried her face in her hands, Reagan sat on the couch next to her and wrapped her arms around her. "How can I help? Do you want to talk about it?"

Reagan held her as she cried and wanted to cry herself when Sydney said, "Cancer."

"Oh God, I'm so sorry. What can I do? Do you want me to take you to the airport?"

Sydney looked at her for the first time since the phone rang. Her tearstained face was blotchy and red. "No, thank you. I'll drive myself. I need to pack." She shrugged off Reagan's embrace and headed into the bedroom.

"Please. Let me help you," Reagan said as she trailed behind her. "You don't want to pay to park in extended parking for however long you're going to be with your mom."

Sydney pulled her suitcase from under the bed and started dumping clothes into it. "I'm not."

"How?" Reagan scratched her head, confused.

"I'll call Aliyah and leave the car with her. It was a shared car, so she'll handle selling or scrapping it. It was the plan the whole time."

Reagan had to be misunderstanding, but a sick feeling was rolling over her skin like stinging nettles. "You're…not coming back? At all?" Her voice cracked, and she hated it.

"I'm sorry, but I…can't do this anymore. I need to be with my mom. I need to focus on her and her treatment. This gives us a chance to have a clean break rather than pretending all summer that we have a chance of making it work."

Reagan's knees sagged, and she stumbled until her back hit the wall behind her. She watched in a daze as Sydney shoved everything she owned in her suitcase in a matter of minutes and quickly stripped off her T-shirt and pulled on underwear, jeans, and a sweatshirt. Reagan certainly hadn't thought this was how she'd see her naked for the last time. But Sydney had already made up her mind, and her mom was an excuse to make the break official earlier than expected.

Reagan jumped when Sydney laid a hand on her cheek. "I really am sorry. I need to be there for my mom right now. Breast cancer took her sister twenty years ago, so she's a mess. I know she can beat it, but I don't know if she does, and I need her. Noah needs her." She lightly pressed her lips to Reagan's, but rather than melting into her like she normally did, it took everything in Reagan not to dissolve in tears. "A little piece of me will always love you, but I think, in time, you'll see this is right."

Then, she was gone.

Reagan wanted to scream. Throw things. Go back in time and scream at her grandfather's grandfather not to join the fucking Army and instill in every subsequent generation the need to serve.

Her heart was breaking for everything: Alice and the struggle she faced, the difficulties Sydney would have to work through as she supported her mom. Noah having to face the realities of mortality sooner than he should. And more than all that, the eradication of the possibility of her and Sydney having a fairy-tale ending. It didn't matter what her heart wanted; Sydney's clear head and devastation over her mom were going to overrule the love she held. So she cried for everything and hoped someday, she'd be able to figure out how to put the pieces of herself back together.

PART III: THE ACCIDENTAL INTERLUDE

Munich Franz Josef Strauss Airport, Four Years Ago

CHAPTER EIGHTEEN

Reagan stood in the United customer service line and tamped down her impatience. She knew it wasn't the airline's fault that a massive snowstorm had descended upon Europe in February, but it *was* their fault that they hadn't staffed up in anticipation of massive numbers of stranded travelers. At least she was nearing the end of the long-ass line that stretched down the concourse; granted, she still had the corral part of the queue to go.

Jesus. This was probably going to be another forty-five minutes. She'd been trying to get through on United's customer service phone line, but that had been busy every time. She couldn't even wait on hold for an agent.

At least she was only three people from where line doubled back on itself. They inched forward. Two people. But as she felt giddy with the movement, she recognized a familiar profile that had her stomach plummeting to the center of the Earth with Jules Verne. Three people ahead and engrossed on her phone was Sydney Adams.

Fuck.

The Sydney Adams, who'd completely broken her heart six years ago and never looked back. Right fucking there in an airport line in Munich.

Sure, they'd kept in touch for a while. In the beginning, it was texts about logistical items. Then, they'd texted about her mom. A lot. How chemo and radiation were going. Her lumpectomy. How sick the chemo had made her. It was weird. They never spoke on the phone. No matter how badly Reagan had wanted to beg Sydney to reconsider the bolded period she'd placed at the end of their relationship, she hadn't called. Sydney had needed someone to spill her fears to, and, like always, Reagan had given her whatever she'd needed. And she'd wanted to know how Alice was.

Looking back, she realized she'd needed to keep their connection for a little while longer back then. Slide back into friendship before the cremated remains of their brief romance scattered into the ocean between Boston and North Africa.

After Alice had gone into remission, their texts had become less frequent. It could have been because when Reagan had left Morocco, life had gotten busier. She'd been selected for the foreign area officer program, which meant more training. Or maybe it was because Sydney didn't need her once her mom was healthy. Maybe she'd found another girlfriend. Whatever the reason, Reagan had been relieved because texting had felt like pulling off a scab every time.

Sydney was past her now. *Whew.* She could breathe again. It wasn't going to last, but she could use these few moments to gather herself. Should she say hi? It felt weird to ignore her, yet nothing productive could come from talking. Sometimes, it felt like Sydney was firmly in her past, but now she felt like an open wound, still red and raw, even six years later.

Reagan pointedly looked out at the terminal as she continued to agonize about whether to say something. She was contemplating stepping out of line and going to the back, despite how ridiculous that would be, versus asking Sydney to have a cup of coffee, maybe get a little closure.

Did she *need* closure?

Light fingertips grazed her forearm. "Reagan?" Sydney's tentative voice said.

Reagan turned and faked shock. "Sydney Adams. Wow," she said, trying to sound nonchalant.

Sydney tossed her hair that somehow still looked perfect despite the hectic mess of travel on a day where half the continent had been shut down. Reagan caught a whiff of cherry blossoms as her hair fluttered back into place. "I don't understand how you're standing next to me in an airport."

Before Reagan could answer, a large white man behind Sydney cleared his throat and jutted his chin at the gap of about two people between Sydney and the next person in line.

Her eyes widened as she said, "Oops. Sorry." She mouthed, "See you soon," as she shuffled forward.

Reagan appreciated the moment of reprieve as her heart and head tried to reconcile their reactions to having Sydney less than a foot away after so many years. Her head wanted her to be angry and hurt. And she was, even after six years. But her heart felt a bubble of happiness. They'd been friends first, and she'd never had a friend quite like Sydney. Granted, some of that might have been the ridiculous attraction always simmering, but she'd felt a closeness to her that she'd never experienced before or since…and it was impossible to forget.

When Sydney made the next turn in the line, Reagan watched her scan the faces until her eyes fell upon Reagan, and she didn't look away until they were within hearing range again. "So what's a girl like you doing in an airport line like this?"

Reagan chuckled reflexively. "I would have gone with, 'Of all the airports in all the towns in all the world, you had to walk into this one.'"

Sydney smirked. "Although I love the near *Casablanca* quote, that wouldn't have been a question, would it? You could've said nothing."

"I would've answered if we'd had the time. But we didn't. And we don't now." Reagan nodded to the line moving before the guy behind Sydney could comment again.

She huffed and moved past. "Fine, but this isn't over."

How could they be so playful—flirty—after all the hurt between them? Reagan couldn't deny the joy at seeing Sydney but feared tearing off that scab. Again.

Sydney kept looking around between them, even before she made her next turn, and every time they made eye contact, something fluttered in Reagan's lower belly. Simply excitement about catching up with an old friend.

And if she believed that, she could sell herself oceanfront property in Missouri and become her parents' neighbor.

As they approached again, Sydney said, "So…"

Reagan wanted to play with her, to prolong answering for no reason other than to annoy her, but instead, she gave her the truth. "I'm going to see my family while PCSing from Poland to the US embassy in Riga. Lithuania," she clarified at Sydney's furrowed brow. "At least, I was. God only knows how much leave this debacle will waste." She huffed, irritated because she wanted to see her parents, and her youngest brother, Jasper, was supposed to be home this week as well. "What about you?" But as soon as Reagan spoke, the line moved again.

Sydney pressed her lips into a thin line as she took half a step forward and stopped. The man behind her cleared his throat again, and Reagan thought she heard her mumble, "Fuck it," under her breath. "Please go ahead, sir." She motioned for him and the other two people between them to pass.

When Reagan was standing next to her, Sydney said, "Hi." She bit her lip and rubbed the hollow at the base of her throat. Her tone was more nervous than before, but when she really looked at Reagan and made eye contact, her full smile appeared.

Reagan hated as much as she loved the way her heart tripped. "Hi," she finally said, wondering if she sounded as shy as Sydney. "So what are *you* doing in this airport…of all the airports in all the towns in all the world?"

Sydney's features softened. "I was visiting Noah. He's working at an investment bank in Switzerland, and I'm heading home."

"Boston?" A little knife stabbed her heart as she said the word. It wasn't the place specifically that had broken them up, but it felt that way, and Reagan hated the city because of it.

"Yeah. Mom is living there now too. We lost Grandma two years ago, and Mom was having a hard time, so she moved closer to me. But it's been great."

They chatted until only two people remained between them and an agent, and Reagan felt like she'd slipped through a wormhole and fallen back in time. It didn't make sense how they could easily slide back into their former camaraderie, but they had. And she wasn't ready to go their separate ways because why wouldn't she want to torture herself? "Do you want to grab dinner together once we rebook? I suspect neither of us is getting out of here tonight."

There was that grin again. "Maybe we should check on the hotel situation first. I think there's a Hilton connected to the terminal. I'm sure they're busy, but I'd like to get a room before they're gone."

"That's perfect. You want to walk over there together?"

"Meet you by that column?" She pointed to one in the opposite direction from the never-ending line.

Reagan had been waiting for a few minutes when Sydney met her, jaw tight and brows drawn. "Not a good rebook?" She was frustrated too, but no one could control the weather.

"Friday, which is supposedly good, but I *need* to get home. My mom has an appointment on Thursday. I messaged my assistant to look every fifteen minutes to see if anything opens up sooner. I don't even care if I don't get a credit for this flight. I just need to get home."

Reagan was curious, but asking what the appointment was for felt too personal, so she simply said, "I'm sorry. I'm out on Friday too, but as long as I get a room, I feel like it's a good outcome, given this storm."

Sydney huffed. "I know. But I need to be there for Mom. It's… dicey. She has an oncology appointment, and she doesn't have anyone else with Noah here in Europe."

"Oh no." Reagan's heart hurt. "It's back?"

"Maybe. Probably. Fuck. We don't know much of anything yet. But that's what she's supposed to find out on Friday. And I can't *not* be there. Except I'm not going to be." She ran her fingers through her hair and shook it out.

"Shit. I'm so sorry." The words felt empty and useless, but what else could she say? She laid her hand on Sydney's forearm where it was draped across the handle of her roller suitcase and squeezed.

Sydney pressed her lips together and cleared her throat. "Let's go check on the hotel, huh?"

"Sure." Reagan forced a smile and dropped her hand.

They walked in an uncomfortable silence that Reagan wished she could fill but only listened to the sounds as their heels clacked and echoed in the empty corridor. It was surprisingly quiet compared to the loud chaos and disorder that had surrounded them in the terminal, almost as if the zombie apocalypse had happened.

They walked into the eerily deserted lobby. Reagan gestured for Sydney to go first. If someone deserved their choice of room, it was Sydney, given everything she was dealing with.

When Reagan was called up next and the hotel clerk quoted the price for a *quaint* room, she sharply inhaled. No wonder no one was there. They'd probably all looked on Orbitz and saw that this hotel was price gouging. But she didn't want the hassle of going somewhere else. And if she was honest, she wanted to spend more time with Sydney.

"Meet down here in fifteen?" Sydney quirked an eyebrow. She still had a slight furrow between her brows that signaled her stress, but something about her posture had Reagan a little more at ease.

"Sounds perfect." She smiled. She couldn't help it. She hated what Sydney was going through, but being near Sydney made her *need* to stay close. What was it about her that made Reagan forget all the pain, all the lost years, and just…enjoy?

CHAPTER NINETEEN

The ding of the elevator drew Sydney's eyes from her phone. Again. It wasn't that Reagan was late. It was more that Sydney had talked to her mom for five minutes to check in and share the bad news and couldn't sit still after that. She'd unpacked her bathroom bag but didn't want to unpack too much in case she could catch an earlier flight. She didn't need the stress of trying to pack her bags perfectly within the weight allowance.

That had been hard enough the first time.

But as Reagan walked closer, her breath caught. How could she be even more beautiful than six years ago? Over the years, Sydney had thought—or maybe had tried to convince herself—that Reagan wasn't as beautiful, as perfect, as she remembered. But watching her walk off the elevator, still so lithe and confident, had her pulse spiking. She hoped her cheeks weren't flushing.

"Hey," Reagan said. Her voice quivered a little.

Sydney exhaled sharply and tried to find her own voice. "Hi." She smiled. She wouldn't have been able to stop herself if she'd tried. Her body's responses were like a dog of Pavlov's. It was embarrassing. She was stressed as fuck about her mom and not being able to get home. She'd chatted with Noah, and he was going to try to get a flight home too, and knowing he was also trying to get home took a tiny bit off her. She prayed it wasn't cancer, but if it was, her mom had beaten it before and could do it again. And this time, Noah could be there too. She wouldn't have to carry all the weight alone.

Okay, that was bullshit. She'd leaned on Reagan much more than was fair the last time. Especially since she'd rejected all overtures to stay together. And now, with Reagan standing in front of her, she wanted to apologize for being so callous. She didn't regret her decisions, but she regretted hurting Reagan.

"Ready for dinner?" she asked, hoping she hadn't waited too long to respond.

Reagan nodded, so Sydney motioned for her to go first. Walking into the hotel restaurant, Sydney was surprised to see it hopping, given how dead the lobby was.

Sydney said, "Think everyone who didn't want to pay three thousand euro for a room is here getting full and drunk to help them pass out on the terminal's cold floor?"

"My thoughts exactly."

Same wavelength, as they'd always been. Sydney laughed and shook her head. How easily they slipped back into it. Like muscle memory.

"Though…you paid three thousand? Mine was only one," Reagan said. "Were you rude to the person at the desk?"

She shrugged, a little embarrassed and wishing she hadn't mentioned her rate. "Well, they had the presidential suite available, and what can I say? I've gotten a little bougier over the years. They told me it has great panoramic views of the airport and surrounding area. If I'm going to be stuck here, I might as well have a nice room."

Reagan shoulder bumped her as they walked. "You *have* gotten bougier."

"Hashtag sorry not sorry?" Sydney grinned.

Reagan rolled her eyes as they paused at the check-in podium.

"Good evening," the host said in German as he approached. Sydney tried to remember the correct German response, but before she could, he said, "Good evening," in English.

Sydney hated being the American who didn't speak a word of the language of the country she was in. Studying French for Geneva didn't help in Germany. "Evening. Table for two please," she said as Reagan started speaking German. Damn. When they were seated, she said, "I forgot you've been stationed here. I'll let you take the lead in ordering." She forced a laugh that sounded nervous. Of course she was nervous, but she didn't want Reagan to know.

"Most Germans speak English, especially at an airport hotel. And it would be rude of me to have a conversation you can't understand."

"Yes, but it's also rude to go to the country and lack basic conversation capabilities. Though in my defense, I wasn't planning on this stop."

"Okay. Let me greet the server, and I'll explain your German is rough and ask if they wouldn't mind using English."

"Thank you," Sydney said, relieved that Reagan could be polite for them both.

The server arrived, and before Sydney had even looked at the menu, Reagan ordered a bottle of pinot noir and cheese spaetzle. Sydney wasn't entirely sure what it was, but since it had cheese in the name, she was game to try. And she'd always trusted Reagan's culinary tastes.

"So you live in Boston with your mom?" Reagan said.

"Well, she's in Boston, but I bought her a condo in an active adult community, though we're only a few blocks apart. It's been great living close to her again. Especially after...everything."

Reagan looked away and chewed her lip. She looked uncomfortable, as if she wanted to say something but didn't.

"You can ask me anything."

Reagan cleared her throat and took a sip of wine. "I always wondered, did you have to put off starting your job to stay with her?"

Sydney sighed. She'd agonized over the decision while making it. "No, not when Mom actually moved to Boston. Her town in West Virginia was small. The nearest treatment center was more than an hour away and wasn't well ranked. I hated essentially forcing her and Noah to move, but it came down to finances. She couldn't work, and she refused to let me put off my new job. That was fine because I really needed that paycheck. We managed to get her covered under Massachusetts' public health care, and although we struggled for a while, we made it."

It was a small modicum of comfort to know that if the cancer came back, they wouldn't have to worry about the cost and could do all the traditional treatments, plus the complementary therapy they couldn't afford last time.

Reagan gave her a sad smile. "I'm sorry you all had to go through so much, but at least you had each other."

"Yeah." Sydney smiled, thinking of her grandma and all the homemade chicken soup they'd eaten because she'd thought it had magical healing powers. "Grandma hated that she wasn't there but maintained that she was too old to move. She did come up all the time and cooked for us and took care of Mom while I was at work. Mom actually moved back to West Virgina once she went into remission, but after Grandma…" Sydney's throat felt thick, and she really wanted to think about something else since her mom's health was so uncertain. She coughed. "How are your parents?" she said, needing to change the subject.

Reagan laughed as she said, "They're fine. Still in Missouri, misguidedly thinking Ronald Reagan was the best president we've ever had, but at least with Trump and almost the entire GOP falling into his cult, they've denounced the party as a whole. They now proudly call themselves Independents. I think my coming out *probably* helped there too, as they got more comfortable with it and heard some of the vile things that people they once respected said about us."

"It's probably a little too Pollyanna-ish to hope for, but I'm optimistic that this country is going to all move that way. But I say that from my privileged status of living in a progressive blue state."

As they ate the spaetzle—like mac and cheese but with fried onions and homemade noodles, similar to what her grandma used to make—the conversation flowed as it used to. Sydney felt transported back to California, when this had been normal for them.

Reagan was mesmerized by the size of the snowflakes outside the restaurant window. They were so big, she could see each individual flake, even though the wind had picked up. "Beautiful, isn't it?" she said pointing.

"Yeah, you could almost forget how horrible and unfair the world sometimes is." Sydney's words dripped with sadness.

There were so many truly abhorrent things going on in the world. "What do you make of this whole coronavirus? Think it's going to amount to anything?" Reagan asked.

"I can't imagine we're going to be too impacted. It seems like it's pretty isolated, doesn't it?"

"Yeah, but they found the first cases six weeks ago, and it's now all over. Even the US." Reagan wasn't terribly worried for herself, but it was hitting older people harder, and her parents weren't young.

"Time will tell, I guess. Hopefully, it doesn't get too bad."

"For sure." Reagan took a sip of wine as they slipped into another silence that felt more comfortable than it had a right to.

"I want to apologize," Sydney said out of the blue.

"For what?"

"For six years ago. I owed you more of an explanation than I was able to give at the time. And then I used you as my pseudo-confidante. I needed someone to talk to, but I'd just broken up with you, and forcing you to stay involved because you felt bad wasn't fair. At all."

That caught Reagan off guard. All evening, they hadn't talked *their* past. They'd caught up on what had been going on for each of them as individuals but not about what they'd been to each other or how that had abruptly ended. She'd thought it was an unspoken agreement to not go there. They were in the middle of a restaurant. Admittedly, a nearly empty one now. Part of her wanted to understand better, but the rest felt like it would be too much. "That's ancient history. We weren't meant to be, right?"

"I still hate how I treated you. What I didn't say." The muscles in Sydney's jaw were tight, that wrinkle between her brows deeper than usual. Reagan resisted the urge to run her fingers along her jaw and across her forehead to encourage them to relax.

"It was a stressful time. Your mom was fighting cancer. Your brother was too young to help. You were balancing a lot. And our timing was impossible. You don't have to carry guilt over me."

Sydney took a deep breath and sighed. "I don't ever talk about my dad. It took us knowing each other for years before I even told you he was killed in action. But that wasn't really true in the traditional sense—he wasn't killed by enemy fire—but I didn't fully know what had happened until I talked to Mom after my graduation. The cancer made everything worse, but I think...I know, it was the truth about my dad that really spooked me. Mom always encouraged me to make sure I could stand on my own two feet and never rely on a partner for security, but my dad was a real piece of shit, and the Navy really fucked us. I just didn't know."

Even with the explanation she'd heard in West Virginia, Reagan had never fully understood why Alice was so against all things military. "What really happened?"

Sydney sighed and took a long, perhaps fortifying, sip of wine. "My dad…"

She trailed off, and Reagan thought she might need more encouragement. "He was still killed on duty, right? That must have been horrible." Sydney's right hand was sitting on the table beside the bread basket, so Reagan grabbed it and squeezed. She meant it to be brief, but Sydney flipped her hand under Reagan's and squeezed back. Didn't let go. *Okay.*

"He was killed while deployed but not on base or on duty at all, which is why…ugh. He'd snuck off base, and the details after this are not entirely clear, but what the Navy determined was that he'd illegally left to meet a woman. Evidently, he'd routinely been leaving base to drink, get laid, and gamble in an illegal ring. But the woman's brother found out she was secretly seeing an American and became enraged. He tracked them down and murdered them while they were in bed. I honestly don't know how the Navy found all that out, but because these actions were deemed willful misconduct, they determined that neither Mom nor me nor Noah were entitled to any survivor benefits."

Reagan grimaced. That explained so much more. "That's so fucked-up. The military sometimes…makes the wrong decision. Even if they had all the right intel and your dad was in the wrong, it's not like the three of you ever did anything. You'd been relying on him for everything, and he threw it all away. I'm so sorry."

"It ruined my mom's life. She'd believed that he was taking care of their future when really, he'd been gambling it away and eliminated any survivor benefits we were eligible for. I know he's half of my DNA, but if he came back to life, I'd punch him in the throat. He left us bereft with massive debt. It's why Mom had to move so many times before we moved in with Grandma. It's why she ingrained in me the need to stand on my own. She was betrayed in the worst way possible, and every time she turned around, it got worse. He wasn't a bad person because he was in the Navy. The Navy isn't bad because it denied us benefits. But the fact that all of it happened really fucked my mom's head up. And it, in turn, fucked me up."

Reagan hadn't let go of her hand. She hated that Sydney and Alice and Noah had gone through all of that. "I wish I had better words. But they shouldn't have treated you like that."

"Mom tried to appeal. She got an attorney. But they denied it. It felt as though we were somehow at fault for Dad's transgressions. I'd known about the gambling and the lying, but Mom, on her last day in California, told me the rest. I'd never really thought about why we hadn't received more benefits from the government, but…how *do you* trust working for an organization that operates like that? That punished children for the sins of their father? Denied them survivor benefits, health care?"

Reagan didn't know. She felt nauseated at how they'd been treated by the country she served. How could she answer? "I didn't know that could even happen. I'm so sorry you went through that. That your mom went through that. Fuck, it's no wonder she hated me."

"She never hated you."

Reagan scoffed.

"I swear. She wanted to, but she couldn't. Because you're you. But she *was* worried about me. About what I would be throwing away if I tied my future to yours. And I don't think she was necessarily wrong."

Reagan shouldn't have been surprised by those words, but they still felt like a sucker punch, and she schooled her features as best as she could to not let Sydney know she'd been affected.

She hoped Sydney hadn't noticed. "I mean, I love my life in Boston. I have an amazing condo and a job that, while exhausting, compensates me incredibly well. I paid for Noah's college. I made partner in record time. I love having the money to do whatever I want whenever I want. Provided my workload doesn't prevent it." Sydney let out a big sigh. Bit her lip. Reagan's eyes were glued to that lip as it slid from under her straight teeth. "But sometimes, I still wonder what a life with you would have looked like."

Reagan's gaze jumped from Sydney's mouth to her eyes. She hadn't noticed them drifting closer, but it was very apparent now. Taken off guard by the thought and their proximity, Reagan's mouth went dry, and she stumbled finding two simple words: "You do?"

"Of course. My life plan didn't include you, but I loved you with all my heart."

Reagan's heart skipped. Sydney had said "loved," but was she still having regrets? Could her finally being honest about her dad and trauma mean something?

It was probably the wine clouding Reagan's mind, but Sydney looked so beautiful. Her eyes were so vulnerable and open. Her skin so soft and warm. But Reagan knew it wasn't just the wine. She struggled to take a breath because sitting there with Sydney in such an intimate setting, she had to admit that she'd never fully gotten over her. That was bad. Bad, bad, bad.

"Pardon my interruption, ladies," the server said with only a slight German accent. "We are preparing to close for the evening."

Reagan looked around the restaurant and guessed her look mirrored Sydney's surprise to see that they were the only people left. She became acutely aware of the silence.

"I hate to end your fun, but everyone wants to get home with the weather. The worst is supposed to hit in the next few hours."

Reagan leaned back and said, "Of course. Of course. I'm so sorry. I didn't realize we were the only people left."

"We normally would let you stay for a little while longer, but…if you aren't ready for bed, I can offer you a bottle of wine to take up to your room."

Reagan felt her eyes go wide at the singular *room*. "Oh, we're not…um."

The server looked between them. "Or rooms. I just assumed. My apologies."

Sydney pursed her lips and shrugged. "What do you think? I don't have another bottle in me, but I could do one more glass. We don't have to finish the whole thing."

Reagan wanted to go up to Sydney's room more than anything, but at her recent revelation, knew that was a terrible idea. She didn't want to say good night, but it would be a mistake if she went up. She'd already pulled the scab off her wound and needed to let it start healing.

Unless…unless there was some type of hope for them. Reagan didn't even want to consider it but couldn't help herself. She winced and looked up at the server. "Could we have a minute or two to discuss?"

Sydney's face fell, and Reagan understood. They'd just had a really open moment about Sydney's past, but Reagan couldn't get on the roller coaster of Sydney again unless she knew they were on it together. "Does us running into each other again mean something to you? Or make you open to something…more?" Reagan finally said.

"What do you mean?"

"Fuck, I don't know. I'm having so much fun with you. I can't believe we shut this place down." She laughed and knew that, no matter Sydney's answer, she wouldn't regret this dinner, but she couldn't let it be more, unless… "Could this be the start of something?"

Sydney stared at the table. "I still live in Boston, and you're still moving to Latvia or whatever. I don't think anything has really changed, has it? You can't get stationed in Boston?"

Reagan sighed. She'd known, but she had to give it a try. "No, no Army bases in Boston. I should probably head back to my room. This has been fun, but I think this evening will just go into a new chapter in the history of us, to be shelved in the back of the library."

"Well, fuck. I've had so much fun tonight. I don't want to never talk to you again. Can we stay in touch? Like, an occasional email or text or something?" She bit her lip. "Or would you let me friend you on Facebook again?"

Reagan had agonized over unfriending Sydney years ago, but she couldn't keep stalking her social media. It wasn't healthy. She didn't want to hurt Sydney, but she had to protect herself and her own mental health. "I'm sorry, but I don't think that's a good idea. I…being here with you, like this, has made me suspect I've never fully gotten over you. I didn't realize what's been missing, but now I know. I've been carrying the hope that someday, we would be able to make a go of things when our circumstances changed. Now, things have changed, but it's still a no for you. I can't go down that road again, so I think it's better to end the night here." It was all true, but each word felt like glass in her mouth.

Sydney's face was red, and her eyes were closed. "I understand. I'm sorry, I've had a really great time tonight too. I wish, I truly wish, things could be different." Sydney signaled for the check. "Don't worry about this, I'll take care of it." It was like she could tell Reagan needed to get away.

"Thank you," Reagan said as she stood.

"It's been…" Sydney trailed off as she stood too.

"It *has* been…something." Reagan paused to gather her thoughts. If these were the last words she would ever say to Sydney, she wanted to make them count. "I don't regret it. It was nice seeing you."

"Same. I don't regret seeing you, either."

Reagan pressed a kiss to her cheek. "Take care of yourself, okay?"

"I will. Be safe wherever you go next. I can see that general star in your future. You're glowing with it."

Every fiber of Reagan's being screamed for her to take Sydney in her arms and kiss her until their flights on Friday, but instead, she squeezed her hand and walked as quickly as she could to the elevators.

It was a hard truth to swallow that she'd been sabotaging her previous relationships because she still had feelings for Sydney. It was a little pathetic that it took an evening of laughing with Sydney for that realization to hit. That wasn't how she wanted to live her life. She wanted to get married and have someone to walk through life beside. Share everything, both the good and the bad. Knowing for sure that Sydney was never going to be that person, that they could never have the future Reagan dreamed of, she *needed* to move on.

She gave herself until Friday to wallow. To order room service and read smutty books on her Kindle, but when she got home, she was shaking everything off. It was time to put Sydney into the dresser of her past and slide the drawer closed.

PART IV: THE NOW

Washington DC, Present Day

CHAPTER TWENTY

Sydney was reaching the end of her cup of coffee, and she still hadn't gotten over the shock of seeing Reagan again. Her smile probably looked ridiculous, but it felt so damn good being near her. She'd known when she'd moved that Reagan could, at some point, end up there for a year or two, but in a city of more than seven hundred thousand, she hadn't believed they'd ever see each other.

Yet here they were, sitting in a coffee shop, catching up. "I can't believe that after all this time, we actually both live in DC. Are you here in Logan Circle too?"

"I'm a few blocks south." Reagan shrugged. "I've been here for about a year and a half."

"I can't believe we haven't run into each other before now. I'm a couple blocks west. I've been here for about two years."

A flicker of…was that hurt…crossed Reagan's face. "Small world, I guess. Smaller than it used to be for us, anyway."

"Yeah." Sydney checked her watch. Shit. The idea of walking out and never seeing Reagan again was devastating. "I really hate to say this, but I have to go soon. I need time to prep for some meetings this afternoon." She sighed, weighed whether she should extend another invitation. She wished they could have stayed in touch after Munich, but Reagan had been clear that they couldn't. She wanted to honor that, but she also really wanted to see her. The worst that could happen was Reagan would say no. Maybe things had changed in the last four years. "Would you want to get together again? Maybe grab lunch. Or brunch. Or even coffee again." She rushed to add, "Just as friends, I mean," when a look of discomfort flashed across Reagan's face. Why hadn't she mentioned her girlfriend? That was something she should mention. She resolved to bring it up the next time it made sense. That fact needed to be out there. Not that she'd do anything with Reagan anyway. She'd hurt her enough as it was, and Sydney was certain that Reagan was probably moving away again soon.

Reagan chuckled. "Sure, brunch or lunch or coffee would be fun. It's too bad you aren't part of the *civilized* world where we get off for President's Day." She smirked. "I'm just planning to relax all day." She yawned and stretched her arms behind her.

"Do you think it's a little ironic that you talk of being a part of a *civilized* world, yet your entire profession exists to do battle? That doesn't exactly feel civilized to me." Sydney smiled to show she was kidding. Mostly.

"I'd say my particular profession is more like peacekeeping. Plus, as an attorney, isn't your entire job to fight with people? I mean, you were miming sword fighting earlier." She took what appeared to be the last sip of her tea, given how far she tilted her head back.

Sydney lost her train of thought watching the muscles in Reagan's throat work, but she chastised herself. She had a girlfriend and shouldn't be ogling anyone, especially not someone with whom she had a long history. "Oh no. I do battle for a living, but my weapon is a pen rather than a sword. But I am jealous that you have off today. The absolute last thing I feel like doing is a mediation meeting on a contract dispute on exactly what constitutes force majeure."

"That sounds horrible. I'll be thinking of you when I have a hot toddy in front of my fireplace with a new romantic thriller." Her half smirk was irritatingly sexy.

"That cuts deep, Reagan." Sydney clutched her chest and pretended to pull a knife from her heart. "Anyway, how about brunch next weekend?"

"Sure." Reagan checked her phone and shrugged. "I'm free both days. Saturday?"

"Now that I'm thinking about it, I might have something with my girlfriend and the congresswoman she works for next weekend, but I think it's Sunday. Let me double-check." Sydney pulled her phone out of her briefcase, proud of herself for finding a way to casually mention her girlfriend.

"Girlfriend?" Reagan said as Sydney navigated to her calendar app.

"Uh, yeah. Viviana and I have been seeing each other for a few months. She's an aide for Congresswoman Meyers from Indiana." She cleared her throat and knew that was like a blinking light saying she was nervous. Even though she had nothing to be uncomfortable about. She finally stopped hitting the wrong buttons on her phone. "Yeah, she has some kind of breakfast fundraiser on Sunday that I committed to, but Saturday works."

"Congresswoman Meyers? She's that surprisingly liberal democrat from Indiana, right?"

"That's her. Viviana's been with her since her first campaign."

"Ah. Well. Back to brunch, how about Sunny Side of Life just off the circle on Rhode Island?"

Sydney exhaled, relieved that the mention of her girlfriend hadn't made things weird. And she couldn't believe she was making plans to do brunch with Reagan in six days. She hadn't seen her in four years, they hadn't made real plans in eleven years, and now, after a serendipitous moment because her normal coffee shop was closed, she'd run into Reagan again.

As she walked to her office—despite the very cold January morning—she wondered if Reagan was uncomfortable with the girlfriend situation. She'd seemed surprised but didn't act upset. After all these years and so much hurt, Sydney was pretty sure they both knew they weren't meant for anything more than friendship, but it was the first time she hadn't been single when they were spending time together. Not that she and Viviana were particularly serious, but they'd decided to be exclusive about three months ago.

Sydney didn't cheat or pretend to be something that she wasn't. Okay, maybe she'd pretended that seeing Reagan again hadn't shaken her to the core, but that was different. That was proper decorum. She was nervous to spend time with her again because despite the years since they'd last seen each other and the awkwardness of their last interaction, they'd clicked like always. And Sydney would count the days until she could see her again.

❖

Sydney looked at her phone again and took another sip of wine to quell her irritation. Viviana had already texted three times to let Sydney know she was going to be late and then later. At least she was *finally* in a taxi and nearly there. Sydney had been sorely tempted to get up and leave the restaurant but had instead ordered a glass of wine and pulled out her laptop.

Sitting at a table in a nice restaurant and working made her feel like even more of a workaholic than she actually was, but she was working on a big case where one of her clients hadn't disclosed a latent defect as part of a sale, and she was trying to salvage the situation as best as she could. She couldn't afford to waste a minute. Especially since Viviana was running so late but swore she still wanted to do dinner. It was ridiculous that Sydney was sitting in a Michelin star restaurant with her laptop and a manila folder spread out on the table in front of her rather than a spread of French food.

"Are you doing okay, madame? Is there anything else I can get you while you wait for your other party?"

Sydney felt guilty monopolizing the table for so long without ordering anything. "Thanks, Pierre. I was going to order another glass of wine, but let's go ahead and do a bottle. I'm expecting my girlfriend any minute, and I'm sure she'll want a drink as well."

"Of course, madame. I will be right back with that." He nearly clicked his heels as he bowed his head and walked away.

Sydney had gone back to the response she was working on and lost track of time again when Viviana said, "So sorry, darling. I didn't mean to keep you waiting for this long." She leaned down and lightly brushed her cool lips across Sydney's cheek before sitting across from her. "Why do you have your laptop out *here*?" She looked around the admittedly fancy restaurant with a sneer, as if she smelled something unpleasant.

Sydney's jaw clenched instinctively, and she let out a sharp breath. "You are"—Sydney checked her Cartier watch to verify exactly—"fifty-six minutes late. What would you have me do? Twiddle my thumbs?" She hadn't meant for her tone to be quite so sharp, but Viviana's judgment was entirely uncalled for.

"Sweetie, I didn't mean anything by that." Viviana grabbed her hand and squeezed. "I'm sorry." She smiled, but it looked a little fake. Sydney suppressed her irritation as she slid her laptop and folder back into her briefcase. "What are you drinking?" She pointed to Sydney's empty glass.

"Amarone. I ordered a bottle." She really wished Pierre would hurry. Everything Viviana was saying was grating, and Sydney hoped a little more wine would smooth her frustration.

As though she'd summoned him, Pierre approached and held out the bottle for Sydney's approval. "Perfect," she said, just as Viviana said, "That looks good, but can I please get started with a vodka martini, dirty, with three blue cheese olives? But please bring me a wineglass when I switch to this."

"Of course, madame."

When he left, Viviana said, "You will not believe the day I had."

Sydney really wanted to tell her about the roller coaster of a day she'd had after running into Reagan that morning, but Viviana didn't give her a chance as she launched into a monologue about the congresswoman and a bill she'd been working on for months, and they thought they had the votes for but found out just before it was formally introduced that they didn't, and blah, blah, blah.

Sydney tuned her out and relived every minute of her time with Reagan. She'd always been beautiful, but that morning, even dressed casually in distressed jeans, a heavyweight flannel jacket, and her hair in a messy bun, she'd been radiant. When she'd taken that jacket off to reveal a tight-fitting, long-sleeved, burgundy Henley, Sydney could easily see that she still worked out.

"Sydney? Hello?" Viviana's knuckles rapping at the table jolted her back into the moment.

Shit. "Yes, sorry."

"What do you think?" Her voice was impatient, her eyes wide as she stared.

"I'm sorry, what did you say?"

Viviana rolled her eyes. "Can you come early with me on Sunday to the breakfast with the congresswoman?"

"Uh, probably, sure. Why?"

"She asked me to handle the prebreakfast logistics, but I'd rather ride with you since we'll probably be coming from the same house." Viviana didn't even pause or acknowledge Pierre when he set their food down. "And I'm going to need a stiff drink once this is behind us."

"Uh, yeah. I can do that. But you know I can't drive, right? I sold my car three weeks ago."

Her face fell. "Oh right. I forgot. Well, we can just play it by ear, I guess."

Sydney's chest felt a little heavy at the thought that Viviana was trying to use her as a designated driver. Weird in a city where there were taxis on every corner, plus Uber and Lyft.

"Well, enough about me. How was your day?"

"A little strange actually. I ran into—"

"Oh, and another thing. That jackass Bobby Ray Vaughn…"

Sydney did a quick flip through her mental address book and was pretty sure he was a pasty, overweight white guy from Kentucky. Or maybe Arkansas. Regardless, she knew he was a dick and had some *very* conservative views of the world. Sydney tuned out again as she marveled over the amazing potatoes dauphinoise she'd just taken a bit of.

When Viviana paused and took a bite of pasta twirled on her fork, Sydney hopped on the silence, hoping to get back to telling her about running into Reagan so it didn't seem like she was trying to hide it. "So anyway, back to my weird morning."

Viviana nodded, but as soon as she started to chew she said, "God, this is amazing. It's no wonder they have a star."

"Yeah. It's fantastic. Anyway, I had to go to a different coffee shop this morning because mine had a water main break."

"How annoying. And you didn't find out until you got there? You'd think they could push out a text blast to their regulars or something."

That seemed like it would be a big ask of a small coffee shop, but Sydney didn't want to get bogged down in the details. Plus, Viviana got prickly when someone disagreed with her. "Anyway, I was in this weird cowboy coffee shop—"

"Ugh, that sounds horrible."

"Actually, the coffee was good, but the weird part is that I ran into an old…friend. I've known her since my study abroad in Italy back in college."

"I didn't know you'd done a study abroad in Italy. Where at? I *love* Italy."

Italy wasn't the point. It stung that Viviana didn't realize that. "Yes, Naples. But Reagan was stationed there at the time, and we were pretty much inseparable."

"That had to have been amazing. Imagine all the food you could eat in a semester." She looked dreamily at the ceiling.

Again, not the point. "Yeah, it was great. Though, I didn't have much money back then, so my meals weren't extravagant."

"Mmm," Viviana said, her excitement clearly tapering off. She had a penchant for the ritzy and exclusive. She wouldn't have enjoyed the months Sydney had been in Italy.

"Well, anyway." Sydney was starting to feel like a broken record. "I'm having brunch with Reagan on Saturday morning."

"How nice. I have a Women's League meeting then, so I can't join, but it's good you have something else to occupy your morning. Want to come back to my place?"

Sydney sighed. Viviana's entire demeanor didn't have her wanting to spend the night, but she *was* long-term material. She checked all the boxes Sydney wanted in a wife, and this self-involved version wasn't the Viviana she'd been seeing for months. Viviana was really stressed with that bill they'd been working on, which had to be the reason she'd been so different lately. "Sure."

A short time later, Sydney lay in Viviana's bed thinking about slipping out and going home after an unfulfilling evening of a tasty dinner but subpar conversation followed by brief and mediocre sex.

Maybe she should have tried harder to explain her history with Reagan, as she was sure Viviana would care that they were exes, but she'd been so dismissive all evening. She wasn't always like that. It had to just be the bill that had failed. Viviana had always been a little self-absorbed, but she was also attentive and sweet. Most of the time. Okay, some of the time. Just not recently.

Sydney didn't sneak out of bed and go home, but she also didn't get a lot of sleep either.

CHAPTER TWENTY-ONE

"Major Jennings, ma'am, can you hold on a second please?" Reagan turned and saw Sergeant Baker running down the hallway toward her. She'd almost escaped. It was Friday afternoon and a little after four. She was ready to get the hell home and because of the Pentagon's design, she had a bit of a walk. "Sergeant, what can I do for you?" She really didn't want to get waylaid. She had a perfect evening planned. She was going to head home, open a lovely Brunello she'd received as a Christmas present two years ago from her youngest brother, Jasper, have some aged cheddar cheese, and finish the sapphic romance she was reading in front of the fire. The perfect cozy evening to recharge. The name of the book escaped her, but it was about an artist-entrepreneur and a chocolatier, and it was getting *good*. Very-sexy-stuff good.

And it took place in Chicago, where she was heading in a few weeks for the wedding of an old friend, so it felt like reconnaissance for her pending trip. She'd traveled a ton but never to Chicago. Otherwise, there was no reason to open a fancy bottle of wine, but something about this week had her walking on air. She'd gotten a little intel that her below-the-zone promotion paperwork was moving along, and it should be official soon. Hopefully. Lieutenant Colonel Jennings had a lovely ring to it. And was one step closer to General Jennings.

She was making the right connections to make it happen. She'd been networking her ass off, and thankfully, it was paying off. It was why she'd landed at the Pentagon, after all.

"Ma'am, you missed a signature here on your leave form. I was about to send it up, but I did a second pass."

Oops. A twinge of guilt flittered across her. "Thanks for getting this squared away, Baker. Much appreciated." She'd probably missed the signature while distracted by thoughts of Sydney.

She couldn't believe they'd run into each other—again—completely by chance. For the fourth time in their lives. She wasn't a mathematician, but it just didn't seem statistically possible.

Regardless, this time, she knew better than to let her heart—or her libido—get involved. Neither could be trusted, particularly where Sydney was concerned. She'd felt a surge of misplaced jealousy when Sydney had mentioned a girlfriend, but the more she'd thought about it, the more she'd realized that it made things so much easier. It was a little like when they'd first gotten together, and Reagan had shut her feelings off because of DADT. Of course there would be a little attraction, but that didn't mean they had to act on it.

They were adults, and Sydney was clearly off-limits. Reagan didn't have lustful thoughts about women who were off the market. Well, other than Emily Blunt. Clearly a thirst trap.

"Anytime, ma'am. My pleasure."

Reagan shook off thoughts of Sydney and looked back at Baker, who'd gone a little red. She was pretty sure Baker had developed a crush on her from the minute she'd started at the Pentagon. She'd done nothing to encourage it, but anytime she thanked her for anything, Baker got flushed and embarrassed. Reagan wasn't interested at all. It was flattering, kind of. But Jesus, Baker was twenty-one or twenty-two, and it was *very* illegal in the Army for an officer and an NCO to fraternize. So for a multitude of reasons—including that she'd feel like a pedophile—she'd never cross that line. But Baker's stammering made her smile a little on the inside.

She wasn't *not* out at work, but she also didn't flaunt her sexuality. She wasn't hiding it, but since she wasn't dating anyone, it never came up. Baker apparently had good gaydar. Once she'd signed off, she said, "Thanks, Sergeant Baker. Have a great weekend. And once you file this, you should get it started, okay?"

"Yes, ma'am. I'll head out as soon as I hit send."

Reagan's train ride was uneventful, and when she got home, she unbloused her pants, took off her boots, and pulled her hair out of the restrictive bun it had been up in for too many hours. At least she was in her OCPs today and not her dress uniform, but it still felt so freeing to get the most restricting pieces off. Once she took off her OCP blouse, she went and opened the bottle of Brunello she'd been dreaming about.

She lamented, as she did almost every day, that she didn't have a dog or a cat to greet her. Her house felt so lonely sometimes. When she'd been in Morocco, she'd befriended a stray street dog that had ended up half living in her home, but she couldn't bring her when she'd left. It had broken her heart, but she had, at least, been able to convince her driver there, Mallal, to adopt Dory, the scruffy mutt.

She still kept in touch with Mallal, and Dory was still alive but had grown more cantankerous in her advanced age. Reagan was planning to take a side trip to visit them on her way to Poland later that year. Okay, it was a complete detour, but whatever. Mallal had been her driver and Dory her baby for the two years she'd lived there. She loved them both.

She carefully poured the wine into her favorite decanter to keep the sediment in the bottom of the bottle and gently swirled it. The aroma was mouthwatering, and she walked away to let it open while she changed, which sometimes felt like shedding a second skin.

She decided to call Jasper to thank him and catch up since it was his thoughtful gift that she was about to enjoy.

"Reagan. My favorite sister. To what do I owe the pleasure?" It was ridiculous but completely Jasper that he always answered his phone like he was in a Jane Austen novel.

"Good sir." She tried to channel some Jane herself. "I have opened the luscious bottle of Brunello that you bequeathed me twice Christmases ago, and I wanted to talk whilst I have my first sip."

Slipping back into twentieth century he said, "Ooo. I drank my bottle of that a couple of weeks ago. Are you decanting it?"

"I'm not a heathen."

"Of course not. I'd only give you a bottle like this. I love Brad and Ryan and their Stepford wives, but they'd never appreciate it like you."

"Don't be mean about Genna and Jacqueline. They're perfectly fine."

"So heteronormative but fine. They're probably still trying to compensate for finishing second in their academy classes. Unlike us. Valedictorians all around." She heard a clap and was pretty sure he had just high-fived himself. Dork. Though she was sure one of the reasons they'd grown so close was that they were the queer members of the family. Jasper was bi but had a preference for men. She was about as gay as they came. Their parents were probably in therapy trying to figure out how they ended up with fifty percent queer kids. "Anyway, how's the wine?"

She hadn't actually taken a sip yet but used that moment to do so. The color was beautiful, and the bouquet made her mouth water. She took a sip, and it didn't disappoint. "Fucking fantastic."

"I knew you'd love it."

"Oh, I do." She took a sip and couldn't stop a sigh.

"Stop orgasming over the wine, sis, and tell me what's new."

"Well, we're down to three weeks before I see you in Chicago for the half marathon. And stay for my old friend Quinn's wedding." She still hadn't gotten over her friend connecting with her long-lost love randomly in Chicago after she'd retired, mending fences, and eventually falling back in love. It was the stuff of romance novels, but she was so happy for them.

"Oh, yeah. Are you going to bring me as your date or what?" His voice sounded pouty. "I mean, everyone loves a man in his whites. Just ask anyone who's seen *Top Gun*."

"It's going to be February. You'll still be in your blues. Plus, it's a civilian wedding. We couldn't wear our uniforms. It'd be weird."

"Fine, but the world is missing out. This gentleman is sexy as fuck in his whites. Okay, his blues too. Are you sure we can't wear them?"

"Jasper. Number one, I can't take you because you're my brother—"

"Whom you never see," he interjected.

"True, but it changes nothing. Number two, they've never met you. Number three, it's just weird. I want to see you. It's why I'm staying at your house. But weddings are expensive. I firmly believe you shouldn't take a date to a wedding unless your date is close to the wedding party, or you've been dating for a long time. We aren't dating."

"But we've *known* each other for a long time. I'm practically your oldest friend."

"You're my brother. Who is my friend, but you don't know Quinn or Kirby."

"Look," he said. "I'll spring for a super fancy gift. Or I'll double your cash in the envelope. It's gonna be great. And I miss you. I just want to spend time with you."

His voice was a little whiny, but Reagan did want to spend more time with him. "Okay, okay. I want to spend more time with you too. I'll text Quinn tomorrow and feel her out. And you are going to have to pony up a serious gift."

"Girl," he deadpanned, "I am the best gift giver around. Note the delectable glass of wine in your hand."

"Fair. I'll see what I can do to secure your invite."

"I'm sure she'll understand. I'm stationed at her last duty station, aren't I? It bonds us."

"You are. It's why she lives in Chicago, which led to her and Kirby running into each other after so many years." A piece of her that always wondered if she and Sydney were meant to eventually reconnect had ignited when Quinn had told her that she and her first love were having another go. But after so many failed attempts, she'd be a fool to go there with Sydney and let her heart get ripped out. Again.

Plus, Sydney had a girlfriend.

"But what about your boyfriend?" Reagan couldn't take *two* dates, and it felt pretty shitty to leave Jasper's boyfriend at home alone while they went to a party.

"He has to work. Being a chef is a pain in the ass. So we can go to the wedding, get drunk at the open bar, and Uber home. Probably before he gets home. It'll be just like the old days." He laughed.

"What old days? We've never been stationed in the same city. We haven't even lived in the same state since I left for West Point." Sometimes he just made stuff up.

"Maybe I'm trying to create old days."

She scoffed. "I'm almost forty. I think it's too late."

"Stop rounding up. And it's never too late. Get me an invite."

She would try. She was going to stay in Chicago for a few extra days to spend more time with him anyway, but it would be great to go to the wedding with him too. She was so grateful that as they'd gotten older, they'd moved past the sibling rivalry and formed a true friendship. She loved her other brothers too but cherished the closeness she shared with Jasper.

❖

Sydney was leaning up against the wall in front of Sunny Side of Life looking gorgeous in a black jacket that looked more fashionable than warm and aviator sunglasses that were sexier than they had a right to be. Although everything in Reagan begged her to be careful about spending more time with Sydney, her body's immediate reaction to seeing her was dangerous.

"It's a little cold to be standing out here, isn't it?" Reagan said.

Sydney looked up from her phone. "I've only been here a minute, and they wouldn't seat me until you got here. We have reservations, though, so we can head in."

Reagan held the door for her and was enthralled watching her slide the arm of her sunglasses into the front of her shirt between her breasts. It was an odd thing to be distracted by, and Reagan shook herself to break free of the spell.

Once seated with menus in front of them, Sydney said, "Are we mimosa-ing this morning?"

It seemed unwise to blunt her defenses with alcohol. But champagne barely had any alcohol, right? "Why not?"

"Excellent."

Their eyes met and held for too long until Reagan looked away and took a sip of water. While staring into her water, she said, "So how was your week? Did you take down the workmanship warranty guy you were on the phone with on Monday?"

"You remember my case from Monday?" Sydney said; her voice wavered a little.

What was that about? "Well, I was annoyed with you at first for making me listen to your conversation." She winced. "My patience leaves a little bit to be desired before I've mainlined my caffeine. And while we drank, we talked about him and what a dick he was and your other client who lied and how you were trying to minimize the damage to him. I was curious how both of those turned out." Reagan shrugged. It seemed like a natural question to ask anyone given the context of their conversation from Monday.

And given she was afraid to touch on any subjects that were *too* personal.

"I just sometimes bore people with my job. It's fascinating to me, and I get a little exuberant and think my friends are also fascinated when really, they're politely plotting their escape." Sydney pressed her lips together and rolled them in, which made her seem more timid than she'd been when they were younger. She hadn't ever been timid, and Reagan wondered what had happened in the intervening years.

She hated the thought of Sydney being less bold. "Your friends don't sound very nice." When Sydney's eyes went wide, Reagan realized that what she'd said might have been a little harsh and softened. "I mean, they should support you, let you vent when you're frustrated. That's a little crappy if they don't."

Thankfully, Sydney laughed. "You're maybe not wrong. Regardless, both cases are progressing. The warranty period attorney and his client are in the wrong, and no amount of blustering is going to change that. I'm just waiting them out. The other one we'll have to wait and see on. My client was wrong, so I'm doing damage control, but there's only so much I can do. How was your week?"

"Eh, fine. Boring. I'm working on a big operations order before I PCS later this year."

"You already have orders to leave DC?"

Was it her imagination, or did Sydney's shoulders slump when she asked that? "Yeah, I'm headed to Poland later this year."

Sydney rubbed the base of her throat. "When?"

"September," Reagan said, unsure how to interpret her reaction to the news.

Thankfully, the server arrived to take their orders to break the tension. A potato skillet with over easy eggs for Reagan and cinnamon roll waffles for Sydney.

Reagan lost herself in the conversation and felt like they were in a wrinkle in time. She had to pinch herself to remember that this wasn't a date. They weren't in California, and it had been more than a decade. It was so easy to slip back into the old rhythm with Sydney, but she couldn't let herself.

"What else are you doing this weekend?" Sydney asked as she took her last bite of waffle.

"I'm training for a half marathon that I'm running with my brother in a few weeks in Chicago, so I have a fourteen mile run tomorrow. Today, my job is to hydrate and relax." Reagan loved distance running. It was as much of a mental game as it was a physical one. As most sports were, she supposed.

"Jesus. How long does that take? And isn't the entire half marathon, like, thirteen miles total?"

"Yes, the race is thirteen point one, but my training plan takes me over the distance in preparation. This is the final long run before the race in a few weeks. If everything goes well, it'll take about ninety minutes, so not bad for a Sunday morning."

"Ninety minutes of running isn't bad to you? Holy hell. The only fitness activity I do that lasts that long is the occasional ninety minute yoga class. Well, and the kind of fitness activity we can't talk about," Sydney's face flushed, and Reagan choked on her sip of mimosa, flashing to athletic hours they'd spent in bed together years ago. "Normally, I stick to the sixty minute yoga classes."

Still coughing, Reagan squeaked out, "So the yoga classes I took you to stuck, huh?" The thought of having introduced Sydney to something that had become a part of her routine made Reagan feel warm all over. Or would if she could stop coughing.

"Yeah, I think they've made me a little less clumsy over the years. Though at first, I did them simply to have an excuse to watch you work out in tight clothing, but they really did grow on me."

That didn't help Reagan's coughing. Though she was happy to see Sydney a little bolder than at the start of their brunch. She just wished Sydney didn't use it to flirt with her.

The server dropped off the check, and Sydney snatched it before Reagan even had a chance to reach for it. "I was going to get that," she said.

"I invited you, remember? And unlike when I was in school, I'm financially stable these days." She handed the check and a fancy-looking credit card to the server without even looking at it. "As my job and life got more and more stressful, the benefits of my yoga practice grew exponentially. Even my mom got into it for a while."

"Oh." Reagan smiled thinking about her. "How's Alice doing these days?"

A shadow crossed Sydney's face as she signed the check, and Reagan's stomach dropped, fearing the worst. Thankfully Sydney said, "She's okay. But I miss her."

"Oh? You moved to DC without her?" Reagan hated how her heart hurt at the thought that Sydney wasn't as married to Boston as she'd claimed to be back in Munich. When she'd used it as a reason that they could never be a thing. She wanted to ask more, press the issue, but the thought of what the answer might be made her feel like she might lose the potato skillet she'd just eaten.

Sydney looked a little pale too. "Do you want to walk? It feels a little stifling in here all of the sudden." She took a sip of water and stood.

"Sure." Reagan guessed she was going to get some type of explanation after all.

CHAPTER TWENTY-TWO

Once outside, Sydney took a deep breath and let it out. One of the reasons she'd wanted to have brunch with Reagan was to try to explain how she'd ended up in DC, but when it came up, the look of hurt in Reagan's eyes had cut right through her. She didn't think she could explain anything while Reagan was staring at her, so she'd suggested a walk.

She put on her sunglasses to block the sun, particularly bright as it reflected off the piles of snow along the street. And they gave her a little protection from Reagan as well. She tucked her fists into the jacket pockets to shield them from the cold and started walking down P Street with Reagan at her side, their shoulders occasionally brushing.

"So, DC and Mom." She took another breath to steady herself. It was amazing how much she'd learned about controlling her emotions using her breath through yoga. "When I saw you in Munich, we were worried the cancer was back."

"I remember. I'm sorry I never checked in. I wanted to know, but I just couldn't handle staying in contact."

"I don't blame you. We've hurt each other more times than we can count, me more than you." Sydney consciously loosened her neck muscles. "She did have cancer, and the timing of the diagnosis was shit with covid. And to make matters worse, we found out at her first consultation that her oncologist had moved to DC six months before. This doctor was at the top of her field and on the leading edge of traditional cancer treatment and complementary care. We met with the oncologists in Boston, and they were fine but nothing special. Everything was locking down, what, a month after we saw each other?"

"Yeah, something like that."

"We knew we needed to decide right away on whether we wanted to stay in Boston and see the new doctor or see if her old doctor would accept her as a patient in DC. Mom was worried about me moving and losing my job, not being able to afford my condo. When I convinced her that my job would work with me, she told me that what she really wanted was to see her same oncologist." Sydney remembered the terror of those days like they were yesterday. Even if her job had threatened to fire her, she still would've brought her mom to DC for the best treatment, but she couldn't say those words to Reagan. They would've been needlessly cruel.

"So you all were able to see her doctor, and everything turned out fine?"

"Yeah, we had a few scares. She had a stint in the hospital when she caught covid. It was a bad time to be immunocompromised, but thankfully, she pulled through…" Sydney trailed off, overcome with emotions she hadn't been expecting.

Reagan lightly placed a hand on her shoulder. "Was Noah able to be here with you?"

Sydney cleared her throat as she shook her head. "No, he was here for the diagnosis but went back to work. I convinced him he shouldn't stunt his career by quitting his job. I told him I'd let him know if it was time to come back. If it was time to worry. But when she got covid, he couldn't get back because of lockdown."

"I'm so sorry that you had to go through that on your own, Sydney."

She nodded. Sniffed. She really didn't understand why she was feeling so emotional. Her mom was fine now. Sydney missed her, but she was fine.

"Stop for a sec," Reagan said and pulled her into a hug. "I know that must have been so hard to go through on your own." she whispered.

Sydney melted into the hug. It felt so *right* to be in Reagan's arms again. Comfortable. Like she'd never left…reminding her that it wasn't right at all. "Thank you," she said as she took a half step back.

"Anytime," Reagan said and smiled softly.

Sydney took a second to think about that. She couldn't imagine being that vulnerable with Viviana. That was probably just because she'd only known her a few months, whereas she and Reagan had known each other for more than fifteen years. And had shared a lot of emotionally intense moments. She just hadn't had many with Vivana. Yet.

Sydney tipped her chin away from Logan Circle, the way they'd been walking before the hug. "Do you want to keep walking?"

"Sure," Reagan said. They kept heading toward Dupont Circle, but it felt like Reagan was walking a little closer now. "So why are you still in DC, and where is your mom?"

"When I approached my boss, he said they were thinking of opening a DC office. I took that on while Mom was starting chemo. Probably an odd decision, given how much work it was, but with the covid lockdown, it was manageable. I never thought I'd leave Boston, but the DC office is mine. I can't leave it. And I like it here. All the history and monuments and everything. Historic homes." She gestured around them to all the old brownstones and neoclassical architecture. "It's like Boston but a little friendlier. And Mom? She'd apparently just started seeing a guy in her building in Boston before she'd been diagnosed. She finally told me about him right after she went into remission, and after about a year and multiple visits back and forth, she told me she wanted to move back. So she's…" Sydney laughed and shook her head. "Shacking up with a guy for the first time in her life. Her words, not mine."

Reagan laughed. "It's hard to picture Alice saying 'shacking up.' I was a little hurt when we ran into each other, and you told me you'd been here for a few years after I'd tried to convince you that you *could* live somewhere other than Boston, but I get that you'd move here for your mom."

"I'm sorry. I know it seems a little hypocritical, but in my defense, we were always talking about moving to other countries, which wasn't a possibility."

"That's not even…" Reagan growled. "I asked you to *try* long distance, and you wouldn't even…" She threw her hands up in the air but kept walking.

"I know. I was afraid. I couldn't stand the thought of relying on anyone. I'd never had any financial security, and I'd promised myself I would get it. And be able to take care of Noah and my mom too. And you know I was messed up about all that with my dad. I was unsure who I could trust, so I didn't trust anyone. But you know long distance wouldn't have worked because there would be no real end to it. We'd have had to do long distance on and off for years on end. I've tried it before and couldn't imagine handling it if something happening to *you* like it did with her. It isn't tenable. Not for fifty percent of the next twenty years. You have to know that."

"I don't know that. At all. We're two very intelligent women. We *could have* found a way if we'd tried, but you wouldn't give us any time to figure it out." Reagan's voice wasn't angry despite the anger her words implied. She sounded sad. Sydney wanted to hug her but knew she couldn't.

"I'm sorry. I wish it could have worked out differently," she finally said.

"Yeah, me too. Look, I've had fun, but I'm going to head home. I'm not feeling much like walking anymore. I'll see you later." Reagan turned and headed in the opposite direction before Sydney even had a chance to respond. She wanted to stop her, say something, but what could she say?

Looking back, a part of Sydney wished they'd tried long distance, but it would have only prolonged the inevitable. She'd needed to be with her mom, and as far as Sydney knew, this was Reagan's first time back in the States after Morocco and Lithuania and Latvia and Poland. Would they have been long distance the whole time? Sydney didn't think she could have survived worrying. Wondering every day if Reagan had been hurt if she didn't hear from her. Her lifestyle was much more dangerous than Harmony's ever was.

Sydney didn't think she could have survived that constant gnaw of fear. Or would Sydney have joined her and lost years of climbing the partnership ladder and building financial security? She still hated that she'd let her fear rule her, even though it wouldn't have changed anything.

Regardless, she was trying not to allow fear to control her anymore. She was putting herself out there on the dating market. She'd met and dated a handful of other people before Viviana. She had a stable life in DC, which was what she'd always dreamed of. A life where she didn't worry about how to pay all the bills and still eat. She couldn't give up that stability or control, but that didn't mean she was ruled by her fear.

Sydney was in a funk for the rest of the day, even after she returned home. She hated how things had gone with Reagan on their walk. And she was missing the sweet and attentive Viviana of their earlier days. She was fairly certain that once things settled at work after all the stress with the failed bill and pending election, Viviana would return to the person she'd been when they'd first started dating.

❖

Sydney met up with Viviana the next morning at the fundraising brunch fifteen minutes before guests were supposed to start arriving.

"Babe, so glad you made it," Viviana said with a huge smile as she ran to greet her with her hand extended. She pressed a kiss to her cheek. It felt a bit fake. Sydney hadn't realized it until that moment how Viviana always put on more of a show in front of her colleagues and friends. It sent a chill down her spine.

But she plastered on a smile and said, "Of course I did."

The fundraiser passed in a blur of faces and names. A few stuck out as potential clients, so they traded cards and promised to follow up the following week. That was the point of having an upwardly mobile, well-connected partner, right? The ability for them to support each other in their career aspirations?

But it struck her as a little quid pro quo. So transactional.

Her mind regularly drifted back to brunch with Reagan the day before. They'd left it weird, and Sydney hated that. She wasn't sure how to extend an olive branch again. The thought of that being the last time they spent time together hurt more than Sydney thought it should.

"How was your day yesterday, Sydney? What'd you do?" Viviana asked as they were heading out to grab a drink that Sydney didn't want. They'd barely spoken at the event, and Sydney wasn't sure why Viviana had even wanted her there.

"I had brunch with that old friend I was telling you about."

Viviana grabbed her hand as they walked. "Oh right. I forgot. How was that?"

"It was good to catch up with her. She's someone I never thought I'd see again, but it was a pleasant surprise."

"How exciting. Are you going to stay in touch with her now?"

That was the question, wasn't it? It was so nice being with her but also so dangerous. Reagan was leaving in a few months, and Sydney neither wanted to get attached nor wanted to hurt Reagan again. "I don't know. Maybe. We're both busy." She shrugged and tried to play it cool.

"I don't know about her, but you certainly are. Almost too busy for me half the time." She laughed, but it had an edge to it that Sydney didn't like. Viviana was the one who canceled plans regularly. But she didn't want to fight, so she let it go. And hated herself for it a little bit.

CHAPTER TWENTY-THREE

Reagan had been waiting for this week in Chicago for what felt like forever. She'd flown in Friday evening and had taken off the whole week to hang with Jasper, and it had been amazing. The half marathon was beautiful and had felt good in her body, and she'd nearly beaten her personal best she'd set when she was twenty-five. She and Jasper talked about running another half in the fall or maybe scaling up to a full, but it was going to be a busy year prepping to move to Poland.

Hanging out with Jasper and Andrew had also been good for her soul. Andrew was so kind and softened Jasper's cynical edges. And Jasper made her laugh like no one else, which she really needed after her emotional roller coaster of weeks avoiding Sydney's texts.

She wanted to see her but refused because protecting herself was more important than giving in to her impulses. She responded but always had an excuse not to meet. Luckily, she'd been busy with work and training for the race. She could hang out with Sydney once or twice more before she left, and that would be that. She could finally move on and not have Sydney floating in the back of her mind anymore. She thought she'd gotten that closure in Munich, but that possibility of what-if had reared its head once she knew Sydney was living mere blocks away. She hated herself for all of it.

"Lookin' sexy, big sis," Jasper exclaimed when he came into the room.

"You're looking pretty dapper yourself, little bro."

He was in a slim-fitting, dark charcoal suit and vest with a gray shirt, but his tie was a colorful pink paisley with matching pink cuff links.

"I love this tie on you. Whoever got it for you had excellent taste."

"Aw, thank you. Wait, didn't you buy it?"

She shrugged but certainly had.

"Your chiffon dress matches my suit, and these rosy pearls match my tie and look great with your skin tone, by the way. Did we secretly coordinate, and I didn't realize it?"

"Great minds think alike, I guess. Unless you've been snooping in my bag?" She cocked an eyebrow.

"I'd never do that. I love you, but I'd never recover if I discovered a strap-on or something in your stuff." He faked a gag, and she punched him in the arm.

"You really think I'd bring a strap-on to your house? I've only used those with serious girlfriends." She rolled her eyes, and he laughed. "Are you ready? The car is downstairs."

"Madame?" He offered her his elbow, and she slid her hand into the crook. She'd ordered a black town car for the evening so they wouldn't have to worry about drinking too much or waiting for a Lyft.

"I'd thought it was a little strange that Quinn's wedding was being held at a planetarium but..." She gestured to the Chicago skyline with the sun descending behind it as she stepped out of the car. It was breathtaking. "It all makes sense now."

"It's my first wedding here, and I don't regret a dollar that I spent on the 2008 Dom Perignon Rose that I added to the card you already planned to give them. This is going to be a fantastic night."

An usher met them at the door and escorted them to the room where the ceremony would take place, so she dropped her voice to a whisper. "That sounds ridiculously expensive, Jasper."

"It wasn't cheap, but you said they got together in 2008, right? When Don't Ask, Don't Tell was still fucking up the lives of service members around the world? Seems like a union to celebrate since they—and you—helped pave the way for me. I've been able to be out from my first day at the Academy." The usher opened the door to a room lined with floor to ceiling windows overlooking the skyline as the sun continued its slow descent. "And attending a party here? I'd pay a few hundred dollars per plate to do it. It's a worthy splurge."

"You are a generous soul." It was sweet that he appreciated the struggles of Kirby and Quinn and even Reagan herself serving in silence until DADT was lifted. "And I love you for it." She pressed a kiss to his cheek.

"Reagan?" A shocked voice with a slight southern twang said.

She spun. "Sydney? What are you doing here?" A jolt of jealousy surged through her seeing Sydney on the arm of a tall, willowy brunette who looked like a model, complete with a brooding expression on her beautiful face.

"I'm friends with the bride. One of them, I mean. Kirby." Maybe she was thrown by seeing Reagan, but she was nervous as she rubbed the base of her throat. She looked fantastic in a navy cocktail dress with a plunging neckline. Her hair was in an updo with a few strands curling around her face that accented her neck and shoulders perfectly.

"Oh, she's a banker or something, right?" Reagan reached back into her memory to remember what Quinn had told her.

"Yes. My firm represents Kirby's bank in a lot of matters. She and I became quite close going through some hairy deals a few years back. Do you know Quinn? Military connection or something?" It looked like Sydney's date wanted to drag her away, but Sydney stayed planted in front of them.

Reagan nodded. "Yeah, even though she was Navy, and I'm Army—"

Jasper coughed, "Go Navy, beat Army," and looked around like some stranger had said it. She wanted to punch him.

"We were both intelligence officers, and our paths crossed several times before she retired. Eventually, we became friends and commiserated on quite a few things. How we'd both served under DADT, relationships, the life of a female officer." Reagan almost said more but since that was probably the girlfriend, she didn't want to say too much.

"Ah," Sydney said, her face a little pink. However, her girlfriend's face seemed to be turning red. Was she angry?

Trying to change the subject, Reagan also realized she was being rude. "I don't know if you remember my youngest brother, Jasper? You met briefly at Thanksgiving eons ago."

Sydney shook his hand. "Nice to see you again."

He squinted at her and looked at Reagan as if trying to place her.

"Jasper, this is my...old friend, Sydney. We met years ago in Italy when I was stationed there."

"Ah, right. Sydney. Great to see you again." Reagan could almost hear his brain engage the moment he realized *who* Sydney was and why she'd been home with Reagan for Thanksgiving years ago.

They all stared at each other awkwardly until Sydney's date cleared her throat, clearly irritated that she was the only one not figuring out the weight of this moment.

"Sorry. This is my girlfriend, Viviana Lyons. Viviana, this is Reagan and Jasper Jennings. They're both military officers."

Jasper extended his hand and Reagan followed suit. "Nice to meet you, Viviana," Reagan said.

"Likewise," she replied, but her face didn't agree with the words. Her grip was also limp and quite disappointing for a woman in a pantsuit and power heels. She had a bit of a Shane from *The L Word* look to her but with a more pinched expression and longer hair, but that same, *I know I'm the hottest thing in this room* vibe. Reagan didn't like her. That aura of superiority was a turnoff.

"Come on, sweetheart." Viviana pulled Sydney's hand.

Sydney shrugged and said, "Well, we should probably grab seats."

Reagan was grateful and yet felt horrible. She'd been trying to convince herself that Sydney was happy and close to getting engaged to a great woman. She was off-limits. But her girlfriend seemed like a first-class bitch.

"Us too," Jasper said and nearly yanked Reagan away. "Oh my God, she was so horrible," he whispered as they walked to the opposite side of the room. "But, damn, Sydney is beautiful. I barely remembered her at first, but you did good with her."

"Are you being serious right now? She broke my heart. I just followed her around like a puppy begging for her love. Which she gave me until it wasn't convenient." She needed to keep reminding herself of that. And if *Viviana* was the kind of woman Sydney wanted, Reagan would happily stand aside.

"Sweetie." Jasper squeezed her hand. "I'm sorry. I know things didn't end well with her, but I didn't realize your feelings for her, exactly. I didn't realize that you *loved her*, loved her."

"I wish I didn't. I mean, I wish I hadn't." That was a terrible slip of the tongue. There was no way she still loved her. For sure not. *Right?*

"Mm-hmm," Jasper said as he pulled her into a row of chairs near the front, rows away from where Sydney and *Viviana* were. Ugh. Why would someone as sweet as Sydney allow herself to be tied down by someone so unpleasant?

"She looked like she smelled someone's fart, didn't she?" Jasper said.

Reagan burst out laughing. "Why was she so unpleasant?"

He shook his head. "No clue."

"Why is Sydney with her?" Reagan said more to herself than Jasper, but he didn't have time for a response anyway as the processional music started, and the officiant signaled for everyone to rise. Quinn appeared, looking much the same as the last time Reagan had seen her, with a slightly shorter woman with a pixie haircut on her arm. They were both in long white wedding gowns and looked so happy. So in love. Reagan's heart ached. She was happy for Quinn. She'd been through so much, and she deserved happiness. And it looked like she'd found it.

The ceremony nearly brought Reagan to tears as Quinn recounted how much Kirby coming back into her life meant to her. She had always seemed a little lost when Reagan had known her, but looking at her now, she seemed completely happy and in love. Then, Kirby ripped Reagan's heart out when she talked about how grateful she was that they'd found their way back together.

It made the pain of heartbreak with the only woman she'd ever really loved—the one who was sitting on the other side of the room holding the hand of a tall troll—more poignant. More real. It wasn't fucking fair. Yet, she hoped for nothing but a lifetime of happiness for Quinn and Kirby. They clearly deserved it.

She wanted to make a quick escape to the restroom to freshen up but instead tried to blot the tears welling at the corners of her eyes before they fell. Jasper squeezed her hand, and she squeezed back. She was happy to have her favorite wingman. She leaned into him. "Thank you for coming," she whispered.

He handed her a handkerchief. "I've always got your back."

Once the ceremony was over, Jasper and Reagan made their way to the bar. She needed a drink, something stiff. "Can I get a Blantons? Neat." She was surprised that they had it, and yet, she realized she shouldn't have been. Quinn had mentioned something about Kirby being a bourbon woman.

"Make that two," Jasper said from beside her. "Such a beautiful ceremony, huh?"

She nodded and made a sound of assent.

"And I didn't even see you looking around to find Sydney and the snake."

She laughed. "The snake?"

"She has an untrustworthy expression and is long and thin. Seems appropriate." He shrugged and subtly gestured with his glass toward an open balcony door. "Isn't that your girl? Standing out there all alone? Maybe you should go say hi? And look, she needs a drink. I'm sure you remember what she likes."

"I've been ignoring her texts for weeks. The last thing she wants is to talk to me."

"I saw the way she looked at you earlier," he said. "She wants to talk to you. Trust me."

Reagan couldn't believe that was the truth, but at his prompting, she ordered a glass of wine, and at his nudging, she started walking toward Sydney. She paused at the door, unsure if she was making the right decision, but when she looked back at Jasper, he was shooing her to go.

Sydney either heard or felt her because she turned as Reagan approached. Her face softened, though that could have been at the drink in Reagan's hand.

"Here, you, uh, looked thirsty. I got you the amarone from their selection of reds." It sounded lame, but what else could she say?

"Thank you." She took a sip and sighed. "Mmm. I can't believe you remember what I drink."

As if she could forget. Reagan just shrugged and looked at the water.

They stood in silence for a moment before Sydney said, "It was a beautiful ceremony, wasn't it?"

"They're clearly meant for each other. Crazy how they found each other after so many years." Reagan realized her mistake as soon as she said it. The parallels between their stories were uncanny, and she didn't want to go there. "Fuck," she mumbled.

"What'd you say?"

Had Sydney miraculously not heard her? She could only hope. "Nothing."

They stood in silence again, looking back toward the skyline all beautiful and illuminated like fairy lights. "I can't believe we each know one half of this pair. Such a small world. Sorry you can't get rid of me." Sydney chuckled, but it sounded sad.

"I'm not trying to get rid of you."

"But you've been avoiding me." She ran her fingers through her hair and continued to pointedly *not* look at Reagan.

"I'm not." But as Sydney spun to look at her, she couldn't continue the lie. "Okay, I am, but it's not because I don't want to see you." Sydney cocked her head. "It's because I do, and I know that's not a great idea."

"Oh."

Reagan felt compelled to elaborate. "I mean, you know how we are with each other. We think we can be friends, but I'm just not so sure we can. And you have a girlfriend. And I'm leaving for Poland in a few months. I can't put my heart through all that again."

"I see," Sydney said. "I mean I understand, I just thought maybe we could try. You know?" Her face looked achingly sad, and Reagan wanted to comfort her. Wrap her in her arms and tell her…something.

But what could she say? She kept her hands to herself and said, "I didn't mean to ghost you. I just don't know how to—"

"Hey, sweetheart, I got you a glass of wine, but it looks like you already have one," an irritated voice interrupted.

"Sorry, Reagan brought me a drink. But I appreciate you grabbing one too."

Why had she brought Sydney a white wine? Unless her tastes had really changed, she barely tolerated white wine.

Viviana's face pulled into a tight frown, and Reagan nearly laughed thinking about Jasper's fart comment. "I'm sorry, I'm just not feeling very well, sweetheart. Can we just go back to the hotel room?" Her face changed from irritated to puppy dog eyes, and Reagan wanted to barf.

"I haven't even said congratulations to Kirby yet. I need to at least give her a hug. Can you hold on for a little longer?" She took Viviana's hand, and Reagan thought she might actually be sick. Could Sydney not see she was being manipulated? She deserved better.

Viviana's sigh sounded like she'd just gotten off a thirty-six hour shift, and someone had told her she'd have to work another twelve hours because her relief had called off. *Dramatic much?* "I'll try."

Reagan couldn't handle any more. "Well, I should get back to Jasper. God only knows what kind of trouble he's getting himself into. Great seeing you, Sydney. Maybe we'll run into each other again in DC." She wanted to hug her, but that was out of the question for so many reasons, so she stepped back and waved. "Viviana."

"Raelynn. Nice meeting you," she said.

Reagan wanted to say, "Nice meeting you too, you pompous, egotistical ass." But she didn't. She only smiled when Sydney said, "Actually, it's Reagan." This time it was Sydney pulling Viviana away rather than the other way around.

When Reagan rejoined Jasper, he'd found his way into a circle of two sets of women. All four were beautiful and laughing at something he'd said. He was midsentence when she approached and stopped his story to say, "You don't look happy. Did things not go well?"

She looked at the group. "Sorry to interrupt."

"No need. Jasper told us you were talking to your long-lost love, so we've been waiting to hear how it went," one of the women said.

"Ugh. Crashed and burned. She has the worst girlfriend ever." Reagan couldn't help her eyeroll.

"Ugh. Horrible," said another woman with long, wavy brown hair. "I'm sorry. Well, hang out with us. We're all nice, I promise."

"Reagan, this is Skye, Bailey, Ellie, and Hayden. They're all friends of Kirby's," Jasper said as he gestured around the group.

"Great to meet you," Reagan said, happy to have a few other friendly faces.

She and Jasper became the foursome's fifth and sixth wheels for most of the evening, and Reagan focused on the conversation and the romanticism of the night. The toasts made her smile and feel nostalgic about the what-ifs. She and Sydney probably could have made it work in a hundred different lifetimes with a hundred different backgrounds. Unfortunately, they had too much fighting against them in this one.

Sydney barely had a hold on the lid of her anger by the time she and Viviana finally got to their hotel room. It had taken forever to get a Lyft, which only compounded her annoyance. As soon as the door closed behind them, she couldn't hold it in anymore. "If you didn't want to come to this with me, you could have stayed home."

A weird look flickered across Viviana's face before she settled on a contrite expression. "I'm sorry, babe. I think my period is about to start, so my stomach is upset, and I'm super irritable. I'm sorry if I embarrassed you in front of your friends. I just needed to get out of there. I didn't know I was going to feel so bad."

Although Sydney suspected she was being manipulated, Viviana did at least look sorry. Sydney sighed. "Do you need some ibuprofen or something?"

"No, I took some already. And my period hasn't started. It just feels like it is. Maybe I should take a bath and relax and see if that helps. You know how bad my cramps are. You can join me if you want." She arched an eyebrow as she unbuttoned her suit jacket and started on her blouse.

Sydney was still so irritated that she didn't feel a flicker of attraction as Viviana slowly opened her maroon silk shirt and revealed her smooth skin and pert breasts in a sheer black bra, so she turned away to make herself a cup of chamomile tea but changed her mind and grabbed the small bottle of red wine from the minibar. Fuck it. This was *not* how she'd seen this evening going.

Viviana, apparently irritated that her overt seduction attempt had failed, said, "And why didn't you tell me that your *old friend, Raelynn,* is actually an ex and not *just* a friend?"

A bolt of rage shot through Sydney's chest, and she took a deep breath before she turned. Viviana was standing in just her sheer black bra and panties, a sight that would normally excite Sydney, but she just felt disgust. "Her name is Reagan, not Raelynn, please stop pretending you can't remember. You have the best memory for names of anyone I've ever met, so I know you're just being an asshole. And if you recall, though you probably can't because you are so absorbed in your own stuff lately, I tried to tell you more about her weeks ago, and you blew me off."

"That's not true," Viviana protested, her lips pouty. "I always listen to you." Her voice had a whiny tone that Sydney normally gave in to, but tonight, it grated and enflamed her frustration.

"You used to listen, but the longer we've been together, the less you seem to. It was the night you were an hour late to dinner and got mad because I was working at the table while waiting for you. I told you about brunch, and you proceeded to tell me all about how you had Women's League that morning. I tried multiple times, and you were distracted by the fact that we'd met in Italy." Sydney could see the moment she remembered.

Vivianna stepped closer. "I'm sorry I wasn't paying enough attention to you that night."

That night? Try every night, Sydney thought but kept silent, wanting to keep the peace while they had to stay in the same hotel room, at least.

Viviana pulled her into a hug. "I'm sorry, Siddybear. Can I make it up to you in the tub?" She tipped Sydney's face up and batted her eyes.

Sydney hated that nickname and hated how Viviana thought she could be so horrible and then expect to make everything better with sex. "I'm tired. I'm going to drink this wine"—she held up the little mini-bottle and took a swig—"and go to bed. But you should have your bath. I know you need to relax."

"Fine." Viviana turned and walked into the bathroom, closing the door before Sydney could respond.

She suppressed a growl of frustration. Why was she still putting up with Viviana? She didn't have a ready answer, but she needed to really think about it as it was becoming apparent that Viviana was not the person she'd pretended to be when they'd first met. Back then, Viviana had always asked about her day and remembered what they'd talked about. She'd brought Sydney soup when she'd had a cold and texted every night just to say she was thinking of her.

Had any of that been real? She couldn't help but compare the Viviana she'd been spending time with lately to Reagan, who'd never shown a bit of disingenuousness. Every second they'd spent together had been real. Of that, Sydney was certain.

CHAPTER TWENTY-FOUR

Sydney hadn't seen Reagan since the wedding in Chicago two weeks ago, and she'd resisted texting. Yet she'd been hitting the cowboy café regularly. The water main break had introduced her to the superiority of the coffee from the cowboys, so she'd switched her daily location.

It had nothing to do with Reagan.

Absolutely nothing at all.

Yet, when she saw Reagan looking sexy as fuck in her camouflage uniform, her hair pulled up in a neat bun, walk into the café, her stomach jittered. Her heart fluttered.

Reagan smiled when she saw her, and that meant more than it should have. "Hey," she said with a soft smile as she approached after ordering. "Fancy seeing you here."

Sydney adjusted the collar of her blouse and smoothed her suit jacket, hoping Reagan couldn't tell she was nervous. "Well, as you said, they have the best coffee outside of Italy. After coming here for a few days and then going back to my normal place, I realized they weren't as good." She shrugged, trying to play it all off. "So here I am."

Reagan smirked. "I'm glad you've seen the light. How've you been?"

"Good. I mean, busy. Really busy. But work always is. I've been working a lot of hours just trying to keep my head above water." Viviana certainly had something to do with how many hours she'd been working lately. She hadn't felt the same toward her since the wedding—probably longer than that—so she'd been using work as an excuse to never be available.

Reagan set her hat on the table between them. "What's going on at work? If you can talk about it, that is. I've heard about attorney-client privilege on TV, but I don't know what you can actually talk about."

"I can talk generally unless a client has directed me otherwise. I normally err on the side of caution. But some of this is in the press already, so remember that guy I mentioned that violated one of the representations in his contract, and the buyer found out?"

Reagan nodded. "Yeah, the guy that you were trying to do damage control for."

"Exactly." Sydney's heart lifted a little that Reagan remembered. She paused to collect her coffee, then hurried back.

"What's new in that case? I don't normally read the business news," Reagan said.

"Well, despite my best efforts to minimize his losses, which would have been a lot less than litigating this thing, he wants to fight, so I am preparing depositions and court filings in preparation to go to trial." Sydney rubbed her jaw, trying to convince it to unclench since the thought just pissed her off. "Between us," she whispered, "I think I'm going to fire him as a client after this. This is the final straw, and he can find some other sucker to represent him."

"I'm sorry, that sounds horrible." Reagan winced and grabbed her order and winced again as she sipped.

Sydney laughed, watching her. "I can't believe you still do your daily shot of espresso, even though you don't like it. How about you? What's going in your world?"

"I'm in a little bit of a holding pattern. I found out earlier in the year that I was going to get a below the zone promotion—meaning I'm getting promoted a little before I'd normally be eligible—but I'm stressed that it isn't going to come through before I'm supposed to PCS to Poland."

And like she'd been splashed with a cold bucket of water, Sydney woke up. Reagan was leaving again, like she did every other year, like she would always have to until she retired, and Sydney couldn't. Despite being continuously so drawn to Reagan, nothing had changed.

❖

Sydney had put Viviana off for as long as she could, but she'd already committed to attending this fundraising dinner for the congresswoman weeks ago. She was beginning to feel like nothing more than arm candy these days, and if something didn't change, she needed to end what was quickly starting to feel like a farce.

She'd been on her own most of the evening, chatting with donors and discussing all the important work Congresswoman Meyers was doing nationally. She was fighting the fight on abortion rights, trans rights, blah blah. Not that it wasn't important work, but Sydney wasn't a politician and didn't appreciate being trotted out like a pony so Viviana could talk about her impressive attorney girlfriend who was "around here somewhere." By the time they were heading back to Viviana's place in their town car, Sydney was at the end of her rope.

"Thank you for coming tonight, Sydney. I appreciate it, and I know Congresswoman Meyers does too." Viviana grabbed her hand and squeezed. "It feels like it was pretty successful, though I'll know for sure tomorrow."

Sydney blinked. This was the first time Viviana had expressed appreciation in a long time. Maybe since they'd made themselves an official couple. "No problem," Sydney said, even though it felt like a problem. "I wish we could have spent more time together. I always feel a little deserted at these things."

Viviana huffed. "You know I've got to work the room."

"I'm just saying, it would be nice if we could work the room together. It's exhausting for me. I don't work in politics. This isn't my wheelhouse."

Viviana looked pointedly at the driver and back to Sydney and with clipped words said, "Can we talk about this later?"

Sydney sighed, resigned. "Fine." She hadn't even wanted to go to Viviana's house that evening, but Viviana had insisted. They rode in silence for a while before Sydney said, "At least it's the weekend. This week has been so long."

"I know. I've had so much planning for this event. I'm ready to relax for a day before I get back at it."

Sydney wondered if Viviana would let her vent too. "Me too. I'm so annoyed with this client of mine. He's really making my life impossib—"

However, Viviana pulled her phone out of her clutch and said, "Talk to me," without a word to Sydney about having to take the call.

How had she gotten here? How could she be with a woman who was so self-absorbed that she constantly made Sydney feel like she didn't matter. And conversely, she'd been running into Reagan with moderate frequency, and Reagan always listened to her. She always knew what was going on with Sydney's cases, what Sydney could share anyway. Reagan didn't take phone calls in the middle of a story. She didn't home in on one little piece of the story that had nothing to do with the point. She listened, made Sydney feel like she *wanted* to be there.

Why was she trying to force something with a woman who clearly didn't care about her just because she checked the right boxes and used to pretend like Sydney mattered? Nausea rolled through her as Viviana's tone got loud. This was wrong. It was all fucking wrong. It was like Viviana had slowly been chipping away at her self-worth over the past few months without Sydney's realizing, and suddenly, everything was clear. Reagan, with her unwavering thoughtfulness, cleared her vision, and she could see exactly how horrible Viviana was. She had to get out. Get away.

Viviana was still chatting on the phone when Sydney leaned forward and tapped the driver on the shoulder. "Excuse me. Could you please pull into that McDonald's ahead?"

"Yes, ma'am."

Sydney pulled out her phone and requested a Lyft.

When they pulled in, Viviana said, "Hold on a sec, Steve." She pulled her phone away from her ear. "What are you doing? We just had dinner."

"I need someplace to wait for a Lyft, and this looks perfect." As the car came to a stop, Sydney opened the door and got out, moving to the trunk to grab her overnight bag.

Viviana said, "Steve, I'm going to have to call you back," as she got out of the car. "What are you doing?"

"I don't want to do this anymore. You don't treat me like a partner, Viviana. You did at first, but lately, you've been treating me like I'm irrelevant. And for some reason, I took it. For months. You ticked all the boxes for the person I thought I wanted in a partner, but there are other things I need. Someone who actually listens to me, who treats me with respect. Who remembers the things I tell her about my world, and that's not you. I'm sorry." A weight lifted with every word.

Viviana's brows furrowed, and her mouth opened and closed a few times before she said, "It's not like I hit you or lie to you or cheat on you."

"It's sad that you think treating me right is *not* doing horrible things. But you ignore me, treat my friends poorly, and are disrespectful when I'm speaking. I feel like an accessory to your life. Like a necklace to show off. You like the idea of me but not the actual me. You probably can't name one thing I'm stressed out about right now, can you?"

"I mean…you're stressed about Congresswoman Meyers losing the next election and what happens to the country, aren't you?"

"I'm as stressed about that as I am about the destruction of rain forests or the possible extinction of elephants. My *actual* stressors are related to my *actual* life. Things I am working on day in and day out, and you have no idea. So I'm done. I've sacrificed my confidence and self-worth long enough. So please let me know in the next few days if I left anything at your house, and I'll do the same. Otherwise, this is over."

In the most perfect timing, a black Chevrolet Tahoe pulled in. She matched the plates to her app and said, "This is me. Viviana, I wish you all the best, but it won't be with me."

Viviana stared at her, mouth slightly agape, as Sydney opened the door to the Tahoe and swung her bag in. As her driver pulled away, it felt like she'd taken off a too-tight jacket and discarded it. Every inch of her felt relief, and she couldn't wipe the smile off her face.

❖

Reagan walked in and saw Sydney at what was becoming their normal table at Coffee and a Kick. She wasn't quite sure how it had happened. It wasn't like they'd ever talked about it or anything, but somehow, they'd started spending about twenty minutes together every morning while they waited for their coffee and as Reagan sipped her espresso. Once that was done, they took the rest of their drinks to-go.

This morning, however, Sydney looked a little extra peppy. Reagan couldn't quite put a finger on it, but Sydney had seemed sadder than she used to. Reagan thought perhaps it was missing her mother and brother. But this morning, something was different, like something that had been dragging her down had been removed. That seemed doubly odd on a Monday.

"Good morning," Sydney said as Reagan walked up to the table, her smile bright.

"Morning. You're looking awfully chipper. Did you have an amazing weekend?" Reagan glanced at her left ring finger to verify she hadn't gotten engaged. Reagan would have been devastated if that was the root of her good mood, given how horrible Viviana was. But to her relief, that finger was still bare.

"Nothing special. I just...I don't know, I'm feeling optimistic again." She shrugged and pushed Reagan's two cups toward her.

"Thank you," Reagan said as she picked up her espresso and winced at her first sip. The first person to arrive had taken to ordering for both of them. It was easier since they were on a limited time schedule during the week.

Reagan had been trying to convince herself that seeing Sydney almost every morning was like an allergy shot, small exposures in order to build up an immunity. Clearly, it hadn't been working. She was still so attracted to her that she could have singlehandedly written a chemistry book on attraction, but it had to work eventually, right?

And maybe things were getting a little better. She could talk to Sydney without a lump in her throat. She could watch her shake out her hair without flurries of butterflies in her stomach. That was progress, and she was going to celebrate every win.

It was a little masochistic going to a place every morning that made her heart ache, but the one morning she'd skipped their unofficial coffee date, she hadn't stopped thinking about Sydney all day, which was worse. She was a mess.

At least she was going to be in Poland in half a year, and this whole chapter would be behind her. And in the meantime, she'd keep catching up with Sydney in twenty minute increments. Long enough to get a buzz, but not long enough to form an emotional attachment.

Right.

When Reagan realized they'd been staring at each other for too long, she coughed and said, "I was texting Quinn this weekend. She and Kirby are back from their honeymoon in Portugal, Spain, and Greece."

"Oh wow. They've been gone for this long? That's more than a month."

"She said they were trying to make up for all the vacations they didn't have a chance to take over the ten years they weren't together. It's sweet, huh?" she felt a little misty about how romantic it all was, yet it also stung. Especially while sitting in front of her own long-lost… *not* love.

"It really is. Gives you a little more faith in the institution of love, doesn't it?" Sydney's eyes went a little soft, and Reagan's espresso roiled in her stomach. She'd once begged Sydney to believe in the power of their love, so knowing that someone else's love story gave Sydney faith made her want to throw up.

She downed the last sips of her espresso in one gulp. "Sure. Yeah. Sorry, I forgot I have an early meeting this morning, so I need to get going. I'll catch up with you later, okay?"

Sydney's eyes went wide as Reagan jumped up and grabbed her cover with one hand and her tea with the other. "Sure, yeah. It was good chatting."

She gave the same awkward wave she did every time they had coffee and fled as fast as she could while seeming casual.

She'd just have to take a break from these tête-à-têtes. She couldn't keep doing this. Stopping would break her heart, but it just hurt too damn much. She adjusted her cover on her head and pulled her sunglasses from a breast pocket as she pushed out the door. The strong wind out of the east was making her eyes water, and she carelessly swiped the tears off her cheeks as she briskly walked to the train.

It was definitely the wind making her eyes tear up and not the thought that this encounter might have been the last she'd see of Sydney Adams.

CHAPTER TWENTY-FIVE

Sydney had gone back and forth about going to the damn Army Birthday Ball. A client of hers owned the hotel in DC that it was being hosted at and had insisted that she and the other attorneys on the assignment attend. She'd said no at least seventeen times, had tried to come up with excuses that she was going to be out of town, but the businessperson in her knew that she should attend. It was important to Kimberly, her client, and so she acquiesced and rallied her team.

She told herself that it was unlikely that Reagan would be there, which she couldn't actually convince herself to believe. With her lofty career goals, Reagan wouldn't miss a networking event like this. However, with more than a thousand people, there was a strong chance she and Reagan wouldn't run into each other, right?

Reagan had made herself pretty clear when she'd stopped coming to coffee a few weeks ago. Sydney had continued to go to the cowboy place because they did have the best coffee but hadn't seen Reagan since the Monday after she'd broken up with Viviana. She didn't even remember what she'd said that had made Reagan hop up and run out, but that was the last she'd seen her.

Sydney had texted just to make sure she was okay. Reagan's response had been to the point: *Everything fine. Just had a change of schedule and can't make it. Sorry, but please take care of yourself.*

Sydney let it lie. She hated it. She wanted to check out other coffee shops in the area. She wanted to do anything to reestablish connection but realized she had to let go. She knew that she couldn't uproot herself and move to Poland. Her life, her law practice, were in DC. She could do long distance for a year or two while Reagan was in Poland, but what happened after that? Maybe Reagan would come back to DC and maybe not, but, even if she did, that would only last for a year or two before the Army sent her somewhere else. Fundamentally, not much had changed, and she was hurting Reagan by continuing to contact her, so she'd accepted that she needed to let her go. She committed to herself that if she did see Reagan at the ball, she'd duck away.

So as she checked the soft curls in her hair that she'd had professionally done that afternoon and made sure her earrings were securely through her ears, she took a few deep breaths and reminded herself to stay strong. Reagan would have no idea she was there. It was going to be up to Sydney to protect them both. She stayed resolute as she got into the town car Kimberly had provided. She stayed resolute as she stepped out at the entrance to the grand ballroom. She stayed resolute as she walked into the room and realized how hard it might be to recognize Reagan.

There was a sea of dark blue, with non-uniformed people mixed in, but by and large, there were a lot of people who looked an awful lot alike. She also felt panic that she might never find her colleagues. Thankfully, Kimberly saw her first and walked over.

"Glad you could make it," she said and pulled her into a hug. "I love this dress."

Sydney had spent a fair amount of time trying to find the right one and had settled on a dark maroon, one-shoulder gown with a slit to just above her knee. It was a flattering cut, but she had spun in front of the mirror six or eight times to make sure it would swirl correctly around her ankles.

"Thank you, and thank you for the invite. I've never been to something quite like this." She gestured at the expanse of uniformed soldiers.

"It's something, isn't it? Oh, let me introduce you to my husband. Eddie, this is Sydney. She's the fantastic attorney who handles all our acquisitions." Eddie was a handsome black man and was unexpectedly in a formal-looking Army uniform. He and Kimberly made a striking couple, both tall, with textbook good looks. She was in a deep purple dress that coordinated with the purple on his jacket lapels.

"Great to meet you, Eddie. I didn't realize you were in the Army. Kimberly hasn't mentioned that."

He let out a deep laugh. "I'm not sure if she's embarrassed to be married to a public servant sometimes." She lightly slapped his arm. "Don't say that, honey. She doesn't know us well enough to know that's entirely untrue. I'm not embarrassed, but I don't talk about my husband's job to be discreet. That's it. I'm incredibly proud of him." She lovingly ran a hand across the side of his chest without all the tiny medals. "Do you know if your team is here? We should grab a drink. This is a cocktail hour, after all."

They grabbed a drink, and Sydney was relieved to be wearing a dark gown so she could drink red wine without being worried about small spills. She mostly stayed with Kimberly and Eddie and eventually caught up to the other three attorneys who she worked with on this account, and they chatted as they walked through the silent auction and sat for dinner.

No sign of Reagan, and Sydney let out a small sigh of relief as dinner was served. However, things started to go a little sideways during the dessert course, when the formal portion of the evening began.

The emcee stepped on stage and made a few jokes before introducing Major Reagan Jennings. Sydney couldn't focus on anything when Reagan stepped onstage in her formal uniform. She hadn't ever seen her in anything other than camouflage, which was hot, but this... this was a lot fancier. And so much sexier.

What was it about a woman in uniform—okay, this woman in uniform—that set her blood boiling with need? Reagan's hair was up as it always was in uniform, except for a few intentional strands curled around her face. That formal jacket had too many medals than seemed like they could squeeze on the front. Everything about her called to something deep in Sydney, including the confidence she exuded standing there, and Sydney crossed her legs tighter and willed the throbbing to stop. This was ridiculous.

Even after Reagan stepped down, Sydney couldn't focus. She had no idea what Reagan's speech had been about. Kimberly asked her something, and she just smiled and nodded. The rest of the program vanished in a blur of Sydney's spiraling, incoherent thoughts.

When the formal program finally came to an end, Sydney jumped up and went to the restroom. She wanted to splash cool water on her face, but that would destroy her makeup, so she looked in the mirror and focused on breathing. After a few minutes of slow and mindful breaths, she felt like her heartbeat had finally returned to normal.

She decided to grab one more drink and chat with her colleagues and Kimberly and then call it a night. The event went on for a couple more hours, but there was no way she could handle staying there for that long. She could do fifteen or maybe twenty minutes more, max.

She got in line to grab a drink and pulled out her phone to see if any important work emails had come in during her near meltdown earlier. "For someone vehemently opposed to the Army, I'm a little surprised to see you at a ball celebrating its birthday," a voice whispered in her ear.

She spun around and found herself face-to-face with Reagan, who was standing closer than expected. "Oh, hi," she finally managed, despite her mouth feeling as though she'd shoved it full of cotton balls. "And I'm not vehemently opposed. I just don't think it, as an institution, can be trusted," she said weakly.

"That's very different indeed." Reagan's smile grew as she leaned back and took Sydney's dress in. "I like this dress. A lot."

She swallowed hard and wished Reagan had let her get her drink before ambushing her. And to think, she'd been the one who didn't want to blindside Reagan. "You don't look bad yourself." She couldn't help herself and ran a finger across the rows of tiny medals on Reagan's left breast. "This is impressive."

Reagan went a little red and looked away. "They're nothing. Uh, anyway, what *are* you doing here."

"A client insisted that I come. This is one of her hotels. I did all the legal when she bought it and fought a contractor who tried to dick her over on the renovation."

"Makes sense. I can't imagine you choosing to come to an Army ball on your own." Reagan tilted her chin toward the bartender waiting for her. "You're up."

Sydney ordered another glass of red wine and turned to Reagan. "At least let me buy you a drink. What're you having?"

Once Reagan had her bourbon, she placed a light hand on Sydney's lower back and gestured for her to move to the side of the room. Sydney knew she should go back to her people, but faced with Reagan, she couldn't walk away.

"Your presentation was great," she said.

"Really? I think you're the only one who thought so. It was boring as hell."

"Uh, well…" *Caught.* "Okay, so maybe I didn't *exactly* listen to every word, but it seemed good. You looked confident up there. I was just a little distracted."

Reagan tilted her head to the left. "By what? Counting all the uniforms in the room?"

"Not exactly." She chewed her lip as she tried to come up with an evasion.

"Then what?"

Sydney took a long sip of wine. Fuck it. "How amazing you look in that uniform. I've never seen you in a uniform other than your camouflage-y one. But this is…" She pointed up and down Reagan's body. "Fucking hot."

Reagan's eyes went wide, and her jaw slackened. "Oh…wow. Uh."

Sydney shook her head and mumbled, "Sorry. Shit. I just couldn't figure out what else to say so I told the truth. But you look amazing, and I'm not sorry to have noticed." She boldly made eye contact. Perhaps with more bravado than she should have.

"Where's your girlfriend tonight?" Reagan said.

"I broke up with her a few weeks ago."

"Good. She was kind of horrible," Reagan said, a slow smile spreading across her lips.

"She was. I should've done it sooner."

They stared at each other for what felt like an eternity, not even breaking eye contact as they both sipped their drinks. "Let's dance," Reagan finally said.

That seemed like a bad idea, given the weird bubble they were in. "Don't you want to finish your drink?"

Reagan lifted her glass and shook it. The ice clinked together, but there was no liquid. Sydney looked into her own glass. One sip left, so she drained it.

This was not a good idea. "Sure."

The Army band was playing a rendition of Elvis's "Can't Help Falling in Love." No one was singing, but the song just contributed to the bad decisions being made in that moment.

Reagan placed her hand chastely on Sydney's lower back, which was covered by her dress and pulled her close. Although Sydney's heels were slightly higher than Reagan's, Reagan was still taller, and Sydney eventually settled with her head resting on Reagan's shoulder.

"Have we ever done this before?" Reagan whispered.

Sydney leaned to look at her. "What? Pretended like we aren't attracted to each other around a thousand soldiers? Absolutely, yes. Well, maybe not this many," Sydney said, thinking of Reagan's promotion ceremony back in Naples.

Reagan chuckled. "Definitely a lot fewer back then. But I mean this." She pressed her hand harder into Sydney's back and jiggled the hand she was holding. "Dancing."

"Ah. No, I don't think so. At least not like this." She leaned back into Reagan's chest and said more softly, "I like it, though."

"Me too," Reagan sighed.

"I think you're the most romantic person I know, Reagan." She felt Reagan pull back a little bit, so she lifted her head again.

"What do you mean?"

"I just mean, since the minute we met, you've orchestrated all these crazy romantic moments. Our getaway to le Cinque Terre, for example, and that picnic on the beach the first night we saw each other in Monterey. I mean, you couldn't have planned this moment out to be more romantic than it is. Well, maybe if there were fewer people around, but still..."

Reagan looked around. "Huh," she said. "Let's get out of here for a sec. Maybe some fresh air? Do you want to go for a walk?"

That wasn't what Sydney was expecting. "Sure?"

Reagan stepped away and released her hold on Sydney's back, but rather than releasing her hand, she interlaced their fingers as she led her toward an exit. When they were in the hall and had made two corners heading away from the ballroom, Reagan said, "Sorry, it was a little hot in there, wasn't it?" She ran her finger inside the collar of her pleated white shirt and neck tab.

"It was." Sydney saw a small bead of sweat rolling from the base of Reagan's updo, so she wiped it away with her index finger.

"Thank you," Reagan whispered. "I..." She closed her eyes and dropped her forehead to Sydney's. Sydney's eyes slid closed too. "I don't know what I'm doing here, but I need to kiss you. Is that okay?"

Sydney nodded but didn't open her eyes even as she felt Reagan's lips slide across her own. She dug her fingers into Reagan's hips and pulled her flush against her, then stepped backward until she was pinned between Reagan's body and the wall. Reagan groaned and deepened their kiss.

Sydney thought the pressure of Reagan's hips was about the only thing keeping her upright as Reagan's tongue danced along hers. Sydney's hips tilted upward, searching for friction. Reagan slotted her thigh between Sydney's legs, but it wasn't enough.

Reagan tore her mouth away, and Sydney blinked her eyes open, trying to focus on Reagan despite the bright hotel light blinding them. "Fuck," Reagan whispered and looked up and down the hallway. "Anyone can see us. Although being gay isn't illegal anymore, dry humping in a public hallway is arguably conduct unbecoming an officer."

She took a step back, and Sydney's body cried for her return, but she swallowed it before it could come out. Reagan took a step to the left and tried a door handle. The door swung open into a tiny linen closet. Reagan tilted her head and shrugged.

Without words, Sydney grabbed her hand and pulled her into the room, slamming the door closed behind them. She pushed Reagan against it in a smooth motion as she sought Reagan's mouth with her own once again. Her fingers fumbled with the little chain holding the fronts of Reagan's jacket together, but she couldn't figure out how it worked. "What the fuck?" she mumbled.

"Mess dress is bullshit," Reagan said as she pushed Sydney's fingers out of the way and unclasped the little bastard on her own. She also undid her cummerbund, allowing it to fall to the floor.

Sydney untucked her shirt and slid her hands up Reagan's torso until she found her breast.

"Fuck," Reagan moaned.

"Ssh. We aren't in the hall, but we still don't want someone to hear us." Sydney had less to lose than Reagan did, but she didn't want photos of them to surface somewhere.

"Sorry," Reagan said as she slid her hand down Sydney's hip and thigh until she found the slit in Sydney's dress, and her curious fingers started their journey back up, taking her dress with them. When

Reagan's fingers grazed Sydney's sex through her underwear, it was her turn to groan, and she tried to bite it back. Reagan seemed to sense her inability to do so and kissed her, swallowing it.

Sydney pinched Reagan's nipple through her bra before pulling the cup down so she could feel her skin but lost what she was doing when Reagan pushed her underwear aside and ran a finger from her soaked hole up to the top of her clit and back. "Oh my God," she breathed.

Reagan wasn't done though and traced that path a few more times before saying, "Can I go inside?"

Sydney laughed. "Are you kidding? Please. Anything you want."

Those seemed to be the right words as Reagan reversed their positions and slid one of her long, perfect fingers into her. Sydney bit the back of her own hand to hold in the cry that she so desperately wanted to loose.

Reagan planted a trail of kisses along her neck from below her ear to the top of her dress that was too tight for Reagan to pull down, but Reagan's fingers continued to slide in and out. When her thumb found the top of Sydney's clit and made slow circles in time with her hips, the telltale tingling started in her fingers and toes, quickly drawing inward until they shattered in her chest and broke her into ten thousand pieces. Reagan kissed her again, absorbing her cry as her orgasm ripped through her.

"Fuck," she whispered.

"I think I already did that," Reagan said and laughed.

Sydney couldn't stop her own laugh, even as Reagan's fingers were still deep within her, and that small motion and the contractions of her inner muscles sent another tiny orgasm jolting through her.

After a few breaths, Sydney tried to find the top of the slit in Reagan's long skirt. But she pulled out of reach.

"Please don't pull away," Sydney pleaded. "I need to touch you."

"I can't here," she said.

"Please." Sydney was desperate with the need to feel her.

Reagan pressed her lips together and Sydney watched her chest rise and fall. "I have a room. Will you come up with me?"

"There's nowhere else I want to be. Tonight. Other than with you." Sydney's chest felt tight. There was nowhere else she ever wanted to be other than with Reagan, but she'd added the additional words to make her seem less desperate. Less infatuated.

Reagan tucked her shirt in and put her cummerbund back on, straightened her jacket before she attached that little chain holding her jacket closed. "How do I look?"

Sydney swiped at a little lipstick smeared below her lip. "Perfect. Me?"

"Well you have an, 'I've just been thoroughly fucked in a linen closet' look to you, but I don't know what we can do about that."

"What? I can't see someone I know looking like I've just been fucked." Sydney adjusted the top of her dress and shook out the skirt.

Reagan lightly kissed her. "I'm just kidding. You're fine. Your hair is a little messy, but just come back to my room, and no one will ever know." She smiled wolfishly as she opened the door.

They rode the elevator in silence, but after the doors slid open, a need bubbled in Sydney. "Do you ever feel like you need to twirl?"

Reagan laughed. "I've never felt that need, but I know you do." She bowed to Sydney and took her fingers overhead. "Madame," she said with a fake British accent, and Sydney twirled the whole way down the hall until they got to Reagan's door.

She collapsed into Reagan's chest, dizzy, and laughed. Reagan wrapped an arm around her waist and walked them into the room together.

❖

Reagan awoke with a head on her shoulder, limbs wrapped around her. When she first blinked, she didn't realize that anything was amiss. Everything just felt...right. But that feeling of rightness had her eyes widening—it had been a long time since anything felt this right—and looking to the side to see whose head was on her shoulder.

Oh right. Sydney. Last night had been fucking fantastic. But where did that leave them this morning? She couldn't *date* Sydney for the next few months until she left and then say good-bye again. She just couldn't do it. *Fuck.*

She gently disentangled herself from Sydney and slid off the side of the bed, padding naked across the room until she grabbed a robe out of the wardrobe. She pulled the other robe off its hanger and laid it across the bed for Sydney. The last thing she needed was Sydney walking naked into the living area.

She used the bathroom and brushed her teeth, then set herself to making a pot of coffee. Colonel Washington had hooked her up with a nice suite because his wife owned the hotel, and Reagan wondered if the wife was Sydney's client. She assumed she had to be. Such a weirdly small world. She'd meant to track him down the night before and thank him and his wife but had gotten distracted.

As much as she wanted to regret the previous night, she couldn't. It felt inevitable that they'd fall into bed again.

Reagan jumped when a warm torso pressed against her back through the robe, and arms wrapped against her midsection. "Good morning," Sydney whispered into her neck, and Reagan's stomach clenched as Sydney traced her thumb up and down Reagan's torso through the silky robe.

She turned so she could wrap her arms around Sydney and greet her properly. "Good morning." They kissed. And kissed. And kissed. Until Reagan wanted to pick her up and carry her back into the bedroom but forced herself to pull back. "How'd you sleep?"

"Fine. I probably would have gotten a better night's sleep if *someone* hadn't woken me up twice with her fingers and then her head between my legs." Sydney smirked.

"Fair, though I would've slept better if you hadn't woken me up that one time sliding your clit back and forth across my thigh while you slid your fingers into me from behind." Reagan felt hot, and her clit twitched just thinking about that.

"Hmm. I guess we both could have allowed the other more continuous sleep, but I don't regret a second. Do you?"

"No. And I'd love to have you right here on this tiny table, but I think we should talk."

Sydney's rosy cheeks went a little pale. Reagan wanted to say it wasn't bad, but it wasn't going to be good. Not really. Or maybe Sydney would think it was. She wasn't sure.

"Okay," Sydney said slowly, drawing out the word.

"Do you want coffee?"

Sydney nodded, so she poured them both coffee from the small pot and dumped powdered creamer and sugar in, wishing she'd had the foresight to bring tea.

"Sorry, I'm sure it's not up to standards, but it's the best I can do in the moment." She handed Sydney the mug and ran her thumb over Sydney's fingers as she took it.

"I'm sure it's fine. I can deal with non-bougie coffee on occasion."

They settled on the small couch. Reagan took a deep breath and went for it. "What did last night mean to you?"

"What…what do you mean?"

"Well, we fucked in a linen closet and had a lot of sex in my hotel room. What did it mean to you?" Reagan hardened herself against the words she was going to say next and told her heart to shut the hell up. "Even though you were at the Army ball last night, you still don't trust the military, right? Because of your dad and everything surrounding his death?"

"Correct."

"And you're still committed to staying in DC for work, and you can't work from anywhere else?"

"Correct," she said, her voice a little quieter.

Reagan forced herself to keep pushing, even though she felt sick to her stomach. "And you still aren't willing to consider trying something long distance in the short term until I'm back in DC?" It seemed asinine to be so shortsighted, and Reagan had to push down her anger because she truly didn't understand.

Sydney hesitated. Really hesitated. Rolled her lips in and inhaled, her nostrils flaring. "If you made it back to DC, that would be short term too though, right? Because you'd be moving on in a year or two?"

"Possibly." Reagan sighed. "Probably."

Sydney deflated. "I used to be afraid of long distance, but I would do it for you. But without a long-term idea of how we could be together, I just don't see a world in which that works."

Reagan stood and matter-of-factly said, "Okay, well that's that. We clearly have no future beyond my stint in DC. I can't—I won't— beg you to love me again, to be willing to work with me and figure out a way since you're unwilling to do so. Even though I could maybe figure something out." She hated projecting this nonchalance as though none of this mattered.

"I don't want you to sacrifice your dreams just to be with me. You've been pursuing this since childhood. I won't stand between you and that dream." Sydney's eyes looked bigger than normal as they filled, though no tears fell.

"That's neither here nor there," Reagan said. She knew it wasn't necessarily an either-or issue, but she wasn't willing to fight about it. She hoped that her new plan wouldn't backfire. It couldn't make her feel any worse than she currently felt, could it?

Sydney's shoulders had drooped. "Do you want me to leave?" she said without looking up.

"That would be easier," Reagan said. "But it's not what I want. Do you want to leave?"

She looked up again. "No."

"Good. The way I see it, there's still something combustible here." She pointed back and forth between them. "I'm available, and so are you, now, right?"

Sydney nodded.

"So we can keep fighting it. We can avoid each other like I've been avoiding you. Or we can lean into the fucking skid. The sex is fantastic. Let's let it run its course with the knowledge that it has an expiration date later this year no matter what." Reagan knew she was playing with fire, and it wasn't a good idea for her heart, but she was so tired of fighting it. She no longer had the strength to.

"You're really okay with that?" Sydney said, her voice tentative.

"Okay is relative." Reagan prayed she'd be okay with it. "But it seems like the best choice given the hand we've been dealt. Do you agree?"

Sydney's face looked sad, but she said, "Yeah, I guess so."

Reagan didn't know what Sydney's reservations could be, given the facts she'd laid out, but it wasn't like this was what Reagan wanted. She really wanted Sydney to be willing to take a chance on them, but since Sydney had shown time and time again that she wasn't, this seemed all she could do.

CHAPTER TWENTY-SIX

Reagan arrived at Sydney's brownstone at seven on the dot, looking good enough to eat in her uniform but with a bag of Chinese carryout to actually eat. It had been three days since the ball, and Reagan had texted earlier asking if she wanted to get together. Sydney had been horny since they'd parted on Sunday, and no number of self-delivered orgasms had taken the edge off, so she'd readily agreed.

But faced with food that smelled amazing versus Reagan, Sydney had an internal war about what she wanted first. "Come on in," she said as her stomach let out a loud grumble. That settled it, she supposed.

Reagan laughed. "Glad I brought dinner."

"Me too. Come on. Let me get this unpacked in the kitchen, and we can make plates." She set the paper bag on her gray granite counter and started pulling out container after container. "How many people did you think you were feeding, Reagan? You have enough for the whole block."

Reagan shrugged. "I know what you used to like, but I don't know if your tastes have changed, so I got a sampling."

The spicy, greasy smell had Sydney's stomach growling even more. She didn't take the time to pull out plates and opened a waxy bag, pulled out an egg roll, and took a huge bite. "Oh my God, this is so good," she managed.

Reagan snickered. "It's not going anywhere, you know. You don't need to eat like a vacuum." She opened a container of some type of sauce. "Here, try it with this."

Sydney felt a little embarrassed, but she was starving, so she dipped and took a smaller bite. The sauce, however, felt the need to escape, and as she was closing her teeth, she felt a drop hit her chin. She reached to wipe it off, but Reagan said, "Let me."

She leaned in and kissed just below Sydney's lip, her tongue flicking along Sydney's skin. "Yum," she said, her eyes hooded.

Sydney's need surged, and she knew that the food was going to get cold. She dipped the egg roll into the sauce again and held it for Reagan to take the last bite. As soon as she swallowed, she said, "Well, I've had enough to hold me over for a while. Do you need something?"

"Just you," Reagan said and pulled her in and kissed her like she hadn't seen her in months. She slid the food down the counter and lifted Sydney onto it without breaking their kiss.

Before Sydney had a chance to react, Reagan had her skirt pushed up to her hips and was pulling her panties off as she dropped to her knees. "Is this okay?" Reagan asked.

"Yes," Sydney said as she grabbed the shelf behind her for support as Reagan's tongue found her center. "Yes, right there," she heard herself say as Reagan slid two fingers into her.

Sydney wrapped her legs around Reagan's shoulders and encouraged her forward, but it only took a few breaths before she was crying Reagan's name.

Sydney worried she might slide off the counter before she recovered, but strong arms wrapped around her and cradled her, and she was lifted off the counter. "Where's your bedroom?" Reagan asked.

"Upstairs," she said and pressed her mouth to Reagan's neck, incredibly turned on at the idea that Reagan could lift her and carry her up the stairs.

Reagan set her on the bed and took a step back. She grabbed the zipper pull on her blouse and pulled it down, flicking open the Velcro pieces as she went.

"What's that uniform called again? I keep thinking of it as your camouflage, but I know that's not its name," Sydney said, wanting to call it the right thing in her head if she was going to be seeing Reagan in—and out of—it more often.

"OCP. Operational Camouflage Pattern. So it does at least have the word camouflage in it." Reagan slipped the blouse off and then pulled her beige T-shirt over her head before undoing her belt and the button fly of her pants.

"I want to help you, but honestly, it's been so long since I've taken a uniform off you, I'd probably slow you down."

"You probably would," Reagan said as she bent at the waist, pulled her pants out of those elastic band things that kept them looking fluffy at the bottom and untied her boots, sliding her feet out and walking out of her pants before Sydney realized what was happening. When Reagan stood again, her uniform was pooled on the ground, and she was in just her underwear. "I thought you might have used that opportunity to remove your own clothes."

"You don't want to take them off me?" Sydney said, teasing a little, but she'd also been enjoying watching Reagan strip.

"Not that I don't want to, but for expediency's sake…" She trailed off as she stepped closer and slid Sydney's suit jacket off her shoulders and down her arms. "But this is fine too," she said and lifted Sydney's blouse up and over her head.

Sydney pulled Reagan's mouth down to hers as she undid Reagan's bra. She palmed one breast and ran her hand back and forth until the nipple hardened beneath her touch. She scooted up the bed and pulled Reagan with her, desperate to feel skin against skin, but before Reagan had a chance to settle on top, Sydney rolled them over and straddled Reagan's waist.

"I love you like this," Reagan said. "Urgent with need, sliding your heat back and forth across my stomach. Fuck, it's hot." She released Sydney's bra and lifted each breast as though checking their weight.

"I love it too, but what I want more than this is to taste you. I've been dreaming of it each time I've played with myself since Sunday." Sydney unzipped the skirt that had been bunched around her hips since the kitchen, but rather than pulling it down and breaking contact with Reagan, she pulled it over her head and tossed it to the floor.

Sydney leaned down and grazed her breasts back and forth across Reagan's, allowing their nipples to brush several times before pushing lower and relearning everything about Reagan with her mouth.

Seven hours and several orgasms later, Sydney lay with her head on Reagan's chest, Reagan's fingertips tracing a path up and down her back.

"I should probably head out," Reagan said.

"What? You aren't going to stay?" Sydney felt hollow all of a sudden, and she didn't want to admit why.

"No. We aren't dating. It's just fun, and I think that's what happens after fun sex. I go home, you know?" She started to slide out, so Sydney sat up.

"Yeah, that makes sense." Sydney wasn't sure why she'd been envisioning Reagan staying the whole night, but it really did make sense. They weren't dating. This was all they were. Sex. She walked Reagan to the door and said, "See you soon?" An unfamiliar whine of neediness in her voice surprised her, and she chastised herself.

"Yeah."

"How about Friday night? I should be out of the office by four thirty. I can order pizza if you want to come over."

"Sure. See you Friday." Reagan gave her a kiss that curled her toes and then walked away.

Sydney clutched the front of her robe, squeezing the front panels together as she watched Reagan's taxi pull away from the curb. *So this is what a booty call felt like.*

This was still what she wanted.

Wasn't it?

Over the next two months, she and Reagan slipped into a loose pattern of getting together a few nights a week based on their schedules. Sometimes, Sydney had to reschedule due to work or court obligations, but the beauty of their non-relationship was that there were no hard feelings. Reagan was never hurt when Sydney had to cancel and vice versa. Yet, that looming deadline for Reagan's imminent departure was getting closer and closer. They were down to less than a month, and Reagan was negotiating a contract to sell her house.

Sydney was fine with that. Of course she was fine with that. They weren't dating. This was what she'd agreed to. Just because they met at the cowboy place for coffee every morning and spent several nights together every week didn't mean anything. And they never spent the *full* night. One of them always left and went home before they fell asleep.

Tonight, Reagan was coming to her place again. She was actually cooking dinner. Not that it was anything fantastic, but she'd bought some French bread to make cheesy garlic bread and some cheese tortellini that cooked in two minutes.

She had just put the pot on to boil when her phone rang. "Hey, Mom," she said after swiping to answer and tapping the speaker button. "What's new?"

"Same old, same old. Charlie and I are thinking about getting a puppy."

"Oh my gosh, that would be amazing. I'd love to have a little fur baby brother or sister. What are you thinking about?" Sydney turned on the oven to warm the bread that she'd already slathered with garlic butter and cheese.

"A rescue of some sort. I have my eye on this little pittie, Cardigan. She has such sweet eyes in the photos, it breaks my heart. We're going to meet her tomorrow."

"Text me a photo. I love her already."

"I will when we hang up. You'll get to meet her soon if you're still planning to come up here in a few weeks?"

Sydney had planned that trip as a way to distract herself shortly after Reagan left. She could admit she was going to miss her...as a friend.

"Yeah. I bought my tickets. Are you sure you don't want me to stay in a hotel? With Charlie and a new puppy and everything, it seems like a lot."

"You will absolutely not stay in a hotel. We have plenty of room," Mom said with a definitiveness that made Sydney chuckle. "And anyway, I think you're going to need a little mothering. Are you still just hanging out with Reagan?"

Sydney had surprised herself when she'd told her Mom about Reagan coming back into her life out of the blue again. She certainly didn't tell her they were casually fucking a few days a week, but her mom probably had already made that assumption. "Yeah, we're having dinner together tonight. I'm cooking right now."

Her mom sighed heavily. "I'm worried about you."

"I'm fine, Mom. I know what I'm doing. And we're down to a few weeks before she leaves again." Sydney wasn't actually sure she knew what she was doing, but to not dwell on Reagan's approaching departure, she started aggressively wiping the breadcrumbs off the counter. Had some gotten under the microwave? She lifted it up to check. It certainly seemed that they had, the little bastards.

"And how are you feeling about that?" her mom asked when Sydney didn't offer up anything more.

"I…" She weighed how much she wanted to say. "I'm going to be fine. I knew this was coming. It's what we want. Our lives aren't compatible." She wanted to share the dread that grew larger every day that passed, but she was afraid saying the words out loud would make them too real. And she didn't want her mom to worry.

"I don't know if that's entirely true, but you're an adult and can tell yourself the story you want. Now this is the fourth time you've reconnected, right? After Italy, California, and Germany?"

Sydney sighed. "Yeah. I think this might really be it. I just have a feeling that this is our last hurrah, you know?" The thought of never seeing Reagan tightened her throat, but there just wasn't another choice. "But, wait. Are you softening your stance against the military?"

"I don't love that Reagan is in the Army, but you're a grown woman now who is secure in life. And I know she's a good person. I don't know if she's your soulmate or not, but having seen you two together, have you ever considered that maybe this *is* your time? You're financially stable. You have no one tying you to DC. Noah is in Europe. We still all visit each other."

"But I *am* tied here. I like being only an hour flight from you. And my work is in DC. Without work, I have no stability."

"I know I instilled a strong work ethic and the value of financial security, but if work is your entire life, you need to rethink your priorities. But I'm going to get off my soapbox. I'll let you stew on all of this on your own. I just wanted to check in on your trip. But I should go because Charlie just got home, and we're going to go to dinner."

"Perfect timing. Reagan is almost here anyway. See you in a few weeks!"

"Love you," her mom said and hung up.

If Sydney's fingers shook a little as she placed the phone down, it was probably because she was nervous at messing something up cooking. Not at the thought of Reagan being gone soon.

Reagan walked in when she arrived as they'd taken to doing: sending a five-minute text and no need to knock. Sydney wasn't even sure when that had become a thing exactly, but it worked out well because she was pouring the tortellini into the pot as Reagan walked in. "In the kitchen," Sydney yelled when she heard the door close.

Reagan came in, grabbed her hips, and lightly bit her exposed shoulder. Warmth flooded Sydney's midsection. "Smells amazing," she finally said as she released her and stepped back.

Sydney hated how badly she'd wanted Reagan to wrap her arms around her and press kisses to the back of her neck. "Thanks." Sydney laughed, trying to divert her attention from wanting something she couldn't have unless she could figure out how to make major changes she didn't know if she was capable of. "I was going to make brussels sprouts in the air fryer, but I haven't figured that contraption out yet, and I thought there was too much chance I'd burn the house down, and I have *plans* for this evening that don't involve a firefighter."

"A sexy firefighter, short hair, maybe a smoke smudge on her cheek, could be fun though, right?" Reagan said and winked.

Sydney wanted to throw up at the jolt of jealousy that raced through her. "Ooo la la," she said to cover it up and quickly turned back to the pot to stir the tortellini that didn't need stirring. Getting the strainer from the drawer into the sink was the next task to keep from looking at Reagan. *Fuck.* "So how was your day? Stave off any nuclear wars?"

"No nuclear winter prevention. My day was…stressful but not because of work. Do you mind if I pour a glass of this?" She lifted the bottle of wine Sydney had breathing on the counter.

"Of course. Pour me one too?"

Reagan poured, and Sydney drained the pasta and plated their food. As they settled at the table, she said, "So what made your day stressful?"

"I got an offer that was fifteen percent over asking on my townhouse. Cash and no financing, appraisal, or inspection contingency." She took a bite of the tortellini and groaned, and Sydney had to suppress her own groan at the sound.

"Isn't that a good thing?" she stammered.

"This is delightful, by the way, and yes, it's fantastic, other than me then becoming homeless three weeks before my actual PCS date. They want to close next week. I could live in a hotel, but that feels so…I don't know, cold? A sad way to spend my last few weeks in DC."

"Oh." Sydney took a bite to give herself a moment to think. It was a terrible idea, but she wanted to spend every second she could with Reagan. "Why don't you stay here? I have the room, obviously."

Reagan's brows rose, and her cheeks went an adorable pink. "You wouldn't mind? I really don't want to impose."

"Not an imposition at all. I'd love to have you. And we already spend a few evenings a week together anyway. It only makes sense." If Reagan hadn't been watching, Sydney would have given herself a pat on the back for her nonchalance.

"I guess it will just give us both an extra hour of sleep since "home" is down the hall, right?" Reagan laughed, and Sydney felt taken off guard and didn't like it. But of course, Reagan would expect them to sleep in different rooms. Why wouldn't they? The real question was, why was Sydney so devastated by it?

Sydney knew she knew the answer but was too much of a coward to admit it to herself. She couldn't give the thought a patch of land to grow in. "Perfect, huh?"

❖

As Reagan stood at Sydney's kitchen counter, chopping an onion for the black bean tacos she was making for dinner, the premonition that this was the last chance she and Sydney had to make it work washed over her.

Her few remaining weeks living in Sydney's guest room had been speeding by with a double edge of pain and pleasure. She hated leaving Sydney's bed night after night, but it was like a death by a thousand paper cuts. But she *couldn't* sleep next to her. Not when she was softness and warmth and inviting and everything Reagan had never been able to replace. And not with their expiration date looming.

The end wasn't just coming. It was really already there. Tomorrow night—in just over twenty-eight hours—Reagan would be boarding a United flight to Munich—of course—and then on to Warsaw. And although it wasn't like she wasn't ever going to be in DC again, something in her told her this was it. Maybe it was the fact that Sydney *still* wouldn't even *consider* trying, even though they both were at points in their lives and careers when they could make it work. And it made her so incredibly sad.

She blamed the watering in her eyes on the onion.

The front door slammed, and Sydney yelled from the door, "Honey, I'm home," just like she used to do back in Monterey when times had been simpler. Reagan found it hard to swallow around her heart.

Sydney's heels clicked on the hardwood of the kitchen as she walked in. Her breath tickled Reagan's neck when she pressed a kiss to the sensitive spot right behind her ear. "Something smells good. Though, are you sure you don't want to go out to dinner for your last night in the States?"

"Positive. I'm going to be eating out all the time for the next few weeks until I'm settled in a house in Warsaw." She finished the onion and turned to Sydney. Damn, she looked amazing in that dark pantsuit. Powerful and sexy and confident, especially with the red button-up shirt that showed just a hint of cleavage. Reagan fought the urge to unbutton just one more button. She sniffed. "I'm going to miss seeing you in a suit every day."

"Oh my God, are you crying?" Sydney swiped at a tear making its way down her cheek. "What's wrong?"

"No, no, I'm not crying," Reagan lied. "It's the onion." She pointed with the chef's knife. "It made my eyes burn." She sniffed again.

"If you're sure." Sydney stared, and Reagan wondered if she was seeing through the bullshit but waited her out. "I'm going to go slip into something more comfortable."

That was a real shame. Reagan could stare at her for hours in that suit but understood changing. She'd taken off her uniform as soon as she'd gotten home, exchanging it for leggings and an oversized sweatshirt and taken her hair out of its tight bun, swapping it for a loose ponytail.

While Sydney changed, Reagan cooked the onion and garlic before adding in the beans and seasonings and did the rest of the taco prep. She was just plating three tacos for each of them, along with rice and beans, when Sydney came back looking much more comfortable in her own leggings and long-sleeved T-shirt.

"I don't know why you keep your air-conditioning set so low. We wouldn't have to bundle up inside in September if you set the thermostat to a reasonable seventy-one or seventy-two," Reagan said as she carried their plates to the table. Sydney grabbed the bottle of wine Reagan had breathing and brought it, along with the glasses she'd set out.

"I don't like to be hot. And I like to bundle up." She shrugged and smiled and poured. "How was your promotion ceremony yesterday? You were out awfully late. I didn't even hear you come in. How'd it feel getting called lieutenant colonel all day?"

Reagan had wanted to ask Sydney to come and pin her, but it would have been weird to have her fuck buddy do it since her dad and Jasper had flown in for the occasion. "It was good. Though Jasper punched me really hard in the chest when he put the new rank on. I think I'm going to have a bruise." She rubbed at the spot between her breasts.

"I can kiss it for you later and make it better." Sydney's voice was sultry, and Reagan wanted to forget dinner and drag her to the bedroom and make love to her all night.

No, not make love. Have sex. Fuck. "I might take you up on that," she said instead.

"Such brutes, though I guess that's the military, huh?" Sydney laughed, but Reagan felt a little sick.

"Brutes? We aren't *brutes*. Or mindless savages." She could hear the frustration in her voice, and Sydney's face fell. Reagan tried to release a little of the anger. "I think you've always had this vision of my profession as a bunch of gung ho commandos, but that couldn't be further from the truth. I have a master's degree in defense analysis and speak multiple languages. I was the assistant defense attaché at the US embassy in Lithuania for two years. My entire career revolves around *avoiding* conflict through diplomatic means and maintaining friendly relations with local military counterparts. I network with high-ranking military and senior civilian officials for most countries in Europe. I was in the wedding party of the deputy prime minister of Liechtenstein when she married a few years ago. I'm about to go be the deputy chief of the Office of Defense Cooperation. Embassies are quite civilized. My job is probably *as* civilized as—I would actually venture to say *more* civilized than—yours."

Sydney let out a nervous giggle. "I'm sorry, I was just joking around. I don't know how I envision your job, but I'll admit, that wasn't it. It all sounds impressive. And movies always make working in an embassy seem glamorous."

Reagan didn't want to ruin their last night together, but Sydney was just so frustrating with her biases. She took a deep breath and said, "I didn't mean to snap at you. I'm sorry. You've just always had this negative opinion of everything associated with the military because of your dad, but I've never understood how to show you that the military isn't all bad. We do a lot of good work, a lot of humanitarian work in places all around the world. I will always be angry about what happened to your family, but your hatred of us as a whole just doesn't make any sense."

Sydney set down her fork. "I don't hate you, but the system is flawed."

"Of course it is, but what system isn't? Are you trying to say you think our legal system *isn't* flawed? Our justice system *isn't* flawed? We have the highest incarceration rate in the world!" Reagan flung her arms out to the side as frustration bubbled out of her again.

"You're right, our justice system certainly isn't perfect."

"Then why do you assume the entire military is all bad?" Reagan paused and took a sip of her drink before she quietly said, "I don't gamble, I don't cheat, I don't lie. I don't know how to prove to you that I'm *not* like your dad. I would never hurt you the way he did. Never." She made eye contact with Sydney and refused to look away.

Sydney's voice cracked. "But you could still die. You could still leave. Mom only admitted it to me once, but she never stopped loving him, even when she hated him for what he did. The anger helped her deal with the loss, but losing him broke her in a way she never recovered from." Sydney exhaled so hard, Reagan could feel it from across the table, and tears built in Sydney's eyes. "What would I do if you died?"

"Don't you see I *am* leaving tomorrow? You're losing me anyway. And I could die, military or not. I could get hit by a car or have a heart attack or be, I don't know, abducted by aliens." Sydney laughed, but Reagan didn't know if she was going to laugh or cry. "You could die. But love is worth the risk." She couldn't believe she'd dropped the love word. She'd been fighting the feelings for months. Since she'd run into Sydney in the coffee shop, really. And long before that.

"I know you're not my dad. That you'd never intentionally hurt me."

"Would it help if I showed you my bank account, and you can see that there are no unexplainable withdrawals like there would be if I was gambling away my life?" It was a silly offer, but Reagan didn't know what else she could do to prove to Sydney that she was trustworthy.

Sydney sniffed. "I know you're not my dad. You've never done anything to make me think you were, but the distrust is so ingrained. It makes me afraid, and I don't know if I can trust my own judgment." She blinked, and a tear fell.

Reagan stood and grabbed her hand. "Let's leave the tacos for now." She settled them on the love seat and took Sydney's hands. "What would it take for you to be brave? To trust me? To trust in the power of us? I've never known anyone like you. What would it take for you to take the leap and fight for us?"

Sydney looked at their joined hands and said, "I don't know."

Reagan ticked one finger up. "What are the fears that have always held you back? One, that your work is here, and you can't go gallivanting around the world with me. Well, that's debunked. If covid showed us anything, it is that most work can be remote. At least sometimes. And being the managing partner of your DC office? I bet you could work remote most weeks and just come back occasionally."

She ticked her second finger up. "Two. That you need to be financially independent? Look around you. You *already are.* You probably have more accumulated wealth than your mom had in her entire life. And it's not like I'm asking you to quit your job. You could easily still work. And finally." She lifted her ring finger up to join the other two. "That I'm like your dad, and the military is going to screw you over? You already acknowledged that I'm not like your dad, and you know I would never hurt you, and all systems are flawed. It's not just the military. All I ask of you is to keep an open mind. Please."

Sydney continued looking at their joined hands without saying anything. Reagan ran her thumb along Sydney's jaw, and she finally looked up.

"Are you done with dinner?" Reagan asked.

Sydney nodded.

"I'll give you space and go clean up."

A nod again. Still no words. Probably not a good sign, but Reagan hoped she was really thinking. She hadn't meant to lay herself bare again. She thought they'd have sex and go to sleep, and she'd leave tomorrow, and that would be that, but as the words started to tumble out, Reagan knew she'd made the right decision. She would have always regretted it if she hadn't.

CHAPTER TWENTY-SEVEN

Sydney grabbed her half-full glass of wine from the table and yelled to Reagan in the kitchen, "I need a little fresh air. I'm going up on the roof patio for a bit."

She heard a muffled, "Okay," on her way up the stairs.

To say she was reeling would be a complete understatement. She'd been struggling with Reagan's impending departure for weeks, but she knew she had to let her go. She couldn't tell Reagan she wished they could be more when she knew she couldn't do it.

But Reagan had decided to shoot down all of her excuses like a sniper, not a diplomat. She'd never even considered the option of working remote, but it was true. Her entire office worked from home for a year and a half after covid had hit, and they did just fine. But would her boss let her? Would she want to?

Her entire identity revolved around being a corporate lawyer, and a lot of that included networking to continue to generate new business. She couldn't do that if she was on the other side of the world. It wouldn't be possible. Yet she and Reagan had been separated by oceans and continents for the better part of a decade and a half, and none of the distance had dampened their need for one another even one iota. The second they saw each other again, they fell back into a comfortable friendship, with more heat than a hydrogen bomb.

Her thoughts battled in circles, and she lost track of time staring at the night sky. Watching the bolts of lightning and listening to the accompanying thunder was so mesmerizing that she jumped when Reagan leaned against the railing next to her.

"Sorry," she said softly. "I didn't mean to scare you."

"You didn't. I was just lost in my thoughts," Sydney said. Reagan looked so beautiful in the light shining from the streetlights below. Her face had lost the tightness, and Sydney wondered if she wasn't upset anymore. Had she resigned herself? Somehow made peace with... something?

The thunder continued all around them and was getting more intense. She knew they should go back inside before the skies opened up and loosed what looked to be a wild September thunderstorm, but she didn't want to. She wanted to hold on to this moment with her arm pressed against Reagan's, watching the lightning.

She could feel Reagan's eyes on her. "How are you f—"

But Sydney cut her off when she kissed her. She couldn't resist for another second. She didn't know what she could promise. Nothing in that moment, but she needed Reagan to know that she loved her. Even if she let Reagan walk away tomorrow, she had to show her. She needed Reagan to feel the emotions she was too afraid to say, so she channeled every bit of love into that kiss.

She didn't rush. She pressed their lips lightly together, and when it felt right, she opened her mouth and lightly grazed her teeth across Reagan's lower lip. When their tongues touched, Reagan groaned and dug her fingers into Sydney's hips, pulling her closer.

Sydney saw a bright light flash behind her eyelids with a gigantic boom of thunder right on its tail. The lightning was getting closer, but still, they kissed. Neither flinched at the thunder growing louder and louder, battling the thundering of Sydney's pulse.

She ran her fingers through Reagan's hair as she pulled her ponytail loose, and Reagan tilted her hips into Sydney, beginning to rock them.

A drop of rain landed on Sydney's forehead, and she pulled away to look at Reagan, but the unfiltered lust in Reagan's eyes pulled her back in. They kissed and kissed and slid their bodies back and forth, creating a little friction beneath their clothes.

Even when the rain started to come down in earnest, they kissed. Reagan spun Sydney so the railing pressed into her back as Reagan palmed her breast through her shirt and squeezed. She planted a trail of kisses along Sydney's jaw, down her neck, and back up again even as their clothes and bodies got soaked. Sydney had no idea how sexy kissing in the rain could be. It cooled her boiling skin and made her even hotter as she captured Reagan's mouth once again, but when the next clap of thunder shook the deck beneath their feet, both of them pulled back, breathing hard.

"We should probably go in before we get struck by lightning, right?" Reagan said.

"Yeah." She wanted to stay out there for hours but also wanted to live to see the next day, even with what that day was going to bring, so she reluctantly took Reagan's hand and pulled her back toward the sliding glass door. "But we should do this kissing in the rain thing again," she said without thought, realizing after she'd said the words that it might be impossible.

To distract her, as soon as she slid the door closed behind them, Sydney spun Reagan against the door and kissed her again. This time, she didn't start slow. She took Reagan's mouth as if it had always been hers and kissed her like it was the last time they'd ever kiss. Reagan was the one to break it, to bring Sydney back to reality. It wasn't fair how beautiful she looked, even drenched. Her hair was flat, and water was dripping from it. She had droplets still all over her face.

"What would you say to a shower? As hot as kissing you is, between being soaked to the bone and your frigid AC, I'm a little chilly." As evidence, she lifted her arm, pulled her sleeve up, and showed Sydney the goose bumps that peppered the entire length.

"Oh God, I'm so sorry. Of course." Sydney moved quickly downstairs and into her bathroom where she started the water in the shower. When she turned, Reagan was standing there watching her, somehow already completely naked. "Wow," was all she could manage.

Reagan's nipples were hard, and she had apparently gotten waxed because where she normally had a perfectly manicured bush was now completely bare. A bead of moisture sat at the front of her labia, and Sydney's mouth went completely dry. "Did you do that for me?"

"I thought I'd try something new for our last night. Do...you like it?"

"I fucking love it," Sydney said as she closed the distance between them and ducked her head to take one of those tantalizing nipples between her lips. When Reagan's hips pushed into Sydney, she slid a finger between Reagan's thighs and found her hole, tracing around it a time or two before running up her drenched slit to her clit. "You are so wet. You feel amazing."

"You need to get these clothes off. Now," Reagan said as she stepped back. "And I want to watch."

Sydney thought about doing a little striptease, but that felt like it was going to take way too long so she quickly dispatched her clothes and moved back into Reagan's space. She went onto her tiptoes to rub her nipples back and forth across Reagan's. Goose bumps broke out along Sydney's arms again but not from the cold.

"Fuck," Reagan said, her voice quivering. She walked her backward to the water. "Watch out for the edge of the shower behind you."

Once under the rain showerhead, Reagan pressed against her despite the shower being quite large. She lathered up her hands and began to wash her, starting with her neck and shoulders. She massaged Sydney's back and arms, and Sydney thought she might melt into a puddle. She was pretty sure the moan she released when Reagan massaged her calves was louder than the moans she'd had while they'd been kissing.

"You are awfully vocal this evening, Sydney. Do you think I can make you scream my name tonight?"

"I kind of want to scream your name right now," Sydney said as she slumped back into the shower glass, her knees too weak to hold her body up without support.

"Hmm. I had no idea how much you liked having your calves massaged. I wish I would have known sooner." She found another really good spot with her thumbs, and Sydney groaned again. This time louder.

"Fuck, Sydney." Reagan stood and pressed her fully against the shower wall as she started touching Sydney in earnest. "I need you." Several of Reagan's fingers slid into her as she lightly massaged Sydney's clit with her thumb. Sydney's hips began to pump and thrust against her hand. She gasped for air as she did exactly what Reagan had asked for and screamed her name as she came.

While Sydney tried to catch her breath, too tired to do anything other than lean and breathe, Reagan quickly washed herself and turned off the water. "Let's get you into bed, hmm?"

Thankfully, she was starting to catch her breath, so they dried each other off with Sydney's fluffiest navy blue towels and tossed them on the floor.

Sydney pushed down on Reagan's shoulders when they got to the edge of the bed to encourage her to sit on the edge before dropping to her knees between Reagan's spread thighs, her pussy open to Sydney's blazing gaze. When Reagan ran her hand along Sydney's face, the caress felt loving. Her eyes radiated love as she bit her lip. Sydney watched her chest rise and fall for two breaths before slowly, agonizingly slowly, taking Reagan's clit into her mouth.

Her sharp intake of breath turned into a groan as Sydney slid two, then three fingers into her. Reagan dropped back onto her elbows as Sydney slid her fingers in and out. Slowly at first, but she increased her pace as Reagan's hips started to move, encouraging her to go faster. She wanted to slow down and savor but decided they had as long as they wanted that evening since neither of them had to work in the morning. She let Reagan dictate the pace until she cried Sydney's name as her inner muscles clenched around Sydney's fingers, and her fingernails scratched along Sydney's head.

When Reagan's aftershocks slowed, Sydney pulled her face from between her thighs and took in the beautiful picture that was Reagan lounging back on her elbows, chest heaving, eyes hooded, cheeks flushed. She wouldn't have been able to stop herself from saying, "You are so fucking beautiful. The most beautiful person I've ever known. Inside and out," even if she tried.

Reagan's eyes widened. "Come here."

When Sydney leaned in, Reagan kissed her sweetly. So achingly sweet. Reagan sat up and pulled Sydney down until she was straddling Reagan's lap. "Right back at you by the way," Reagan said before deepening their kiss. Sydney started to move her hips, searching for something to provide a little pressure, and Reagan didn't make her wait. She ran her fingers up and down both sides of Sydney's clit until Sydney's head tipped back.

She wanted all the sensation, but she needed another couple of minutes before she'd be able to come again, and inspiration struck. "A few weeks ago, I ordered something online, but with supply chain issues, it got delayed until yesterday," she said quickly, a little embarrassed and unsure why.

"Oh?" Reagan said, her tone telling Sydney her curiosity was piqued.

"Yeah. Do you want to give it a try?" Again, that nervous, three-times-normal-speed delivery. Why was she so nervous? If there was anyone Sydney could trust with this, it was Reagan.

Reagan's fingers stilled, yet provided a little pressure along the sides of Sydney's clit. "Are you going to tell me what it is?"

Sydney's nervous laugh was cringey to her ears. "It's a double-headed dildo that you don't need a harness for."

"Oh?" Reagan said, turning one syllable into several.

"Yeah, one end is shaped a little more for, uh, holding, and the other end is shaped more for, uh, thrusting. What do you think? Want to give it a whirl?"

Reagan's free hand touched Sydney's wrist that she didn't even realize was at her throat. She hated that tell. "Why are you so nervous? It's not like we've never used a strap-on before. We did a bunch back in Monterey." Reagan's fingers started moving again but with the lightest pressure and the subtlest of movements.

"I'm not." When Reagan leveled an incredulous look at her, Sydney said, "Okay, I'm a little nervous. That was a long time ago. And we aren't the same as we were. And it's a different style. And I'm afraid it seems a little pathetic that I bought a new toy for us for your last night here. Ugh. I don't know." She dropped her head onto Reagan's shoulder, unable to look at her anymore, but Reagan guided her chin back up with her hand and smiled at her.

"Of course I want to try it with you. Do you want to give or receive?"

Sydney laughed and blurted, "Both. But maybe receive first. Then give? If you want?"

"Oh, I want. Do you want to grab it?"

Sydney climbed off Reagan's lap and padded naked into her closet and pulled out the box she'd hidden there earlier. She pulled the dildo out of the package, along with a bottle of lube, and went to the bathroom to wash it. Her breath was shaky as she caught her reflection. She could do this. She really wanted to do this. She just needed to settle herself.

When she walked back into the bedroom, Reagan had slid up the bed so her whole body was on it, and she was slowly caressing her own sex. Sydney lost her breath but managed to squeak, "Starting without me?"

"No way. Just trying to get myself ready."

Watching Reagan pleasure herself was certainly getting Sydney ready. "Ah," she said and remembered to squirt lube onto the end of the dildo that she was going to slide into Reagan. She worked it up and down the length as she walked across the bed on her knees.

She slid two fingers into Reagan first and then three to make sure she was ready, working them in and out a few times, but when Reagan's hips started to move, she withdrew and placed the head of the dildo against Reagan's opening. "Let me know if this doesn't feel good, okay?"

"I will. It's a little big, but I can tell it's going to feel amazing." Reagan tipped her hips up, and Sydney applied pressure until the tip started to slide in. She worked it back and forth slowly, turning it from side to side to make sure nothing was sticking.

Reagan apparently got tired of going slow and pushed her wrist, driving the dildo all the way in in one swoop. She laughed. "Slow is for sissies." She took the lube and squeezed some on the other end.

Sydney laughed too. "I didn't want to hurt you."

"You didn't. Now come here. I'm dying to come inside you." Her eyes darkened at the words, and Sydney immediately did as she asked. "Lie on your side."

"My side?" Sydney said, unfamiliar with most positions other than missionary and cowgirl.

"Yes. If you don't like it, we'll try something else."

Sydney lay on her side, and Reagan snuggled up behind her like they were going to spoon. Reagan lifted Sydney's top leg and draped it over her own legs, and Sydney felt weirdly exposed.

Reagan must have felt her tense. "Relax," she whispered as she planted kisses along Sydney's neck and upper back.

Sydney forced herself to relax. Reagan slid an arm under her and cupped her breast. Squeezed her nipple. Twisted. Sydney groaned at the press of the head of the dildo against her entrance. She could feel Reagan's hand behind her guiding it as she slowly started to press into her and began shallow thrusts.

Once the dildo was firmly seated, Reagan reached that hand around and began to rub light circles on Sydney's clit. "Oh God," she heard herself say as she began to move her hips too. "How do you feel this good?" she said.

"It's just us," Reagan said as she continued to pepper kisses all along her neck and upper back while slowly thrusting in and out. "I love the way you feel, I love the way you smell, I love the way you taste." As she said taste, she bit the top of Sydney's shoulder where it met her neck. Just a nibble, but it drove Sydney crazy, and she began to move her hips more purposefully.

Sydney cried out when Reagan slipped out of her. "What are you doing?" she said.

Without speaking, Reagan rolled Sydney onto her back, her hips on a pillow she hadn't even realized Reagan had put there, and quickly settled on top of her, spreading her legs with her knees. "Is this okay?" she whispered.

Sydney nodded, and Reagan slowly slid back into her. Reagan looked at her as she began to pump her hips with a deliberate slowness that Sydney thought might drive her mad but had her squirming with need within seconds. "Oh God," she gasped.

As her eyes started to drift closed, Reagan said, "Stay with me. Please?"

Sydney struggled but opened her eyes and tried to focus on Reagan, whose gaze nearly brought her to climax with its intensity. Sydney bit her lip in an effort to keep her eyes open when they desperately wanted to slide closed, but she didn't want to break the connection.

Sweat was beading on Reagan's forehead, and Sydney was pretty sure it was beading on her skin as well as Reagan maintained that excruciatingly slow pace but reached between them and began to massage her clit again.

Sydney's hips began to move faster, pushing Reagan to keep pace, which she finally relented and did. Thunder cracked in the background as Sydney bent her knees and braced her heels against the mattress for leverage.

The last thing she saw before her orgasm ripped through her and tore her into a thousand pieces was the love in Reagan's eyes as she cried out Sydney's name.

❖

When Reagan woke, it was still dark, illuminated only by a small stream of light from the moon. She tried to slide away from Sydney, hating the feeling of the lost connection. God, she fucking hated doing this. Her butt bumped into something firm, rubber, and she accidentally knocked the dildo off the bed.

The sound of it hitting the floor was apparently enough to wake Sydney. "Are you leaving?" she croaked.

"That's the agreement, right?" Reagan said, tears welling in her eyes. Her face was in shadow, so she hoped Sydney couldn't see. "We don't spend the night." She hoped with all of her heart that Sydney was thinking about her plea earlier.

Sydney sat up and tucked the sheets under her armpits, cleared her throat, rough with sleep. "Please...please don't leave."

Reagan's heart clenched, her throat tightened. Staying was dangerous, but the vulnerability on Sydney's face in the light of the moon caught her body in a vise. Without true thought, she climbed back into bed and pulled Sydney in as the little spoon. Sydney wiggled her hips until she found the exact right spot and sighed. "Okay," Reagan said, even though she knew this was only going to make tomorrow even harder, but she prayed that maybe this meant Sydney was thinking about the possibility of a future.

They came together twice more during the night. It seemed to Reagan that they both knew that this *could* be the last time they ever made love   she couldn't deny anymore that was what they'd done—so each time they found each other felt a little more frantic than the last. She hoped this wasn't the last time, but that was in Sydney's hands.

As Reagan started to wake up on Saturday morning, there was a surprising sensation between her legs. When she had enough awareness to lift her head, she realized blond hair was fanned across her stomach, and Sydney's face was buried between her thighs. Reagan dropped her head back on the pillow and slid her fingers into Sydney's hair as she enjoyed every second of her beautiful wake-up call.

They had an idyllic morning. Sydney cooked breakfast, and they lounged in robes, not talking about when Reagan had to leave for the airport, even though it was coming up in too few hours. However, after a midmorning *nap*, lunch, and an early afternoon *nap*, Reagan had to bring up the subject. "My car is going to be here around six, which is quickly approaching."

"Are you sure you don't want me to take you? It's no big deal." Sydney wrung her hands as she spoke. "I'm happy to."

Reagan laughed. "You don't even have a car."

"Well, no, but I have a driver on retainer who would take us out there and bring me home." She was chewing on the inside of her lower lip.

"My Lyft is already scheduled, and it'll be reimbursed by the government. I wouldn't be able to do that with your car service. Thank you, though."

Sydney's face fell as she said, "Right. Makes sense." Did she really just want to spend those few additional minutes out to Dulles together?

Reagan's heart hurt. As the witching hour got closer and closer, Reagan had one more thing she needed to say. "I told you I wasn't going to beg you again, but at risk of my pride, I feel like I need to say a few things."

Sydney nodded, and they both leaned back into their own corners of the love seat, but their feet met in the middle as they looked at the other.

"I swore to myself that I wasn't going to get emotionally invested this time. You've broken my heart multiple times, and yet, I convinced myself that I could stay strong, even while sleeping with you. But the problem is, my heart has never been free from you. And I'm in the same spot as before." She felt her eyes welling up and tried to swallow the tears.

Sydney grabbed her hand. Squeezed it.

"I'm not going to harp on the reasons that we could work. I've tried to make my case, and I hope you'll think about everything I said. Because I want to be with you." She squeezed Sydney's hand again as she made eye contact and emphasized every word. "I. Want. To. Be. With. You. But I can't keep living like this. I haven't ever let you go, even though I've convinced myself that I've tried. But this is it. I mean it. It has to be. I can't keep holding on to you when you're determined to push me away."

Reagan paused to gather her thoughts and see if Sydney wanted to say anything, but she was just looking at Reagan with silent tears tracking down her face, pale except for the red blotchiness in her cheeks.

The tightness in Reagan's chest was almost too much to bear, but she wasn't going to leave anything unsaid. "I love you, Sydney. I always have. The walls I built never held you out. I think they just trapped you inside my heart. Please think about joining me in Poland. Or doing long distance. I'm only going to be there for two years, and then, I'll come back here to you. I only have five years left before I qualify for retirement. I would give my career up for you then without grabbing that gold star. Because *you* are more important to me than some goal I've had since I was a child."

"I would *never* want you to give up your career for me," Sydney said, her voice unsteady.

"It wouldn't be *giving anything up*. *You* are worth it. *We* are worth it. But honestly, I don't think you believe in us enough. Maybe it's that you don't believe in love enough. You aren't that starry-eyed girl I first met in Italy who really believed in true love. I sometimes wonder what would have happened if I hadn't refused to break the rules back then. Would that girl have been brave enough to be with me? To figure out how our love could work?" Reagan swallowed a sob and knew the hardest part was coming. She closed her eyes to steel herself. "The really funny thing is that *I* wasn't, but now *I* believe in *us*. But this is it for me. Either you fight for me—for us—or I'm done. There is no reason that we can't work if we're both willing to make a few sacrifices, and if you can't see that, I can't keep opening my heart for you. If I see you somewhere, I'm not saying hi. If I come back to DC in two years, I'm not going to text you or live in this neighborhood. Because I have to move on from you."

Reagan kept her eyes squeezed tight, but she could feel the couch shaking from Sydney as she cried harder. Heard her sniffles. She blinked her eyes open and felt like her heart was being ripped out as Sydney was full-on crying now.

"Please say something, Sydney. I feel like I'm laying myself bare here." Reagan needed to know what she was thinking. Jesus.

"I don't know what to say. I feel like my emotions have been all over the place for months with what my head wants, what my heart wants, and I don't know what to say. I don't know what to do. I need some time to think. Is that okay?"

Reagan hadn't expected Sydney to fall into her arms and profess her love. When Sydney had to make hasty decisions, they'd never gone in Reagan's favor. But she'd been hoping a little bit that Sydney might, finally, be ready to move forward. She suppressed her disappointment and nodded.

"It isn't a no, okay? I just...I need to think about what you said last night. I see where you're coming from. But I just have this fear that lives inside me, and I don't know how to get past it. How to get out of my own way." Sydney swiped tears with her free hand carelessly, as though they were just nuisances.

Reagan's phone started to vibrate on the side table. "That's my car. I have to go. I'm sorry. I thought we had more time."

Sydney licked her lips and nodded. "I know. Be safe, okay?"

They both stood, and Sydney walked her to the door where her bags were already waiting. "I will. You too? Let me know once you've had some time to think."

They awkwardly held hands in front of Sydney's door, tears rolling down both their faces. Reagan had so much more she wanted to say, but she knew she'd already said it all. She prayed Sydney had listened.

A horn sounded from outside. She pulled Sydney into her arms.

Sydney squeezed her tight, and Reagan committed every sensation to memory in case this was the last time, which she couldn't deny it probably was. She squeezed her eyes closed against the tears that she couldn't stop. "I love you," she finally said. "Please don't let me go."

She pressed a kiss to Sydney's cheek and stepped back, needing to put distance between them before she became a blubbery mess. She turned, grabbed her deployment bags, and tried to blink through the tears as she walked to the black SUV sitting on the street in front of Sydney's townhome and into the next phase of her life that she prayed would include Sydney.

CHAPTER TWENTY-EIGHT

Sydney leaned against the balcony rail of her mom and Charlie's apartment, staring at the Boston Seaport and farther into the distance at Long Wharf. Her mind drifted to the first time she'd seen Reagan again in Monterey, and Reagan had drunkenly twirled her at the top of the Fisherman's Wharf. She tightened her hold on her jacket and buried her neck in the scarf she was wearing as a shiver ran through her.

It was a different wharf, before she'd learned the truth about her father. And it had been one of the best nights of her life. Her throat felt tight as she realized that Reagan had been present for nearly all of the best nights of her life.

It had been almost a month since Reagan had left, and Sydney was struggling to get through every day. Every time she closed her eyes, she saw Reagan sitting in front of her, crying and telling her she believed in them and asking Sydney to believe too. Sydney hadn't been able to form any response. She'd wanted to. She'd known she was destroying Reagan by not speaking, but terror had seized her vocal cords.

When Reagan said she loved her as she was leaving, a tumbler had fallen into place in her own heart, and everything had become crystal clear about her need to be around Reagan, her desire to sleep next to her. She still loved her too. She probably always had. But she couldn't formulate the words.

She knew what she wanted to do, but fear had her mired in the status quo.

Sydney's mom bumped her shoulder and held out a glass of wine. "You're looking broody over here. What's going on?"

"Thanks, Mom," she said as she took the glass. When she'd planned this trip to visit her mom to cheer herself up after Reagan had left, she hadn't admitted to herself that she was going to be nursing a broken heart rather than just sadness. "Just lost in my own world, I guess."

"I can see that, but what thoughts are racing around in your brain? You're wearing your spiraling face."

Sydney sighed. "Reagan. And how we left things. I texted with her a few times. I know she made it and is doing fine.

"I was going to wait for the right time to talk to you, but…" She shrugged. "Have you made any decisions about what's next?"

She shook her head and took a sip. "Fuck, I don't know."

"Okay," her mom said. "So let me get this straight. She loves you?"

"Yes."

"Do you love her?"

Sydney closed her eyes and hung her head. "Yes."

"I see." Her mom paused. "I think I made a mistake talking to you about your father when I did."

Sydney's chest hurt at the look of grief on her mom's face. "Oh, Mom. You couldn't have known how it would affect me." A little worried as the color drained from her Mom's face, Sydney said, "Let's sit," and guided her to the chairs.

"I wasn't fair to you or Reagan."

Something felt off about this conversation. Like something had fundamentally shifted in her mom without her knowing it. "Have you forgiven Dad?"

"That's…complicated. He gave me you and Noah, the greatest gifts of my life, though I'm still hurt by his actions. He made our lives infinitely harder than they needed to be. But I share some blame in that I allowed him to treat me—us—in a way I shouldn't—"

"Mom, no. *You* didn't do anything wrong."

"Oh, I know that. But. I could have taken action and didn't, and I think that fed some of my hatred. Because I wasn't strong enough to do what I knew was right. And that also fed the hatred. But I've realized over the years, after beating cancer twice, that hatred and anger don't serve me. All it does is make me afraid. Your father made mistakes.

The military made mistakes. But we all make mistakes every day. My timing back then is one of mine. One that I am so sorry for, and I can only hope you can both forgive me and try to push past whatever role it's still playing in your fear of a relationship with Reagan."

Sydney felt shocked to the bone. She never thought her mom would forgive. "Truthfully, it plays a role in my inability to commit to her, but it isn't the only reason."

"What else is holding you back?"

"What if she gets hurt? Or killed? Like Dad. The military is dangerous, and what if no one tells me?" Sydney's heart started to beat faster and made the bottom of her throat feel fluttery.

"Oh, Sydney. Your father was killed because he knowingly engaged in illicit behavior. He would've been fine if he could've kept it in his pants while deployed. And Reagan isn't in combat, right? Didn't you say she works mostly in diplomatic positions?"

"Yeah…"

"So not much more dangerous than any other profession."

Sydney nodded. That was probably true and similar to something Reagan had said to her as well.

"And I'm not sure why you think no one would tell you. In the unlikely event that something happens to her, I'm sure you would be listed as her next of kin, and you know at least part of her family now, don't you?"

Sydney nodded again. Her mom had a point.

"Are you still worried about financial security? I know I engrained in you to not rely on anyone else—perhaps to an extreme—but I'm pretty sure with your skills, you are marketable anywhere, don't you think?"

"Interestingly, that's the area I'm fine with. In a rare moment of bravery, I talked to my boss about what a hybrid work situation could look like. I got him to agree to let me work remotely and just come back for a few days a month to check in, meet with clients, mentor junior associates."

"That's great." Her mom smiled.

"I'm a good negotiator. It's why I'm a good attorney. And Reagan dismantled a lot of my arguments for staying in DC, including reminding me that the pandemic taught us that a lot of us lawyers could work remote."

"So what's the problem?" Her mom's eyebrows were drawn in confusion.

Sydney paused, searching for the truth. "It's a big change."

"*O*kay," Mom said, dragging out the word again.

"Don't judge me. What do I do if it doesn't work out?"

Her mom placed her hand on Sydney's wrist on the table. "Then you lick your wounds and come home. Go back to your old work schedule. No big deal. Is that really what's keeping you from the great love of your life?"

"I…" Sydney hadn't been aware of how empty her existence felt now that Reagan was gone—she certainly hadn't noticed it before Reagan had come back into her life—but it was. She'd been so busy charging toward her goals that she'd never stopped to ask herself if she was happy. She knew she'd been happy when Reagan was with her.

They both stared out at the harbor for a while and watched the Ptown ferry pull in before her mom said, "You know, you claim you're a good negotiator, yet you haven't made a single argument as to why you can't be with her."

"I…" Sydney couldn't formulate an answer. There wasn't one.

"I think it's because you *want* to go to Reagan. You know it's the right choice. No matter what you're telling yourself. Your head and your heart both want it, and it scares you. I'm sure you already know this, but Reagan is not your dad."

"I know that. I know." Sydney did know it but didn't know what else to say. She couldn't believe her mom felt guilty about her timing in telling her the circumstances of her dad's death. She had so much she needed to unpack emotionally from this conversation. But later. When she was alone.

"I'm not an expert at love, but what I can tell you is, I don't have a single regret about being brave and taking the leap with Charlie. I have a loving partner for the *first time* in my life. And I'd miss the hell out of you, but you have to *live*. I'm here if you want to talk more, but I'm sensing you need more time to think. Let me know if you come up with any logical reasons *not* to go."

Her thoughts were spiraling again but this time about trying to figure out if her fear of Reagan was unfounded or not.

Before she went to sleep, she opened the selfie on her phone saved from the night of her and Reagan's first kiss in Florence and ran her fingers over Reagan's face. So long ago, yet it could have been a month. What was she afraid of? It wasn't a fear of commitment. It was a fear of being hurt. No one else had ever had the power to hurt her the way Reagan did, and it scared the hell out of her.

Sydney had a fitful night of dreaming about Reagan and felt like she'd been up for half the night. Every time she slipped off to sleep, she pictured Reagan hugging her and telling her she loved her, but rather than walking away, some unseen force pulled her backward into the SUV as she screamed. Every time, Sydney woke up with her heart pounding.

However, she *was* asleep when a banging woke her up. She was disoriented but heard, "Sydney, you need to get up."

Mom?

"Huh?" she managed as she shook her head.

"Are you dressed?" Definitely Mom. "I'm coming in even if you aren't."

"What? No, I'm in pajamas," she said and tried to push herself up as her mom opened the door. "What's wrong? Is it Charlie?"

Mom sat on the bed. "No, Charlie's fine. It's Reagan. Or it could be. Something's happening at the US Embassy in Poland. Terrorists or something."

All of the air in Sydney's body left her. She couldn't breathe. She thought she was going to throw up. "Wha—what?" she finally managed.

"Come on. We have it on in the kitchen. Charlie and I were having coffee and watching *Today*, and they cut in with special coverage."

Sydney stood and grabbed the pajama pants she'd taken off to sleep and stepped back into them, pulling them up as she followed her mom to the kitchen.

The sound of the emotionless male anchor saying, "At this point, we don't know much but there was an attack on the United States Embassy in Warsaw, Poland at approximately twelve p.m. local time. A terrorist group that may be backed by the extremist Russian Imperial Movement stormed the embassy with automatic weapons and explosives and were able to gain entry. At this point, we know at least three US service members have been killed, but we don't know how many people, civilian and military, are still inside, whether there might be hostages, or if any have escaped or been released."

An equally emotionless female anchor said, "Such a terrible tragedy this morning. We'll be standing by to provide updates once more information is known, and in the meantime, I will be praying for every person in that building and their families." The anchor paused briefly. "Everyone has heard of an embassy, but a lot of people don't actually know what they are or who works there."

Male voice again. "Embassies are diplomatic headquarters for US interests in a foreign country, and although we don't have a headcount of how many people were in the embassy at the time of the incident, it can be assumed that a significant number of US military and civilian personnel as well as Polish nationals are currently being held."

Sydney didn't even notice her mom holding her hand until she pulled on it. "Come sit. Breathe. We don't know anything yet. Everything could be totally fine. Reagan might have been at lunch, or she could be home sick."

Her voice sounded faraway, like she was speaking through a fog. Charlie might have sat a cup of coffee in front of her. It didn't matter. All she could see in her head were dueling videos of what the rest of her life would look like with Reagan by her side versus a life without her, and in an instant, she knew. Whatever the risk of getting hurt, whatever dangers were present, she needed to be with Reagan. She *belonged* with Reagan.

"I have to go. I have to go right now," Sydney said and grabbed her phone, checking for flights to Warsaw as she walked back to her room.

The bed sank as her mom sat next to her, placed a hand on her arm. "Please take a breath here and think. You can't go charging into a country where we are being attacked by terrorists. Maybe you should see how this all plays out first. Find out if Reagan is okay."

"It doesn't matter. I need to be there. Nearby. Even if I can't see her." She sorted the flights that popped up by arrival time in Warsaw and found a flight with only a short layover in Paris. "This is the one. There're only two seats left. I'm booking it."

Her mom pulled the phone out of her hands. "Please take a second. Twelve hours ago, you were walking around like a zombie, not sure if you wanted to go to Reagan or not, and now, you're frantic to get there because she *may* be in danger. Do you even have your passport?"

"Yes, and all this made something click. Reagan is worth anything. Everything. I've been a coward and too ignorant to see it. But I see it now. My heart, my mind, my soul all want the same thing. They've *always* wanted the same thing. And I'm terrified for her and what she's going through. But for the first time in my life, I'm not terrified for me. You were right. She was right. And she'd better fucking be all right for me to tell her that." Sydney was nearly hyperventilating as fear and love and terror and excitement were coursing through her. "Now, please give me my phone back so I can book this ticket and pack."

Thankfully, she didn't need a visa. She tried to text and call Reagan while she packed and then again on her way to the airport but no answer. The text showed up green rather than blue, which meant the text didn't go through. She tried not to panic. Reagan had to be okay. She prayed Reagan would respond before her plane took off. It didn't happen.

She streamed CNN on her phone at the airport and on the plane, right up until she had to turn it to airplane mode, but luckily, her first-class pod had a TV that she could stream the news on. Still no changes. It appeared that the terrorists wanted the US to facilitate the release of twenty-five Russian soldiers who'd been captured in Ukraine. The anchors continually reminded her that the US didn't negotiate with terrorists, but the prisoners were also not being held by the United States and therefore, couldn't release them. They were at an impasse.

Jesus. These people were American citizens on a US diplomatic mission in Poland and were being held by terrorists. They were going to figure out something, right? They had to.

In the third hour of her trip, Sydney realized she didn't know how she was going to track Reagan down when she landed. She knew she worked at the embassy, but it wasn't like she could walk up to the gates that were still being held by terrorists and ask for Lieutenant Colonel Jennings, and she had no idea where Reagan lived.

But she knew one of Reagan's brothers. Jasper. There couldn't be that many Jasper Jennings in Chicago, could there? She paid for the

Wi-Fi on the flight and found his contact information. It was creepy just how much information she could get on someone for the small, one-time fee of fifty dollars. She'd call him when she landed.

The next hours of the flight were agonizing. No developments on the news. She tried to focus on a book but couldn't. She tried to watch a movie but couldn't handle not having the news on in case there was a development.

The jolt of the jumbo jet bouncing against the tarmac woke her, and for half a second, she couldn't remember where she was or what was happening. Then, it all came flooding back. Shit. What was going on at the embassy? The TV had gone off. She pulled out her phone and took it out of airplane mode as they were still taxiing.

Why did it always take cell phones an eternity to find service in a new country? She willed it to go faster as she tried to take calming breaths. Her hyperventilating wasn't going to help anything. She still had to get through this airport and to her connecting flight.

Finally, it connected, and immediately, a CNN alert popped up.

"Hostage Crisis at American Embassy in Poland Over"

Oh thank God.

Sydney opened the article and skimmed to see if any more details were available. Apparently, the terrorists had been able to override the security cameras in the embassy for a short time, but the US had hacked back into them, and once they could see what was going on inside, a special forces team had stormed the building and taken out the terrorists. It was still sad, as at least three Marines at the gate had been killed, and twenty more embassy personnel had been injured, but they were mostly embassy security. Not a deputy officer in some cooperation office. Sydney couldn't remember her actual title, but she knew it was something like that. She prayed that was a correct assumption.

While still taxiing, she called Jasper, hoping that even if he didn't answer, he would have more time to call her back. Straight to voice mail. Ugh.

"Hi, Jasper. This is Sydney Adams. You might remember meeting me at that wedding a few months ago in Chicago and that long-ago Thanksgiving at your parents'. I've been...uh, friends with your sister for a long time. Anyway, I'm hoping you remember me. I saw what happened at the embassy on the news, and do you know if she's okay?

I tried calling and texting her a few times, and she hasn't responded. Also, I'm on my way to Poland, but I don't know her address. Do you have it, and could you give it to me. Please? I really, really need to see her. So please…please call me back. I'll be in Paris for a couple hours and then just a few more until I'm in Poland."

She gave Jasper her phone number and hung up, hoping she didn't sound too frantic, but leaving a message for someone she barely knew about something that was literally going to change the rest of her life had made her a nervous wreck.

While sitting at the gate, she typed a couple of quick texts. One to update her mom on her progress and the other to Noah letting him know she was in Europe and that she'd explain everything later.

Everything from boarding to deplaning was a sleepy blur as Sydney tried to nap on the shorter flight from Paris to Warsaw, but it wasn't good sleep. Her heart soared when she turned on her phone and saw she had a voice mail from an unknown number that looked like Jasper's.

"Hey, Sydney. I definitely remember you. Reagan is fine. She's out of the embassy. She wiped her cell phone right before one of the terrorists took it, so right now, she doesn't have a phone. She says she's going to replace it tomorrow. She's at the Warsaw Grand Hotel in room twenty-five-oh-four. Give her a huge hug from me and tell her I'm coming to make sure she's fine in person as soon as I can get leave approved."

By the time Sydney dragged her carry-on from the gate to immigration, cleared customs, called a cab, and arrived at the hotel, she was sure she had to look like she'd been hit by a bus. She had no idea how many hours she'd been traveling after crossing so many time zones, but her mom waking her up felt like it was days ago. She was surprised to see two armed police officers standing at the entrance to the hotel, though she probably shouldn't be. They said something to her in Polish, and she opened her mouth a few times, realizing she didn't know a word of the language.

At her blank expression, one of the guards said in accented English, "Are you a guest?"

"Checking in." She smiled and tried to look disarming since she didn't have a reservation.

"The guard inside will check your bag." One of the guards opened the door for her, and she pulled her bag in.

As promised, another guard riffled through her roller board as well as her laptop bag, going so far as to make her turn her laptop on, but once she was cleared, she headed to the elevator. A sliver of her wanted to get her own room and clean up before she went to Reagan's room, but she couldn't resist the stronger urge to see Reagan that second. After the security at the door, Sydney was a little surprised that she didn't need to scan her room key to get upstairs and worried the hotel wasn't secure enough, but that was a problem for another day.

The doors slid open, and as she walked down the hallway, she had a moment of self-doubt. What if Reagan didn't want to see her? What if she'd waited too long, and Reagan had resolved to move on? What if… but she was in front of twenty-five-oh-four.

Even if Reagan turned her away. At least she would be able to see for herself that she was okay, so she knocked and hoped for the best.

CHAPTER TWENTY-NINE

A knocking on her door pulled Reagan out of a deep slumber. It had been a long twenty-four—she checked her watch—make that, twenty-six hours. She rolled off the couch, heart beating rapidly, unsure why she'd flopped there and not in her actual bed.

Reagan approached the door cautiously. When she checked the peephole, she blinked, rubbed her eyes, blinked, and checked again to be sure her eyes weren't deceiving her.

She pulled open the door and scanned the hallway. "Sydney? What are you doing here?"

"Thank God you're okay." Sydney stepped forward in the dim entryway and hesitated. "I had to see you. Can I...hug you?"

Reagan still felt dazed from the shock of seeing Sydney and from having just been woken up. She wasn't sure what was real, but Sydney seemed like she desperately needed the hug, so she nodded, not entirely certain that she wasn't a hallucination. However, as Sydney's very real arms wrapped around her, Reagan melted into them. It had been a horrible day, and Reagan hadn't realized just how much she needed comfort. God, she'd missed her.

"I've been a mess for what feels like days. I've never been so terrified." Sydney stepped back as she trailed off. "Can I come in?"

"Of course." She stepped to the side to let Sydney roll her small suitcase through and closed the door behind them, still dumbfounded as she secured the deadbolt.

As they stepped into the brighter light of the main living area, however, Sydney grabbed her face. "Oh my God. What did they do to you? Are you okay?" She ran her thumb lightly under Reagan's eye where she assumed a bruise was probably forming. Reagan closed her eyes and felt herself sway slightly as Sydney's fingers caressed her skin. When she felt the light brush of Sydney's lips against her cheekbone, Reagan's eyes popped back open, and she took a step back.

"I'm sorry," Sydney stumbled. "I know I don't have the right to do that. But are you okay? What happened?"

Reagan led them into the sitting area, and as Sydney sat on the couch, Reagan started pacing. "I'm okay. I promise. There will be investigations over the next few months to determine exactly what happened, what intelligence the terrorists were operating off of, and how they were able to hack our systems and overcome our defenses…" Reagan stopped pacing and stared into Sydney's eyes. "We lost some good people today—those Marines…I said good morning to them when I arrived yesterday." Reagan cleared her throat and looked away. "Overall, we were lucky, and the rescue and evacuation mission was successful. And most of us made it out okay."

Sydney grabbed Reagan's hand and pulled her to the couch. "But other than the black eye, you're fine? You swear?" Sydney's face was pinched with concern as her eyes swept over Reagan's body, ostensibly searching for any other hidden wounds.

"I swear. This is superficial." She pointed at her face again, and then took Sydney's hand. "And I'm happy to see you—you have no idea how happy—but why *are* you here?"

She sighed. "I don't know if I should start at the beginning or with the punchline."

Reagan wanted to hear the whole story but also needed to know if Sydney had hopped on a plane as soon as she'd heard the news because she loved her or because she was worried. It could be both. But she hoped against hope that it wasn't *only* the latter. "The punchline please."

"I love you. I should never have let you walk out of my house without telling you that last month."

The warmth that flooded Reagan's chest could have melted the polar icecaps, and she wanted nothing more than to pull Sydney into her arms, but Sydney wasn't done.

"I hate that I did that. But I was so terrified. I've had a clear vision of my life since childhood. I never planned to fall so madly in love with someone that she consumed my thoughts and nourished my soul. And I certainly didn't expect her to have to move every year or two. And it took me a little while to figure it out."

Reagan wasn't sure if Sydney had noticed, but she'd started tracing little circles on the back of Reagan's hand, so she started to graze the inside of Sydney's wrist with her index finger. Butterflies in her stomach started swooping. She wanted to hug Sydney. Hold her like she'd been dreaming of for weeks. But she couldn't until she knew more.

"When I was sitting at Mom's kitchen island this morning—or was it yesterday morning? I'm so jet-lagged, I don't know—and saw what was happening, I had the realization that my life could go one of two ways. I could be fine without you. Maybe a little lonely but fine."

Reagan's chest tightened hoping Sydney wasn't going to do this to her again. She didn't breathe.

"But the life I saw with you…was everything. It was filled with laughter and adventure and love as we explored the world together. And I realized in an instant that was what I wanted. What I needed. The only life that would make me *happy* because once I'd seen what we could have, it was the only choice. I'm so sorry it took me so long to figure it out. I was so obtuse. I knew from the moment you left. I think I've always known, but until I had that vision of us, I was paralyzed by fear. You're not my dad. I know that. And, yes, your career is inherently more dangerous than mine is, but the fear of you not being in this world anymore made me realize that, no matter what happens, I would be devastated if something happened to you, so I want to spend every second that I can with you." She looked at Reagan, and it felt like they were looking into each other's souls. "If you'll take me back. Please?"

"Come here," Reagan said and pulled Sydney into her lap. "I love you. When I heard the explosions and the terrorists stormed the building, all I could think was, 'I hope I get to tell her I love her one more time.'"

"Really?" Sydney's smile grew, her dimple popped, and a hint of her southern twang appeared. "Because the first thing I thought was 'I can't believe I didn't tell her I loved her the last time I saw her.'"

"I love you. I love you. I love you. And I love that you're here and that you want to be with me. I don't have words to tell you how happy

I am that you're here." She pulled Sydney's face down and kissed her softly at first, but it quickly deepened as the need for each other, the need to reassure themselves that this was really happening, the need to reassure themselves that they were still alive, overtook them.

They showered and made love for hours, both slow and sweet and fast and furious. But every kiss, every touch, every swipe of the tongue spoke their love.

Finally exhausted, Reagan was on her back with Sydney's head on her shoulder. "How long before you have to go back?"

Sydney sighed as Reagan played with her hair. She'd always loved that. "Probably four weeks or so. I'll have to talk to my boss, but I think four weeks and maybe three days or so every fourth week after that."

Reagan sat up, and Sydney fell back onto her elbow. Whoops. "Wait, you're telling me you already arranged remote work before you'd even gotten here?"

"Please lie back down." Sydney pulled on her arm and settled back on top of her. "Yes. Because looking back, I knew I was going to do it. I love you so much and have for the past fifteen years. I'm sorry it took me so long."

"I love you. No matter how long you waited, I'm glad my heart and I finally get what we've always wanted. You. Us."

EPILOGUE

Washington DC, Eleven Years Later

"Are you nervous?" Sydney said as she stepped behind Reagan in the mirror and pressed a kiss to her neck.

"No, I feel like I've been building toward this since high school when I joined the student counsel to beef up my West Point application." That wasn't true. She was nervous as hell. But a colonel didn't show her nerves. Plus, having Sydney and Jasper there made her feel a lot better. Along with her parents, Alice, her other brothers, and decades of friends. "Are you nervous about swapping out the epaulettes?"

"I'm really not sure why you had to pick your service dress for this shindig. The Velcro on your other uniform is so much easier." She clucked her tongue and shook her head.

"True, but the photos are better in service dress. Plus, you know you love me in this uniform. You think I'm sexy." She nodded her head and flicked an invisible piece of lint from her medals rack over her left breast.

Sydney bit her lip. "True. Though I'll admit that your mess dress is my favorite by far."

A laugh bubbled out of Reagan. "I think you have a fond spot for that uniform due to a particularly unmentionable tryst in a hotel linen closet a long, long time ago."

"That may be true, but you've certainly given me ample opportunities to see you in it since then at every Army, brigade, inauguration, whatever ball." She scoffed playfully.

"I can't deny I also love seeing you in a ballgown. It does unmentionable things to me." Reagan turned and pulled Sydney into her arms.

"Even after knowing me for twenty-six years, I still do unmentionable things to you?" She ran a finger down Reagan's jaw.

"You absolutely do. If we didn't have to meet with a four-star general in approximately two minutes, I would take this moment to show you exactly what you and that sexy pencil skirt suit do to me. But I promise I'll show you later."

"I'm going to hold you to that," Sydney said as she kissed Reagan lightly, thankfully careful of the makeup they were both wearing as it would be unseemly for them to exit with smeared lips.

"On an unrelated note, you're sure you're okay with Brussels, right? I could have taken that West Point commandant job, but this one is better for me, career-wise. Especially if I'm looking to make four star someday." She'd promised Sydney that she would try to get more stateside assignments and after Poland she mostly had, but this NATO position was too good to pass up.

"I promise. I told you it was fine when you asked the first time and the second. And again after you accepted the position formally. I think it's too late to back out. Janie is going to love her international school, and our au pair wants to be closer to home for a while. Plus, Brussels could be fun. And it's only six hours ahead of DC. I made that time difference work when you were in Poland. And Naples. And your title as the deputy whatever of NATO is hot." Sydney kissed her again, and Reagan pulled Sydney's hips tightly against her own.

"It's actually the deputy US military representative to NATO, if you want to get technical."

Sydney nodded and leaned in for another kiss when a knock sounded at the door. "Ma'am, it's almost time," the master of ceremony said.

"Saved by the knock," Sydney said.

"More like thwarted," Reagan grumbled. "But let's go find Janie. Hopefully, she's still with Dad, and he isn't teaching her any other sordid secrets from his time here."

Thankfully, Janie and Reagan's dad were already in their seats in the front row with the rest of Reagan's family and Alice and Charlie. Alice grabbed Reagan's hand and squeezed. "I'm so proud of you."

"Thanks, Alice." Reagan leaned down and hugged them, but it looked like it was time. She gave her a light kiss on the cheek and whispered, "I love you. Thank you," before taking her place at the front.

"Are you ready for this?" General Blackmond said.

"As I'll ever be, sir." She smiled to tell him she was mostly kidding.

"I've been watching your career for a long time. You're ready for this." He patted her on the shoulder as they began.

"Good afternoon, ladies and gentlemen, and honored guests," the officiant said. "Today we honor Colonel Reagan A. Jennings on the occasion of her promotion to the rank of brigadier general. Before we begin, we would like to recognize several distinguished attendees in the audience. We are pleased to extend a welcome to Colonel Jennings's wife, Sydney, their daughter Janie, and Colonel Jennings's father Colonel Brian Jennings, retired."

The officiant paused and took a breath. Sydney smiled, flashing her dimple, and Reagan knew she could take on anything with Sydney at her side.

"Attention to orders," the officiant said.

Reagan snapped to attention and prepared to accept the star she'd been working toward for her entire professional life. Her heart couldn't be fuller with Sydney, Janie, and the rest of her family there to witness this achievement.

She felt like she'd gotten everything her heart had ever wanted and was excited to see what life brought next.

About the Author

Krystina has been a lover of romance novels since she was probably too young to read them and developed an affinity for sapphic romance after she found her first one on a shelf in a used bookstore in 2001. Despite a lifelong desire, she never made the time to write her own until the COVID-19 pandemic struck, and she had extra time with no daily commute or work travel.

Krystina grew up in Florida but, after spending six years in the military, finds herself now calling Chicago home—though she frequently travels so often for work that she forgets what city she's in. She works in real estate and lives with her wife and their two rescue pit bulls. When not working, traveling, or writing, Krystina can be found reading with a glass of wine in hand, doing yoga (occasionally with a glass of wine in hand), snuggling with her fur-babies, or trying to convince herself that it's not too cold to go for a jog outside.

Books Available from Bold Strokes Books

Can't Buy Me Love by Georgia Beers. London and Kayla are perfect for one another, but if London reveals she's in a fake relationship with Kayla's ex, she risks not only the opportunity of her career, but Kayla's trust as well. (978-1-63679-665-9)

Chance Encounter by Renee Roman. Little did Sky Roberts know when she bought the raffle ticket for charity that she would also be taking a chance on love with the egotistical Drew Mitchell. (978-1-63679-619-2)

Comes in Waves by Ana Hartnett. For Tanya Brees, love in small-town Coral Bay comes in waves, but can she make it stay for good this time? (978-1-63679-597-3)

Dancing With Dahlia by Julia Underwood. How is Piper Fernley supposed to survive six weeks with the most controlling, uptight boss on earth? Because sometimes when you stop looking, your heart finds exactly what it needs. (978-1-63679-663-5)

Skyscraper by Gun Brooke. Attempting to save the life of an injured boy brings Rayne and Kaelyn together. As they strive for justice against corrupt Celestial authorities, they're unable to foresee how intertwined their fates will become. (978-1-63679-657-4)

The Curse by Alexandra Riley. Can Diana Dillon and her daughter, Ryder, survive the cursed farm with the help of Deputy Mel Defoe? Or will the land choose them to be to the next victims? (978-1-63679-611-6)

The Heart Wants by Krystina Rivers. Fifteen years after they first meet, Army Major Reagan Jennings realizes she has one last chance to win the heart of the woman she's always loved. If only she can make Sydney see she's worth risking everything for. (978-1-63679-595-9)

Untethered by Shelley Thrasher. Helen Rogers, in her eighties, meets much-younger Grace on a lengthy cruise to Bali, and their intense relationship yields surprising insights and unexpected growth. (978-1-63679-636-9)

You Can't Go Home Again by Jeanette Bears. After their military career ends abruptly, Raegan Holcolm is forced back to their hometown to confront their past and discover where the road to recovery will lead them, or if it already led them home. (978-1-636790644-4)

A Wolf in Stone by Jane Fletcher. Though Cassilania is an experienced player in the dirty, dangerous game of imperial Kavillian politics, even she is caught out when a murderer raises the stakes. (978-1-63679-640-6)

New Horizons by Shia Woods. When Quinn Collins meets Alex Anders, Horizon Theater's enigmatic managing director, a passionate connection ignites, but amidst the complex backdrop of theater politics, their budding romance faces a formidable challenge. (978-1-63679-683-3)

One Last Summer by Kristin Keppler. Emerson Fields didn't think anything could keep her from her dream of interning at Bardot Design Studio in Paris, until an unexpected choice at a North Carolina beach has her questioning what it is she really wants. (978-1-63679-638-3)

StreamLine by Lauren Melissa Ellzey. When Lune crosses paths with the legendary girl gamer Nocht, she may have found the key that will boost her to the upper echelon of streamers and unravel all Lune thought she knew about gaming, friendship, and love. (978-1-63679-655-0)

The Devil You Know by Ali Vali. As threats come at the Casey family from both the feds and enemies set to destroy them, Cain Casey does whatever is necessary with Emma at her side to bury every single one. (978-1-63679-471-6)

The Meaning of Liberty by Sage Donnell. When TJ and Bailey get caught in the political crossfire of the ultraconservative Crusade of the Redeemer Church, escape is the only plan. On the run and fighting for their lives is not the time to be falling for each other. (978-1-63679-624-6)

Undercurrent by Patricia Evans. Can Tala and Wilder catch a serial killer in Salem before another body washes up on the shore? (978-1-636790669-7)

And Then There Was One by Michele Castleman. Plagued by strange memories and drowning in the guilt she tried to leave behind, Lyla Smith escapes her small Ohio town to work as a nanny and becomes trapped with an unknown killer. (978-1-63679-688-8)

Digging for Destiny by Jenna Jarvis. The war between nations forces Litz to make a choice. Her country, career, and family, or the chance of making a better world with the woman she can't forget. (978-1-63679-575-1)

Hot Hires by Nan Campbell, Alaina Erdell, Jesse J. Thoma. In these three romance novellas, when business turns to pleasure, romance ignites. (978-1-63679-651-2)

McCall by Patricia Evans. Sam and Sara found love on the water, but can they build a future amid the ghosts of the past that surround them on dry land? (978-1-63679-769-4)

One and Done by Fredrick Smith. One day can lead to a night of passion…and possibly a chance at love. (978-1-63679-564-5)

Promises to Protect by Jo Hemmingwood. Park ranger Maxine Ward's commitment to protect Tree City is put to the test when social worker Skylar Austen takes a special interest in the commune and in Max. (978-1-63679-626-0)

Sacred Ground by Missouri Vaun. Jordan Price, a conflicted demon hunter, falls for Grace Jameson who has no idea she's been bitten by a vampire. (978-1-63679-485-3)

The Land of Death and Devil's Club by Bailey Bridgewater. Special Liaison to the FBI Louisa Linebach may have defied all odds by identifying the bodies of three missing men in the Kenai Peninsula, but she won't be satisfied until the man she's sure is responsible for their murders is behind bars. (978-1-63679-659-8)

When You Smile by Melissa Brayden. Taryn Ross never thought the babysitter she once crushed on would show up as a grad student at the same university she attends. (978-1-63679-671-0)

A Heart Divided by Angie Williams. Emma is the most beautiful woman Jackson has ever seen, but being a veteran of the Confederate army that killed her husband isn't the only thing keeping them apart. (978-1-63679-537-9)

Adrift by Sam Ledel. Two women whose lives are anchored by guilt and obligation find romance amidst the tumultuous Prohibition movement in 1920s California. (978-1-63679-577-5)

Cabin Fever by Tagan Shepard. The longer Morgan and Shelby are stranded together, the more their feelings grow, but is it real, or just cabin fever? (978-1-63679-632-1)

Clean Kill by Anne Laughlin. When someone starts killing people she knows in the recovery world, former detective Nicky Sullivan must race to stop the killer and keep herself from being arrested for the crimes. (978-1-63679-634-5)

Only a Bridesmaid by Haley Donnell. A fake bridesmaid, a socially anxious bride, and an unexpected love—what could go wrong? (978-1-63679-642-0)

Primal Hunt by L.L. Raand. Anya, a young wolf warrior, finds herself paired with Rafe, one of the most powerful Vampires in the Americas, in an erotic union of blood and sex. (978-1-63679-561-4)

Puzzles Can Be Deadly by David S. Pederson. Skip loves a good puzzle. Little does he know that a simple phone call will lead him and his boyfriend Henry to the deadliest puzzle he's ever encountered. (978-1-63679-615-4)

Snake Charming by Genevieve McCluer. Playgirl vampire Freddie is on the run and a chance encounter with lamia Phoebe makes them both realize that they may have found the love they'd given up on. (978-1-63679-628-4)

Spirits and Sirens by Kelly and Tana Fireside. When rumored ghost whisperer Elena Murphy and very skeptical assistant fire chief Allison Jones have to work together to solve a 70-year-old mystery, sparks fly—will it be enough to melt the ice between them and let love ignite? (978-1-63679-607-9)